Kate Worsley's first novel, *She Rises*, won the HWA Debut Crown for Historical Fictio͟   ͟   ͟   ͟   ͟shortlisted for a Lambda Literary Prize in the͟   ͟   ͟   ͟   ͟   ͟Lancashire and now lives on

Praise f͟

'With slow, quiet intent Kate Worsley builds a tense atmosphere of looming horror. This book demands to be savoured, even as it clamours to be devoured'
The Times

'Kate Worsley has a wonderfully fertile imagination . . . Her wily prose curls around the story she is telling, like a creeper'
Katie Ward

'A wonderfully atmospheric and deeply unsettling novel, full of images so vivid they seem to leap off the page. Worsley's fiction is something to savour'
Sarah Waters

'A rich, wonderfully uneasy pleasure. Exquisitely written and deeply original, with secrets that are tightly layered, always surprising and teased out with impressive control'
Bethan Roberts

'Beguiling, and written with a piercing eye for style'
Eva Dolan

'A spellbinding evocation of the rural uncanny'
Historical Novels Review

'I loved the brooding suspense of *Foxash* – both the unspoken and the fear of speaking dominate its claustrophobic setting'
Jonathan Myerson

By Kate Worsley

FOXASH

SHE RISES

Kate Worsley

FOXASH

TINDER
PRESS

First published in Great Britain in 2023 by
TINDER PRESS
An imprint of HEADLINE PUBLISHING GROUP

First published in paperback in 2024 by
TINDER PRESS
An imprint of HEADLINE PUBLISHING GROUP

1

Cataloguing in Publication Data is available from the British Library

ISBN 978 1 4722 9491 3

Designed and typeset by EM&EN
Printed and bound in Great Britain by Clays Ltd, Elcograf S.p.A.

MIX
Paper | Supporting
responsible forestry
FSC® C104740

Headline's policy is to use papers that are natural, renewable and recyclable
products and made from wood grown in well-managed forests and other
controlled sources. The logging and manufacturing processes are expected
to conform to the environmental regulations of the country of origin.

HEADLINE PUBLISHING GROUP
An Hachette UK Company
Carmelite House
50 Victoria Embankment
London EC4Y 0DZ

www.tinderpress.co.uk
www.headline.co.uk
www.hachette.co.uk

For one we have lost

'A weed is a plant out of place'

Donald Culross Peattie (1896–1964) botanist and painter

'Sir: you know this hope is such a bait, it covers any hook'

Ben Jonson, *Volpone; Or, the Fox*

Growing Season
No. 1

28th January

I thought he'd be here to meet me. I had it all crystal clear
in my head. Letter said to come down twenty-eighth of
January. Ticket was a single, same as his. Caught the ten-
to-eight mainline, same as he had, three month back. I'd
pictured him that day, arriving here about teatime, with the
rest of the men from the Special Areas. Cold, hungry, tired,
piling into an Association truck in a fog of white breath. All
those nights since, I've conjured him up, stood here waiting
on me. I'm not after a truck. Just my Tommy.

He's not written to say either way, of course. Not written once, bar that Christmas card. A robin, perched on the
handle of a spade dug deep in snow. Crinkle edges. *Greetings
from the Association.* And just *Tommy*, no *love from*, no news.
Not that I wrote and asked. I learned early, never ask, never
expect nothing, and that's what he liked about me, right
from the start. No where you been, or what you been up to,
or where did that 10/- come from? Tommy'd rather twist
your arm off than give an account of himself.

And he knows I've never been on the railways before.
Leastways, not the mainline. My pluck lasted about as long
as the poke of barley twists I bought on Durham platform.
There's no earthly power keeps Lettie Radley away from a
confectioner's barrow. Even as Mrs Chilvers had waved me

right round the corner and up the hill, I'd not really believed that I was leaving. It was only on the big train, squeezed in with a party down from Edinburgh – yes, their fine leather gloves and trimmed hats did for me, their scented soap and bright complexions. And the baby. Their big, silent baby, with its big, blue eyes. When the lot of them trooped off to the dining car I swiped their copy of *Titbits*, and after they came back I peeped and sucked and swung my legs at the lot of them.

By the time I had to change at Peterborough I was pretty low. A fresh bloke in the pinstripe got on, his cheeks pitted like a copper kettle with the chickenpox or whatever. Yarned me all sorts, he did, starting with his leg and Verdun, and then the drapery business and the little place he likes to stop off where there's willows and a viaduct. I didn't take anything off him, not a nip, not a tab, just a sugared bun or two. But after a while his talk got me pepped again. I'd nod, and smile, and look out the window at the green fields, the telegraph poles flashing by, the birds on the grinning wires. All I felt then was joy. Our past was vanishing behind us; already it seemed to mean nothing. We'd escaped. And I was on my way to Tommy. To claim a future I'd hardly been able to believe in until now. When I caught my reflection, I couldn't stop dimpling.

Quite a job it was, keeping him at bay. He helped me off with the cases, tipped the porter for carrying the tea chest. He'll be sat back down in the fug now, off to London and the big shops he sold to. No harm in any of it, of course; though Tommy wouldn't have understood. Even so, I'd wanted him to clock the fellow, see him touch his hat, touch my elbow as I stepped down on to the platform, good foot first, in my green plaid he'd always liked so much. In my stockings and shiny button shoes, all fresh out of hock thanks to the Association advance. This perky little hat too. His sister Monica's best, in fact – not that Tommy'd remember – I knew she'd never redeem the ticket.

Both platforms are empty. And beyond the platforms there's only fields and hedges and cloud and wind. No houses. No trees. No hills. No snow, or slush or soot stains. All flat and wet, green and muddy. Soft. It sets my teeth on edge. Who builds a station in the middle of a field anyway? There's only the station and the stationmaster's house, the signal house, the two platforms, with steps down to a tunnel connecting. I watch for him: the steps, the station building, the steps again. Rain comes in great, windy gusts, rain that splatters my smooth stockings and powdered face. They said it'd be warmer down here, and it is, a little. There's a sweet, rank smell in the air too. The smell of the South.

When I ask after the Association my voice sounds tinny, like an announcement. The Manningtree stationmaster snorts unpleasantly under his moustache. He's back in his stuffy little room before I've worked out what he's said: *Best fetch up in the Ladies Waiting Room, miss, Association's a rule unto itself. They'll be along in their own good time, I reckon.*

I huddle too close to the banked grate, lose myself in the familiar scent of damp wool and cheap coal, and I wait and I wait and I try not to think about why Tommy might not turn up. All this planning, all this way, Association can't send us back now. I'm standing on one spot, but I still feel like I'm moving. The air seems to rush past my ears and the room shimmers. I've never travelled this far for this long in my life and I seem to have left myself behind.

*

It takes an age for the Association trap to come. Tommy's not in it and the trap driver's about as friendly as the station-master. By the time we're away and out of the woods that big empty sky has shuttered down to an orange sliver over the high, bare hedges. And everywhere flat and no one and nothing to see. Just a paring of moon overhead, around every promising corner another long, straight muddy lane. We'll need to get somewhere sharpish, though. I've been due my monthlies all week, cramping on and off since dinnertime, and my rags are right at the bottom of my bag. I'm gearing up to ask how much further when he pulls hard on the reins and we come to a halt, just before the lane enters a dark tunnel of trees.

Down on our left I can make out the gleam of a low picket fence. Tucked behind it, the silhouette of a neat cottage, low and wide, with a steep roof and a squat chimney, dim in the rising dusk. The wind-rinsed air fills with a scent of woodsmoke and bruised apples. Here it is at last. The fairy-tale home they promised us.

Wordlessly, wearily, the driver dumps my luggage on the verge, and I step down, clenching and praying for everything to stay in place. My heels sink into clumpy grass, I stagger, and up floods a stench of mud and leaf mould and worse. Then, before I know it, the trap's rattled off, swallowed up in that tunnel of trees. Was I supposed to have tipped him? Too late now. Here's the gate. Our gate. With no one stood by it.

The dark's never bothered me, Tommy knows that. I'm not the afraid one, am I? And this isn't even proper pit dark. Not alley dark, or cellar dark. Not any kind of dark we've ever known. No, it's wide open country dark, weighty and huge. It's alive. And it's all around.

I have to tug off a glove, and pull down Monica's hat to shut my ears to the rustling and the whispering before I manage the sneck. Through at last, on to snaggy grass and a rough concrete path. I sweep my feet like a skater in case I walk into some invisible nastiness. There's no door to be seen, just a pair of casement metal windows, set wide apart, their panes bare and lightless. I feel my way to the right, and down the near side, my palm scraping raw brick and mortar. This wall is blank too. At the far corner I meet a faint butchery stench, like something died a while back. Then the full force of the wind hits.

Never mind, I tell myself. We've got ourselves far away from Easington, and just in time. We've our own place again. This is our fresh start. Come daylight, we'll see what we can see. The rest of the settlement must be down the lane there, through those trees. The shops, the pub, all of it. A picture house. And we shall have this place to ourselves. Just the two of us, like we've always wanted. Never mind that it's out of the way. It'll be safer. Less talk.

Dead ahead, out in the wide, blowing blackness, a distant light flares and blossoms. It breaks up into dozens of glowing fragments, like some gigantic church window. That's the glasshouse they promised us too. Its ribbed frame scores the yellow light inside into a shifting kaleidoscope of diamonds, squares and slivers. And it's huge: cavernous as a dance hall, bright as a motion-picture screen and entirely empty inside, save for a single moving figure holding a lamp.

I grab hold of Monica's hat before the wind does and set out, across grass, and cinders, and mud and more grass. My poor shoes. And my foot, cramping. At the corner of the glasshouse I bump into a water butt taller than me. Ducking behind, I straighten my hat and brush off my coat, tug my handkerchief out for a lick and a spit.

He's hanging the lamp up, on a low rafter down the far end. The light rocks jauntily, over neat lines and low ridges

7

of earth dotted all over with small green shoots. Poking up around his feet are three bright rows of clustered green leaves. Solid, lacquered and luminous, they could be giant lime sherbets, fresh cracked from the frame.

I've not seen that dark jacket before, with its big, baggy pockets. Those loose matching trousers of stiff drill, muddied up to the thigh. Or the wide brown felt and the high boots. Must be Association issue. Four years married, and I've never seen him in anything other than his Sunday suit or his pit clothes. Or his birthday suit.

Tommy's taller, somehow. Straighter. Stronger. I will him to turn round and see me framed in the doorway. To tear off his hat and stride towards me and take me in his arms. But the metal door won't pull open, or push neither, it snags my coat sleeve and as I'm struggling to free it a hand falls heavy on my shoulder.

'Oh! You're . . . you must be . . . come in, come in.'

It's a country voice. Deep but soft. And flustered. A woman's voice.

She tugs me inside, into warm, still air, all paraffin and damp and soil. Ducking behind me, with a practised heave of her shoulder, she slides the door shut on its runners.

'Best keep weather out.'

Her face is long, and lean, like a horse, her skin as creased and dull as reused brown paper. She pulls off that wide hat, and her bobbed hair, coal black with strands of grey, curling and clumped and flecked with dirt, swings forward to her jaw. Tucking it hurriedly back behind her ears, she smiles shyly down at me, her wide-set dark eyes fixed on the lace at my throat. Under her snarled brown pullover I see the clear swell of large solid breasts.

Stupid, stupid of me.

I can't help myself. 'What are you doing here?'

Her arm jerks nervously and she drops the hat. As she snatches it back up, I see her clock my shoes and my stockings, muddied as they are, my trimmed cloche and my powdered cheeks and my reddened lips. It's a hungry look she has. Craven with it, like a kicked dog. She looks me up and down, quite speechless. And I feel better, somehow. This one won't know it's all fresh out of hock, will she, only cornflour and cochineal. That I'm near fainting with tiredness and vexation and my monthlies. This one won't know the first thing about me. About either of us.

Slowly, I re-pin Monica's hat on the side of my head. Best voice this time, and pray the powder hides my blushes.

'Direct me to Mr Radley, if you'd be so kind.'

Her whole wizened face crinkles up. She tucks her hair back behind her ears again and this time she beams down at me, showing all her teeth, white and strong, like a dog's, like she whets them on bark.

'Of course I shall, my love!' she says, joyous and lilting. 'You're our Mrs Radley, aren't you? Of course you are. And haven't we been proper looking forward to your coming?'

This one doesn't look shy now, not a bit of it. She looks like she knows an ancient secret I don't, oh yes, many secrets, and maybe she'll tell and maybe she won't.

Wiping her right hand carefully on her trouser leg, she smiles, then holds it out like some sort of a blunt implement. What sort of a woman shakes hands? She squeezes my hand deliberately, like you'd test a loaf for freshness. Her hand is huge and her grip is firm and dry. But, once she releases me, those dark eyes are wide and searching and nervous again.

From over by the house, Tommy shouts my name.

Three paces off he stops dead. His shadowy figure is the spit of hers. But that was his voice all right. That's the way he's always said my name, off hand, on one note. *Lett-ie.*

Firefly. As though he doesn't care. The shivers come, my knees go; only then does it come over me, in a rush, how close I've been to giving up, without him.

He clears his throat. Shoves his hands in his trouser pockets the way he does, poking both thumbs at you; though of course I can't see, in the dark.

My Tommy Radley. I'm smiling like a fool. I want to thump him.

'All right,' he says.

It's how much he keeps hidden, that's what turns me over, makes my chest tighten. The caution that is his constant shadow.

'Hello, Tommy.' My voice hides nothing, never could.

Before that one catches us up with her lamp, he's taken me by the hips and tugged me up and against him. This strange new place has soaked him in strange new smells, musty as an empty larder beneath the scorched cotton reek of that stiff Association jacket. His stubble is loud with grit, and his throat, hot and slick, pulses against my forehead.

He'll have been outdoors since first light, in the chill damp air. He'll have hurried, far and fast, to meet me. Much too far to walk, along those lanes down to the station, and after a full day's work. In the country dark. Three whole months Tommy's been alone down here, waiting on me. Labouring in this strange, bleak place: out in the cold and wet, turning in every night stiff and weary to a narrow barrack bunk.

I clasp my arms around his neck and press my face between his lapels, smother the resentment, the impatience, the triumphant dissatisfaction. Under cover of my coat, his hands search out all the softness that's left on me: my backside, my breasts, my backside again. Three months he's been away – how much longer since he came this close? Those soft full lips murmur against my chilled ear: that choked, urgent whisper when he doesn't want anyone else to hear.

'Lettie, ah, Lettie. *Lett-ie. Lett-ie. Lett-ie.*'

Then he stills in my arms as his whole frame braces. Only his eyelashes blink hot and wet against my forehead and his thudding heart matches mine beat for beat. This has never changed, for either of us. He only has to come close and stay there, and something rekindles inside.

Now I just need to get us safe indoors. I just need to see his face. It was what had made up my mind, when the Association letter arrived. He'd stood there in Monica's doorway, letting in the draught. The letter flapped in his trembling hand. He held it out to me, held his head high, and held my gaze.

For how long had it been since Tommy'd met anybody's eye, if not in anger? The more he'd tried to fake it, the more it showed. I'd looked at that poor, drawn, chalky face, seen the fresh hope flicker in his eyes, and I'd wanted to cry: the pain and fear and worry of moving away, I knew it would be nothing compared to what our life had been before, the worry and the waiting. How could it be worse? For either of us.

*

There's a man stood at the corner of the cottage. A great long lash of a man, twisting his hat in his hand, watching us.

He lopes over, and he stands much too close, holding his lamp high, grins down into my face like he's known me his whole life, knows me inside out. He's the spit of scarecrow woman – big bones, long legs, dark eyes. Same greying curls and creased skin and gleaming teeth. But this one's not shy of me, not one bit.

Adam Dell, he says his name is. And grins again, wide and slow. Oh now this one's alive, I think. This one's all here.

'Pleased to meet you,' I say. And I'm dimpling, despite myself.

'Now then,' he says, with a little jolt, as though he'd only now remembered he had more words inside him. 'You must blame me, Mrs Radley. Not young Tom here.'

I have to listen hard, watch his lips move, because they don't all talk the same down here in Essex. He's got that same chewy, sing-song way of talking she has, nothing like the stationmaster.

'Most days we cadge a lift partway, but we had to make do with Shanks' pony today, isn't that so, Tom?'

Tommy's silent, of course. He's stepped back, out of the light, a shrunken shadow of the man I married, next to this old Adam Dell, tall and straight and full of sap.

'This time of year, Association'd have us at it all night if they could. I did try and say to Mr Bridgewater—'

Tommy jerks with a pantomime shrug. 'Ha!' he says explosively. 'Ha!'

Dell grins down at him, and waggles his hands too. 'Mr Bridgewater, eh?'

Marra talk. They must have gone through training together, then. Shared a billet, a tab, a drink or two. What else might Tommy have shared with him? This man's easy, avuncular manner might lower anyone's guard. Though surely not Tommy's. And especially not now.

'The wife's introduced herself, I trust? She's been watch-ing out for you since dinnertime.'

She makes a rakish silhouette, with her long, trousered legs and wide hat tilted, hands in pockets, and the glass-house behind her spilling rays of light on the dark ground.

As she comes over, her feet shift and scuff, she's wary as a wild thing.

Dell takes her hand, that great mitt of hers more than a match for his, grins again. 'Now look you here, Mrs Radley. See this hand? These are the greenest fingers in the whole world. A natural-born grower is my Jean. This woman can make anything grow—'

She casts him a pleading look, like some giant fettered pony. Dell smiles fervently back at her, and bends to kiss her hand. Tommy stands rigid, just outside the rim of the light. When you were First Man in the pit, I think, you'd have spat where you stood, to see a grown man fawn over his woman like this.

As if on cue, she unfurls, helpless, blushing. They tear their gaze from each other, only to turn it on me like I'm the second coming, their twin faces joyous.

'You'll sup with us tonight, the pair of you,' simpers Jean. She paws at Dell's chest, tousles her head on his shoulder. 'You'll not even think of taking her to that canteen, Tom.'

'Oh no,' I say, prim as. Tom, indeed. It's Mr Radley to you two, whoever you are. 'Don't you go putting yourself out on our account, Mrs Dell. We'll get ourselves indoors. Tommy can fetch us back a couple of fried fish and some chipped potatoes from up the road.'

Two portions, large. I'll nip up and change these rags sharpish, set a fire, check my face, comb out my hair. He'll pull me on his knee and let me pick out the crispy bits before the grease soaks through, while the newspaper scalds my thigh. And when he's balled up the wrappings and thrown them on the fire, I'll let him kiss my fingertips, one by one, tart with vinegar and salt, and watch the flames flare blue and yellow.

'Fried fish?' Dell ducks his head to hide his smile.

There's no fried fish shop round the corner, is there. No blessed nothing out here, by the looks of it.

Jean flings out both arms as if to herd us down the lane. 'We can do you better than fried fish, Lettie. There's more than enough for all of us. Eh, Ads?'

Dell nods, grinning still.

'Very kind, Mrs Dell, I'm sure,' Tommy says, in that jerky, pantomime way he has with strangers.

And she's off with the lamp, arm in arm with Dell. Tommy lowers his head and follows smartly behind. I've no choice but to go with them, or I'll be stranded out here in the wind and the dark.

Just before they head round to the lane, the Dells stop at the rear of the cottage and raise the lamp before a low door framed by thick-stemmed briars, hard pruned. Dell lifts the latch, and a large white chicken bolts out between his legs and flutters off across the grass. He holds the door open. Jean stamps her boots and tugs them off. Then she shucks on a pair of well-worn carpet slippers waiting on the mat, peers back out into the windy blackness and, in a huge, cawing voice, yells: '*Flo!*'

A white scud in the dark. And before I can move, the chicken is making swift, painful darts for the button fastening the shoe of my bad foot.

'No, no, my darling,' Jean croons. 'Don't you go bothering young Mrs Radley.'

She scoops the chicken under one arm and heads inside with the lamp, leaving the door wide open. Tommy's not said a word. He's crouched down beside the step, busying himself with his boot laces.

Dell stands close. He rocks on his heels. 'You make a good door but a rotten window, if I may say so, Mrs Radley.'

I dimple up, but I swear, once Tommy and I are back on our feet, I'll never humour another old bastard ever again.

Dell swings his lamp high again, and to the left of the door is a pair of narrow metal windows, each with three single square panes. To the left of them, a second door, bare of briars and exposed to the elements.

'This is us, see.' Dell speaks slow, as though I'm backward. 'We're holding number 95, and that's you next door, holding 94. Now come on in. We're ever so glad to have you as our neighbour, and that's the truth. There's him who does the tractors and such, of course, a way further up towards Central and the rest of them. But it's been just the two of us down this end of the estate for far too long, we reckon.'

He flashes that grin once more, for luck, and ducks inside, leaving the door ajar.

Only now does Tommy straighten up. We watch their light flare in a larger window to the right. It spills out and shudders over the grass, pushing at the darkness. Inside, we can hear the chicken purr and whistle. Jean talks back to it, high and girlish. Dell chuckles.

Tommy stands at my back. He doesn't have to speak. He doesn't have to move a muscle.

*

Ever had one of those rotten headaches, laid up proper, and had to put a hankie over your eyes, soaked and fumey with lavender water? Soon as we go inside, that tiny hallway drenches me in just that same startling sweetness. Their kitchen is stacked fuller than a florist's window. Dozens of pungent pastel blossoms stagger to stay upright, shelf upon shelf of them. Pots of hyacinths are lined up on a dresser on the far wall: fat, drunken fists of waxy lilac and white.

Clusters of yellow narcissi are ranked all along the window-sill and the mantelpiece, more hyacinths, blue and pink, pink and blue, on and on.

I don't remember the last time I saw a fresh flower, truly I don't. Not even a snowdrop. I used to watch for them in the backyard at St Clement's. Nothing but bare flags out there, hardly a crumb of earth, you think they'd give up. But then one day, they'd return, always, my precious tiny pearls.

Jean watches my face. 'Yes,' she murmurs. 'She's a country girl at heart, just like you said, Tom.'

Tommy lounges restless against the dresser. The lamp-light catches a faint flush and rounding of his cheeks as he bends to sniff a blue hyacinth, waxy and stiff. Pit stoop's gone, the pallor too. My heart turns over again. Yes, I think, Tommy's been like a shuttered pit himself all these years: unnaturally still and silent. But coal doesn't rot when there's no call for it. It lies there, locked away, useless and taunting. It just needs digging out.

'Oh, Lettie loves her flowers. Always on at me she was, terrible.' He folds his arms with a hard little chuckle. 'Couldn't pass a stall without nagging.' He adds, in a final spurt, 'Won't have to waste any more of my money now, will she?'

Jean nods vigorously. 'That's right, Tom. No call for spending what a body don't have on what a body don't need, not here.'

'Now these here bulbs of Jean's,' intones Dell, in reverent tones. 'They're what gets us through the dark months. We've scarcely room, as you can see. But they remind us, don't they, Jean? Spring is always just around the corner.'

Reassured, she wraps her arm about his waist, and worms her ruddy cheek up against his. Tommy's tapping his heel against the dresser, looking about, everywhere but at me. That face of his – mud-smeared, sheened with exertion, ruddy with weather – is a bright mask.

Dell grins. 'You'll not believe this place in a few months' time, Mrs Radley.'

Jean gives me her moist stare again, like a hungry dog. 'You never told us she had such pretty hair, Tom.'

Candyfloss head is what Tommy used to call me. He'd aim to catch me unawares, just so he could press his great seamy palm into the pale puff of my hair. Afterwards, in the mirror, I'd see myself outlined with a faint halo of soot.

I fluff my hair and flash the dimples around. 'Well, you know, folk do say I have a look of Valentine Fox.'

Their faces are quite blank. These two might have never been near the pictures in their lives.

'I don't know about that.' Dell's dark eyes glitter with amusement. 'I'd say this one's a dandelion clock, come to life.'

Jean giggles. 'Wouldn't take much to blow her away, now would it?'

'Do sit down, Mrs Radley,' says Dell, all dignity. 'You must take us as you find us, mind.'

Their table is bare pine, dark with grease. No cloth, no paper, nothing but a couple of clumped-up brown paper bags, and a ball of twine and a sticky jam jar with the knife left in. A curving length of red rubber hose and a broken piece of chalk and a grubby teaspoon and a newspaper parcel tied with string and sat on its own damp bottom. My stomach turns. Only the real slatterns down Pit Bottom live like this.

'Very kind, I'm sure.'

I take the chair next to Tommy, nearest the dresser and the bracing scent of the hyacinths, and reach, discreetly, to undo my shoe strap. Long time since I wore anything but clogs. But that chicken of hers is back, stalking about underneath the table. I draw my feet in.

Jean plonks bowls of stew where she can, and hands me a spoon with a spidery crust of something green on the back. Dell holds a square shop-bought loaf to his chest, sawing off slices and offering them out on the point of the knife. I take one.

'Well, now, what a long way you've come, Lettie.' Jean folds her slice and splashes it in her bowl. 'However did you manage, all alone?'

I tear off a morsel and pop it daintily in my mouth. 'Oh, you know. It was a very comfortable journey, Mrs Dell. Most stimulating.'

'Hmm.' She sucks sceptically at her crust. Her upper lip is cross-stitched with creases. 'But you'll have left everyone who knows you, your family. Won't they miss you, all the way down here?' She waits, her eyes wide and avid.

Tommy doesn't miss a beat. 'It's a different world down south, that's for sure.' He lays down his spoon. 'Now here's a poser for you, Lettie. How long you'd think an Essex summer lasts?'

At last he lets me look back into his eyes, that are clear and bright and guileless.

Yes, he's told them I like flowers, which is true. That I'm a country girl, which is not. He's clearly not told them about me being from the St Clement's home. No one ever treats you the same once they know you've no family behind you, do they. He won't have told them anything about himself either, then, not anything important. That's my Tommy. It's far too early to show our hand, to anyone. If ever.

I lay down my spoon carefully, next to his. 'Why, Tommy, I couldn't say.'

At that, his muddied brow knits together. I watch them

appear at last – those familiar furrows in his forehead. One two three four, like ripples in sand. I used to be able to read them the way other women read tea leaves, or palms. And I shall again.

'Thirty-six week.' Dell sounds triumphant. 'February through October.'

Jean leans forward. 'He means in the glasshouses, Lettie.'

'*Thirty-six week*,' he repeats.

'Gosh,' I say, dimpling up.

It does the trick. The Dells take turns telling me about what a good life they've made for themselves here. About the climate – sunnier – the soil – sandier – the Association – fairer – than anything back home. Back home being somewhere down in the West Country. Which accounts for the chewy way they talk. I'd thought all the Foxash smallholders were from the Special Areas, like us – Glasgow, Tyneside, Lancashire and South Wales. The Dells seem to have moved about plenty, although what did it matter, because the way they tell it, they had nothing, until they came here. It all belonged to whatever family they worked for. That being the reason why they'd moved all the way over here, when they heard the Government was doing something for people who had nothing of their own. Tommy and I both nod at that.

Turns out he's not been training with Dell after all. Dell's been one of those training him. He's what they call a 'pace-setter', brought in by the Association at the very start of this settlement here at Foxash, on account of his 'extensive horticultural experience'. He took over his own holding straight off. Nowadays he makes £600 a year. He'll be able to buy a piece of his own land back West before long.

He and Jean reminisce about the early days, three years back, when the holdings were just rectangles, marked out with string on posts, in the used-up fields of the old Foxash farm bought with Government money. The way they tell it, Dell built most of this entire estate single-handed: the outbuildings, and the poultry houses and glasshouses and pigsties. Laid the drainage pipes. Dug the wells. Spread manure. They laugh. Cartloads of manure.

All the while, though, I can feel them looking me over the way you might inspect market produce. Keen, but not keen to show it. Her eyes flicker all over me: my frock, my hair, my home manicure. He turns that melting smile on me every chance he gets.

Did I know the Government is now backing the Association's estates across the country? It will mean national food security can be assured. And if everything goes to plan, they'll set up a whole load more estates out in the colonies. Then they'll be able to ship all the redundant men and their needy families from the Special Areas out there and off their hands altogether. Yes, the Dells have swallowed the whole brochure: back to the land, and back to work. An end to hunger, idleness, poverty and degeneracy.

When Sanders was spouting this stuff at our interview – *as man cultivated the earth he drew from it* something *virtues*. Something something *the dignity of labour, the beauty of growth* – talking of Tommy and his marras, idle and poor, like they were the scum of the earth, I saw how Tommy's fists clenched tight behind his back. Now he nods along, obedient as a well-trained dog. And when Dell takes a breath, Tommy chips in, to recite more of their achievements for them. Two breeding sows and thirty blue pigs for fattening to bacon, 125 laying birds. Two dozen geese and twice that in poultry. Mr Adam Dell is the best pig man on the estate. Big deal here, apparently, pig breeding. Thirty-eight different market-garden crops over a twelve-month period. On average.

Three months the Association's had Tommy to itself.

He's spilling over with words, complicated new words at that. Those final months at his sister Monica's, he'd never said more than a how do to old Mr Chilvers downstairs, to anyone. The morning he left, blacking his boots on the step, I'd heard him parrot: *Association don't just take a man's labour and pay him off when they're done with him. It's a hand up they're giving us, see, not a hand-out.*

And see how the Dells gaze back at him, fond as loving parents. Lord Sanders had that look on him too, by the time he left. *Here's a good un.*

Tommy clasps his hands earnestly before him on the table, to match Dell's. Dell's hands are slender and tanned, with long, tapering fingers whose broad, pale nails are reeded like acorns. Tommy's hands are blunt, reddened slabs, his fingers that short and wide he could never close his hands to make a fist. I can see the hot, fresh blisters rising. These years without work have softened his skin. I remember that first afternoon he took me up the back of the church, those hands were as rough and dry against my throat as the warmed stone against my back. I'd flinched, even started to prise them away. That's when I'd noticed the finger on his right hand. The little finger, lopped off at the first knuckle. A part of him must have gone missing, I'd thought, some accident maybe, down there in the dark of the pit. And I'd closed my hand around his. *I'll hold on tight to this one, and we'd be all right. I'll be all right.* But he'd pulled away, breathing hard, and stuffed both hands in his jacket pockets. He might have walked off then, and never come back. He didn't, though, did he? Couldn't tear himself away.

Oh but you're mine, I tell myself. *You are. Aren't you?*

'Lettie?' Tommy pauses. 'I said, we've done well to have fetched up down this end of the settlement, next to the Dells. They've a lot to teach us.'

Dell nods sagely, accepting his due. 'Collecting eggs before we could walk, weren't we, Jean? You know, we've been crying out for fine young men like your husband, who are keen to learn. Those Special Area fellas they've been sending us – twice your age, hordes of kids – they tell us they're skilled, but they don't hardly know one end of a chicken from the other.'

'*Pfft*,' scoffs Tommy. 'Was the same for us in the War. When they sent the conchies. Worse than useless, they were.'

Dell nods. Then, with a sidelong glance at Jean: 'Tell me, Tom, wasn't it pigeons you and your dad specialised in, on that allotment of yours? Oh, and chrysanths, of course.'

If he hears any slur, Tommy doesn't show it. 'You see, Lettie,' he says to me, brisk, respectful, 'gains you a fair advantage, a specialism does. Adam here was the first to lead on winter lettuce.'

Dell braces his hands comfortably behind his head. 'Lettuce does us very well, all things considered, doesn't it, Jean? Although' – he rocks slightly, grinning – 'it doesn't always do, to put all your eggs in one basket, we've found.'

Jean lays down her crust and gazes wordlessly at him, her cracked lips parted.

Tommy whips out his tabs, taps the packet over and over on the table and lights one in a flurry. 'Well now, Dell, you cut, what is it now, over two thousand lettuce, priced at—'

Dell shrugs. Then he grins.

Tommy tucks his packet away and gives the tabletop a loud slap that makes us jump. His shoulders are braced, his pale eyes intent.

'Ha! Never you mind what it comes to. Hear me, Adam? I'll beat that easy.'

Dell sits silent and still a moment more, bestowing his calm, winning smile on one and all. Then he reaches round the table to yoke a heavy arm around Tommy's neck. 'Ah yes,' he says fondly. 'You'll see, Mrs Radley, Tom's got his own ideas about how to run this place. Haven't you, Tom?'

Jean smiles that cringing smile at Tommy. 'Course you have, Tom.'

'That's the joy of this place, Mrs Radley. A man gets to be his own master. We work hard, course we do, no one gets anything for free in this life. But you've got your independence now, haven't you, son? Up to you now. Show your lady wife what you're made of, eh?'

Tommy lifts his tab to his mouth once more.

'Lettie.' Jean's voice is sharp. 'You're not eating.'

Tommy plucks a flake of baccy from his lip. 'She'll have filled up on toffees. Our Lettie's got a right sweet tooth.'

Jean tuts. 'You Special Area girls are all the same. You need some proper nourishment inside you.'

'When Tom first got here,' says Dell, 'he could barely hold a blessed trowel, let alone pick up a bale, remember?' He gives his indulgent guffaw. 'What was it she had you living on up there, Tom, thin air?'

Before either of us can reply, a mass of white feathers and red beak rears up from the mantelpiece. Jean pats her shoulder smartly and the chicken topples towards her with a loud cluck and rustle. But Tommy is up and standing and there to catch it. The chicken tucks in its wings and feet and neck and sits very still in his arms, a china ornament rescued from certain shattering. Jean turns to take it from him and for one long moment, as we watch Tommy settle it in the crook of her arm, her breast rests heavy against the back of his hand.

'Hello, my lovely,' she croons, lowering her head. 'Have we woken you up, Flo? Come on, say hello to our new friend.'

Flo fixes one shiny, bulbous eye on me. Tommy sits him-self back down next to Jean. He hunches over his bowl, all elbows, like a hungry child. I watch her stroke the chicken's smooth, oily neck, gazing vacantly over my head, up at the shadowy shelves behind me. Something hot inside me shifts, and pools.

I lay down my bread.

'Mr Dell?' I say, polite as I can, and try not to wince as I slip the button of my shoe back into its loop.

He raises his head and gives me that big, soft, enquiring grin.

'If you could let me have that lamp there, Mr Dell, I need to step out for a moment.'

*

He builds a fine outdoor nettie, I'll give him that. Roomy. Dry. Very little in the way of draughts. The night air sits thick and damp in my throat. If Tommy's been eating here most nights, where's he been sleeping?

Each square of newspaper tears easily away from the loop of twine, mushroom soft and just as fragile. I hold them to the lamp to read, out of habit. It's a foreign language.

MOLASSINE LAYING MEAL . . .

3'6 WEEKLY BUYS A MEAD . . .

COMBINE WITH GOVT. DURING RAT WEEK . . .

Rat week.
I tug off more sheets.

Intercrop the Nursery Bed.

Dreadnought, Bunyard's Exhibition Early Long Pod . . .

In the end I put down the lamp and shut my eyes and do my best. Just my rotten luck. I tell myself I should be glad of my monthlies, glad I've not messed that up at least. But I never feel clean any more, not properly.

I wipe my eyes and straighten my clothes and sprinkle straw down the hole, waiting for the four crumpled balls of newspaper to warm inside me before I lift the latch.

*

When I finally get Tommy away, out into the dark and the wind and the cold and the mud, he takes a deep, long breath, the sort of breath he never used to manage without coughing his guts out. He holds it for longer than I think possible and then raises his face to the stars. In and out he breathes, like a bellows, like he's stoking himself up, or reaming himself out. He lets the last breath out long and slow.

I move a little closer and slip the point of my little fingernail into his buttonhole, smooth his lapel. 'That's better. Fresh air, eh?'

He grunts.

Shivering prettily, I clasp my elbows.

'Tom, is it now?'

Tom had been his ma's name for him, long before he was born. Only his sisters use it now.

He raises the lamp high between us, swaying slightly. And I see how tight and grey his jaw is, how tired and worn out he must be by his long day outdoors and all this talk. I should have kept my mouth shut.

I take the lamp from him, find the latch. 'Best get indoors, pet.'

It's clear someone's lived here before us, but not recently. Not lavishly or even well. There's a kitchen, just the same as theirs, but in reverse: coal range to the right, big windows to the front, door to the stairs on the back wall to the left. They've left us a table, just as Jean said, and two battered chairs and a dresser. There'll be a bedstead upstairs too. With a mattress. Tommy had grinned at that: the Association won't need to have ours sent down after all, Lettie. Meaning, Monica can sell it on.

Front to back this place is no bigger than Monica's front room. And we've damp here too, and mildew, and mouse droppings. The ceilings are lower, but the walls are scuffed, and the corners bracketed with spiders' webs. Lino throughout, yes, but unswept and torn in places. Off the small hallway, to the side of the back door, is a scullery, with indoor pump, as advertised. It's tiny, though, nowhere to set up a copper. Some dark shelves under the stairs. But where's the electric, we were promised electric. I can't see any sort of switch, or fixing. When I came back from nettie, Jean told me we'd have had water closets if the Association hadn't been warned off by the locals; they'd insisted we weren't to have better than they have themselves.

I shine the blessed lamp everywhere I can, but this is all there is. And one of Jean's hyacinths perched on the front windowsill. Pink as a baby's bottom.

Tommy slumps against the kitchen door. He doesn't act the fool. Pull me on to his lap. Nuzzle my neck. He just stands in the doorway, letting in the draught. That's my Tommy back, right there.

I'd get off work at Crampton's, the other girls clacking off down the hill, and me left there like a lemon, thinking my eyes were playing me tricks. But he'd be there, stood still in the shadows. Then out he'd come. Stooped. Hands in pockets. Forehead furrowed. That bright face, full of want. I don't let myself remember what I've done these past months and years, just to get that look back.

But I can't seem to stop.

'You've not been here at all, then?' And then: 'You've been stopping at barracks?'

He wipes at his mouth with his handkerchief. Now we are alone together, he seems nonplussed, like a child whose game has taken a wrong turning.

'Aye. Been waiting on you, Lettie.' He gives me a steady look, wipes his mouth again.

There is something different, but I can't put my finger on it. Something pent up, yes. A constraint. A forbearance, perhaps. Hope flares back up in me.

I set the lamp down on the table, claim it as my own. 'She's laid us a fire too, isn't that kind.' I bustle over and cock my finger under the latch of the stair door, give it a jiggle. 'Look. A downstairs and an upstairs.'

I even start to whistle. *I love you, a bushel and a peck.* This is the Lettie he likes, scooting about the place, chattering on, brass shining, fresh flowers.

Tommy stuffs his handkerchief back in his pocket. 'It's what you wanted, Lettie.'

'Oh yes! It'll be grand once I'm done with it.'

I wiggle my way across the room. 'It's ever so dark, though, isn't it? Without—' Without the electricity we were promised. In the middle of nowhere. Next door to the pair of them.

He pulls the door to behind him and swallows a cough. 'It's getting on, Lettie.'

Someone's already carried in the tea chest. All Tommy has to do is lever it open to get at the bedding. I'm glad of the hammering and splintering. It keeps the silence inside and the darkness outside. Because I used the quilt to line the chest to keep everything from breaking, I have to lift all the pieces of our old life out of the chest before I can get to it. Kettle, fry pan, teapot, cups. Mending bag. Dustpan and brush, worn to a slant. The pot. Spoons, forks, knives wrapped in newspaper. It looks like someone else's rubbish.

Tommy picks up the bedding. I take up the lamp and lift the latch and go gingerly up into the narrow, musty space.

There's one room. A dormer window to the front, bare boards and sloping whitewashed eaves. The bedstead and mattress take up its whole width. A tiny cast-iron fireplace at the foot of the bed, some pegs for clothes, and a small cupboard door in the wall opposite, to the left of the bed-head. Tommy squeezes past the end of the bed to crank open the window latch. As he lights up, the clammy night air floods in.

I dust off the mattress and make up the bed. I hang up the green plaid he liked so much and the ruined stockings, and get into bed in my slip. I lie down on the left side, my side. Three months I've slept alone, in the middle of our mattress on the floor. Huddled up in my overcoat, and still I'd slept sounder than I had since I don't know when. I'd even started to dream again.

When he hears me tug up the sheet, Tommy flicks out his tab. He pulls the latch to and undresses where he is. Under his long johns, I glimpse his shoulder blades, his ribs and the ridge of his spine. Muscle is coating bone again, smooth and concealing. Rubbing him down used to be like running a cloth over a boulder.

He snuffs out the lamp. As he makes his way over, my body flares and curls to him. It's like striking a match you thought might be too damp to spark. He lies himself down flat on his back, left arm stiff as a poker over the blanket between us, and stares into the darkness, the silence. Only inches between us, but he could be hundreds of miles away.

I shift on to my back. 'Good to stretch out in a proper bed, eh, Tommy?'

He tucks in his chin.

'Sheets not damp, are they?'

I draw the blanket up over my shoulders. We'd never had many blankets, we'd always had coal. And I try to hold my breath, stay very still.

'No word, then?' he says finally.

Those mornings at the pump. The queues I've stood in. Nothing. This whole three months will have been worse for him. He'll have been wondering, waiting. Maybe we'll never know if we'd had to leave at all. I turn my head from side to side so he can hear the pillow rustle.

He pulls in a long, steady breath.

'It's just us here, Lettie. You know? Rest of them from our area were from the docks, and they went over north of the river. Another settlement there, Newbourne.'

No one around to ask awkward questions. No one to write home and let on where he is. He'll be safe. He's telling me we can start again, just the two of us.

Next door, a latch drops loudly. A drawer shunts shut, the other side of the wall. Feet scutter on bare boards. The Dells' voices rise and cut out, but I can't make out whose is whose. I feel hot all over. They could be right here in the room with us. We hear a high giggle, then nothing. Nothing, until the dull, unmistakeable thud of a bedstead, against the wall at our feet, over and over.

I heave the bedclothes up loud as I can. 'You'll be back to the Central first light, then?'

'Aye.'

The thudding doesn't stop. I rustle the sheet again. 'I am glad to be here, Tommy, you know. Aren't you glad?'

Tommy's rigid, staring up into nothingness.

His hair, cut. Socks, darned. Seconds, served. What is she to him? He's never strayed before, I'll say that for him. But then he's never been away before. No, it's ridiculous. I know better than to let on, though, not even with a look. He can't be questioned. His chest tightens, his eyes go blank, and he can't breathe, he's back down there in the dark.

'Night, Lettie,' he says.

Then it comes to me, in a hot wave of shame. He'll have smelt it on me straight off, trapped inside my coat earlier, now wafting up between us – that rusty, rotten tang of stale blood.

I press my legs together. But his breathing is already slowing, exhausted, sleep is sucking him down. *It means a lot of hard work, of course. Naturally, you'd expect that.* I tuck the sheet over my cold, exposed ear, and listen to the pounding of my own blood.

*

We'd both been stuck so long it was like asking the slag heap to grow legs and run away. Doesn't matter how you try, his marras would say, once you've been in the pit, she's got a hold on your throat. And we knew well enough how people spoke about them who had gone down south. They didn't speak of them. Do a moonlight flit, least you get respect.

But it had been like that longing to have a tooth pulled, even if you can't afford the dentist, let alone the gas. If everything's rotten – the gum, the ground, this rotten place – it should be easier, shouldn't it, to pull it, to go? And then a thought would come that would make me take my hand from my aching jaw, because what if I'd got it the wrong way round? What if we were the rotten ones, and we were only taking our own rottenness with us, to poison somewhere else?

The day of our interview, the streets had been emptier than ever. It was pouring down. The clock gone from mantelpiece, no pit buzzer no more: the man from the Association might arrive any minute. I knew they'd all be watching out from behind their windows. I should have done more to the place, for days I'd been making lists in my head. Monica's three-piece was back where it should be and our mattress was wedged behind her kitchen door, if only it had stayed fine, I'd have put it in the yard. The table was set. I'd borrowed a chair from Mrs Chilvers downstairs for him and I'd got tea and sugar and if he wanted fresh milk he'd have to whistle for it, no one has fresh. I couldn't let myself think about the look they must all have on their faces, because it was hard enough to wipe it off mine.

I was trembling hard and it made me so cross I was wishing I'd never even told Tommy. This is our chance, you know, I'd said, when I showed him the leaflet. I'd stripped it from the window of the butcher's up Argyle Street after Daniels cheeked me again. That had been the Wednesday, three whole days after, and I'd heard the way talk was turning. So I'd dared him. Told him I'd not forgotten the gambler in him, the chancer I'd married.

Tommy Radley, hewer, king of the pit. First man down the shaft every shift, first to move from pit to pit, to work where there was gas or water or a weak roof, to get the best rate, get ahead. Silent, sleepy-looking, stony-faced Tommy Radley, who'd play pitch and toss in the woods all night long, and play to win. And if you were fool enough to take him up on a game of cards, he'd fold you in half. Bluff you till kingdom come.

You're my First Man still, I'd told him. There's plenty of gilt left on that gingerbread, if you know where to look.

He'd not said a word. But off he'd gone. And he came back from dole with it all on a piece of paper. Gave me a flash of that look. Then his mouth twitched and out came someone else's voice. *Well, what do you think of it, now you've read the particulars?* I wasn't going to give him the satisfaction. We were well beyond larking. If I'd played along, I think I might have have crumpled up and cried, and never stopped. But before I could turn away he was mumbling into my neck, thick with the pitmatic.

It means a lot of hard work, of course. And then he was stood behind me, snatching up my hands and clapping them before us like I was a dummy. *Naturally, you'd expect that. When do I start?*

He hadn't touched me in so long. His lips were soft and warm, all across the nape of my neck and behind my ear.

That was when I told him about the allotment too. Not said whose it was, mind, just that no one seemed to be working it. Let him work it out, I was thinking. Believe it was his idea. I never thought we'd be in with much of a chance, even so. I must have been still hoping, even then, something might turn up.

They had us up before their selection panel, the pair of us. He had to borrow a pair of socks and I tacked him on a set of cuffs and a collar. I'd steamed my hat, but when I sat down I saw I'd have to take it off and I hadn't been able to get my hair to wave. Then there was a physical inspection for Tommy, that we hadn't known about, and I wanted to weep then, for what they would see when they stripped him, how would they know what he had been?

All those years he'd faced down any bugger. Flying out pit gates on that fancy bike of his, never mind he'd worked a double shift. Chin up, cap down low like a fighting man, you'd be a fool not to get out of Radley's way. Not that he was ever one of the likely lads. Tommy never went looking for trouble, kept himself to himself, but oh, Crampton, and the salesmen fellas, when they saw him waiting on me across the street, they scattered like pigeons.

Will you walk out Saturday, then? Chin up, pale eyes steady, mouth petal-soft, slightly pursed. My knees folded and my palms stuck to my skirt.

I'd have done anything rather than walk out. Always tried to hide it, how my bad foot throws my right hip out. Turned out he really went for it. *I could spot you a mile off, bobbing about in that shop.* Next Saturday, I made him a trail of sweets wrapped in shiny paper, got him chasing after me all the way back down to our canal bridge.

You run like you're hobbled.

Have to catch me if I trip then, won't you?

My First Man. The year we married, he was making over £3 a week. That bike of his was a Jack Adams, cost him £8, all his savings. He said he'd buy us a tandem, if I'd learn to ride. He was saving for a motorcycle. Imagine. After the first lockout, he was one of the lucky ones, they had him back. But on £2, even as First Man. After the second, £1 14/-; then 5/- a day before offtakes. No man alive can hold his head high on that. Or step out smart with cardboard for boot soles. Let alone look a body in the eye.

And so I'd watched him walk blind, these three years. Back from gates every day, back from Guardians every week with our relief vouchers in his hand, back from nothing to nothing and his step slower each time. Him and all the rest of them, disappearing inside their clothes, inside themselves. If you go on strike and win, you're a hero; if you lose, you're nothing, and a fool to boot. *You never hear the spark of hobnail on cobble no more, do you* Monica would say to me, after we'd had to give up Shiney Row and move into her front room. *And if you do, it only spells trouble.*

He fixed himself up as best he could for the interview. Shaved so close his face was dish-rag soft. Oh yes, Tommy was ready. I could see it in the set of his jaw. It would be the Association *v* the Radleys. But I wasn't. My rag of a frock hanging off me, my pitwife bun, Monica's half-cocked housekeeping. How would they know how we had once lived, or who we could be, given a chance?

A smart, steady step rang out in the yard. Alongside it a lady's heels tapped, fast and light. My breath puffed fast and white. I could see too well how the place would look through a woman's eyes. The only other cup was chipped. Tommy never found a new pane. I never got anything for a fire.

At first he'd tried to keep his dignity, and hadn't I wanted to curse him for it? We both knew they wouldn't have us if he kept that up. He soon buckled under. What choice did he have? Was made to repeat himself over and over, knuckles whitening behind his back. Lord Sanders noted down everything on sheets of creamy paper with his fancy fountain pen, only he didn't have the faintest, did he. Sat there in his punched brogue boots. Fanning out his brochures.

Last Friday in every month, I wanted to say to him, the means test man has sat himself down at the table, and without being invited, neither. Three years now, every month. And all he's ever needed to see is one page, but no, he has to flick back through the whole book. That £1 we started out with, and the £76 we'd built up – and we'd bought a lot that year too. He'd always pucker up his lips at that. Not long, it was £68. Clothes, and coal, and things which had worn out. £50, £48. Trying to manage without drawing. £20. £19. Matter of time and it was £6, £4, £2 . . . He pawed down the page and he never once looked us in the face. Ill-mannered pig. I'd be giddy with anger by the time he left. Notice there's not enough chairs, Mr Sanders? No cushions? No mirror? That's thanks to him.

All that striving, and we knew we were failing. We were helpless, and we knew it. And so did Sanders.

And as for that lady wife of his, eyes glassy with curiosity. The state of this place is Tommy's sister's fault, you know. Friday nights, our place always looked bright. When we had our own place. There was brass to polish, cushions to plump. Rugs everywhere. I'd have got something special for tea and supper, stowed his pit clothes in the box under the sofa and made myself neat and clean. I had a bob to set then, not this wispy little nest in the nape of my neck. And on Saturday nights we'd go to the pictures, no matter what. Don't crane your neck about like that. It's not like we'd always had nothing.

Tommy's trying not to cough, stood awkward at my elbow because Lady Sanders had his chair, not knowing he had hold of that cup so the chip showed. Remember, pet, I wanted to whisper, when you were on a foreshift, how I'd get up before dawn with you? Warm your coat and boots, put up your bait and tea, sit with you a while. And when there were no more shifts, but we couldn't sleep, I'd mash the tea, and bring it back to bed. We'd listen for the knocker-upper, knowing he wouldn't be stopping outside ours, tensing anyway. And long after that, when there was no more tea, I'd heat some water and bring the kettle back to bed to warm our feet and we'd lie there and talk until our stomachs made us get up.

I aimed the dimples at Lord Sanders and made sure you never clocked. *Yes indeed, sir, we're dead on our feet here, as you can see.* But inside I was shouting: you lot can keep your sympathy, your sneers, your pity, your charity: it's all the same to us.

They came straight on back up afterwards, Mrs Chilvers, with Tommy's sisters at her back, crowding in, and me having to sit myself down on her ladyship's chair that was as warm as a hand on my bottom. I was swallowing hard, trying to plug it, that hole the woman had opened inside me with her rallying talk and her considerate smile, each prying remark that dislodged a new sift and dribble of shame. Tommy carried on rooting about on the mantelpiece and patting his pockets. He'd have thumped you rather than admit it, but there was a plummeting inside him too, I could tell.

He blew out his match and turned to face them. Fold them flat, Tommy.

Pfft, he said. Mrs Chilvers held her breath. His mouth twitched. *It means a lot of hard work, of course*, he told them. *No time to write.*

I told them, those pitwives who'd never got over a St Clement's girl taking their precious Tommy. Now I'd be taking him away for good. We've a brand-new cottage all to ourselves, I told them, in a jolly little place too, a 'thriving settlement' a world away, down in the sunny, civilised, fertile South. Running water indoors and our own front door. Electric. Windows that open proper and shut tight. I'll have a parlour again. And an oak sideboard and a three-piece, and a wireless. There'll be a parade of shops, and a regular Saturday dance. I'll cook hot every day, smarten myself up, have something over for extras, have a bit of fun.

And I beamed and dimpled and cooed enough for both of us. I meant it too. Because this Association scheme isn't just our crack at that gilt on the gingerbread. It's my chance to get my Tommy back.

I always had hope, you see. Always knew I had more than him. Never was one to give up. Never even thought of hope as something to be kept alive; it was just what you did. Because what else could you do?

*

I open my eyes. There's no curtain, but there's no lights either. No moon, not even any stars. I close my eyes again. Makes no difference. My rags will have to wait till morning. I turn on my side.

After a while I can't tell if I'm floating, or falling. I'm in the dormitory, with the whisper and hiss of nine other little girls at St Clement's. I'm squished up next to Mr Robert's daughter, in the bed we shared above his butchery. That's him sawing and hacking away out there in the yard. Scrabble, scratch. It stops, then starts, then stops again. A tremulous hooting somewhere down the lane. Four, five times. It stops too. Then something closer, by the gate perhaps, like a baby crying, crying and crying. And now a terrible collapsing noise, right below the window, a deep, grating rumble that goes on and on. The earth, grinding and shifting in its sleep. Some wild animal, trapped. I'm lying in the dark with Tommy, trapped. I inch closer to him, put my hands to the warm blank wall of his back and bury my face between his shoulder blades.

Down below, a door slams and the latch rattles. Tommy's boots slip and spark, round the house, through the gate and out into the lane, until I only think I can hear them. A blackbird starts to sing, then stops. I feel my way down the stairs and light the lamp where he's left it, with the matches, on the windowsill in the scullery. There's his mirror again, and his strop and razor. His brush stands on end, its bristles soft and wet.

I find my cardie and my fresh rags and shut myself in, stand at the sink and lift my slip. Just in time. Each warm, bloodied ball drops into the sink like a raw yolk. The rattle and suck of the pump is terribly loud. The first gouts of water smell swampy. I rinse my fingers, shake them off, and then start to roll the first rag.

Outside, the light is blue grey and indistinct. More than the one glasshouse out there, at least three, dull with dew and stretching long into the mist. Hoar frost bristles on black sheds, on the crests of muddy ruts and on grass and bare branches.

There'll be no knocker-upper, will there. No women calling or running water, no poss-sticks thumping or street hawkers calling or engines whistling; no steam sirens or children at play or babies wailing. Only this huge, solid silence, as though I might have imagined those sounds in the night.

Jean's neat little fire lights easy as anything. As I watch the flames dance, something unclenches in my chest. I find my own twist of tea. My own tin of milk. I dig out the kettle and take it through to the scullery. Once I'm warmed through, I'll wrap up in Tommy's big old coat that he's left on the back of the door and shake out my stockings and brush off my shoes and walk on down the lane through that tunnel of trees. Established settlement, they'd said. That means a parade of shops. A pub. A picture house. I'll buy myself some scented cachous, and a lace camisole. He could get himself a cane again, a decent hat and some dancing pumps. We'll eat jelly for tea again, with forks.

When I take the filled kettle back through, the kitchen has filled with smoke. I drop to my knees in front of the range and feel for the damper, but more and more smoke pumps out. I close my eyes, my mouth, but it fills my lungs, the room. Eyes smarting, I feel my way to the hallway and push open the back door.

'That range got the better of you?' Jean's voice is rich with a cheerful pity. 'I meant to warn you last night. There's a knack, you know. Here, take my hankie.'

I press it to my eyes. Before I know it, she's propping my front casements wide and is down on her hunkers.

'See this flap here?' She cranes her head round, eyes screwed up against the smoke.

'That one?' I point at random and hurry to the hallway to find my shoes. I've never let anyone see my right foot, the ugly twist it has, the purpled scaly mass that grew with me, and the way the skin has calloused over the hump. Not since the girls at St Clement's, not Tommy, not in all these years. Especially not Tommy. I hardly limp at all with my shoes on.

I wince as I fasten the button. The unfamiliar shoe strap has cut a raw, angry mark across its bulging bridge.

When I return I see a tiny black kitten has snuck in with Jean. It stretches and curls, festooning itself with cobwebs, and snags at the cuff of her dungarees, mewing, until she scoops it away with the edge of her boot and it curves on its side again like a worn-out boot, and thrusts out a blood-stained rump.

'They're welded wrong, look. Mine's just the same. You prop it open, like this.'

She takes from her bib pocket a length of metal that will do the trick. I can keep it. She'd put it aside specially. She squints up at me.

'Lettie, you're pale as a pint of mushrooms.'

For a long time in the night there'd been a sound like a baby's cry, not through the wall, but from outside, in the dark. On and on, and no one coming. It's the upset of moving, I'd told myself.

Jean cocks her head. 'Was it the pigs? The noise they make rubbing up each other at night.' Her eyes widen. 'Foxes. Am I right? At it all night this time of year. We'll have half a dozen cubs down that lane come March, just you see.' She wipes her hands on her thighs, sets to fixing the prop in place. 'Don't worry, I'll show you how to deal with those little devils. Anyway.' Her face brightens. 'Third time lucky.'

'What?'

'You Radleys. You're our third set of neighbours in, what, two seasons?'

'Is that right?'

She snorts. 'Last lot did a flit. Wife wasn't up to it. Said it wasn't her cup of tea. Never did a stroke of work. I'd see her out brushing the path, waiting for someone to pass the time of day.' She shakes her head, and starts to remake our fire, her broad back hunched and her fingers supple and fast as snakes. 'Said she'd left all her family behind, and she couldn't write as she didn't have her letters. Took them all back to Wales to live with her mother. Silly girl. Older than you, she was too. How old are you?'

'I'm twenty-six.'

'And no kids. Not long married then?'

'Don't you worry about me, Mrs Dell. I'm a sticker.'

'Jean, please.' She surveys me for a moment. Then she coughs hard, with her pale, cracked tongue out, the way a man would, and flaps one hand. 'Water, Lettie.'

The kitten shadows me right into the scullery, butting its tiny head against my ankles. Those balls of blood are still in the sink, each sat in its own pale pink pool. If I could have got that fire going myself, I'd have had them burnt by now. I splash the first swampy pump into Tommy's shaving mug, shoo the kitten out and pull the scullery door to behind me.

I set the mug down at her side. We had a dodgy range once before, I could tell her. Tommy stuck his hand up the chimney, pulled out a seagull. Long dead, but you'd never know. With its wings neatly folded by its sides, and its head nestled in its breast, like it was sleeping, like those Egyptian mummies they found.

We'd get to chatting, then, wouldn't we. She'd never leave us alone. She'd be in and out the whole time, the way they were back home. All this space, all this emptiness and quiet, and still no privacy.

Before I can stop her, she's up and marching through to the scullery with the mug. I hear her put it down in the sink. She's in there an age. I don't know where to put myself.

Out she comes, bobbing and smiling. I've never seen anyone so grateful for a swallow of water.

'That better, then?'

'Oh yes, *much*. Oh yes.' Her eyes are shining.

I open the back door smartly.

'Well then, thank you ever so. Best get on.'

Pausing on the freshly muddied doorstep, she shoves her hands deep in her pockets. 'I've filled your back boiler for you, so you'll have hot water soon enough. But you'll need to keep those windows open till this smoke clears.' She gives me that moist, longing look. 'Best come over to mine, don't you think?'

*

There's a big glass jug, with yellow cream floating on fresh blueish milk. A bowl full of curls of real salted butter, I can see the grains. A mound of strawberry jam on a saucer, glistening with whole fruits. Another bowl, stacked with cubed white sugar. A fat square loaf of shop-bought already hacked about, with another untouched on the board beside it. I can't think when I last bought so much food. With marmalade at 8/½d. Butter 10d/lb. Breakfast has been nothing but bread and butter and cocoa.

'Tom's been in for his fill this morning already. Why don't you feed yourself up a bit, Lettie?'

Can't she see we'll choke on any more charity? Especially from her.

'That's very kind of you, but I can't stop, see. I'm off down the shops directly.'

'Shops?' Jean's eyes widen. 'There's the central depot, but that's for the holding – supplies, tools, you know. No, what you do is, you make yourself up an order.'

She plucks a pencil from the crowded dresser and smooths out a paper bag. 'Here, write down what you need. Warden's assistant, Mr Bridgewater, he takes an order down to Manningtree for us once a week. Ask him nicely, he might have something back for you today if he's not too busy. He'll be along in a bit with Tommy for the inspection.'

As I touch my hand to my empty pinny pocket, she adds: 'Oh, you shan't need to pay up front. It'll go on a blue chit at the end of the month, with anything Tom orders in the way of equipment and the like, from the depot. Keep an eye on your chits, mind. We know you Special Area types.'

Before I can bridle, she goes on: 'He'll drop off outside the gate, once a week. Co-op used to deliver down this end, but now the estate's filled up with families the round's too long. So they say. We had a confectioner's van too, you know, in the early days. You should have seen the little ones run when they rang their little bell.' She turns to fork at the pan sizzling on the hob. 'You'd have liked that, I expect.'

I can't help but breathe it in, the sweet, harsh stink of bacon.

'What's up with your foot then?'

'Nothing's up with my foot.'

'Born with it, were you?'

'Born with what?'

She stops prodding and turns to look at me. She seems about to say something, then change her mind. 'Long as it doesn't get in the way of you doing your work, I suppose. You know why they put you down here, with us, don't you?'

'Because you're—' What was that word Tommy used last night? I make it sound ugly. 'Pioneers.'

'Pacesetters.' Her smile is brief. 'No. Because it's just the two of you.'

I keep my face hard. 'Is that right?'

'We've just the mechanic and an orchard worker up the lane. They put the families up by the Central nowadays. Makes sense, I suppose. Company for each other.'

43

'I suppose.'

She turns back to the hob, cracks in an egg. 'You'll get a sight more done on the holding without little ones, that's for sure. How long did you say you've been married?'

'Not long.'

'No.'

'Little ones will come along soon enough, eh?'

'I suppose.'

I stare mutinously at her back, at the dirty piece of string tied around her non-existent waist, the soot and worse all over her dungarees. She's not even tucked a tea towel around her middle.

Fly spots and cobwebs on the windows too. Petals are browning at the edges. White roots finger out from under the pots. I look away, and up, at the two rows of broad shelves that run right round the walls, stacked solid with bottles and jars of unnameable preserves and pale fruit, bottled whole. Hunched right up in the far corner, by the door to the stairs, is a shadowy row of harvest dollies. Bell-bottomed, woven in straw, arms clasped at the waist and tied together with red thread. Five of them, at least a foot high, their sheafed heads crooked against the ceiling.

'Reckon you could find a bit of everything we've ever grown on those shelves.'

Jean Dell has eyes in the back of her head.

'Ads says I'd bottle the spiders if I could catch them. You shan't need to buy jam, Lettie, that's for sure. I've plenty. Tom loves his jam, doesn't he? Proper pitman.'

Her heavy stride sets everything on the table rattling. All her movements are too large, like she's outside in all that open space still. She slides a huge oval plate with a blue border on to the table in front of me.

It's a man's portion she's given me. Two domes of bright orange yolk in a pillow of white, three pink rashers, the rind golden and crispy and oozing speckled fat. Perfectly cooked, and the plate is shining clean. Impossibly perfect, like food in a dream. Far too perfect to eat.

She stands over me, breathing heavily. It's how the Sisters used to linger by a desk, or a bed, exerting their will although we had no choice anyway.

I shake my head. 'Now, Jean, you shouldn't have.'

'Oh come now.' She pulls out a chair. A big, shaggy cat peels off with a yowl, leaving the seat scummed with brown fur.

'Ooh, no, Sammy'll kill you if you sit on his cushion. Come here, Sammy love. He's our best mouser yet, on account of missing that left eye, see? A devil with toads too. As long as he doesn't drop them on his blind side. You'd laugh to see it – they just hop off again. One summer he disappeared, we were worried sick, turned out he'd been out in the fields following the flayer, came out the other end all bound up!'

She settles him back and turns the milk-jug handle towards me. 'Now this is from my lovely old Nanny Queenie. Three little kids she had, just three weeks back, and all girls, luckily. There's one not found a home yet, if you—' She pours the tea, slopping it on the saucer. 'Sit yourself down, do.'

'Three sugars, like Tom? Isn't this nice, now. You and me, we'll be company for each other, shan't we, you'll get to know Queenie, and Sammy, and Flo, my girls—'

'It's Tommy,' I say abruptly. 'No one calls him Tom.'

She sets down the sugar bowl. Watch that tongue, Leticia Radley, the Sisters always said. You'll cut yourself one day.

I don't care. It's the only weapon I've ever had. But I don't need a friend, do I. Not some slatternly, nosy old witch next door. Just my Tommy.

'Like I said, I really must be off. There's ever such a lot to be done before I can even think of having a sit down. You needn't have put yourself to such trouble, not on my account.' I cast a deliberate look around. 'Not when you've so much to set to rights in your own place.'

*

Outside again, in the thin morning light, amid the cawing birds and the rising scent of wind and manure, I see where I've landed us. This perfect plot. Our four-acre Eden.

The land slopes slightly, from north to south. To the left are the Dells' glasshouses, four of them, clean and gleaming with a dozen or so naked young trees behind, fanned out along the hedge to the north. We've just the one glasshouse our side, greened and mouldering with broken panes. What looks like the remains of another behind it: low walls framing nothing, a rickety stack of glass panes piled beside it. Nothing to mark where our land stops and the tussocky field starts but a few low posts and some sagging wire.

We have a wash house each, and there are two – no, three – tarred black sheds their side, in front of the glasshouses. They have a series of sturdy pens for livestock, pigs here in front and chickens and goats down the side, teeming with movement now, the squawks and squeals starting up at the mere sight of me. We have two sheds our side, greening and broken down like the glasshouses, with tarred roofs torn and flapping. And the remains of what must have been our livestock pens.

The Dells' holding runs away to the east in regular furrows, some tufted green already, some boasting rows of little glass wigwams a couple of feet high. Our holding is as barren and colourless as the fields around us.

She has strung up a washing line, propped twice, between the house and a stunted little tree next to the netties. That would do four families easy, back home. Between the netties and our houses are twenty yards or so of rank grass. Three dewy tracks cross it: one from their nettie to their door, one from the sheds to their door, and another one from round the corner of the house. Our side is untrodden.

Nothing else. Not another building in sight. No wall or fence or hedge between our two holdings. The only real division, and even that we will have to share, is a cinder path that runs from the back of the netties straight down between the holdings all the way to the orchards at the bottom. Beyond that a hedge, a flat field, another hedge, and more fields.

*

I picked up the clods of mud and chucked them out the door. I wrapped a rag around the end of a broom and got all the cobwebs. Wetted another to rub off the fly spots. I found the key to the back door when I was wiping the top of the frame, locked it and slipped the key into my pinny pocket. I made a lot of noise after that. *I love you, a bushel and a peck* . . . Scrubbed that step. Swept those stairs. Opened all the windows and sang some more. When I opened the little door in the bedroom I'd thought was a cupboard I found another, much smaller room under the eaves. Six kids they'd had in here, all told. There are four wooden trays of earth, freshly watered, set out on newspapers in front of the window. I let them be. I'd used up the hot water in the back boiler so I put the kettle back on. Then I opened the front casement. And toppled her hyacinth out on to the grass.

I've burnt up the shovelful of small coal she left beside the grate and shut the windows and it's still no warmer than outside.

Coal, I write with her pencil on her paper bag.

Soda, after I've unpacked the suitcase.

I'll give her a list.

> *4 x Mousetraps*
> *Mothballs*
> *Flea powder*
> *Soda*
> *Tea*
> *Sugar*
> *2 x Loaves*
> *2 x Carnation*
> *Flour*
> *Doz Eggs*
> *Yeast*
> *2 x Saveloys*
> *2lb Mince*
> *1lb Bacon*
> *Cheese*
> *5lb Potatoes*
> *2lb Onions*
> *Dripping*

My stomach growls.

> *Cocoa*
> *Marmalade*
> *Oxo*
> *Tapioca*
> *Currants*
> *Tin salmon*

Tin peaches
Cream
Butter

I cross those last three out.

Margarine

There's not much space left. I wonder what that lot will cost. Lady Sanders had taken great pains to warn me how much more expensive we Special Area wives would find it down here.

With the table pushed under the window like that we could fit a sideboard opposite the range. It might block the door to the stairs, but Tommy could rehang the door to open the other way. I unroll one clippy rug before the hearth, another to catch the mud at the door, and take both the smaller ones upstairs.

2 x Turkey carpets

I sit back down by the range to look at the smooth, clean surfaces, the bare walls, and have a rub at my foot and ponder on Jean. Mr Crampton, the salesmen, Mr Roberts, Mr Bridgewater might have looked me over all right, ate me up with their eyes, least they were looking at everything but my foot. And she saw what was in the sink.

I go over to the front window to check if Tommy's back yet. All this time I've thought he'd be close by. Turns out the men on the settlement, new and old hands, work together on the communal Central farm through the winter months to top up their earnings and produce the seedlings and stock needed for their own holdings. They have to clock on every morning. Then they're hired out for haymaking and harvest and beet singling.

The sky has clouded right over and the light has dulled. Nothing to see anyway, but the muddy lane and beyond it more of those fearful fields, ploughed over and frosted grey.

At least the windowpanes are new, and clear as the big one at Crampton's we had to polish twice a day, on account of noses and fingers. Towards the end of a winter afternoon, when it got quiet, I'd rest my foot against the counter rail and gaze out, just to see my own face looming back at me, glamorous as on the big screen: my hair a gleaming halo, my eyes huge and dark, my vamp's mouth.

I move forward and back, trying to see myself again. It's as though the glass isn't there at all.

Curtains, I think. *Nets Pelmet Eiderdown Dressing set Birdcage Clock.*

Wireless Cake stand Cigarette box
2 x Cinema ticket
1 x Jockey Club perfume
Dancing shoes

I wipe my armpits and clean my nails and check my rags again. I find a nail and hammer it into the wall with the heel of my shoe so I can hang Tommy's mirror up by the scullery door to suit me. I sweep up the flakes of plaster and then I fix my face. There's just enough left in the bottle to do my cheeks as well as my lips.

1 x rouge
1 x face powder

I brush my coat and hat and hang them up behind the door. In the shadows is Tommy's suitcase, that I packed for him three months ago. When I pick it up, it's not empty. And when I open it up, there are his clean drawers and pressed shirts still. I shake out the top shirt. It's been badly pressed and it reeks of onions. I bundle it back up and flick the clasps shut. Then I hear male voices in the lane.

*

I open the door, straighten my stockings and step out across the lumpen grass. The wind plucks at my skirt as I reach the cinder path. It rushes between my thighs and about my throat. Tommy drops his gaze to the ground and jingles the coins in his pocket.

The visitor lowers his pipe and looks me over, his mean, wet little mouth hanging open. He's a short man, nearer my height than Tommy's, in a smart long coat and a dark-brown homburg. His sandy moustache twitches.

'How do you do.' That wireless voice gets me standing a little straighter. 'Mr Bridgewater, assistant warden.'

'How do you do, Mr Bridgewater. I'm Let— Mrs Radley. Ever so glad to see you, Mr Bridgewater. You see, we've simply nothing in, as yet, and how am I to do for my dear husband here?'

Got that straight from Lady S. *How do you manage? You must mind awfully. Dear husband.*

'Dear Mrs Dell next door – she's been awfully helpful – she says as how it's you takes in the orders for us?'

Mr Bridgewater lodges his pipe back under his tache and sucks hard. Forward is as forward does. 'I take it you are enquiring about your Co-operative order?'

I nod dumbly, let my curls tease my cheek.

'That is standard Association procedure nowadays, indeed,' he says, face stiff as a frozen sheet. 'Have it ready for me before I leave, I'll see what I can do.'

He busies himself with his clipboard. He'll go home and chew on that pipe, though, bet you anything.

'Now then, Radley, you have your rotations?'

'Certainly, sir. Right here.' Tommy tugs some dog-eared papers from his jacket and holds them out, eyes lowered.

Back home, the crawlers who doffed their caps to the managers and said *good day, that spot of rain we had last night was just what the roses needed*, they felt eyes on them every day, going to work when no one else was, the men on their door-steps, the women pulling back their curtains. There were blacklegs got their windows smashed, the wife's face cut to ribbons by flying glass.

Mr Bridgewater struggles into a pair of wire specs, juggling his pipe and his clipboard. 'Good man. Someone was paying attention.' He disentangles his specs from his remarkably tiny ears. 'Now, Radley, we walk the bounds, as the old boys say.'

'After you, Mr Bridgewater.' Without a backwards glance, the pair of them set off down the cinder path.

'Oi!' I shout. This wind whips about so, it's hard to catch my breath. 'Oi! Mr Bridgewater!'

He stops and turns. Tommy keeps walking.

'What am I like? I had my list right here. In my pinny pocket. Look.'

He has me come to him, of course. He watches me pick my way through the long grass, my frock blown tight against my swaying hips, my cold nipples. After a quick look at Tommy's receding back, he snuffles up close, his pipe breath rank in my face. There's a bit of will-he, won't-he before he plucks the list from my hand.

He sniffs. 'There's not much to you, Mrs Radley. You sure you're equal to this work?'

'You needn't worry, Mr Bridgewater. Full of vim, I am.'

Another sniff. 'I'll say.'

Neatly sidestepping behind me, he trails his gloved hand across my rump before moving off.

*

Tommy'd watch men like Bridgewater from his spot out there on the street corner; watch them lean against the counter and wipe their sweaty palms on their trouser legs, while I did my bit with the cellophane and the ribbons. He'd walk me smartly along the streets for a bit. We'd get away somewhere quiet, between lamp posts, and he'd take hold of me under the elbow. *If I'd known you were like that I wouldn't have come. Why's that?* I'd ask. *'Cos I wouldn't.* He'd hold me tighter, I'd feel his fingers still twitching for half a brick to smash Crampton's window. I couldn't have pulled away if I'd tried. He could have tucked me under his arm like a stuffed toy.

Picking the last of the dead flies out from behind the window hasp, I hold my pinny pocket open and drop them in. Down the holding they've gone, in and out the sheds, around the orchard and back to the house, Tommy nodding and trailing a few respectful paces behind. Now they are right under the window. All I can see is the top of Bridgewater's homburg.

'As you know, it's good brown earth we have here at Foxash. Your holding is well drained, level, with a nice little slope away there to the south. But this soil is in poor heart, I'm afraid. The last fellow having made rather a precipitous departure. There'll be a remission on your first year's rent, of course. No stable manure worked in last autumn, see, and that end section, should have been dug over—'

Bridgewater breaks off for Tommy's mumble.

'No matter, Radley, I've booked Mr Thompson and the tractor. Marvellous, that machine, does an acre a day.'

Bridgewater recites figures like they're the Lord's Prayer, his officious voice rising clear as a bell. The £260 that's our 'working capital' for the year: for buying implements, seeds, fertiliser, livestock, all that. The monthly allowance on top, for living expenses. What we'll get in income through the central depot from selling pigs, poultry, eggs and vegetables and so on will be 'computed' to allow a 'balance', which will be 'credited to our account'.

It's good to be reminded of what a fortune the Association has gifted us. £260 in the bank. Our pot of gold at the end of the rainbow. That's what we are worth now. How careful we'd had to be, not to breathe a word of it before we left.

'Ours is an extremely generous scheme, all things considered. And you are extremely fortunate to have been chosen, I must say. Now remember, your success from here on in is entirely up to you, Radley. You have your freedom here, and complete initiative. Also, remember we operate co-operatively. Your neighbours will share their knowledge with you gladly. There is no reason why a good man ready to be helped and who will work sensibly should not earn £400 a year. Many present tenants are doing so soon after taking over their holdings. You with me, Radley?'

'Indeed, Mr Bridgewater.'

'Today marks the start of the joint trial period, for you and Mrs Radley. That takes us to – the twenty-fifth of April, if I'm not mistaken. Take note, Radley, that of the men who have retired from the scheme to date, over 85 per cent retired at the end of the joint trial, having discovered that their wives could not accommodate themselves to the new surroundings. Couldn't endure the peace and quiet, would you believe. However, if your lady wife proves satisfactory, then at the end of your first year, when you come off the dole, we write off half of the gift capital and you'll start to pay back—'

I stop listening.

*

Tommy walks those Association boots right across our clean floor, our beaten rugs, past me, to our shining windows. He brings the smell of the place with him: fresh, green and moist. The colour is high and raw in his cheeks. His nose is rindy with cold, his hair pale tussocks. He presses his forehead to the glass and squints up and down the lane, as though he's checking for any more visitors. Then he rests both hands on the windowsill and breathes in deep. I watch the mist come and go on the glass. He shuts his eyes tight.

'All you need to do, Lettie – all you need to do, mind – is show that man you're up to it.'

To keep his voice this low and steady with me, after my performance outside, it must cost him. It's as though none of our darkness ever happened. As though the slate has been wiped clean, even since last night. There is a sort of blithe, determined hope that I think I recognise, from before, from a long time back. When we used to dart across the surface of new things together, confident, testing. *Are you with me, Lettie?* Our first afternoon at the back of the church. Our one room on Banbury Street, our first morning in Shiney Row.

'What are they going to do?' I say. 'Inspect my house-work?' I fluff my hair and recross my legs. I know he can see me, in the glass. 'Oh, I'll prove satisfactory all right, Tommy.'

After a pause, he says: 'Be a good hinnie. I might surprise you yet, Lettie Radley.'

'Had enough surprises already, thank you very much. You seen what's upstairs?'

He pulls out a fresh packet of Woodbines. No more picking up dumpers outside the Empire.

'Seed trays are Jean's idea. Get us ahead before the plugs come. I've to fix up the glasshouse.'

'Isn't that kind.'

He shakes out his match. 'I'll say.'

Don't turn round just yet, Tommy. We're talking at last, even if it's to our own reflections. Flirting, even. We haven't done either, in so very long.

He lights up, still gazing out of the window. 'You be nice to Jean. She's all on her tod down here. Poor old thing.'

'Poor old thing?'

'You heard. They're soft, these Dells. The pair of them.'

Keen old Jean, squatting on her haunches to fix our stove. She's harmless: a foolish, lonely old bird. She'll be soft on Tommy – who wouldn't? Wanting to take him under her wing. Mother him. Nevertheless.

I tuck up a bit of undone hemming on my skirt. 'Don't know anything worth knowing then, do they, the Dells?'

'Don't know anything worth knowing,' he says quickly. 'Beyond this place.'

Tommy knows very well what I can't ask out loud.

'Don't know nothing about hard work. I tell you, Lettie, I'm out there, digging away all weathers. First sign of rain, Adam's off under cover, counting seed or some such.'

And in one quick stride he's in position behind my chair, rocking on his heels, his hands gripping my shoulders. In one long breath, his words are unspooling themselves.

'He thinks he's on top, but he's a fool, Lettie. The Association's taught me new methods he'll not even look at. There's trickle irrigation, and hot benches and powders and treatments like you wouldn't believe. He's no idea. I can order any tools I like, and treatments. I get a whopping discount. I'll outcrop him easy. The yields, Lettie, they're something else.'

'Giant tomatoes!' he says, bending over. 'Huge cauliflowers!' His voice is thick in my ear. 'And cucumbers. I might specialise in cucumbers.'

I grasp his stubby finger and give it a squeeze. 'That'll be my surprise, will it?'

'Don't be like that, pet. We're set up here.' As though this was his idea, his doing.

I let the heat of him soak into my back, loosen my shoulders. I might have slept easier these past months, alone in the middle of the mattress, but I've not once been warm, have I, not through and through.

Tommy's right thumb comes to rest in the hollow at the base of my neck and he strokes the skin lightly once, twice. My pulse throbs in time with his.

'You're with me, Lettie, aren't you?'

I remember how he'd enter me before a shift, when there was nearly no time. Quietly, desperately, working his way deep inside. All this chancer stuff Tommy does, the marra talk, it's not idle boasting, it's not just about getting by. It's to convince himself. To convince me. He'll never, ever admit it, but he needs me to believe in him. To hold him tight in the dark. Now more than ever.

I put my mouth gently to the clear blister on his forefinger. 'Course I am.'

'We'll scrape some gilt off the gingerbread, you'll see.'

I squirm round, trying to see his face. 'That's a promise?'

Tommy nuzzles into my neck, one hand feeling for the hem of my frock.

'Might have a nibble right now.'

He strokes up the back of one knee. That syrupy, undone feeling I've not had in so long floods through me. The force of it surprises me.

I bat his hand away. 'Might you now.'

And now I'm scared all over again. It's been so long, I've forgotten the to and fro. I watch the furrows appear, one by one, and I can't read them at all. His eyes are hazed over, pale and impenetrable as the high, clouded sky.

But I can hear the pride. All that talk last night, the marra rivalry. I never imagined he'd really want this life, winding up like the Dells, out here in the back of beyond. But what else is there for him? Datal and shift work, didn't matter how hard he worked, he never got paid more. Once he got sent to the face, even as First Man, it was still piecework, they paid him for breaking his back. It'll be the same here; the harder he works, the more we'll have, only the work is far lighter. After pit work, digging soil must be like forking jelly. He gets decent garb, gets to stand up straight in nothing but sunshine and rain. His allowance every week no matter what, and all that capital. Tommy'll take the Association, and the Dells, for all he can get. We'll be living off the fat of the land. Anything can happen in three months. We've uprooted ourselves once. What's to stop us doing it again?

He pats my shoulders smartly.

'All right then. Best get back out there.'

One soft, dry peck on the cheek, and he's gone.

Soon as he steps out the door, though, it's like he was never here. I used to listen to his boots strike all the way down the street, around the corner, fainter, down the hill, gone. Coming back, I'd know his step before I really heard it, like it was my own heartbeat.

I listen hard, but he's been swallowed up again in all that silence.

*

Tommy pushes half a dozen packets of seed across the table. Says he's not waiting any longer on those promised Association plugs – the seedlings they raise at the Central farm. A smallholder has to be early to market or there's no profit; may as well throw the whole bloody crop on the bonfire. And Jean's giving us their seed for free.

'You had the training, not me.'

'Get Jean to show you,' he says from the hallway, doing up his creaking new Association mackintosh. 'I'm trenching.'

I'd just got the fire going steady, and set some yeast on. I was about to measure up for curtains; I'm after yellow gingham. These windows are black mirrors after dark; anyone could look in and see us, clear as day. Any time I step outside, Jean's there, beaming. Her hide has turned out to be thicker than I'd thought possible. She will call Tommy Tom, and she's overflowing with advice for me.

Trenching warms and dries the soil. It makes the roots descend lower and the plant grow stronger. This land was pasture before, and only the top layer was ever ploughed, so rain collected on the hard pan underneath and soured the upper soil. Even with the aid of Mr Thompson's tractor, she tells me, Tommy will have to trench all hours if he's to get ahead of the season. Although Adam's sure to give him a hand, when he can.

The headache hits as soon as I open the door. Over two years it's been, every month, yet they still take me by surprise. Pain clamps across my forehead and deep into the rotten roots of my back teeth. It's that great, huge sky, pressing down on our heads. The emptiness of this place scares me witless. Not that I'll let on. I'm fine sat indoors with the lamp. But out here, with no street lights, no streets, no walls, no people, I feel as though I've disappeared.

No sign of Jean. The sky is dark with cloud again and it's raining hard. They'll be indoors, sorting seed. Back home no one'd go out on a day like this, on account of having nothing to go out in. I put the seed in the pocket of my Association mackintosh and turn up the collar.

The air inside the glasshouse is dank, private and still, with a tang of unexpected promise. My spirits lift a little. It is the scent of our first summer. After a few months walking out, Tommy started taking me behind the yews up at St Mary's. He'd lay down his jacket, reach out his hand, and promise me the earth.

I look at the puddles spreading under the missing roof panes, the bare earth, the empty benches, the two dozen new trays, stacked, the single, broken-down stool. It's cold as the grave. But Tommy must get that trenching done before he can make this place weather-tight and put in hot pipes. Jean put those seed trays in the box room because its window faces south and it traps the sun. I could take these up there too, when I'm done.

Only there's nothing to fill the trays with. Am I supposed to dig up the earth? Or has Tommy ordered compost? Where might it be? I look out through the glass panes, crazed bottle green with growths. One sweeping glance takes in the whole holding, three hundred and sixty degrees: houses, sheds, horizon and sky. I can be seen too, from anywhere, clear as day. But not heard. The glass stops nothing but my voice.

Tommy's abandoned his spade. He's moved off halfway down the long ditch along the side of the holding, pole in hand, peering in. If I knock on the glass, perhaps he'll turn and see me: dithering and idle. I don't want him to snap at me again. I scan for the Dells, finally see them in the orchard, two mackintoshed figures crouching either side of one of their bare-branched, hard-pruned trees. One of them sinks to the streaming wet ground, sits, and wraps their arms and legs around the tree's trunk. As the other does the same, their legs emerge from the folds of their mackintosh, gleaming white and quite naked. Then they embrace, around the tree. At this distance, through the rain, it's impossible to tell each from the other.

Mr Thompson's tractor starts up again, right outside, with a whoosh that sets the panes rattling. It drags a set of curled metal blades that slice steadily into the crusted earth and turn it over. Once it passes, I can see the Dells again, up again and walking slowly through the trees, hand in hand, heads bowed.

That familiar tension is building in my head. Tommy jabs at something in the ditch. If I can beg some compost off Jean, I can at least get a few trays done.

I crunch to the far end of the long cinder path – the straight and narrow, she calls it – and make my way towards them along the gap between the trees and the brambly hedge at the bottom of the holding. I turn sideways, to squeeze past three greening wicker beehives, and there, looming over the top of the hedge, is a sodden scarecrow, large as life.

It's been dressed in an old nightgown tied in at the waist and cuffed with twine. On one broomstick arm, set akimbo, dangles a mouldering handbag. And topping it off, a battered straw hat set at a jaunty angle. But the face is a hideous blank: a stuffed feed sack, sliced across by an ugly stitched seam.

I shut my eyes against a sudden dizziness. Coloured

lights move and strafe across my closed lids. They fizz like sherbet, pink and yellow and jagged, electric blue.

'All right, Mrs Radley?'

Dell places a hand on my shoulder. He's very tall, close up. I look around for Jean, but it's just me and him and the scarecrow.

'Frightened me half to death!'

He pulls a wry face. 'I think it's meant to.' He leans in close. 'Least they gave over sacrificing humans before you got here.'

The line of the hedge dips and curves.

'Oopsadaisy. Best get you back indoors.'

His sleeve is worn to the weft and very soft.

'That's quite a wiggle you've got, Mrs Radley. I saw you, you know, out with Bridgewater.'

I can't seem to speak. I try hard to keep my balance, but when he offers his arm again, I take it. The local people have set up these scarecrows in every field about, he's telling me. Not in the middle, for to scare off the birds, but at the edge, facing out. For us settlers. To show us we're not wanted here. To scare us off.

'– even when that there's wheat, not pea or cabbage. Drives Jean potty, it does. She's always on at me to go over there and take them down. First year we've had a lady scarecrow, mind. Reckon tramps might be less likely to strip her. Or maybe not.'

I giggle. Then I think I might be sick. He stops walking. Pats my arm.

'Why folk call them scarecrows I never know. It's not the crows you want to watch out for, it's the blessed pigeons.'

Someone takes my other arm.

*

The pain in my head seems to have drained away entirely. I'm floating along quite nicely in a warm, sweet darkness, my nightgown damp between my thighs and my arms akimbo and his pink lips parting, until the seam in my face peels open like a zip and all kinds of horrid things come spilling out, mice and sugared buns, eggs and snails, a torrent of seeds and droppings.

'Lettie?' It's Jean, huge and hunched in the bedroom doorway. Even when she comes into the centre of the room, where the sloping walls meet, she can't quite stand up straight.

'Are you awake?'

I nod but can't speak. My lips still feel numb.

'That was a nasty turn.' She lumbers over to the bedside.

I would turn away, but even the thought of moving makes me dizzy.

'Here you go.'

A cup with a spoon sticking out of it. And a tea towel, held by its four corners, with something light and bulky inside.

'Can you sit up?'

I close my eyes while she arranges the pillow behind me. The mattress dips as she sits down. The spoon clunks.

'Here.'

She nudges my lips with the spoon and tips something warm into my mouth, thick and sticky as tinned milk, and just as sweet. A sharp, sherbety sensation spreads across my tongue. I open my eyes. She gives me the cup to hold. Something green, with foamy bubbles around the edges. It smells like freshly scythed grass.

'Isn't that better? Go on, another sip. You Special Area girls, you're always that run down, it's scandalous. And the Association expects you to jump to it. Go on, drink it all.'

I'm flat on my back in the St Clement's infirmary, that long, shadowy room next to the chapel full of coughs and crying and bad smells. The balled, crusted handkerchief. The figure in black at the foot of the bed. The wide spoon clicking against my teeth. No one to stroke my hair, to hold my hand. I drain the cup. Warmth spreads through me, powerful as port at Christmas.

There's Tommy at the door, smiling back at me.

Dell, smiling.

Jean, smiling.

*

Later, alone in the bed, I put out my arm and find the tea towel. Inside its folds are cool leaves, crisp and soft and large as my hand. I finger them for a while, feel their softness and firm ridges. And then I take a stem and pinch it hard and fold one leaf after another between my fingers. I feed myself chipped potatoes from the cone, sweets from the poke, one after the other, sharp and sweet, until there is just the bitter stump and the tea towel lies limp and empty.

I wake to daylight, and the sound of a steady wind from the west. No rain. Cold air squeezes through the gaps in the casement. The inside of my head, the space behind my eyelids, feels opened up, rinsed out, ready for anything. No cramps. When I check my rags there's very little there. I feel wiped clean. This is the first headache that's not left me dazed and dull, in need of a dose of Andrew's. It's mortifying, though, for them to have seen me like that. Tommy will be cross.

I pump some water and splash my face. He's halfway down the holding, with Dell, leaning on their spades at the start of one of his new trenches. They step apart and start to dig. Even I can see Dell's skill, and strength. He lets the blade drop deep into the earth, and rests his foot on it only a moment before he levers it out, tosses off the earth and plunges it in again. Easy as spooning jelly.

Tommy looks awkward next to him, stunted and amateur. It's the first time I've seen him thrust a spade down, into earth, rather than forwards, into the coal pile. Again and again his blade goes down, just as fast as Dell's, but crooked. The handle lists over as he stomps on the blade. He yanks it out and jabs, again and again, like there's a wild animal there in the furrow, some sort of vermin to be dealt with, just out of sight. He's trying hard, but it twists my heart to see him. Dell puts out a hand, says something, and then they start again, in unison. Still Tommy falters. And now there's Jean, working her way along from the far end. She digs the way her husband does, smooth and easy, and faster than either of them. Tommy's spade gets stuck and he leans on his handle to watch her, his cheeks red and his breath puffing fast. Then he pulls the blade out with a jerk, like a petulant child.

I flush hot for him. Three months training, and he's still floundering. He won't want patronising by Dell, any more than by Sanders. But he'll have to shape up fast if we're to get away with this. As will I.

He's left the loaf all pitmatic too, hacked about straight on to the table, and the knife in the empty jam jar. In the darkness of the passage I find the box from the Co-op. On top is a smooth new share book in my name. No receipt or anything. A basket of fresh veg alongside: leeks, potatoes, two turnips. Hanging on the back of the door is a clean, pressed Association jacket and trousers and a well-brushed hat. A pair of small brown boots, my size, and slick with dubbin. The coal scuttle sits alongside, filled to the brim with good big coals.

I leave the Association suit hanging, and button on my cardigan and pinny. After I've cleared the table and relaid and lit the fire, I take the Co-op box into the kitchen and unpack it. *Tea. Sugar. 2 x Loaves. 2 x Milk. Flour. Doz Eggs. 2 x Saveloys. Cheese. 5lb Potatoes. 2lb Onions. Mince. Dripping. Cocoa. Marmalade. Oxo. Tapioca. Margarine.* I stack the familiar packets and tins neatly on the shelves, with their smooth new newspaper linings, arrange them in twos and threes like I'm dressing a window again. Then I open a can of Carnation and make myself a cup of cocoa, thick and sugared. I cut myself two slices from the shop-bought, layer on the cheese and the marmalade and cut it into four pillowy triangles.

Once the fire's going I'll put on onions, and a tapioca. Tomorrow we can have leek pudding and roly poly. Mince and mash Thursday, pot pie Friday, saveloys Saturday and a Yorkshire pudding and gravy Sunday. Should have got that peaches and cream. But I've got flour and sugar, eggs and shortening. With this good coal, I could bake my way through these three months. Gingerbread. Hinnies. Sly cake. I could make us tablet. Start to fill out my frock again.

There's something sweet in the air already. Jean's hyacinth, back on the windowsill. All the pink buds have come out, straining like trumpets right the way down to the bottom of the stem. I go over to take a sniff, but it's not any stronger close up.

When I go back upstairs to make the bed, I find the tea towel on the floor, with a small brown stump inside, and the door to the little room ajar. I must have reached from the bed and opened it to let in some warmth, some air. Tiny green blades have appeared in the soil trays, a full half-inch high. I see Jean's cup under the bed. Bending over to pick it up, I feel a little dizzy again. There is a crust inside the rim that is thick and shiny and almost black. It smells of treacle. I'm about to put my finger in when I hear the back door go.

Tommy shouts up: 'Need you in the glasshouse.'

He's at the bottom of the stairs, bare-headed, sleeves rolled over the elbow and collar undone. I stare at his bright, flushed, impatient face.

The dignity of labour, the beauty of growth.

They say you'll never catch a pitman outdoors without his cap and muffler: after years at the face they feel the cold more than most. Not Tommy. He might have been born a pitman – and he'd have hated for anyone to know it, his da

67

most of all – but in all this space, under this huge sky, he can breathe at last.

'She's up, then?'

'I'm grand, Tommy, I'll just see to your bait—'

'Pfft. Come on. We need you out there.'

He sees the empty cup in my hand, and nods approval. 'Jean's special.'

'Jean's what?'

'Adam fetched me some when I was in barracks. Cleared my chest right up, that stuff did.'

It's true, I've not heard a cough from him since that first night.

'That's grand, Tommy. What's in it?'

'How should I know?' He is backing up to the open door as though sucked by a great wind. 'Get a shift on. You'll not ruin this, not before we're started.'

His boots rap a little shuffle. '*Lady wife*,' he calls over his shoulder.

*

Dell hands a fresh pane of glass up to Tommy who half lies, half leans on the metal roof struts, his boots dangling several feet above his ladder. I hang back and watch. Dell, long and supple in his faded overalls, reaches Tommy's outstretched hand without even going up on to his toes. He nods when he sees me, takes off his cap to rake back his hair, while Tommy presses the glass into thick ropes of fresh putty. I give my frock a tweak.

'Feeling better, Mrs Radley?'

Tommy speaks for me. 'Up, isn't she?'

'Right as rain, thank you, Mr Dell.'

'Oh yes, my Jean knows a thing or two. Isn't that so, Tom?'

'What's that?' Tommy reaches for his putty pot, jabs about. 'Oh, aye.'

Dell gives me one of his wide, fatherly smiles. 'Jean's Special Area special.'

'Lettie,' says Tommy. 'You want to get clearing off those potting benches.'

'Right ho,' I say.

'Pass us up another, Adam.'

I look around for a brush and pan and get to work.

Dell comes over, and I turn away to wipe my nose on my sleeve. My frock is a mess, all cobwebs and dry earth. I should have put on that Association set. And the boots. He lolls against the potting bench, drumming his knuckles, watching me wipe out the pots. I tear off a fresh strip of newspaper, wrap it around my fingers and rub it, self-consciously, methodically, round and round.

He nods. 'That's right.'

Tommy's ladder thunks against the side of the glass-house.

'Out here, Lettie,' he mouths loudly through the glass. 'Hold the ladder.'

As I walk out of the door to Tommy my hair blows across the nape of my neck, my legs move loosely in my skirt, my back is erect. Dell is watching me still, through the glass.

I'm ravenously hungry.

*

Jean hurries out with a newspaper parcel in her hands, loosely wrapped.

'Oh,' she says, 'you *do* look a lot better.'

My stomach rumbles. I press on it with my hand, and smile back. Her tired old face creases up in delight.

'You were in a state, weren't you? No wonder you didn't want any breakfast.'

'I was feeling queer.'

'And no wonder. You polished that last dose off, didn't you. I'll make you up a couple of bottles, why not. My own recipe, won't cost you a penny.'

'Well, I don't know. What's in it?'

'Nothing but what you need, Lettie. Take a spoonful every morning. If you feel another turn coming on, though, take more.'

'More? How much is too much?'

'It's nothing but concentrated goodness, Lettie. Spring in a bottle. Can't have too much of what does you good, now can we?'

I look at her eager, bashful eyes. The arcing dark hairs on her upper lip. The unfamiliar bliss of charity surges inside me.

'That's very kind, Jean.' It doesn't cost anything to be nice, the Sisters used to say. 'It does taste smashing, your Special Area special.'

'Oh—' She flaps one hand coyly.

'Tommy's cough's quite gone.'

'Oh, that's nice.' She's all flustered. 'Oh, I am glad. Well, it's the least I can do for you Special Area folk, you always arrive in a shocking state. Now then, what I came out for was this.'

She opens up her parcel. Inside is a huge lettuce. The Dells' speciality. Against the newsprint, under the overcast sky, its pale leaves are luminous.

'You finished the other one.'

I'm puzzled for a moment. Then I remember the leaves I ate one after another in the dark until they were all gone, until the leaves grew too small and bitter and I let the pale nubby stalk fall down the side of the bed. This one must be twice as big.

'When did you last eat anything as fresh and green, Lettie?'

I can't think. Monica's kale pudding, no brown sauce, just vinegar. Her pickled onions, that were always soft. I'd watch the kids spit them out behind her back, one by one.

Spring in a bottle.

Every lockout, for weeks and months, they'd left the pit ponies down in the dark. Over a thousand of them. Papers made out it was cruel to do it. But their choppy was better than what we were living on, Tommy said, and anyway, ponies are intelligent creatures. Shetlands, anyway. Galloways have less brains than a chocolate mouse. Once they got a taste for green grass and fresh air, there'd be no way they'd want to go back down.

'Go on. Take it.'

Just then the wind whips my hair out in front of my face. As I toss it back I see Dell, standing full square in the door of our glasshouse. He nods and smiles and goes back inside. Tommy has his back turned still, up the ladder, waiting.

By the time I have the parcel in my arms, my heart is thumping and my mouth has filled with saliva. Jean tucks the sheets of newspaper back in place.

'That's better,' she says, in her sing-song voice. 'Off you go.'

*

The fresh glass is fixed, the old panes are scrubbed and the trenching is done. Tommy's gone off whistling down the lane with Adam to pick out a gilt, and I'm to get on with the seeds. The boots, stiff and new as they are, fit snug and secure. With the mackintosh and hat on too, outside feels like inside. Every step, over grass or mud, or puddles, it's as smooth and warm and steadying as the foyer carpet at the Empire.

Rain flows down the outside of the glasshouse in a thick curtain. It squeezes through the cracks and drips in syncopated rhythms on to empty pots and dead leaves and bare earth. Inside, just me and the smell of linseed oil and fresh compost. I tap my feet in tune with the raindrops. *We're in the money, we're in the money, let's get it, spend it, keep it rolling along.* I'll show that Bridgewater. I take rapid handfuls of compost from the pile on the bench and shove them into the new trays, fast as I can, although I have to stop every so often to scratch my shins because I've bites coming up all the time.

1 x Lysol.

I sprinkle the seeds like sugar and shower them with more compost and press it down until my nails clog black. *We're in the money, we're in the money . . .*

The door slides open. Jean holds a plate covered with a tea towel in one hand and a steaming cup in the other.

I brush my hands off on the bib of my dungarees. Uncanny, how Jean seems to read my mind. 'Oh, is that for me?'

'Hungry, are you?'

'Ravenous.'

'Yes, well, you'll find it's hungry work.'

Jean sets the plate and cup down on the bench and picks up the packets I've opened to peer at the numbers printed on them. As she puts them back down she folds their tops over in a particular way so that they look like they've never been opened, but so fast I can't see how she's done it.

She frowns. 'You do know which are which, Lettie?'

I feel myself blush. 'Course I do.'

'I think you might have mixed up the packets there.' She pauses. 'It's a bit late, anyway, to sow these ones. You must always sow on a waxing moon, you know.'

'Oh yes?'

A few weeks after the first lockout started, Mrs Baker next door gave me some of her seedlings. I was ever so grateful at the time: it didn't feel like charity, not as bad as giving us food from her pantry. It felt like a gift. I don't know what I did wrong, but before I knew it the stems went thin and black, and the leaves started to snarl up with little growths, like nasty hundreds and thousands. I watered and watered, but the soil went mouldy, with a sort of floury crust, and it started to stink. Those should last you months, she'd said. Once it's ready, don't take more than a handful at a time, break them off at the base, and it'll keep on coming. Spinach, I think it would have been. Or maybe chard. Cress? In the end I'd wrapped the whole mess up in newspaper and put it in the bin. The waste of it still makes me feel shivery.

Jean blinks. Patiently, she holds out the cup. It's more of that thick green tonic, hot and steaming. 'Well, never mind, Lettie. Better late than never. This'll warm you up.'

She lifts the tea towel off the plate.

'This is for you too. Keep your strength up.'

I was never one for lettuce in a sandwich. Nasty, limp stuff. Always peeled it out, as a rule. This one is nothing but: it bulges with velvety, spoon-shaped leaves, downy and delicate. Under the overcast sky, the green of the leaves is sharper and brighter than ever.

I bite through the doughy bread to the crunch of leaves. Sweet, crisp apple, I think. No: light, melting meringue, like that huge one Tommy bought me at Peppinster's in town once, that was filled with fresh whipped cream. Once it's all gone, I keep wanting to swallow, although my mouth is empty.

'We'll put these trays to one side, for the time being, shall we?' Jean says, with a reassuring little smile. 'You never know what might come up.' Then she sweeps the bench clean and sorts through the unopened packets.

'And these will need sowing straight into the ground. Carrot, turnip, beet, parsnip, radish, the underground ones.' She looks around briskly. 'Where's your nursery bed?'

'I'm doing the trays.'

'You haven't warmed your soil, have you? Or sieved it.'

I shake my head. But the more useless I am, the keener she gets. She shows me how to rub soil through a riddle, mixing it with leaf mould and grit. I almost expect her to add shortening and a splash of cold water.

'You're not going to know what's what, though, are you? What I do is, I plane down the top edge of the box, here, and paint it with white lead. Then you can use an ordinary pencil to label them. It won't rub off.'

Jean finds a sieve behind the staging and sifts a layer of fine soil over each box.

'Really fine seed I mix with sand. That way you can see where the seeds have gone to. Onion seed, though, you just scatter on the surface.' Pouring a tiny quantity into her palm, she holds it out like gold dust. 'Watch.'

She bends over, so her shoulders are level with mine, and I can see it in the stilled lines of her face, the pleasure this gives her; it's like she comes alive.

'These ones, you make a hole, deep as the first joint of your third finger.'

'Third finger,' I whisper, with a giggle.

'Not too deep, they'll use up their energy just trying to

reach the surface.' She looks round. 'Don't let that go cold now.'

I pick up the cup. It's sweet and strong and pungent, like hot port and lemon. I wipe my finger around what's left on the inside of the cup and suck it clean. My ears start to ring.

'What's that you say, Jean?'

She looks at me. 'I'm talking to them. Not you.'

Every living thing needs some encouragement, she explains. And I nod, solemn as I can. She fixes the fine rose to the can, lets the water play over the path before she turns it on the boxes. Goes off to find sheets of glass to cover them and overlays them with newspaper. I have to turn this every day, early in the morning, before the condensation drops. And turn the glass every morning, and check again every night.

She pins more newspaper up against the glass to keep off the frost, and lays thorny twigs over the trays. I should really have put the table legs inside clay pots before I started, to stop the mice running up. And prepared a box of cooled soot, a light dusting to keep off the cats and slugs.

'There,' she said finally, 'All done.'

I lean against the bench. 'Oops,' I say, putting one hand to my mouth, feeling the buzz of my lips. 'You're forgetting the soot, Jean.'

Her face shuts down in a flash. 'It's not a game, Lettie. You know it's all a gamble, don't you? You can't make something grow if it doesn't want to. You have to do everything you can. So many things can go wrong, Lettie. Sometimes you never know why.'

I hold myself very still.

'You can draw up all the rotations you like, Lettie, order yourself an orchard if you want.' There's a tremble in her voice. 'But for God's sake don't go making plans.'

She strokes the filled trays, pats them anxiously, like she is putting those precious baby seeds to bed.

I can't stifle another giggle. 'Nighty night, little ones.'

She looks straight at me.

And then Dell calls her name, loud and clear as day, for the rain stopped some time ago. He's standing in the doorway. I can see Tommy behind him, hanging back by the corner of the house.

Jean gathers up her cup and plate in silence. When she reaches the door Dell puts his arm about her shoulders.

'Remember to water them, Lettie,' she says. 'They need a good soaking, to get the roots to grow down. Give them far more than you think is enough. And again tomorrow evening. The ones in the little room too. A good drenching, every day.'

I manage a nod. 'Right you are.'

This time she goes. Dell looks at me a moment. Then he follows her, and slides the door shut.

*

The mornings break steel-grey and still. There is ice in every imprint in the mud; it glints and flashes like so many little windowpanes. It's been dry for days now, but after noon the wind will get up and there will be hail like rain. Swallows – or are they swifts? – fly over high from the north-east to south-west in ones and twos, but the next time I look out the sky is empty.

I splash my face with water from the pump, and empty the pot and take out the ashes and the peelings. I catch a whiff of smoke from the chimney. Nothing smells right, not even the coal. The wind can blow day and night, but this whole place is as rank as the church compost heap. The villagers are ploughing that bottom field; the ploughman's cries and the jangle of the harness drift on the chill air. When I think about that ridiculous scarecrow I feel quite hot. And how cross Jean was with me about the seeds, in the glasshouse. Put me right off going in there again.

Until our chicks arrive I'm not sure what I'm expected to do with myself. The shelves are lined, the curtains are sewn and ready to be hung once Tommy has cut the dowels. I bake. I sit by the fire for ages, catching up on the weeklies. Everything's new and clean, but I might have lived here for ever, everything has its place. I go out front and sweep the path, polish the front window. There's never anyone passing, though. Children's voices sometimes, ever so faint, carried on the wind from the holdings up by the Central. Nothing moves out here, or if it does I never see it. There are strange prints in the mud some mornings. Strange noises at night. I don't care to think too hard about either.

She brought me those bottles of tonic that same afternoon, just as she promised. And half a dozen jars of jam for Tommy. Left them on the doorstep, didn't even knock. Ever since, she's kept herself to herself. That was days ago. I've lost track. They shut themselves up indoors at night, the pair of them, but I hear her, up and down the stairs, using the pump, clattering at the hob, nattering with her chickens. Imagine her at Crampton's, gallumphing into everything. I see her every day, on her way to the glasshouses or the hen-house. But when I do get myself out there she's nowhere to be seen.

Anyway, if I'm feeling flat, it's not her I'm missing. It's Monica, would you believe. On her high horse all morning and nodding off at the table of an afternoon, blowing her nose on her cuff and swiping at the bairns. I miss Mrs Chilvers, droning on in the courtyard. I miss the chatter from the pump, and the voices below the window, and knowing I could just pop to the parade on King Street when I needed anything, and especially when I didn't and couldn't afford it anyway. I miss that lop-faced hurdy-gurdy man who danced with the jointed dummy every Wednesday. I miss there always being something in a shop window to covet. Even the cheapjack, flashing his bright new shilling. I try to hum a hurdy-gurdy song to myself, but I have to stop. I could choke on all this silence.

I don't miss an empty belly, I tell myself, empty cupboards. That lumpy mattress on the draughty floor and always listening out. Tommy's tight, hollow face. I look at my upstairs and my downstairs, my indoor pump and my warm range and my packets and jars and tins lined up, and I remind myself of that tramp Jean told us about, the one they found frozen in a ditch the week before Christmas, before I got here. Just inside that tunnel of trees, to the left of the gate there. What with so many coming down from the Special Areas to try their luck, the dosshouses are full year round, can't put them up. He might have been any of those dozens of men back home, singing their hearts out on the corners, with their caps out. He could have been my Tommy. If we'd not got on here, if he'd had to do a flit, I might never have known what became of him. Still, I can't stop my old life piling up like railway carriages behind me, nudging for attention.

*

Tommy never talks about home. He acts new born, destined to be a man of the soil. *Glad that I live am I*, pedalling home with his marra, high in the pedals and arching his back. *That the sky is blue*. I watch him dismount, fizzing with fresh air and chemicals.

Adam's helped him demolish the old sty and they've

built another one nearby – to leave the parasites behind, apparently. Now he's down there every chance he gets, gazing at the new gilt from the Association pool. Chosen for her many teats, the width of her hindquarters, the evenness of her toes. He's had me boiling up potatoes specially for her, twice a day, and now he wants to try fish meal, the latest thing. He picks the green peelings out of the swill bucket and drops them in the sink. Swaddles her in straw. Grooms her with a stiff brush and dandy oil. Sometimes, when the wind dies down about teatime, I hear him crack his knuckles with satisfaction.

'Oh, she's a fine one, that Rosie,' he says softly as he takes off his boots, and shakes his head fondly.

'Rosie?' I say, startled. 'You called her Rosie?'

He gives me a stony look. 'What of it?'

Perhaps it's what pig men do, name their gilts after old sweethearts. He parrots what Adam's told him. *You want to get to know your gilt, so she gets to know you.* And I want to say: yes, and not just Rosie. You spend more time with Adam than you do with me. I see the way you look at him, when he pats you on the back. *Adam's out of here soon, any road. Means to head back west, buy a bit of land, he'll do it too, claims he cleared £600 last season.* Tommy breathes deep. *And you know what else? When they go I'll get first dibs on their holding, being right next door.*

*

He's not missing Monica, is he? Not any of his sisters, not for a moment. Or having to queue at the Exchange. Kicking the doorstep. Those long, aimless walks he used to take, past all the people pretending not to see him idle. Trying not to breathe in when someone comes round the corner with a parcel of fried fish.

I only ever see him at table. He's eating more here than he ever did, even when he was on double shifts. Mind you, I've had about as much of that loaf as he has. The other day I made him pink lint biscuits as a treat, but by the time he came in there were only four left. I can see he's clocked it, the amount I'm putting away, but he's not said anything.

This morning he pulled a face as I helped him on with his mackintosh. 'You're not dressed.'

I asked him, then, if he'd fetch me another bottle, but he shook me off. 'Get some clothes on and go ask her yourself.'

*

Two days since, I finished that second bottle. I tipped them both up and licked inside the necks anyway. It was streaming with rain, but I could just make her out in the lettuce glasshouse. *If Jean thinks you need it, then you need it. Just go and ask her for more. I'm busy, Lettie, for god's sake.* My mouth was watering like billy-o so I put on my coat and hat and boots and picked up the empty bottles and went out before I could change my mind.

She was stood at the potting bench. I could see she had at least three heads of the bright green lettuce, and some longer stuff like rhubarb or chard, a pile of knobbly roots and different-sized funnels and bottles. Soon as I drew back the door that rich, fresh, clean scent fizzed up my nose and coated my throat like liquid velvet. I was going to just ask her to fill them up, offer to swap her some stottie cakes, brandy snaps maybe. Thought she'd be pleased I'd come to her for a change.

But when I said her name she jerked round, brows fierce and knitted together, and she thrust out her arm, like a policeman at a junction. 'Stop there,' she said.

'I've your empties,' I said, and held them up.

'You can leave them just there. Slide the door to, if you would.'

I opened another Carnation in the end. Although I can't blame her for giving me the shoulder. I've not gone near those trays of hers. Dozens of tiny seeds, muffled under soil and newspaper, waiting. When I swept out the bedroom the broom nudged the door to the little room and I tugged the latch down tight before it could swing right open. My insides plummet just thinking about any of it. Nothing about this place makes any sense to me. It's mess and ugliness and as damp and chill as the grave.

He's polished off another pot of that jam. I wash it out and take it round. I set it down on her step and stand between our doors a while, stare at the little green heads nudging into view in their glasshouse. I don't know what exactly I am longing for, but I've never wanted to eat a leaf of lettuce so much in my life.

I can hear the Dells' voices inside, see the lamp glow faint in the window. It's dusk, but the days are already getting longer. A blackbird starts up. I listen to his song all the way through and again, and then I go back indoors. *If Jean thinks you need it, then you need it. Then go and ask her for more. I'm busy, Lettie, for god's sake.*

No. I'll not beg.

Tommy smokes steadily, staring into the fire. He's missing Rosie. When she didn't come out for her swill yesterday, Dell checked her, said she was brimming, and they roped her up and took her to boar this morning. I watched from the window as they walked her down the lane.

I'll stay up and bake. I could bake all night, there's more than enough coal. Next door will fill with the scent of sugar and currants and bitter yeast, maybe the harshness of burnt crust. Keep her awake. Make her mouth water too.

He stands up, yawns, then comes over to stand behind my chair. He's been sterilising soil and the stink of Jeyes makes me gag a little. Lay your hands on my shoulders, Tommy. Put your mouth to my ear and ask me how I am. He's not like that, is he. He's never been like that. He says he's got to check on the boiler Dell's helped him fit in the glasshouse.

I hear him knock on their door. The door closes and there's quiet for a while and when I hear voices again they are fainter, away outside somewhere.

That yeast is overflowing. I'll have to use it tonight. I'm wide awake anyway. I pull the table out into the middle of the room. Then I go into the scullery for water and I see two lanterns moving in the Dells' glasshouse. They light up row after row of those bright green lettuces; dozens of them, well tended, growing strong. I stand and stare until my feet are numb with cold. Then I make myself some cocoa, have another bun. When I go to rinse out the crockery, all is dark out there.

Later, much later, I hear a tread going up their stairs. And another. Stockinged feet. Their bedroom window cranks open.

I know I won't sleep, but I'm not going back down. I wish I could shut my ears as well as my eyes. I know every sound the Dells make, from the rattle of their kettle to the drop of the latch on the back bedroom window. When they're taking their boots off, I know when his drop to the floor and when it's hers. I still can't tell their voices apart though.

The waxing moon is bright through the window, still uncurtained, edged with frost. I think again of those rows and rows of crisp bright lettuce sitting out there alone, their hearts swelling and their tips unfurling in the moonlight. I wipe my mouth. Tommy's still not back. I go back and sit on the edge of the bed for a while, feeling that hollow ache inside, remembering that glow. And then I stand up and open the door to the little room.

What do I expect to see? Her little plants thriving, sitting up tall and strong in their beds? Holding out their leaves, grateful to me for all my tender care? I've not been in here once, not in all these days. I know I was meant to, of course, but every night I'd realise I'd forgotten, and then I wasn't going to get out of bed again, was I, and anyway, there was always tomorrow. I'd just tell myself they'd be fine on their own, and if they weren't, how would I know what to do about it?

What I don't expect to see is the moonlight streaming in over empty boards.

I know all the night sounds. I'm ready when their cockerel calls. I tell myself that when I open my eyes I'll see sunlight through the poppy-print curtains and the pit buzzer will go off and I'll go down and get the bacon on.

I tell myself there's no need for either of us to stint ourselves, not any more. My monthlies are long gone, but I reckon we're safe, just. When I see his eyelids begin to flicker I try again. I reach down and lace my fingers through his and brush my hair against his cheek. I have to swallow hard. My mouth never stops watering these days. I wake up and the pillow is wet. I've dribbled out the side of my mouth. He yawns, and stretches out his arm so abruptly I have to pull away.

It's been days, weeks now since he's come near me. That first evening, when he put his arms around me, that was the first time he'd touched me in ever so long. He smiles now, though. He nods, he eats, he sleeps, he's polite. It's not like the way we got to be back those last months, when his moods filled the room even when he wasn't in it. If anything, he's more like when he was working up to ask me to marry him. Absent. Watchful. Ever so quiet, and no trouble to anyone. As he would like me to be. I'll just have to wait. If my surprise is a wireless and he's bought it already, then I wish he'd just let on. It's like he's holding his breath.

Although, when I close my eyes, it's not home I long for now, it's not Tommy. All I see is that crisp green lettuce nestled in the damp warmth of their glasshouse, pale against the soft earth. I see them in my sleep. The soft sworl in the middle of each head, where the tips of the leaves thin and darken. The sturdy little ribs that curve to support them. The hidden, solid stalk. I long to touch the meshed tips of those leaves, to nudge them apart. Snap off one of those little ribs. Twist out just one solid stalk and wrap the head in my pinny and carry it away.

Last night I went to the door and stood on the step and stared at their glasshouse in its silver veneer of moonlight. The latch went next door. I heard someone open the door. I don't know who it was. No one came out. They didn't say anything. I went back inside before they could.

I've eaten up the condensed milk. The bread and jam. The cakes and hinnies are long gone and the yeast has gone sour. I've stuck my tongue into the necks of the bottles and held them up to get every last drop. None of it satisfies me. All I crave is one bite of that lettuce. I am that hungry I don't know where to put myself.

15th February

The full moon is high in the window tonight, bright and cold and round as an electric bulb. The dazzle of it floods the room, bleaches the sleeping Tommy to a smooth, white slab, pales his fair hair to dust. A full fortnight now, it must be, we've laid alongside each other, chaste as brother and sister.

I reach under the covers, into his long johns, and I take him in my hand, something I've never done in all these years. He is very warm and a little moist. Like a sleeping bat; something wild and strange and not to be disturbed. I stroke him, firm but gentle, the way you'd stroke a kitten.

'Tommy,' I say. 'Tommy, love.'

When he doesn't move, I take his left hand and close it around my throat. This I have let him do, many times over, for the sake of what follows. My pulse thuds in my ears as I whisper my wants.

He groans and pulls away.

It would be the easiest thing in the world, I tell him. They wouldn't mind, they needn't even know. There are dozens of them, out there for the taking. No one would miss just one. Even one leaf. One bite. If he can bring me just one leaf, I'll be all right again, I know it. I plead with him. One bite will staunch this mouth-watering, sate this hunger, bring us back together even. Yes, we'd be all right again, I know it.

I whisper my wants in his ear, over and over. I can't stop. Just one leaf would do. I tell him I think I might die if he doesn't get me just one leaf. When he doesn't move, I curl down to take him in my mouth, something I have never attempted. He groans again, tells me I'm cracked, tells me to make myself some cocoa, we've not to piss off the Dells, do I want us to be sent back. He turns his back and humps up the blankets so the cold gusts in around my legs, and now he's the one pretending to fall sleep.

16ᵗʰ February

I manage one more day. I wait until the very heart of the night. The holdings are etched in charcoal and pearl, as bright and clear as they would be on the silver screen. It's full moon still. I've seen how its mercury glare coats the transparent panes of the glasshouse with a dazzling sheen, opaque as silver paper. No one will see me in there, even if they woke. The livestock are asleep. And dew will refill my footprints before dawn.

As I close the glasshouse door, warm air flows about my bare arms. The green rows are glowing brighter than ever. I sink down before the very first plant I come to, cradle and lift its limp lower leaves, searching for the thick white stem. Then I grasp and twist and pull and lift it like a bouquet and press my face into its heart. I bare my teeth and flatten my tongue. The outer leaves caress my face as I bite down. Its freshness astonishes me, the crunch and dissolve. I burrow in. Lose myself.

Until I feel the chill on the soles of my feet. The door has opened behind me. I chew once, twice more, then stop. A long moon shadow moves towards me and covers me like a cloak, darkening the pale heads around me. I'm no longer alone. He drops heavily to his knees behind me and I crouch very still, toes braced, heart pounding, legs soft as bread in milk. Then he holds the palm of one hand lightly to my hair. *Candyfloss head.*

It's only when he lowers the full length of him against my back and I take his weight, his heat, and smell the apples on his breath, that I know my emptiness, and my hunger. He touches my hair. *Dandelion clock.* He runs a hand over my right calf and down to my ankle. I let him hold my foot, stroke it. I let him ruck up my nightdress. I raise my hips to him, I lower my face to the ground, I press my cheek into the cool, soft leaves.

*

To the east, over the holdings to the fields and the frost-rimed scarecrow, there is a fuzzy lightness at the edges of everything. I feel myself rise as the sun must be rising, although it's still hidden out there, just, by the curve of the earth.

I pick up the tooth mug, rinse my mouth, dip my fingers once, twice, and run them over my face and neck. The water is stale, but I can't risk pumping fresh, the pipes bang. I have to lean on the edge of the sink. My knees are weak. They drop bits of soil, more is smeared down the front of my nightdress. I remember the other one, folded and ready on the bedroom chair. I can peel this one off and bundle it up under the sink, behind the curtain.

My thighs slide and stick together as I walk naked through the ash-grey kitchen and up the stairs, but all I know is relief. And gratitude. Something has lodged into place. That terrible hunger, gone. I have come back to myself. Though I remain heated and tender, all over. Moon-scorched.

The bedroom door is off the latch. I filch the laundered nightdress through the gap. It shakes over my head with a sound like birds flying out of a hedge. I gather it about my legs to sink down, just for a moment, on to the top step. A rich, loamy scent funnels up between my thighs. I'll have to go back down, wipe myself clean. If I stay down stairs until it's time to heat Tommy's shaving water, he might think I'd only just got up.

Reaching up to pull the door to, I see the flare of a struck match. Then there is only the glowing end of a tab against his bare white chest, its rise and fall.

I couldn't sleep. I went down to splash my face. Indoor water is such a blessing. I forgot to cover the peeled potatoes. I heard the gate banging, a fox cry—

Tommy twists to stub out his tab on the bedframe. One by one the falling lights wink out.

'Where've you been?' His voice, like the movement, is precise, sharp, unclagged by sleep.

'Downstairs.'

Silence.

'You went out.'

'Fox was back.'

'Fox was back.'

'Yes, Tommy, didn't you hear?'

He must know where I went, what I went to get. He won't have forgotten my pleading. I taste that freshness all over again, dissolving on my tongue. Feel again what Adam has opened inside me. How natural, and necessary, it was, worth any risk. And just that once was enough. If only I could explain it to him. See his face. But the bedroom window faces west, and the moonlight is long gone.

It was about this time of a morning the knocker-upper used to rap on our window. Tommy would lie there rigid beside me, hoping against hope, perhaps, that he wouldn't have to go. When there was nearly no time, he'd turn to me. Only at the very last minute would he pull out. It helped him then, I know it did. It was the least I could do.

It will help him now.

17th February

I haven't slept, at all, but Tommy did; a heavy, stupid sleep that was a joy to watch. He's sleeping still. His face always pales and softens in sleep, feels delicate as warmed wax to the touch. *You're with me, aren't you, Lettie? Just the two of us.* He raised the sheet like a flag and took me back, without a word. I kept him inside and he didn't even try to pull out. I ought to think about why, and what that might mean. I ought to keep watching him till he wakes, see his face, his eyes, open. But I don't want him to see mine. I want him to sleep that stupid sleep for ever.

Because I have to be outside again. The sun is coming up, it must be well above the bottom hedge. I'm quite desperate for air, and light, and space. I pull off my nightdress and I feel his slick dried on my skin, deliciously tight like the squeeze of an invisible hand, like the sunlight as it struck my bare forehead when we came out from under the canal bridge that afternoon, unsteady, hand in hand, my hollowness gone, that first time he kissed me with those soft, full lips, the time I lost my hat. Downstairs I cover my singing nakedness with Tommy's overcoat, slip into my boots and open the door wide, braced for the familiar chastising burn of dawn.

The air I draw in is warm and gentle. A mild breeze blows soft on my skin. And there is a new freshness and a brightness to everything. I can see every winking dew bead, every branch and stem, clear and distinct; and for the first time, dozens of pale little buds, sitting quietly underneath the matted brown decay. Dead leaves, that had been pasted to the earth, have dried pale and thin and scud about on tiny gusts. I step out, the grass an emerald carpet cushioning my tread, to look around and breathe.

How had I not noticed the birds? Great squadrons and trailing ribbons flash pale and dark as they twist about in a sky that is high and clear and pale, pale blue, stretch-marked with white cloud. I walk out across the grass on to the cinder path.

There is a sweet delight in every clear, crunching footstep. A low thrum has started inside me. I spin slowly on the spot, bewitched, unable to stop looking. All this has been growing without me, from the buds on the trees to the shoots in the Dutch lights to the seeds, deep in the soil. I see it now, what is there and what is coming and what it will become. How it can be ours. Then, as though they want the whole world to know the good news too, the Dells' geese trumpet and their cockerel blares. The glasshouse door rolls open on its runners.

Before I know what I'm doing I'm waving hard, moving my arm above my head in big, loose arcs. The gentle air bracelets my wrists and strokes the back of my bare legs, and I shiver with delight. It's Jean who emerges, holding her gloves to her forehead to shield her eyes against the bright sun.

I wrap Tommy's coat tight about me. We gorged ourselves in there, Adam and I. Surely we left our mark. Scuffled earth and crushed leaves. The morning light is still hazy, but the edges of everything are getting sharper by the minute. Jean would have seen it all, our rut, if she'd looked. The thought only makes me feel wilder.

Her geese have come staggering after her. They honk and stretch out their wings and necks imploringly and I am transfixed. See those thick, rounded necks, how they plunge deep into the frothing, creamy breast feathers, pin-curled as tight as any Hollywood starlet.

'Your geese,' I say faintly. 'They're—' I touch a fingertip to the cleft of my collarbone, like a feather.

Jean watches me, the hint of a smile playing about her mouth. There is soil in the creases around her eyes, where she's wiped her face. Hatless, with her hair uncombed, she looks even more mannish, more overgrown and unkempt. She examines my hair, my face, the coat, my loose-laced boots, my bare ankles and throat. Then she shrugs.

'That's just what frizzles are like.' She glances towards the house. Their door is closed and Adam is nowhere to be seen. 'Well, Sebastopols is the proper name.' She stuffs her gloves into her belt. 'You look like you've never seen them before, Lettie! Lettie, meet George – say hello, George – and this is Georgina.'

'Hello, you two.'

Jean lets out a surprisingly rich and womanly laugh. I don't remember ever hearing her laugh before. 'At least, we *think* that's George. We can't be sure yet. When they can honk properly, we'll know.'

George and Georgina press themselves together like a pair of bustling vamps and turn on a hapless pullet who has strayed too close. When they flap their wings I clutch Jean's arm. The hymn we sang at St Clement's every spring floods back. I sing it out, all of it:

Glad that I live am I,
That the sky is blue.
Glad for the country lanes,
And the fall of dew.
After the sun, the rain.

Jean joins in, softly, under her breath. We watch each other.

After the rain, the sun.
This is the way of life,
Till the work be done.
All that we need to do,
Be we low or high,
Is to see that we grow
Nearer to God on high.

I sing the last line alone; my voice is strong, steady and true. My breath comes more evenly, and my heartbeat is steadying, and I know myself to be free. Nothing, no one, has power over me – except this.

Everything, anything feels possible. If she asks, why am I wearing Tommy's coat and nothing else, I might laugh in her face. If she mentions a disturbance in the glasshouse, the missing lettuce, I'll remind her about the deer, the foxes, the—

Jean covers my hand with hers, pats it once, then again, says nothing.

I take a deep, deep breath. 'The air, Jean. Smell the air!'

'Yes,' she says, with a little disbelieving giggle, scanning my face. 'That's spring.'

'Spring.' It strikes me like a deep truth, newly revealed.

Jean squeezes my fingers tight. The clear sky floats huge and weightless above our heads. About us is our garden, God given, hedged, fenced, ours to tend.

'New life on its way. Your own little ones to come.'

I look at her.

'Your own chicks and goslings. Piglets.'

'Oh,' I say, a little daunted. 'Yes.'

Her hands hold me tight. 'Oh, Lettie. Don't you worry. Everything's going to be all right, it really is.'

No, she can't have guessed. Seen from here, on the cinder path, there's nothing untoward about the glasshouse. It stands clear and light and wholesome again, carpeted by a soft, thick, seemingly unbroken lozenge of green leaves.

'Oh, I know.' I gaze back into her dark eyes. 'Of course, I know it now.'

I believe her, and with all my heart. Dear, innocent, pure Jean. She believes in me and, somehow, this morning, so do I. I feel washed clean, despite what I did last night, because of it.

'Come on then.'

She takes me back across the path to our side, to our renovated glasshouse with its new boiler and hot pipes. There they are together on the potting bench. The trays from the little room, and the trays she and I planted together. Filled with shoots several inches high, bright, pale clusters of leaves like small green fists lifting into the air.

'I've been bringing these on for you, you see. Shame about the wait. They're only just ready now.'

I take up a tray and pinch a pair of leaves between forefinger and thumb and twist. I feast and feast. She takes it from me when she thinks I've had enough. I wipe my mouth.

'Better?'

I nod, breathless.

'I'll bring you a full head of ours later, shall I? Give this lot time to grow. One a day, every day, how about that?'

I've got her wrong, haven't I? I've been the one full of pride, hiding away, not her. She wants to help me and be my friend. I must find a way to make it up to her.

'Oh, come on now, wipe your eyes. I think we need a cuppa?'

*

Jean can't have poured the water on the boil, and the cup is chipped, but I sip her terrible tea anyway. The thrumming has muted a little, but it's still there. *Glad, glad, glad.* It's as though a grey film has been scrubbed away and I can see this place for what it truly is: a fresh miracle, every day.

Look at her Flo stalking across the table, and that pretty little black kitten of hers, kneading at the patchwork cushion. Look at her four walls of shelves bursting with good things to eat and that fine set of corn dollies high up on the shelf by the stair door, the only things in the room that ever seem to get a dusting. I'll have to get Jean to teach me how to make them, and preserves too.

I've never had anyone to teach me this sort of thing. All we learned at St Clement's was how to do laundry and clippy mats and serve in other people's houses. After I'd got myself away from Mr Robert's nasty box room and into Crampton's lodging house, I'd made up my mind to save and save, because even if I never got married all I ever wanted was a home of my own and never a clippy mat in sight. I'd have nets and a budgerigar, a tea trolley and a chiming clock, everything shop bought and brand new on the HP. In the end we had that, and more, me and Tommy, and it was taken off us again, and what good did it do us in the end anyway? How ridiculous that dream seems now, how childish and false.

This is what I must make for us – a proper home. Messy, perhaps, and nothing like what I've always longed for, the curving walls and the satin and the wrought-iron screens, like we saw on the pictures and in the weeklies. They weren't real, were they? They were sets: sterile, artificial, made of canvas and paint. This is the life I want: busy, and alive, and full of growth and movement.

Jean pulls a face and sets down her cup. 'Sorry, yesterday's milk.'

She rocks back in her chair and tugs the scarf from her throat. I get the feeling she's waiting too. Their bedroom door latch goes. There's the thud of stockinged feet and the stair door opens.

'Ads.' Jean smiles, but she doesn't take her eyes off me. 'She's here.'

Avuncular, ramshackle, bristly old Adam has a gleam on him like that of a freshly shelled nut. Shaved now, washed, eyes clear, curls shiny and clean, red flannel shirt rolled up above the elbows, soft yellow cords belted high and tight. He hums with health and vitality. Eyes bright as a bird's. Lips red and smooth. Makes me think of harvest festival in the chapel at St Clement's, the heaps of freshly cracked conkers, and ripe golden wheat and juicy red rosehips. Last night I had known but not cared who it was that filled me, only that it was what I needed. I want to press my face into him and swallow him whole.

'Hello, Adam.' And I wonder too, at the bright calm of my voice.

'Lettie's been out admiring George and Georgina.'

'Oh yes?' Adam moves round the table to Jean and sits down, takes her hand and kisses her lightly on the knuckles. There is something alert and electric between the two of them, the way the chickens get sometimes, tense to the tips of their feathers. I'm on the outside of it, and I'm not sure I care.

'Or' – she nudges his knee with hers – 'is it Georgina and Georgina?'

'I told her, we're hoping for George. The way he runs at the pullets I'd say he is. Hate to fork out on a gander otherwise.'

Jean pats his arm and stands up abruptly, cracks three eggs into a pan and stands over them, spoon in hand. She stands very still, the way a rabbit freezes in the middle of a field. The silence stretches and stretches.

'Do you remember, Ads, that morning we woke up, soon after they arrived it was, and they were making such a racket. When we went out they'd knocked the roof of their house clean off, there. Do you remember?'

Adam nods. 'They were with just their heads sticking up.' His eyes follow her to and fro. 'Making one hell of a noise too.'

His chin was wet, his lips were swollen, I pushed back his damp hair. He licked inside of my legs. Ran one hand down to my foot and held it steady. I recross my legs, adjust the coat where it's slipped off my knee.

'I know the Association recommend Romans, but we've always had frizzles. Well, you don't need to clip their wings, do you?'

Adam turns in my direction. In a much louder voice, freighted with expertise, says: 'Frizzles don't do a flit, see.'

I nod as though I understand, and watch how his wide lips move against those white, white teeth.

'Little buggers, otherwise, geese, in general.'

'Oh Lettie, honestly?' Jean leaves off slicing bread and leans against the range to look at us both. 'I just think they're pretty.'

She leans forward to stroke Flo, nestled in the middle of the table, and there's another quivering silence.

I should probably leave, and leave now, before Tommy wakes up and finds me gone, before I give myself away. Instead, I lose myself in how plump and sleek Flo is, with her enamelled red beak and powderpuff neck. Her shiny half-blind eye.

'Mind you,' says Adam. 'Geese is the best creature on earth for keeping Mr Fox away.'

'Come here, my gorgeous.' Jean scoops Flo up and settles her on her lap, tucks in her wings. She looks at Adam. 'Why don't you take her a minute, Lettie?'

'Are you sure?' I say. 'Oh!'

Flo's claws scrabble, leaving tracks of pain down my thighs. She settles quickly, though, tucking in her wings and feet; warm and surprisingly heavy. I see how each feather lays upon the next, in an intricate, endless, mysterious pattern. When I stroke her neck, the feathers are denser, at once oily and dry. Her head swivels and her round eye stares at me, steady and unblinking.

'Look at them, Jean.' Adam's voice is soft.

Flo flinches and jerks her head. It's Tommy putting on his boots, scuffling on the doorstep.

Adam leans back and shouts out the open door, 'In with us, Tom, boy!'

Jean puts one hand on my shoulder. I lose myself in stroking Flo, over and over. Flo can't see what's right in front of her. She can only see side on.

Tommy's shirt is untucked; he is uncombed and unshaven, his eyes still heavy and swollen. I'm always down before him, to heat his shaving water, get his breakfast, long before ever he steps outside. *Why is she here?* he will be thinking; he must know I've not crossed this doorstep since that first day.

The four of us are barely feet apart, but we might be standing at the far-distant corners of the holdings. A great, watchful distance has opened between us. Tommy's forehead has furrowed right up. He's no fool. He can feel something's not right in here. He's working it out. It wasn't a fox Lettie heard last night, was it. The Dells have gone out and seen their blasted lettuce missing, how much did she take for god's sake, did they know at once it was her, the fool, or have they called her in and she's confessed? We're in for it now, she's ruined it.

'Oh, your face, Tom.' Jean gives a trilling laugh. 'Lettie'll be with you in a tick. I've had so much to show her this morning we lost track, didn't we? Just settle this for us: is it Romans or frizzles?'

Tommy scrubs at his hair, forming it into greasy clumps. I see his thoughts bunch and reverse.

Adam goes over and squeezes his shoulder. 'Romans or frizzles. Which is it, you dozy beggar?'

Dozy Radley. It's what his marras shouted across the street the morning after we were wed, when they first saw this stuffed-pudding, up-all-night look he gets afterwards. They soon learned not to take advantage, though. He played them off their heads that very afternoon. Once his head clears, and the puffiness goes, his wits are sharper than ever.

'Never mind.' Adam holds out a small brown-paper parcel. 'Jean's made you up some bait. Chop, chop, we're late as it is.'

'Go on, Tom, let her finish her tea, why not?'

Tommy takes the parcel, still uncertain. Then he finally looks at me – wordless, replete, relieved. I want to gather Flo to me and never let her go.

'Just this once, mind.'

'That's the ticket,' says Adam.

I duck my head as he guides Tommy outside. 'Boots, Tom. Don't forget your boots now.'

I kept him inside. And he didn't pull out. We've both upped the stakes, I realise. Does he understand that if we don't make a go of this, there may be three of us turned out on the street? I listen to the sound of their boots, one long stride, one short, disappearing. I want to shout after him: *this is what it's like to gamble, isn't it?* And I start to feel the way I did on the way here, as though my feet may never touch the ground again.

*

Tommy drops his Association-issue bike back in the usual place at the corner of the house, where the growing grass snags the whirring spokes. He is in the scullery, working the pump, when Adam wheels his past. Once he's propped it round the corner, against their end wall, I come out of the tomato house to rinse my hands in the water butt. Adam turns to watch. He takes the measure of my neck, my wrist, my waist, my ankle, the halo of my hair bobbing pale against the sky. I am a jointed doll again, awkward and helpless and moving for him alone. Ever since that first morning with Bridgewater, he might have been watching me like this. In plain sight.

Adam starts walking across the grass towards me. I shake off my hands, go back into the tomato house and close the door. He doesn't look in as he passes. He carries on down the straight and narrow, then cuts across to the back of the lettuce house, where he's been hosing off the Dutch lights before he sets them out over the new rows.

Stand just about anywhere, and you can see right across

both holdings: straight into the glasshouses, down the paths, every furrow, every row from end to end, and through the orchards to the hedge and the bedraggled scarecrow beyond. But this time of day Jean is always round the front with her girls. Tommy sits down to his catalogues soon as his hands are clean, puts his feet up, waiting on his tea. If I don't start it soon, though, he'll be out to check on Rosie. And me.

I wait until Adam has finished coiling the hose and hung it back on its hook. The sun has already dropped behind the hedge. It's chilly this far down the holding, after being in with the tomatoes. I walk just around the corner of their glasshouse. He takes a couple of businesslike strides towards me, rubbing his hands together.

Adam's been with other men all day, and it shows. Tommy is the same. When they get back from the Central it courses through their bodies, that cooperative endeavour. Adam tells me straight off. Today was their last contracted day at the Central until the season ends. After tea, they're off down the Fox to celebrate. Which means from tomorrow the four of us will be here together, all day, every day, working on our holdings from sunrise to sunset and beyond.

'Tom's been keen to get caught up, of course, and I've told him, he'll find he's more than enough to get on with. Everything goes like a rocket from now on.'

I glimpse the ghost of my face in the panes behind Adam. My eyes are huge and haunted.

'That lettuce, for a start,' I say, stupidly. 'That'll need cutting.'

Adam's voice is all business. But he's looking at me the way he checks over his stock in the pens. I want to rasp my tongue over his jaw, and into the curling nape of his neck. Here, in the early-evening shadows behind this, their furthest glasshouse, no one would see us. His tool shed is between their door and us, and the scullery windows are hidden by the nettie.

'I see your tomato plugs arrived today, Lettie.'

'Yes. Jean says she can get me potting two hundred an hour.'

He takes a great, busy breath, like he's about to move off. I fumble the empty seed packets out of my pocket. My excuse for crossing over the straight and narrow.

'You've your plugs now, Lettie.'

'Oh,' I say. 'I know, but I thought—'

He runs one hand over his face and looks away. I press the empty packets into his hands. I tell him I'm a grower too now. I understand what he understands, what Jean understands. I am part of it now, with them, with him. I'm hungry, to learn the work.

His breath comes to me, hot and pure. He smells of apples still, and of sweat and creosote and wet soil. Adam slips the packets back into my jacket pocket, smooth and flat again with their flaps neatly folded, the same way Jean does it.

'We're done with that, Lettie.'

'Yes,' I say. 'Yes. I know.'

'Yes. Good. You've got your plugs now, remember.'

'Oh, yes,' I take the packets out again, look at them, tuck them back in. 'Of course.'

'We're done with that,' he repeats.

'Yes,' I say. 'I know.'

'Good.'

'Yes.'

It is good. It is. It has to be. And now there's nothing to do but walk away.

'Two hundred an hour is nothing,' he calls out after me.

I turn. 'What?'

He's fiddling with the gutter; something's come loose. 'With Tom back' – his voice strains as he reaches up to straighten the bracket – 'you'll double that easy.'

*

Tommy's having a smoke on the doorstep. The back of the house lost the sun ages ago, but he's out in his shirtsleeves, his head bare to the sky.

I crunch up the straight and narrow towards our lit doorway, ever more conscious of every part of my body, moving through the dusk. I remember the whirling carousels at Gala, how effortlessly they would turn, all mirrors and light, and how loud and ugly the engines were, up close.

He stubs out his tab on the doorframe. Harmless orange sparks fall on his boots, but his eyes are as keen as the wind.

'Tea not on yet?' He keeps his tone light.

'Nearly. I forgot to water the tomatoes.'

'You know Adam gave me his bait, dinner time.'

'I am sorry, Tommy, Let me just—'

'How come you were round there this morning?'

'Oh, you know, she was asking about the geese. You wanted us to get pally, didn't you, me and Jean?'

'I wanted you there when I woke up is what I wanted.'

I let the wind whip my hair hard into my burning face. He reaches out and tucks one finger behind the buckle of my belt. Tugs me off balance.

'What about Rosie?'

'Never mind Rosie.' His voice has thickened.

He can see the difference in me, that's all. Anyone could. The good this place has done me. Of course he didn't want me when I was poorly and failing and no use to anyone.

Tea, Rosie, the Fox, will have to wait. We never could stop, once we'd started. That's never changed. He's only had to touch me. And now we've started again all right. My body feels like syrup on a spoon. He runs his hands around my waist and up my back and pushes his fingertips deep into my hair, and cups the base of my skull in both his palms.

I've got my First Man back, you see. The way he was that first afternoon we walked out together: stiff and silent as we passed the faces outside the pubs, the windows of the houses, then doubled up with laughter under the bridge. Tommy, who'd make a game out of anything, and make it last for ever, pull the oil lamp down and back again until I couldn't breathe for laughing. Chase me round the table with the poker and a poker face.

Long before the light comes, I wake to his hot night breath in my hair. Reckless is as reckless does. Afterwards, he sprawls on his back with his hands behind his head. As I dress he tells me his plans, and what he's done, and what he's going to do today, the orders he's placed and how this crop and that crop are coming on. Counting down the days and weeks to the twenty-fifth of April, the end of our joint trial period and the day I earn my surprise. He's still talking as he eats his breakfast, even as he walks out the door. Walking backwards. Can't take his eyes off me.

'Tommy,' I'd said, when we were halfway up the stairs. 'What if we—'

He pulled back his hand from mine. 'What if we what?'

Even then I couldn't ask him: are you sure, how will we manage, if we don't get the tenancy, and even if we do? Are we are risking everything, or staking everything? The truth is, I can't bring myself to think about the consequences, of anything, any more. I got us here, didn't I? I've got him back. I've waited so long to be happy. I take him in, and keep him there, and I let that delicious thrumming feeling take over again. It's hope, I tell myself, not fear.

*

Adam is no different to how he ever was. Now they are both here all day, the early flush of their friendship seems to have steadied. They consult over this and that, head off to the Fox together once in a while; otherwise they keep to their own sides, they come home to their own kitchens for their tea, and then they're off again to their own sheds.

If Adam and I do happen to pass, close enough for it to be unneighbourly not to speak, we fill the air with talk. About the two magpies, mainly. We were opposite ends of the cinder path when we first saw them. We both looked up at the same time. The magpies court up and down the holding. *Seen them today yet?* we call across to each other. We both know exactly where the other is, where Jean and Tommy are too. I tell myself I'm watching for the magpies as I work. Not for him. I don't let myself think I shall have to watch him always now, as long as we stay here.

I have to be out there anyway because I can't breathe inside the house any more. I have to be out alongside Tommy, be at his side always. And work, hard. Work until I sweat and my muscles ache. I lean into the handle of my spade. Tommy looks me over, says nothing, digs harder.

When it was bad, he'd always regret himself. Stay away for a good while, afterwards. It would be agony, the place would never be cleaner, each time I'd never quite believe he would come, but each time he'd be back. I'd hear it in his boots as he came up the street – the regret, the contrition, the longing – and feel a sort of triumph. He'd hang up his cap and set himself down in the front room. I'd make him a pot, fill up the sugar bowl and take myself off. When he was ready. he'd come up behind me. Take my hand and bracelet my wrist with his fingers, run his thumb and forefinger up and down and raise the little hairs. Lean into my nape, lift my hair. Endless soft butterfly kisses on the hurt places. The tickle of damp eyelashes. I'd turn and show him the dimples. Eventually. He'd have a present for me, one of his 'surprises'.

All these years, I've told myself, at least he's mine, just for those moments. Now, if anyone told, it would break this spell for ever. His chest would tighten, his eyes would go blank, he'd be gone, down there in the dark again. He'd take me with him and we'd never come back.

Every morning Jean brings me my lettuce to the door. We stand on the step in the morning air and talk about the day's work ahead. I take each fresh green head from her hands eagerly, unquestioning, grateful. Jean looks at me trustingly, sees the hotness of my cheeks, and smiles. Once I'm alone in the house again I eat it up, every scrap, even the stalk.

When I shut my eyes, it's not Tommy I see, or even Adam. It's rows of those dancing green heads, growing about my feet. That night I went to the glasshouse feels more and more like a dream. I am, if anything, more grateful than guilty. For the morning after. When I woke up to this new life, with the plants. I go out to my seedlings, urge them on, run my palm over their tiny, twinned leaves. I talk to them and they get bigger every day. But I know I can't pick more, not yet.

At night, my ears ring. I'm no longer dreaming of the pit, the old days, its whirring wheel, the tromping boots. Truth is, I can't remember much of anything before that night in the glasshouse. It's fuzzy, muffled, as though it's a long distance away. St Clement's, Crampton's, all of it. Even Turnbull.

Jean's right: it wasn't any sort of life that we had. I was terribly run down. The headaches, that I've had every month since I went down South Shields, have stopped. My teeth don't even hurt. I don't remember ever feeling so well, even the year we married. I'm new born to myself. All day long, all night, I hear a sort of humming chorus, soft and steady. Every so often there's a run of higher notes, along the top, a sort of unfurling. Then a pause, and we're back to a low thrum.

One night it's so loud I go down to the door to listen. Maybe a factory has opened up nearby, and I can only hear it at night when everything else is quiet. Except it's always quiet here, if nothing's disturbed the pens. Maybe they're doing work on the railway line.

I stand on the step, blind and cold. It is clear as anything, rising up from the ground like mist. I fold my arms and my breasts feel tight and excitable. I walk out across the sodden grass until the singing is all around me in the dark. It swells as I walk towards the glasshouse and when I open the door the congregation glows, ripples and pauses. Then they sing out again in welcome. The glass quivers. The glazing bars hum.

Glad that I live am I.

I kneel before them. I hear the unfurling of their dear little leaves. The strain in their tender stalks as they stretch towards me. I caress as many as I can reach, touch their tender heads, and they bow towards me. *We thank you. We love you. We are full of love. Full of praise. Full of thanks. Love us now. Love us.*

As I'm letting myself back in, the front of my nightdress sodden and clammy and clinging, the Dells' door opens.

'You can hear them,' Jean says from the darkness of her doorway. It's not a question.

'You too?'

'Me too. The plants have always sung to me.'

'You never told me.'

'No, I should have, though.'

'I'd have thought you were mad. I did—'

'—think old Jean was mad,' she supplies. 'I know. I know you did. You didn't even try and hide it.'

'I'm sorry.' I'd say anything to keep her happy. Keep her feeding me. She is my first true friend, after all.

Glad that I live am I.

'I'm sorry,' I say again.

'Don't be. It doesn't matter now, does it? Now. You're a grower too.'

20th March

I start to feel the way I'd get Fridays, when I'd gorged on the misshapes coming home. Giddy with it, when I threw away the bag, fit to dance through the night. I'd have to have a sit down half an hour later, when everything drained away.

I'm leaning against the side of the glasshouse one morning, when Adam comes round the corner and sees me. Tommy is right there, trying to get a look at Rosie.

She comes to the rails and we watch him turn her around gently and press his hands down on her hind quarters, rick his neck to look under her tail. Rosie's stayed in her sty for days, isn't feeding. At teatime, I watch him underline, circle and pencil notes in one of those Association manuals Adam won't have any truck with. He folds it shut, trying to hide the softness, the excitement in his eyes. At night, before sleep, I summon up that devout, fleeting look and let myself imagine.

From the other side of the path, Adam hands me an apple, warm from his pocket, and soft, the colour of old paper. He watches me bite, hard, and suck to trap the juice inside my lips. When he nods and smiles and moves on, my head swims with gratitude.

He keeps his distance still. But when he sees me out on the holding, and no one else is around, he'll straighten up and come over and take from his bib pocket another apple from the store, a stiff young onion, maybe a beet, brushed clean. Hold it out, as you would to a horse. I take it and bite into whatever it is then and there. He watches me take the first bite, then moves on.

Chew. Swallow. It's not enough.

*

I start to walk on tiptoe. Wait for something to dislodge. I flinch when I see a vein of red in a cracked egg. My rolled rags stay at the back of the bedroom cupboard shelf.

Sometimes, when he's buried deep in sleep, I reach down for Tommy's hand, limp and hot, and place it between my breasts. Perhaps it's not such a gamble as I think. If we let ourselves believe in this enterprise, that this place can make me a better person. It might make a proper family of us at last. We have a place of our own. A regular income. An empty room, waiting.

Perhaps it wasn't my foot. Perhaps it was that she didn't have any of this. All I know of my mother is that she had to leave me. I don't know why or where she went. Charity paid my keep and, even if charity knew, charity deemed it best I didn't. If we pass this assessment, we'll have a home, and our keep, and I shan't have to leave, ever. If I could forgive myself, then perhaps I could forgive her too. Atone, at least, for what I've done. I wouldn't have to choose. I could have both.

The heaviness of his hand on my ribs always steadies my breath. It's so dark here at night. I wish I could see his face. His eyelids flickering. Not that anything can come of it, I tell myself, any of it. Rotten is as rotten does. But, if by some miracle, it did. I slide his hand down and hold it against my belly.

That spring, when we moved into Shiney Row, when Tommy was still First Man. That would have been the time. We might have managed all right, if it had happened then. Only we'd have been just like the rest of them, and neither of us ever wanted that. *If I'd wanted a pitwife, I'd have married a pit girl.* And I didn't want anything but Tommy. We never once spoke about babies, of course. And I'd known enough to take care, right from the off. I could count days, couldn't I? Tommy was careful too. Kept a fresh handkerchief tucked under his pillow. Two week on, two week off. Got to be second nature.

Just the two of us. It was smashing – who'd want to change that? Although it changed soon enough, with the first lockout. We'd never known life together without a wage before, but we'd been saving hard, and at first it was a delight, having more time together. I could see what a relief it was for him, not having to face the pit. But after only a few weeks, a couple of months, he was different. And I couldn't always manage.

I'd told myself I was run down through worry and want, I'd be back to rights once he got some work. But I knew. My nipples prickled if I even looked at a baby. I was a bit giddy all day, like coming off the merry-go-round. A whiff of chipped potato made me want to gag. Kept swallowing, again and again. Couldn't focus. Couldn't settle.

I didn't have to imagine his face to know what to do. I only had to look at the Co-op book. It was a lockout, not a strike, but no one was getting any sort of relief. All we had was lodge money, 10/- a week, with 3/- going out on the HP, 2/- on the hospital insurance, and there was the rent. Even if Tommy took the longer hours on offer, the wages were far lower. And if he didn't, well, the Means Test was coming in. They'd already stopped benefit to women like me who hadn't paid enough contributions before getting wed. And Crampton's never took back a married woman. No respectable establishment ever did.

I'd have gone ahead and done it anyway, though, to keep him. I knew full well it would have been the finish of the two of us. There'd be no more gilt on the gingerbread, for either of us.

Aloes, Epsom, Beecham's, Glauber's – I sweated it out for as long as I could and then I made a plan. I knew where to go; I wasn't a St Clement's girl for nothing. I was going to sell my precious three-piece to pay for it and say the HP took it back. It was winter; I could tell everyone the van came after dark. But our luck must have been worse than I thought because the HP came and took it anyway.

I sat inside another week but in the end it was a stall down South Shields quay. Wasn't another way I could see. I'd heard the pitwives talk about the quacks there, who sold gentian violet for worms, that sort of thing. Went down the other end of town early early early to catch one bus, then a tram, eleven miles, on a Sunday morning. Got there just as he was putting up the shutters. He was picking little bones out of his moustache and the kipper stink so strong I had to put my handkerchief over my mouth. I didn't have to say a word; he could see the state of me.

I filled my basket with greens and the like and brought it home. At the bottom a big brown bottle, unlabelled. Ergot solution, I think it was. He tried to sell me some Jeyes fluid to flush it out. Got that at home, I told him.

Tommy didn't know a thing about anything. He was out half the time anyway, going from pit to pit, or keeping conk. There'd be small coal in the scuttle, and tuppennies and ha'pennies tied up in a kerchief. Small stuff. Small mercies. On top of everything, his da was on the way out. When the sweats started, Tommy was down there with his sisters, doing what he could. It was what I'd hoped, for him to be out the house, but when it came to it, that's what scared me most. Being alone.

After a while, of course, I was praying that he wouldn't come back. The room flooded with the coppery tang of blood. When the cramps started I just wanted someone to hold my hand and talk to me. After that I went so far inside the pain I couldn't talk, and if he'd come back then he'd have thought I was dead. A bird flew into the window. I thought it would smash. I remember laughing, oh my God what was that. The blood on the glass was bright scarlet, and thin as strawberry juice.

It got dark. I couldn't even move to light a candle. Couldn't make a sound for fear someone would hear. They wouldn't have come over, naturally. Well, maybe when it came to it. But I couldn't take that risk. They'd talk right enough. Mrs Hutchinson's daughter started up on her piano right opposite, and was I glad of that. She plays so badly the dogs get to howling and someone always comes out and has a go, however bad the weather. And then it started raining, hard. I felt something moving through me, something big; it was in bits.

When Tommy did come back, it was all over. *Had a clean-up?* he shouted up when he came in. He could smell the Jeyes. I was glad, meant he couldn't smell anything else. I was very thirsty. *How's your da?* I called back. Told him I had a sick headache, I'd laid tea and he'd find the candle on the mantelpiece. After that, I slept, and I don't even know if he came to bed. I woke up on my own.

Jean beckons me across the cinder path and leads me to their second glasshouse. It's turned much warmer these last weeks, though every time I see Jean she's bundled up in more clothes. Today she has one of Adam's waistcoats on under her coat, and a jumper under her dungarees. A pile of fence posts blocks the gap between their piggery and some tarpaulin-sheeted straw bales. She straddles them easily, and takes my hand to help me over. After that we walk hand in hand.

The glasshouse is a sort of sanctuary now: the air domesticated, the frantic birdsong more distinct, somehow, filtering through the glass. What I always hoped to find in church, and never did. I give her hand a squeeze.

She wants to show me the rows of low, bushy plants, all bearing white and yellow flowers. Strawberries, planted eighteen months ago. Can I see the double crowns? Lots of flowers means lots of berries. They look like they should ripen much earlier in May this year; it will be good to get some cash. She and Adam have been what the Association calls 'on their own' for years and years, and successfully too, but still, she warns, we must never take anything for granted. Tommy calls them country misers. Jean says she's showing me so I understand growers must always plan to tighten their belts at this time of year. She calls it the hunger gap. Plenty of young plants showing. Just none quite ready to crop.

Jean uses only her left hand to sow, to and fro. She rakes the folds of earth over, to put the seed to bed. She tamps it down with the flat of the rake, and a long row of lines appears, like a railway track. She hardly moves, yet within minutes the whole patch of empty soil is done: sown, raked and tamped. It's as though I fell asleep and hours have passed before I woke. She watches me fondly as I attempt to copy her, gently corrects my mistakes. She would teach me everything she knows, if she could.

If this is friendship, I've never really had a friend at all. I only have to shout through the wall if I need her, and I do. Once I asked her for a cup of sugar, just as a joke, but she brought it round anyway, keen-eyed and solemn. I sit at her kitchen table more often than I sit at my own. However many mistakes I make, she doesn't give up. She gave me her mash mixer. She reminds me daily to check the temperature in the egg store.

And what do I do for her? I've must have told her half a dozen times to use salt not soda on her burnt pans, she never does. Once I collected them from her sink, took them back to mine to scrub out, hung them back up. Days passed, she never even noticed. I've got her to go in with me on a flour club, and coal too. The Co-op orders never come with chits but, from what Jean says, Lady Sanders was right, everything's much more expensive here.

I'm itching to go round and sort her kitchen drawers, which are so full they never shut properly, and run a cloth over the windows; there's mould growing in the condensation. But she won't let me touch a thing. Shoos me outdoors again, to show me some new trick. It's not that she's wedded to her own ways, more that she doesn't see the dirt, the mess, doesn't care about anything but what's growing outside. She's stubborn too. Doesn't care to be told neither.

This is neighbourliness, I think. Not eyeing up each other's nets and hands back on hips before you're even round the corner. This is sisterliness. Not Monica, making it clear who'd made that bread, paid for every spoonful of tea. It's as though Jean's house and mine are one, as I'd imagined them to be the day I got here.

I've more to be thankful for here than I'd ever imagined, and I would like to atone for that night, if I could. But what do I have to give her? She's not interested in soaking rosemary to make a wash that might give her hair some shine. She doesn't care about how to keep her lace white; Jean doesn't own any lace.

What I can do is tell her tales, from my life before. The smallest details amuse, or shock her. She makes me feel like a sailor landed on a savage island, handing out beads. I feed her titbits: watching out for the snowdrops at St Clement's. The saucy things young Mr Crampton would say to us girls. About Monica hiding our cushions from the means test man. My pocketing the Association poster from the butcher's window before anyone else saw it. Bite-sized pieces, sugar-coated. Nothing that matters. Nothing incriminating.

Get nothing back, mind. She talks about how she'd knit socks, from when she was very small. Play down the lime pits with a wax doll, that fell on the fire and shrivelled up. A boiled pudding she used to like, that tipped out of the cloth, and didn't break till you put the knife in. *Your ma made that?* I asked, but she spotted a rabbit by the celery and that was it. She's mentioned a village crier once, who went about on a bicycle with a bell. It must have been a dull life they had out in the country, back west. I don't mind. I like the way she screws up her nose and frowns – it's a mystery to her, my world of bait-tins and chipped potatoes, treeless streets and trams and pink rock candy.

'You sold sweets?'

'Made them too. Sherbet. We did hard-boiled – black bullets and rosey apples and soor plums. And jellies – black and rasps and jelly babies. And sarsaparilla tablets.'

She nods.

'You know those?' I ask.

'Sarsaparilla's good for the heart.'

I tell her about the Crampton's uniform, how you always had to stand up dead straight on account of the frilly cap that had two long plumes dangling halfway down your back.

'Like an egret.'

'A *what*?'

'It's a bird, Lettie.'

'Oh. Right. And we had a lovely double row of pearl buttons down our fronts. Sewn with white cotton, though, not red.'

'Red?'

'Red like Nippies.'

'Like *what*?'

It's my turn to goggle. 'Nippies. Lyon's tea house? The uniforms? Jean, how do you not know what a Nippy is?'

I tell her about the day I first saw Tommy, coming off shift. We'd hear their boots ring out as they came up the hill and we'd keep our heads down as they barrelled past; pitmen weren't worth the trouble. Only this day a young lad had jumped up from the gutter for a prank and gone and knocked Tommy's cap off. Tommy never yelled or lashed out. He just stood stock still while the rest flowed around and stared down at the lad until he picked it up and dusted it off and handed it right back.

'Where did you meet Adam then?'

'I couldn't say. He was always around.'

'Was he from the same village?'

'Not exactly. We were on a farm, you see.' She shades her eyes with one hand and squints. 'Is that rabbit back?'

'Tell me?'

'Well,' she says, as though she's only just remembered, 'I suppose you would say we were childhood sweethearts.'

'Yes?'

'Yes,' she says with finality. 'I suppose so. Yes.'

The stories I've told her. And what do I know about her? She's vague about everything but the work. It makes me uncomfortable, to think how much I've told her. It's not fair, somehow. Isn't this what friends do, confide in each other? I get the pain in my chest that would come when the St Clement's girls huddled in corners, twisting their hair and whispering their secrets. I kept myself apart, then, and I don't know why. They'd never let me forget my bad foot; I'd hear them behind me on the stairs: *hobblediho*. We were all orphans together, we all had something wrong with us. They told each other their stories. I could have made something up.

Then I remember all that I've not told Jean, all that we did before we got here, and what I've done since.

I wake to find Tommy sitting up, smoking in the dark. 'What's up?' I ask, from deep, deep in the pillow. I can't think how I'd manage. I want to sleep all the time as it is, ease myself into a furrow, watch the earth trickle and go inside myself.

'Nothing.' But he reaches down under the covers and folds my fingers in his. His hand is icy cold.

Those nights after Turnbull when we lay side by side in bed, wide open to the darkness, without tobacco to fill our lungs or glow between our fingers, terrified of the future. He never reached out to me then, not once.

'What is it?' I sit up beside him, and grip his hand tight. 'What is it?'

Only a few weeks to go, of course, till the assessment. He's a lot of pride, has Tommy. Nothing but contempt for those less fortunate, and only envy for those better off. And not a jot of belief in himself, not really. Even before the lockouts, he used to put the cat in the oven for luck the day he'd start at a new pit. Bow to the moon. Leave his shirt on inside out, if he'd put it on that way in the dark. Just like his da did, and his da before him. Luck is everything to pitmen.

What's a wife to do? Tell him it's our grass that's greener now. We're both growers now, he just has to believe it. Never mind what else he's done, he'll have earned his success, here. Aren't we both working harder than we've ever worked? That'll be it. No wonder I've not needed my rags since we came. I was just the same at Crampton's, until I got used to the pace. We both have to keep our heads, is all.

I squeeze his hand so that he can feel my blisters, and the splinters lodged so deep the skin has grown over them. I work Zam-Buk in every night, but I can never rub away the faint sepia seams of soil.

'Never you worry about the twenty-fifth. We'll be all right. I'm doing you proud, aren't I?'

He says nothing.

I prod his shoulder.

'Giant cucumbers,' I say. 'Big, fat juicy tomatoes.'

His tab end flares brighter; I hear it consume itself.

'You'll outcrop the lot of them. You will.'

He pulls up his knees and braces his forearms against his shins.

'We'll be happy here, Lettie.'

It's not a question, but I answer it anyway.

'Course we'll be happy.'

'It'll be worth it.'

'Course it will,' I say. '*A lot of hard work . . .*'

He doesn't respond.

'You're playing big now. And when you get that cucumber house—'

'Yes,' he says, abruptly.

'What?'

He sighs.

'Nothing.'

'No, what?'

Silence.

I tuck the blankets in around us. 'Want me to guess my surprise? I've a pretty good idea, you know. It'll be either—'

'Everything, Lettie—'

I wait.

'Everything I do. Always. It's all for you, Lettie, you know that.'

After a while I give his hand another squeeze.

'And they'd do anything for us,' he says.

'The Association?'

Silence again.

'The Dells,' he says.

'Oh,' I say. 'I know.'

It's not their charity now that shames me when I think of Jean, and Adam. It's myself. We get through this assessment, I tell myself, I'll get my rags out again, and my rottenness will be behind me too.

Tommy sucks hard on his tab. 'That holding of theirs as good as belongs to us already, you know. Once they leave, and I'm working them both, we'll—'

He breaks off.

'I'm not going back, Lettie.'

'Course you're not,' I say quickly. 'It'll be worth it, Tommy. Big stakes, big returns. You'll see.'

'I know.'

'Anyway, that assessment, it's just—'

'A formality.'

That's what Jean keeps telling us. No one ever gets thrown off. Not once they've invested so much in you. 'What about that lot who were here before us?' I asked once. 'Oh, they did a runner long before the assessment. And anyway, they were different,' says Adam. 'They weren't natural-born growers, were they? Not like you two.'

I squeeze Tommy's arm. 'That's right. It's a formality is what it is.'

He lies himself back down.

'Look, you've rucked the bed up now. My feet are freezing.' I flounce the blankets about a bit. 'You owe me, Tommy Radley. Better not forget my surprise?'

'I'll not forget.' He turns away. 'Go to sleep, Lettie.'

'Tommy—'

'Go to sleep.'

*

All through our courting, he'd never said much. I'd never thought anything of it. Not felt the lack, never having had anyone to talk to. And we'd not needed talk. Once we were married, though, once we were just the two of us, and in bed, afterwards, he'd talk then. Tell me things he never told anyone.

About the dark, what it was like down there. How very alone it made him feel. He'd try and explain to me, those times when you'd turn a corner and your light snuffed it. You might be a matter of feet from your marra and the rest of them, and it wouldn't make any difference because you'd find yourself absolutely, finally, alone. As though no one else had ever existed, or ever would. He would go very still, then, remembering. I'd have to poke him in the shoulder to make him come alive because I couldn't bear it either.

He told me about his first shift. His da got up with him at four and made him jam and bread sandwiches and a bottle of tea. Told him he'd do that for three days and then he was on his own.

He told me he was no scholar. And after four daughters, he was the first, the only son. And all he'd wanted, for as long as he could remember, was to carry a lamp like his da, and risk his neck for his marras like his da, deep down there in a world no one could ever know but men like them.

Only, the minute the sky sliced shut as the cage sank down the shaft, he knew he wasn't going to be able to stand it. That absolute pit-dark. It swallowed him alive. Only stand it he knew he must, for his da. And the wage, of course. His sisters. Stand it he did, shift after shift. Near lost the habit of speech, for fear they'd hear his voice crack. Worked his way up from putter to hewer, jowled the hardest places, right up until the day his da died.

Even then, he'd had to bury his craving for light and air until all his sisters were married off. By then he was earning enough for a diamond jumper and socks to match, to shine up that Jack Adams and take off up and out of town, enough to be able to fill his lungs with sweet, cool air and speed past folk who had never been further down into the ground than their garden spades could reach; always on his own, mind, he never joined the lads and lasses of the Cycling Club. He'd not have anyone see his face as he lifted it to the sky, or the tears stream down his cheeks.

Other pitmen, once they married, wheeled their bikes down the allotments to get their fill of sky and birdsong, came home with carrots and onions draped over their handlebars. It took him even longer to tell me why that wasn't for him.

He'd hide his face in the pillow a while. I'd have to tell him again how much I loved him, no matter what. He'd turn to face me and hold his palm against my hair as though it were glowing filaments. *Firefly*, he called me. And then he'd tell me again, about that November evening, when he crested the brow of the hill, all his muscles on fire, and saw me through the bright-lighted plate glass. *I thought my heart was going to burst.*

I'd have to squirm myself upright. I'd want to open the curtains, dance loose and proud and naked on the bed with you watching invisible at my feet.

Firefly.

Tommy needs the dark then. To not be seen, just held; that's when he can show himself. *I can't be without you, Lettie. I shall take you down there with me, in my pocket, see. Set up you up on a ledge. This hair of yours, see, I reckon it shines brighter than any lamp.*

No one had ever said such things to me. St Clement's had trained us to serve and be grateful. *You weren't worth your keep* Mr Robert shouted after me the day I left for Crampton's. Those nights, with Tommy's arm heavy around my shoulders and his chin resting on the top of my head, I felt precious as a ring, snug in a velvet box.

And then, whenever we were out, the two of us, when we were all sat around in someone's front room belting out *We're so misable, all so misable, a down on Misable farm,* I'd watch him. He'd keep his cap and muffler on, as if he were just passing through; no one ever cut up about it. Tuck himself in by the window, roll and smoke and never trade a tab. Move his lips if there was singing. Wrinkle up his forehead at anyone who spoke to him. *Yes,* he'd say. *No.* Twist his head away to one side. *Pfft.* No answer to that, is there. He had everyone's respect. But no one came close. No one saw him. No one but me.

Firefly.

I was only a St Clement's orphan; I had no one. But none of his pit folk, even his own kith, knew him like I did.

That summer we were fixing up our very first place. One room down on Banbury Street, half a dozen streets away from Pit Bottoms and his sisters, but it felt like a world away. He was on at me for feeding the fire with a cup of kerosene every morning, on account of the chimney was crooked. We were saving hard for a neat little house, high up and well away. But we had enough over to set out on a Saturday around six, when people were beginning to stroll about, for a few glasses of port and a pair of good seats at the Empire. And if ever I got low, he'd press his fingertips to my dimples and kiss my nose, promise me the gilt on the gingerbread.

When we did make it up to Shiney Row, my lord. End of the row, free to do what we liked at last, loud as we liked, upstairs and down. First thing I did was hang that mirror of his by the back door at a height to suit myself thank you very much. He had to squat like a frog to shave. I'd sit on the stairs to brush my hair, and watch the muscles move in his back and shoulders, every morning until they delivered the dressing set with the three folding mirrors and I could watch him check the closeness of his shave from the bed. Those packing cases were full of fresh wood shavings. We had kindling for weeks. We didn't have to stop in bed to stay warm then. But we did, when we could.

And then. He was hewing in the Yard Seam, a hard place, and going steady until they reduced the hewing price. And brought in a long-wall system and mechanical loaders. None of us believed it would come, but it did. Five hundred men sacked and turned on dole. No bargaining. Company just locked them out.

I knew better than to console him, at least. Took his coat, boots, the lot. He tucked the cracket stool under him and I stood myself next to the tub. But he took fast hold of the basin and flannel, washed himself, dried himself, wouldn't even turn around. He always was a restless sleeper, but that night I watched great, guilty shudders pass through him. That pit had got a hold on his throat and wouldn't let go. If bad luck had caught up with him at last, it could be nothing but his fault, his own failing. There was no use trying to tell him different. It was his fault, because he'd been afraid down there, all this time.

And it became my fault, for knowing it.

That first lockout went on, and on. We didn't really believe, I think, those gates wouldn't open again. They had before. *Not a penny off the pay, not a minute on the day.* All we had to do was wait it out. We knew no other life. We kept on eating, even kept taking the Sunday paper long after everyone else stopped. Kicked myself for that, I did, by the time I was cutting it up to put in his boots.

He'd lived from one cavilling day to the next, the drawing of that slip from the bag with his number on it that told him his working place; now he waited outside the library with the rest of them, but they none of them got to the board in time. Any job going went to them as could still afford to buy the paper themselves, at six in the morning. He'd not tell me that, of course, just parrot stuff he'd picked up from reading *Church Messenger* or *Barber's Record*, anything to stop the attendant chucking him out.

He fixed the crack in the fender. He finished puttying the scullery window. He tightened the handle on the iron – the lot. He'd stand by the mantelpiece with a twitchy grin and smoke himself silly. Then he sat down. He sat sat sat until I wanted to kick him up out the door and on to the moors.

And then he just lay in bed, like a bundle of dirty linen. I'd come in and think he'd gone out at last and then find him in the front room, stretched out on the settee asleep and not even washed. If I poked him, he'd stare right through me.

I hated him as much as he hated himself. I couldn't help it. After he'd come, the big man, and taken me away from Crampton's and married me. I couldn't look after him; he wasn't bringing in anything to look after us with. You managed the pit, I'd think, the dark that scared you witless, but lying around indoors is too much for you? And I was filled with a terrible feeling of dread: it had been for nothing, our striving and grafting. Jeering, jealous young Mr Crampton had been right about pitmen. You'd drag me down to Pit Bottoms. Monica's face then, and her sisters. We'd end in the workhouse.

Then came that July day. We were holding on at Shiney Row, behind on everything. Furnishing company wrote to say they'd be taking it all back, £25 of solid oak. And then Monica's girl Nancy turned up with a covered bowl. Mam was going to throw this away, she says, and she thought as perhaps we'd might like it. *We'd be doing her a kindness.*

His pride broke. He sent Nancy on her way with a clout, and then it was my turn. I held my tongue, always had, but trouble is, I've never been able to tell what sort of silence it is, with him. I ask too much with my eyes, that's what it is. I look at him too long. I try to hold my breath, stay very still. Sometimes, even as his hands come up, I can get hold of his wrists, and slowly, slowly, he unclasps. Other times, if I so much as move, I break the spell.

We're sat on our stools, transplanting again. The Easter sun through the glass warms our skin and fills the still air with the scent of soil and roots and leaves. Jean's funny when she laughs. She shows all her teeth and sometimes she snorts like a donkey.

I'm telling her about the ducklings I found at St Clement's. I must have been about six or seven. They'd wandered away from somewhere and got shut in the little close. I didn't tell a soul. They were my secret and I was going to rescue them and be their mother. I picked them up in my pinny pocket and took them into the outhouses. I filled a bowl with water and set them swimming round and round. One two three four five of them, cheeping and bleating and stretching out their scrawny necks.

After a few days I forgot about them, of course. I tell her how they looked when I went back and saw them. I tell it lightly, one smallholder to another. I laugh first, so she'll understand the foolish, ignorant town child I was and how much I've learned from her. Perhaps I want her to forgive me.

Straight away I know I've made a mistake. I may as well have wrung their tiny necks and be holding them out for her now, limp and dripping.

'Jean?'

She cranes her neck away so I can only see the line of her jaw. She swallows hard. She raises a hand to shield her eyes from the glare of sun on glass.

'Those sheets look dry already,' she says. 'You only put them out just before noon, didn't you?'

*

After tea, there's a knock at the door. I know it's her. We don't have callers, and Adam has never come to the door.

Jean shifts from foot to foot. The wind has made a nest of her hair and she's so bundled up she looks more like that scarecrow every day.

'I want to show you something.'

'I'm just washing up.'

'Before the light goes.'

I untie my pinny.

'Never mind that.'

She walks stiffly ahead of me down the straight and narrow, to their side of the orchard. All is neat and still. The Dells' trees were pruned long before we got here. Tommy still hasn't finished ours. The growth is long and whips about, like overgrown divining rods.

Jean kneels beside the first tree in the first row nearest the path. The wind has her words before I do. I wrap my arms tight and lean in closer.

'They look like nothing, don't they? But just you wait, Lettie. See, the buds are coming, the leaf and the flower. Then we'll have the blossom, the scent. My bees will do their work. Come summer, it's a little piece of heaven down here. Good years or bad years, there's always something precious, something new born. The earth will always give back. You just have to keep faith, do you see?'

I don't really understand. But I do want to please her. And atone. I reach out to touch the tree. I smile down at her.

'Take the Blenheim Orange. No fruit for years, and then—' She clasps both hands about the trunk. 'There's this one too. Beauty of Bath. Matures early. Too early, sometimes.'

Jean runs her hand down the trunk to where it disappears into the ground. 'She was our first, you see.'

Then she turns and points at a tree behind her. 'Norfolk Pippin. That was our second. A boy.'

I look around for some excuse to leave and see Adam in his shirtsleeves, standing in their open doorway.

Jean lumbers to her feet, head down, and walks fast to another tree, several rows further in. Her big coat flaps out behind her.

'Jean, wait a minute.'

'You've never replanted a tree, have you, Lettie? It doesn't always take. The soil has to be right. And the hole has to be much bigger than you think. There's a lot of digging. And it's just as much work to fill it in. You can't ram the earth back in any old how. The roots have to be able to breathe.'

I'm still holding the trunk of the first tree, Beauty of Bath. I lift my hand away.

'That's all right. I like to see you hold her. They were our first-born. Beauty of Bath and Norfolk Pippin.'

I want her to stop talking, right there. She has to stop.

'Not a good idea to transplant a tree once it's taken, of course. But the climate's been good here. And the soil. We thought our luck might change as well. Over here, look, this is Wyken Pippin. He was tiny.'

'Jean, I'm sorry. I was foolish, I know that. You don't have to—'

Adam is walking down the cinder path.

Jean goes up to yet another tree, touches its trunk. 'Tom Putt. He was small too, like Pippin.'

She moves on. 'And Peasgood's Nonsuch. She was perfect, was Nonnie, and a good size as well. Just perfect.'

I watch her sit down, shuffle her bum close and curl her heavy legs around the tree trunk.

'I talk to them every day. You've seen me, I suppose? It's foolish, of course it is. My plants talk to me, always have, you know that. Well, I've always thought that, some day, my babies might talk to me too. I still do.'

Jean bows her head against the trunk.

'When I think of the seedlings I've grown. The thousands of plugs I've planted out.' Her mouth works. 'I know what you think, Lettie, but there's no magic to being a grower, not really. Just pop the seed in the earth and water it. Slip the plugs out of their little pots and into the earth and give them a bit of water, sunshine, keep an eye on them, and off they go.

'Oh, I can grow plants, Lettie. I can grow anything I want from seed. I'll raise you all the livestock you like. I've incubated hundreds of chicken eggs, hundreds. Ducklings, geese. Oh, but babies, Lettie—'

Adam reaches us soon after that. He ignores me, crouches down and puts his arm around her shoulders. I look at the pair of them, huddled under the tree. Then I walk back to the house.

Halfway up the path, my knees almost give way. I have to stop myself turning round and shouting. *Don't give me that, Jean. They were only baby ducks. They would have died anyway, if I hadn't found them. You don't know how lucky you are. See what you've got. See what you already grew. Acres of it. You've been a grower your whole life, Jean. What more do you want? Don't think you're missing anything; babies are two a dozen. Any fool can have a baby. Why can't you be happy with what you've got?*

Tommy grabs at my arm. I shake him off. Why doesn't she just give up? Can't she see it's hopeless. At her age.

'Oi, Lettie. What's up?'

'She's making herself ridiculous, Tommy.'

He shakes his head.

'What?'

'What have you said?'

'Nothing!'

'Pfft.'

I stop. 'What does that mean?'

'You know.'

'No, I–' I bite my tongue.

'I don't want to know. Get yourself indoors.' He stalks back to his rows.

*

I eat the last three Eccles that were going stale, with lashings of butter, and crumbs all over *TitBits*. When I've had my fill of dastardly earls and shade trimmings – I've circled one of those Dargue acetylene table lamps – I flick through Tommy's Association handbooks until I find *Apples, Some Good Varieties.*

There are hundreds of varieties: Gascoyne's Scarlet, Newton Wonder, Lord Lambourne, James Grieve. Crimson Bramley. Ridiculous names. Beauty of Bath crops in August. The only Pippin I can find is Allington, which crops late, November through December.

I look at the plate of photographs, at a short man in a trilby and a jacket with breast pockets, like the ones we wear, planting an apple tree. I read the captions. He puts back the *turves*, whatever they are, upside down. He remembers that *the union of stock and scion must not be covered over.* Nothing about how to replant a tree.

The Dells must have brought Beauty of Bath and the rest with them. How could I ever ask now? I wasn't even trying to be mean. I was trying to be a friend.

Thorley's Almanac falls open at April. Tommy's drawn a circle around the twenty-fifth. Next to that he's pencilled *CD 11 Mr B.* His interview at the Central, eleven o'clock with Mr Bridgewater. And next to that a squiggle, & <u>Mr R.</u> The *Mr* underlined, twice. Because if he gets in there'll be no more Radley this Radley that from our Mr B or anyone else. He'll be Mr T. Radley, Grower, Holding Number 94.

He's on tiptoe too. Waiting. If Adam or Jean brings up the assessment he starts to swagger and goes on about 'Lettie's surprise' instead. How I'll never guess. How it'll have been worth the wait.

Of course I've guessed. If it's not a wireless set it'll most likely be a set of teeth. Tommy promised over and over he'd buy me a complete set, like John had got Monica. Said he'd take me to the same man, upstairs on Sinclair Street with the fancy wallpaper. I knew better than to let him anywhere near me. Promises mean nothing, do they. I got the ring. Though I never got the set, on account of that first lockout.

It'll be a wireless. The dream of it kept us going, sat there in our coats and scarves: cosy evenings with Ambrose and his orchestra, getting the gang over again on a Saturday, but instead of spoons and a banjo we'd have Carroll Gibbons or Jack Hylton crooning down our necks. Tommy tried putting one together from parts, but he hadn't the knack, chucked the lot out.

Either way, I can't make myself care much. My rotten teeth have stopped hurting. And I'm used to the quiet. It's never silent here, not really. Always something to watch, or listen to. Something living, however small. All that singing I did, to fill the emptiness.

I look in the tin again, even though I know there's nothing but crumbs. Then I flick back to the breeding table for January.

Date on which an animal served or an egg set on any day of present month is due to give birth or hatch.

I read across the column headings.

Mare, Cow, Ewe, Sow, Bitch, Goose, Turkey, Fowl, Pigeon.

Fowl. Gestation period: *21 days.*

I make myself read February's motto instead, printed in black type across the bottom of the page.

**HURLEY's FOOD will increase
the quantity of Milk in Suckling Ewes
and the Lambs will benefit.**

And the one for March:

**If Pigs are healthy, Pig Powders are not
required, but if they are out of sorts,
HURLEY'S PIG POWDERS will be useful.**

Only then do I let my finger trace across the cow's gestation period: *40 weeks.* I find the sixth of February.

The sixth of February. Tommy's scribbled something about the piglings there, but I can't read it. The numbers jostle and merge in my head. Because her gestation period is forty weeks, a cow that is served on the sixth of February will give birth on the sixth of November. Nine months later.

The sixth of November.

I leaf through the nine pages until I reach November and press my long fingernail into the 6. It leaves a cusping dent, barely there. No one would know it even exists.

Eventually I decide. It takes me the next day and most of the one after that. Best out here, where we can be alone. It's clear and cold now the sun's going. The wind is bitter, whipping the sheets from my fingers. I'm glad; I want my words to be blown away as soon as I've spoken them. I'll know what to do straightaway, I'll see it in her face: whether she thinks I could really manage it, this time; whether she could bear it too. Either way, I need to know before the assessment, so I can decide what to do. There's just time.

I've already left it too late to get this wash in. A wash can be out all day and bone dry, but once the sun sets it's soon sticky with damp again. This lot will have to go straight on to the horse before the range. And then tomorrow morning I'll have to hang it out again.

She seems not to hear me coming down the path. It's the wind in her ears, the pigs jostling. I watch her tip one pail after another into the sty. Ten yards off, I stop. The moon hangs rusty gold, huge and low at the end of the cinder path. It looks too heavy to rise, but it does. I watch it labour up into the sky, separate itself from the tops of the trees at the bottom of the far field. My arms ache.

She's still talking to those sows. Look at them slobbering over her hand. Jean loves that; she'll stand there for ever like that. Look at her face. My bare arms are chilled through, under the heavy linen. I shiver and hurry back to the house.

*

More and more days I spend in the glasshouse. However chilly or windy or wet it's turned outside, the air in here is always still and soft, with a bathhouse whiff. I've done a bit of hoeing. Then the rain stopped and the sun came out and when the heat flooded in through the glass I felt like I was sinking into warm water. Even the yammering blackbirds in the bushes outside couldn't stop my steep slide into sleep.

I let go the watering can and curl up on a patch of dry soil. Each breath is monumental. Each breath sinks me further into the earth. An insect settles on the back of my hand but I can't open my eyes. Let the plants grow over me, I think. Perhaps I'll never be found. I stretch out on my back and let my arms drop to my side. I rest my cheek on the ground. I dream of trays and trays of eggs, watching to see if one moves. Of batter, falling off a spoon. When it drops I jerk awake but find myself still asleep.

The door slides open; slow footsteps. The swish of dungarees. The insect buzzes away but I am snug under-ground. My name. And again. After a long, long time I still cannot reply. She brushes my hair from my cheek.

'Lettie.'

I'm in too deep. Leave me be.

'I think this is it.' I hear the catch in her voice.

I can't move, not even a flicker. My chest rises and falls, my ears pulse.

'Lettie. Open your eyes.'

I can see the browning leaves beneath the strawberry crowns.

'Sit up. Look at me.'

141

My right leg has gone to sleep and my arms won't support me. My tongue is thick and dry.

'Jean—'

'Look at me.' Her eyes swim with tears. 'Yes!'

Straight away the high note of triumph and delight in her voice makes me sick with guilt.

Jean wraps her arms full around my shoulders and kisses my forehead.

'You've fallen, Lettie.'

I close my eyes, imagine she is Adam. Just for a moment.

'You did know, didn't you, Lettie? Does Tommy know?'

Tommy must never know this. Nor Adam neither.

'I didn't— I wanted—'

'To tell me first?'

I wanted it not to be true. But oh Jean: if only I had told you, gently, that evening, been able to soothe away your hurt and envy, my fear, we might have raised our chins to face this together. As true friends. Not like this. Not now. You have stolen this secret from me.

'I'm sorry, Jean.'

'You're sorry? Sorry for what? Don't be silly. This, this is— marvellous news.' She hugs me to her, pressing my head against her wide, pillowy breasts. 'Marvellous,' she says again.

I don't deserve her as a friend, really I don't. Nothing about her words, her manner, seems forced. Perhaps she has already braced herself for news like this, many times over, rehearsed what she might say. Her mind, like mine, will be running ahead. Here I'll be, right next door. She'll have to see me grow it and birth it and feed it. Hear it cry and gurgle and climb into my lap and see its little clothes dancing away on the line.

I press my face against her shoulder. She strokes my hair lightly. Then her hand slows. I brace myself.

'Mind you, it's early days, isn't it?' she says. 'You'd best not say anything to Tommy, just yet. Just in case.'

'No,' I say. 'I won't.'

Share it with me, Jean. Be with me when it's born. Help me look after it. That's what I'd really wanted to say, that evening. I'm not sure I want it, but it won't want me and I won't know what to do. I don't deserve a baby, after what I've done. I'm not fit to be a mother. Although what kind of gift is that, to share something you're not sure you want anyway?

'Goodness, it must be getting on for seventy in here.' Jean labours to her feet. 'I'll open some vents. Can't have this lot getting too hot too quickly. You go and splash your face. Get tea on.' She wipes her cheeks roughly and holds out a hand. 'Up you get.'

In the scullery I work the pump till it squeaks and stare at myself in Tommy's mirror. My face is a mask of itself: spread out, stretched smooth and clear. My skin looks flat, like pancake make-up. My eyes are darker, the colour of irises. I flex my swollen fingers and wrists. I feel up to my neck in water.

Of course Jean guessed I'd fallen pregnant. She only had to look at me. She notices everything that blooms in Foxash, every change. Sometimes I think she can feel everything growing. She just shuts her eyes and she knows.

She can't know everything I've done, though, can she. No one can, not ever.

Yesterday was like high summer. The sun shone all day and the air smelt like moorland heather on a bank holiday. And it was just as Jean had said: the butterflies and birds were all flying north, with the sun. Tommy crunched up and down after tea, diving into the rows to straighten canes and pinch off yellowed leaves. When he was first laid off, and took to gaming down an alley with the others, he'd come back with his fist screwed tight, just like that, tight round his pennies, to stop the rest of his luck leaking out. I'd wanted to go out and kiss his knuckles. But then Adam gave over lidding down the lights and went over to offer him a fresh tab.

We're still not as far on as the Dells, but our holding is nothing like the dump it was. With the Dells' help, we've coaxed the earth bare; it's soft and dark and steaming under the big blue sky, with a green haze spreading fast. We've raked and hoed and watered, straightened rows, tied on labels. Mended fences, repaired roofs. Even the muck pile looks perky. Birds flit over it, anxious and questing. Tiny, those birds are, like babies' fists. Always tugging at something for their nests.

Every morning, I've woken with a start. This place has put you in a trance, Lettie Radley. All those years of being careful, and I'm pacing about, unable to ignore the coiled life in every packet and plug, the swelling forms buried in every row, the relentless growth of everything; wanting to weep over the days and days that I've let slip by. Jean watches me from her rows, bobs her head and comes over to check my work, but neither of us lingers for long. *Must get on.*

After Tommy goes to sleep, and the foxes and the owls stop their signalling, and I'm alone in the dark, rotten and exhausted, I long to tear open those sweet, acrid sacks in his shed, gorge myself and be done with it. I've not forgotten how bad it was, last time. I'd want it to hurt. After all, rotten is as rotten does.

Every night I've made up my mind. I've lain there and lain there, still as a sleeping beauty in her glass box. Until last night. The blackbird started his song, rusty and inter-mittent, and I knew it was too late. I haven't the courage.

*

I go down to light the fire and heat Tommy's shaving water. The day is overcast and windy. I'd pressed his Sunday suit and polished his shoes and brushed his hat and laid them out for him. I call out 'Good luck!' when I hear him slam the gate behind him. I mean it. He deserves a bit of luck, does Tommy. With a wife like me.

I feed the chickens and do the watering, and some last-minute hoeing where it matters. Bridgewater will come back with him to inspect and then he'll say right off whether we're staying or not. He won't need to speak to me, Jean says, I've proved myself just by sticking it. What we've done out there is what counts. I expect we'll guess the outcome soon enough, from the look on Bridgewater's constipated face. I'm on the doorstep, taking off my boots, when Adam comes round their corner of the house, wiping his hands on a rag.

His step slows when he sees me crouched over, bad foot in hand. He frowns. As I slip my boot back on and bend over to tuck the tongue straight, he turns on his heel to give the holding an appraising glance.

He says soothingly: 'Tom won't have no trouble, I reckon.'

I'd forgotten how Adam looms, the tallness and straightness of him, the broad yoke of his shoulders. His skin, creamy as toffee.

I've not once let myself regret that night in the glasshouse. I'd not wish it away, not ever. I'll never go back to before; that night transformed everything. But often, in the deep of the night, I find myself wishing the pair of them away.

Jean taps loudly on her window and beckons to us both. Her face looms up large and pale and strained behind the glass. Adam stares on across the rows, working the rag across his palms. I see a flush rise in his cheeks, and a jolt of fear goes through me. She has told him what is growing inside me and this is to be my reckoning too.

Somehow, I get to my feet. Jean raps again, and he stuffs the rag in his pocket.

'After you.' As I step inside, I feel the touch of his hand, cobweb light, against the small of my back.

'Lettie! Come sit with us.'

Jean has her back turned, stirring the teapot, with Flo huddled on her shoulder as usual. She's brushed her hair. Even her dungarees are clean on. Not pressed, but clean.

'I can't settle to anything this morning.' Her voice shakes a little. 'I'm sure you can't either.'

Adam pulls out a chair and one of the new kittens claws at the tabletop, hanging off the edge like a bat before it clambers on. When he sits, it noses at his shirt and butts his forearm. I walk around to Jean's side and take my usual seat, with the dresser at my back.

'Bridgewater'll expect tea, won't he? I've made scones.'

'Oh, I doubt it.' She sniffs. 'You don't want to start inviting the likes of him in for tea, Lettie.'

Adam makes a scornful noise in his throat, and lets the kitten climb right inside his open cuff and up above his elbow, where it bulges like a new muscle. They're right, of course. The scones, the jam, the ironed tablecloth, it's a bit of gilded gingerbread, as much to get back at Sanders and his wife as to bribe Bridgewater.

'Well, I still need to get changed.'

'You do?'

Adam retrieves the kitten from his sleeve. 'Where's this one's mother got to, Jean?'

The room is full of shadows and dust as always, and smells of rotten apples. I'd started to feel quite at home coming in and out of here, with the mess, the trays of seedlings, bowls of scraps, dirty cups and nowhere to sit. Now I long for the empty quiet of my own neat house, that won't ever be quiet or empty again. Babies belong in houses like hers, not mine.

'I've chitted all that last batch,' Adam tells her. 'Have you seen the weeds coming round the brassica already? Parsnip drills are sprouting too.'

He leans back as Jean pours the tea from a great height, and slops the milk.

She passes me a cup and settles Flo on her lap. 'That's the one with the handle, mind.'

Meaning the one without. I nestle it between my palms, hot as it is.

Jean sips noisily, giving me long, intent, prideful looks. Adam glances at her, then at me, and dips his head. I have to set down my cup and grip the sides of my seat with both hands.

Well before my tea is cool enough to swallow, the door bangs open behind me. Jean hugs Flo to her.

'You Dells slacking indoors again?'

It's not his wireless voice. It's not any sort of voice at all. It's curt, clipped; with the light behind him like that, he could be Bridgewater. Then, in his right fist, I see he's holding a furl of crisp papers, tied up with red ribbon.

Adam's on his feet, instantly, to pump Tommy's hand.

'*Mr* Radley!' He snatches the contract and bats Tommy's hat off on to the floor. 'Youngest fella on the estate too. Jean, quick now, fetch us out something to celebrate.'

Tommy's hat rolls into the hallway. Flo flutters to the floor and Jean covers her face. Then she claps her hands together. 'Of course, of course. Where are those glasses?' She goes over to peer at the dresser. 'Two, or three – Mr Bridgewater not with you?'

Tommy is twirling his hat on his hand. He is grinning, flushed; that little tuft of hair defiantly erect still and gleaming with oil.

'Stopped at depot, didn't he.' He pauses for effect, hushes his voice. 'Fella's got to watch his chest.'

Adam guffaws. 'That's Bridgewater for you.'

I set down my cup carefully in its saucer. Now Tommy sees me. He stares me in the face, unblinking.

It's the look he gave Sanders when he span him that line about his da's allotment and offered to take him up there. What Tommy does when he's about to lay down his hand, even if he turns out not to have the cards. Now that was a gamble. Tommy's no need to bluff now. Not any more.

'That's grand, Tommy. I am pleased. Well done.'

I see his eyes soften, just for a moment. *Firefly.*

He gives me an exaggerated nod, accepting his due, and grabs his contract back off Adam. He rolls it up.

'That one used to say—' He raps the table smartly, once twice thrice, looks from Adam to Jean and back again. 'That wife of mine used to say I was no more good to her than a table.'

I flush right up. 'I never—'

That was Monica, his sisters, said that. After his da died, and the lockouts. They thought he was made of stone, those sisters. I've never, ever said anything like that. Not to him, not to anyone.

Over 85 per cent retired at this point, having discovered that their wives could not accommodate themselves to the new surroundings. I'm not to remind him of that, am I. Or expect to be congratulated.

'Oh, never mind that!' Jean steps between us. She hands two tiny, long-stemmed, dusty glasses to Tommy and Adam and fills each fragile cup to the brim with her apple brandy.

Tommy's breathing fast and light; there's a tic going in his left cheek. Why he had to leave or what we had to do to get here, none of it will matter any more. He's a respectable working man again, only this time with property, and capital, and prospects. And I'm his respectable lady wife.

Adam holds up his glass. 'To *Mr* Radley.'

'Mr Dell.' Tommy raises his glass briefly to Adam, then downs it in one.

Adam sets his glass aside. 'You can go ahead with that cucumber house of yours. Do it the Association way, see if you can make it pay, eh?'

Tommy only raises his eyebrows a fraction.

Adam folds his arms, mock affronted. 'Oh, I see. It's like that now, is it? Our Tom don't need his old friend and helper no more. Seeing as we'll be commercial competitors.'

This is when Tommy is to come back with a bit of marra talk. *Need you like I need a broken leg. You're no more use.* If he can't thank his lady wife, he might thank the Dells, at least, for all they've done to guarantee his success. *Couldn't have done it without you. Here's a toast to you, good neighbours and helpmeets.*

Silently, he gestures to Jean to refill his glass.

I watch her pour and I can't think of anything to say, anything at all.

'Come on now, you two shall carry on pals just the same. Only more so. *Mr* Dell and *Mr* Radley!' Jean giggles. She's found her voice at last. 'Hold up, don't drink just yet, let's have another toast. This'll make your day twice over, Tom, oh yes. Listen now. Shh. There's another special day coming. Hold up, boys, while I—'

She searches the table for her almanac and opens it.

'There. Now take a look at that.'

She shows us the page. The date. And the pencilled circle around the date. The sixth of November. As Tommy leans forward to peer at it, Adam takes another surreptitious, smiling sip.

Jean takes a long, shuddery breath. 'Tom, do you see, just there? A special day for Lettie too. Do you see what that means? And now we must congratulate Lettie, too, on her wonderful news.'

*

I'm glad she's told him. I could never have broken the news myself. He may have kept his face smooth, unflinching, but I know him too well. I could not have brought on the darkening of his eyes. Snuffed out his faith that his firefly was his and his alone. Here in this room, with them, he can't be anything but happy at the news, can't say or do anything else.

But now it's Jean who has betrayed me. And I saw the relish, the flourish, even, with which she executed it. I've seen her break the necks of mice with her bare hands and shatter the ribcages of birds with shot, but I never dreamed plain country Jean might wound me. This is her idea of friendship, of sharing.

I summon the dimples for Tommy. They quiver in and out, I can't hold them.

Adam clears his throat. 'Congratulations, Lettie.' His smooth little bow is comic in its formality. There is no surprise. No jolt of reassessment. He is nervous, though. He wipes his hand on his dungarees before he holds it out to Tom. 'Congratulations are in order, Tom. Yes indeed.'

Tommy looks at Adam's proffered hand. And barks out a sort of laugh. He grips Adam's hand in his, hard and fast, and releases it just as swiftly. Then he pulls out a chair and sits suddenly, clasping his hands tight and bracing his elbows on his knees. The three of us look down at him.

Jean giggles again. 'How about that, Tom, to top it all?' Jean's sing-song voice grows richer and more indulgent by the minute. 'Now give your little mother a cuddle, why not. What better time to be starting your own family? And we'll be right here by your side. Won't we, Ads?'

Adam takes another small sip from his tiny glass. 'Indeed we shall.'

Jean giggles. 'Go on, Lettie, let your Mr Radley give you a cuddle.'

I take up my position next to Tommy. His suit smells of Saturday nights still, under the mothballs and pressing water. I reach for his hand. But Tommy's fists are locked tight together.

'Oh Lettie, don't take on.' Jean presses her clasped hands between her breasts like a music-hall contralto. 'I know, I *know!* All this good news at once. But there it is, Tom, and how lucky we are, how glad you must be.'

The words keep spilling out of her.

'You needn't worry about a thing, Tom. Lettie will make a marvellous mother. Isn't she thriving here? Look at her, stronger every day. Of course, the Association hasn't got the hospital insurance scheme up and running, not yet, but there'll be no need, will there. I shall be right next door to help, when her time comes.'

Tommy tugs at the knee of his trouser leg. He adjusts the crease, then dusts it off. 'What did you always say, Lettie?'

A chill runs across my neck. Please don't start that stuff about being no more good than a table again.

'I don't know, Tommy.'

He takes a stiff breath and stands up. 'I told you, didn't I?' He looks at Adam, at Jean. 'What this one used to say to me, over and over, lockout after lockout?'

They stare back at him.

'*There's always hope, Tommy,*' he intones artificially. '*Never give up, Tommy.*' He clamps his hands on my shoulders and turns me to face Jean and Adam. 'And here she is. My own little mother.'

'Yes,' says Jean, faintly outdone. 'Here she is indeed.'

He gives me a little proprietorial shake. 'We shall be mother and father at last. A proper family. Not everyone can be so lucky, eh?'

'I suppose not.'

I look quickly at Jean. She's glassy-eyed and unperturbed.

'Maybe I should go for a lie down, Tommy? It's been quite the day.'

'Indeed it has.' He can't get me away quick enough.

'In that case—' says Adam, 'I'd best take our Tom down the Fox, get a drink inside him.'

'Oh no,' says Jean. 'No, you can't go. None of you. Not yet.'

She's pressed herself right up against the back wall, in the corner under the corn-dolly shelf, with Flo hunkered up under her chin.

'Oh my dears. What a morning this is turning out to be.' She strokes Flo's feathers, fast and regular. 'Our Mr Radley. And our Mrs Radley. And now, my dear Flo, you wouldn't believe it, would you?' She is almost panting. 'Ads? Ads, will you come here?'

Adam puts down his glass on the table behind him and stares at her. There's a tiny cracking sound. The bowl of the glass rolls free of its snapped stem, spilling its pale liquid. He twists about, to mop at it with his handkerchief.

'Leave that.' Jean claps her hands. Flo squawks and flutters to the floor. Adam turns to fiddle with the glass, trying to get it to fit together.

Jean has to take a breath before she can go on. 'You Radleys don't get all the luck, you know. Oh no. Your little stranger isn't coming alone. No, he's going to have his own little friend, right next door.'

※

Jean cried then. Her face crumpled into a soggy maze. Adam went straight over and held her tight, muttering into her neck. He stroked her hair and clasped her face between his hands and then he kissed her long and hard on the mouth, all over her face, her hair, as though I had never crossed his path. I glanced at Tommy, his face pale, his mouth sagged; he couldn't look away from them either. Their happiness was too much for us. It was like a burning bush, we couldn't help but watch.

Then later, it felt like much later – I'd sat down again and I couldn't seem to get up – there was Adam's voice echoing off the freshly washed glass – 'a miracle, a bloody miracle!' – shouting out to the holding in general, as he dragged Tommy off to the Fox. The racket of geese, and the pigs, the hedge birds, sounded like applause. It carried on long after the suck of their boots faded away down the lane.

The two of us; each with our own little seed growing. I've sat on, and smiled, and said all the right things. *You must be very happy, Jean. Now isn't that the best news. Oh, yes, I am very glad for you. When did you . . . realise?*

All the time asking myself: was it that first night we arrived? Or that same night he came to the glasshouse? He laid himself down on that great lumpen body of hers, that I imagine to be as heavy and wrinkled as a parsnip after a winter in the clump. No wonder he came to me. Watched me. It's better, though, isn't it, for them to have their own baby to distract them. Even if it dies. And there was Tommy thinking he'd get ahead of Adam.

Mean, desperate thoughts, all of them easier than thinking about what's ahead. I've only sat on and on because I can't be alone in the house when Tommy comes back.

'Doubt they'll be home any time soon.' Jean's voice heaves with sisterly solicitude. 'Go for that lie down, why don't you?'

Jean doesn't look tired. She looks exactly the same. Solid, ruddy-cheeked, agile, competent. I can't see anything of what I see when I look at my own face in the mirror: steeped, spread pale and wide-eyed, like I'm drowning.

A helpless anger bubbles up in me. Now they will all be my mirror, whether I like it or not. There will be nowhere to hide.

'You didn't have to tell them, Jean.'

She feathers a curl of hair against her peeling lower lip. 'Well,' she says coolly. 'You weren't going to.'

Jean sees everything, doesn't she. She knows I don't want this baby. But consumed as she is by her own good fortune, does she guess why?

'It was Tommy's big day, that's all,' I say stiffly.

I wasn't going to spoil it for him.

'A happy, happy day for all of us. You've brought us all luck, haven't you? And now this baby of yours will be your reward.'

Her fervour is overwhelming. I remember her almanac, her pencilled circle. How many days and weeks she must have counted. There's a stack of those almanacs high up on that top shelf behind me, propping up her corn dollies. They must go years back, long before the Dells came to Foxash. How can I begrudge her this exulting?

'You'll be November too?'

Jean lays her hand lightly on her stomach. 'I never work it out. Bad luck.'

She'd worked it out for me. Drawn a circle around it, even. Or, had that been for her all along? Only she'd wanted to announce my news herself, first.

'You don't, you see. Work it out. Not until the quickening.'

That old tone of hers, that's not changed. Patronising is what it is.

'The—?'

'Quickening. When Baby first moves.'

Last time, I'd lived in dread of feeling it move.

'When's that, then?' How churlish I sound.

'Not to worry, Lettie. Not for a while yet.'

We have months of hard work ahead. Heavy, back-breaking work. Who knows what might happen?

'You see, I opened up the bees this morning,' Jean continues, dreamily. 'I saw they'd been carrying in pollen, thought I'd take a look. And the queen's survived. I think that was the sign I was waiting for.'

'The others.' I can't help myself. 'Did they – quicken?'

'Of course.' Jean sounds defiant. As though I'm accusing her of making them up. 'Most of them.'

'Oh.'

'But let's not dwell.'

'No.'

I take another mouthful of tea, but it's too bitter to swallow, now it has cooled. I can only drink her tea piping hot; I think it's the water here, the Association had to drill down ever such a long way. Or her goat milk. Jean never has tinned. To think I scoured these cups for her again, with soda and scalding-hot water, only a week back. This one's as stained as ever.

'Adam seems pleased,' I say primly.

Jean leans back, stretching her arms above her head so that her breasts and belly strain against her dungarees. 'Oh yes. Dear Ads. More than pleased, Lettie.' She shuts her eyes. 'Tom's over the moon, of course.'

I look at her blissful, closed face. Maybe she's right. Maybe she and Adam know my husband better than I do these days.

'I told the bees your news too. You don't mind, do you? Bad luck not to.'

So much news. All spent at once. But nothing broken. Not yet. Jean smiles to herself, draws a length of hair across her mouth again and again.

*

Tommy comes back when the moon is high, singing. *We're in the money, we're in the money.* He staggers up with his boots on and sits down so heavily on the side of the bed I can't pretend to be asleep. 'Take a look at that,' he says, chucking something heavy on the bed. 'And that.'

I wriggle myself up and light the lamp. Brochures. Horticultural hardware. Sheds. Machinery. 'Lovely,' I say.

'Hmm,' he says. 'And this one, look.'

'Nice,' I say.

'*Mr* Radley,' he prompts.

'Mr Radley,' I reply.

Both of us and our puppet voices.

He goes to stand up but he knocks his head on the slope of the ceiling and, when he falls back, the brochures spill over the floor and I hear him curse.

'Oopsy-daisy, Mr Radley,' I say, and bend to pick them up.

'Glad, then, are you?' he says, watching.

'Course I am,' I tell him. 'Of course I am.'

He turns away, starts up again. *Get it, spend it, rolling along.*

'You stink of beer,' I say. 'Open that window, why don't you?'

The night air streams in. It sets him off coughing. I pull up the sheet. He comes and lays down outside the sheet anyway and we are both quiet for a good long while. Lying there in the dark. Staring at nothing.

'Are you,' I ask in the end. 'Glad?'

His laugh makes me jump, and something peeps and scutters in the wall by the fireplace. He gets up again and he sticks his head out the window again, not lighting up this time, just sucking in the night air.

'Surprised, I bet?' I say.

'Nah,' he says. 'Knew I'd do it.'

I start to say that wasn't what I'd meant. But he draws his head back in, and coughs. Then he says quietly, so I only just catch it: 'We're set up now, Lettie.'

The way he says it sounds like a question, as though there were still a choice, something I might confirm or deny. As though we might still go home, or go on, just the two of us, even now.

Out comes my best puppet voice: 'We are indeed, Tommy. And I'll be expecting that surprise you promised soon enough.'

*

Only long after he's asleep do I open my eyes wide to what he might have been asking. We're set up, here. It might be different, here. I'm not his mother. He's not his father. And the baby. This baby might be ours, to keep.

5th *May*

Tommy gets his cucumber house within the fortnight. There's not anyone else on the whole estate has one purpose built, just for the cucumber. The Dells have early-season lettuce, we'll lead on cucumber. Never mind the cost, he says gleefully, it'll earn it back within the season, and some.

It goes up in a couple of grey, windy days, on the half-acre down the side of the house that was marked out for poultry pasture, like the Dells'. It's lower and narrower than the glasshouse, but its panes are bigger: a whole twenty-four-inch square. Glass as thin and clean as new ice. Soon as the concrete's set – no duckboards for Mr Radley – he keeps going inside for a smoke. I see him standing there in all the nothingness, looking out through the glazing bars.

Adam, out in his own rows, keeps an eye on progress. Refers to it as Tom's Palace when he knows Tommy is in earshot. Passing me on the path one morning, he gives it a cheerful nod: *Quite the greedy young fellow, isn't he, your Tom?* I bridle anyway. Adam's not beyond a bit of greed himself. Tommy has every right to his hunger, and his ambition. Adam never saw that old hopelessness and doom and panic in his eyes. I don't ever want to see a flicker of it again, or where it leads.

The cucumber house smacks Bridgewater and his mate

from HQ right between the eyes too. I'm halfway down the holding, earthing up the early potatoes, when they come to inspect. They've brought a photographer along, who keeps waving his arms about. I squat back on my hunkers and shade my eyes, watching Tommy tug down his hat and jut out his chin.

Jean's appeared at my shoulder, in that silent way she has.

'That'll be for the Association brochure. *Daily Times* too, I shouldn't wonder.'

'Is that right.'

I keep my voice level. That's only local, I think. No one knew which estate he was being sent to. The Association has dozens. We didn't know ourselves, until the day his ticket came. But Tommy couldn't exactly have refused Bridgewater. I tell myself the chances of anyone back home seeing the *Daily Times* are less than nothing.

'They've asked for you too. Not many of you Special Area wives stick it out this long.'

I grip my trowel tight. If I were in the photograph too, it would be even easier to identify settler no. 1404, if anyone were looking.

Jean pats my arm. ''S'all right, told Mr Bridgewater you weren't feeling well.'

I feel myself flush. 'You've not told him—'

'About our little visitors?'

Her coyness is excruciating. I hear her say it to Adam: *when our little visitor arrives.* His eyes light up.

Jean shakes her head. 'Sure you can manage those last four rows?'

'Oh. I'm fine, thanks.'

She clucks with concern.

'And you?' I ask. 'How's you?'

'Very well,' she beams. 'Really well, you know?'

I smile back. Yesterday Jean told me that she won't be doing any laundry for the whole of this month, just to be on the safe side. Pitwives would do the same, when they wanted to keep a baby; never helped them any, did it. They just got behind.

'Dazzling, isn't it? All that new glass,' she says. 'Listen to my girls, they've been in a tizzy since it went up.'

Very Jean, this is. Happy as a lark, these days, full of this togetherness, but there's still something high-handed about her helpfulness. She'll offer you something coated with praise, or at the very least amusement. Suck on it a while, though, and you'll find the criticism. Am I imagining it, or is there, as with Adam, a new edge? In announcing her own conception, they have trumped mine.

I keep my trowel moving. 'Laying like demons, though, aren't they still?' I say. 'Your girls. Far more than mine.'

'I suppose. For now.' She looks up. 'Although' – the indulgence has returned to her voice – 'once you get that thing going . . .'

'What?'

She nods towards the house. Tommy and Bridgewater have gone inside the cucumber house. It's not the photographer stood there waving his arms about now, it's another man, in a long dun apron.

'Your surprise is here.'

I should have known. The holding could never spare me for the hours it would take to get my teeth pulled and a new lot fitted. It's unthinkable, now, to leave this place at all, let alone for a whole day.

The man wipes his sweaty hand on his apron and holds out his receipt book for me to sign, and sharpish. There's been a proper stand-off in the lane. He'll have to reverse on account of Bridgewater's car, go back to Colchester the long way round.

Tommy's bought us a monster. The bulk of it blocks the entire doorway. It has the smooth sheen of a giant chocolate brazil, and looks just as out of place. We'd always talked about a Philco 444, but it's a huge Marconi radiogram, walnut veneer, four valves. That would have cost him at least £12 all in, plus there'll be the 10/- for the licence. He has never spent anything like that on me, on anything.

'You'll set it up indoors, though, before you go?'

Dimples don't work on this one. There's a lorry on its way up the lane behind him; he wants to get to the turn-off before they do. That'll be my plugs I've been waiting a fortnight for. He bangs the gate shut behind him so hard it swings right open again.

As I go to shut it, I try to catch Tommy's eye. He's turning his hat over between his hands, concentrating hard on whatever it is Bridgewater is saying. He catches the movement of my hips, though, as I walk back along the side of the house. He keeps his face blank for Bridgewater, but his eyes widen. *See what I did for you? See what I got? Promised, didn't I?* And uncertainty, just a flicker of the eyelids: *It is what you wanted, isn't it?* The little boy inside, who's already failed.

Right from the start a wireless was what I'd set my heart on, for the day we got our own place, our own front room. At Shiney Row, a Marconi would have made us everybody's new best friends; we'd have had the whole street trooping round. All those crushing, silent months of lockouts, I'd longed to be able to turn a knob and flood the room, the street, the town, with music. For a conductor to pull our strings and get us up on our feet and dancing, our bodies warm and alive and close again.

I hunch my shoulders and grab my elbows, nod furiously in a pantomime of eager, simpering gratitude, and flit round the corner before Bridgewater looks up.

Jean is there, inspecting from a safe distance.

'Quite something, isn't it? Do you think Adam would bring it in? Bridgewater's still here.'

'Oh no. You squeeze in there behind, we'll manage.'

And we do, just, although she showers mud everywhere and trips over my rugs. We've just got it in place when a horn toots from the lane.

Jean winces. 'All this toing and froing.'

Automatically, I check my hair in Tommy's shaving mirror and blot my nose. This is what I'd missed, all those months, isn't it, and never admitted to her: noise, people, the new, the shiny. The unexpected. I look at her. She's distracted, and uncomfortable, wanting the place to herself. Yes. I'm like you now, Jean, like your girls. I can do without any of it. All I want is to get those plugs in, get back to the still warmth of the glasshouse.

'Come over tonight for a listen, why don't you?'

She smiles. 'Why not?'

If that order is complete, I'll be planting up plugs till midnight. We both know the wireless has come too late.

When I turn round again, Tommy is there, grinning. His Sunday suit and his brushed hair look as out of place as the wireless did. At his feet are four blue enamel tins marked *Kilogrub*, '*guaruntested*'. A hundredweight bag printed with *Karswood Poultry Spice*. Maybe half a dozen cartons of With's Garden Manure. Also a sack marked *Wakeley's Patented Hop Manure*. He'll stack it with the rest in the new shed he's built: the superphosphate, the nitrate of lime, ammonium sulphate, nitro chalk, tomorite, CCF . . . all with their guarantees and testimonials. He'll take another look at the

catalogue and order more. Then head back to the cucs. Or
Rosie.

Jean has her hands on her hips. Tommy gives her a look
that dares her to say it again: *Every penny you spend is a penny
off your profits. Keep overheads down, that's the key. Remember the
hunger gap. Any losses you make will carry over. What if there's a
blight, if . . .*

We watch her depart down the cinder path. *What if?* he
always says to the world at large after she has a go, stubbing
the ground with the toe of his boot. *If if if. We can't live our
life like that or we'd never have anything.* Today he pulls me inside,
bouncy as a flea. 'Look at the size of it! That's the place for
it all right. Looks grand, don't you think?'

It was the only place it could go. Even so, the stair door
won't open properly. 'Grand enough, Tommy.'

'You hadn't guessed?'

'Of course not. It's a wonderful surprise.'

He nods, pleased as Punch. 'I'll charge it up for you,
soon as I've sorted that lot out there. Liven this place up a
bit, eh?'

When he claps his hands together they make a dull,
hollow sound. Tommy looks at me then, just for a moment,
and I know it's because he's reminded himself of the new
life we've made so recklessly, that is on its way whether we
like it or not.

'Those photographs?' I say. 'Who will see them?''

He blinks, rebuffed. Then he shrugs. 'Just the Association. Annual report or something.'

*

This morning I heard Jean slip out very early, so quietly
none of the livestock woke. I saw her from the bedroom
window, kneeling by the first tree in the first row, the mist

still low on the grass. Her head was bowed but I thought I could see her lips moving. The latch went next door and I knew he would be there on the doorstep, watching her too.

The way they've both floated about since she announced her news, it would be easy to think they'd stopped worrying. Although Jean is carrying herself more carefully, the way a tap boy carries a tray stacked high and brimming. And Adam walks in train behind her down the path when she's carrying full pails. Once she sets them down, he turns back. When he sees her heading for the stack of bales, he's there, tugging one out and tossing it into the pigpen himself, as though he'd only just remembered.

One morning, when the wind is strong and gusting, he appears behind her as she's struggling to hang out a sodden sheet. He reaches into the bag around her waist and pegs out the sheet himself. Tommy is with Rosie.

He looks up and sees Adam reach around to shield Jean from the flapping corner, one hand on her waist to steady them both. Their dark, curling heads pressed together, close as conspirators. Tommy's face grows stiff and careful. He can't look away either.

*

He hasn't forgotten her, any more than I have. Rosie Jordison, his first sweetheart. Monica loved to remind me of Rosie. It got so as I'd go through his drawers, sure I'd find something he'd have kept: a ribbon, maybe a lock of hair. If I so much as mentioned her name, his face would slide smooth shut. He'd not walked out with Rosie for long; she took up with another First Man, married him, well before I came along. But she'd clearly been Monica's choice. All the sisters' choice. The Jordison boys were pit royalty. And Rosie longed for sisters; she'd have known her place.

Rosie died, with her first, a few months before he ever met me. None of them ever mentioned her when he was about. If he was reminded of Rosie, and how she died, he'd be reminded of his own ma, and then where would we be.

Many, many nights it took, before he so much as told me her name. Margaret. His face buried in my neck, his hand against my hair. After he was born, the longed-for son, she'd lasted less than a year. His da got the doctor in, but she went on just sitting there, without the strength to lift her needle. She was thirty-seven.

One night his da sold his allotment, the whole lot – hens, spade, rake, everything he'd grown except for a single head of lettuce – no one ever asked him why; and came back with a bathchair. He wheeled her round Wycoller Park every spare minute he had until she died. All this Monica had told Tommy, when he was old enough. I remember the bloody bathchair, he would say to me, but I can't remember her face.

All this I knew by the time I went down South Shields quay. It's not so much that he doesn't want babies, as he doesn't want to lose me. He'd never admit it, just as I'd never let him know what I did, but he'd rather lose this baby than lose me.

I watch Adam's steadying arm around Jean's waist and wonder, does he feel the same way about her.

24ᵗʰ June

It almost never happens now, that we all meet in the middle of the holdings like this. But this noon our paths have crossed. We know we can't linger: the sky is blank hot and there's no breeze; the birds have long since fallen silent. I need to finish off watering in the glasshouses before it gets too humid to breathe, and Tommy and Adam must cover today's soft fruit with damp hay so it doesn't spoil. Pour more cool water on Rosie, tethered under the trees by her brood hut. Jean has been out weeding non-stop since dawn. But here we are.

Adam sets his barrowload of raspberries and goose-berries down in the sliver of shade by the piggery. His back, now the same deep brown as his face and neck, gleams with sweat. Jean, raises her elbows above her burgeoning belly to tug off her gloves and flex her swollen fingers. Tommy has thrown himself down on the grass in full sunlight, wiping one hand across his scorched and freckled chest. An under-ground creature no more.

'We should have a party.'

'Do what?' Tommy squints up at me.

I tuck my hair behind my ears and cock my hip. The old Lettie.

'A proper knees-up. Remember, Tommy? But out here, not indoors.'

All those days in February and March, those windswept, freezing, backbreaking days, I used to long for dusk so I could crawl back indoors. But the house is shut up against flies and wasps, it smells of stale sun and dust and rotten fruit, of warm wool and sour milk. I want to stay out here all night and listen to the plants sing. To arch my back, ease my belly, and fill my eyes with stars.

'A picnic party. You two can carry the tables out here, and we'll light all the lanterns.'

The table linen Tommy's aunts made for our wedding gift, with the pink and blue thread work, that we hid from the Means Test man, I can dig that out. We'll fill every dish we have with berries and Jean can spare some of her cut flowers, and after dusk Tommy and Adam will come singing back from the Fox with jugs of beer balanced on their handlebars.

Jean's frowning. Perhaps she's never thrown a party. Who would she invite, after all?

'Tonight?' she asks.

'Why not?' I spread my fat, tingling fingertips. The hem of my lilac frock doesn't hang quite straight any more, but I can still do it up, just.

'You noticed then?' Jean holds up her basket, full of weeds, her face full of affection.

'Good on you,' says Tommy. 'Too hot to spit, eh, Jean?'

Adam grins at Tommy. 'Jean never weeds before summer solstice. *He who weeds in May throws it all away.*'

Tommy generally rolls his eyes at what he calls her 'witchy ways' – the way she's always singing to the crops and spitting on the weeds. Now he restricts himself to a solemn nod.

'It's Midsummer's Eve tonight, Lettie,' Adam explains, patient as ever.

'Of course it is,' I say, as though I'd known all along. 'What better reason. Tonight, then?'

They take that so seriously, the moon and the sun, the waxing and the waning, the planting and the harvesting. Tommy and me, we just plant, water, hoe, spray, hoe, spray again, crop—

But I have felt it. The swell, split, stretch, the blind search for the light. These past few weeks the growth has been unstoppable. The sky seems always to be wide awake, calling. I do feel extraordinary. As if I've been waiting for this day all my life and now it has come it will never end. As if, anything I ask them, they might do. Anything I want I might have.

Tommy rubs his hands over his sun-baked face. He's been putting in what must be an eighty-hour week. To think what that would have earned him as a hewer. Well, he's going to double that, easy, isn't he. We're out there as soon as it's light enough to see. Picking by lamplight three nights this week past ten, just to get the orders off. We've barrowloads of weeds dumped everywhere, our verges are choked with nettles and broken crates left where they fell, no time to keep anything straight. Tommy and Adam are far too busy, too hot by day, too exhausted by night, to spar over techniques and outputs any more. I see Jean straighten up and look around. Her lips move as she plans and calculates; she catches my eye but we don't even nod because I'm doing the same. We've worked and worked and heaved and sweated and still our babies keep on growing.

My body doesn't want to stop. Do I? If I catch my reflection in the glasshouse panes I can't help but stare. My eyes and teeth gleam; my hair is thick and dense; my skin golden. It feels downy, my flesh: smooth and solid, and taut. And I am wet, all the time. I wipe my thighs before I put on my dungarees.

I want this, now, before it's too late. Us four to sit down and stretch out, together, with our limbs still warm and our faces bathed in lamplight. Unity, cooperation, mutual aid. We have worked hard for the Association, I tell myself, let us enjoy the fruits of our labours.

'We got that big order off, didn't we? So let's celebrate, all this.'

Our success, I mean. Everything we've grown. Everything we've managed to suppress. This equilibrium I want to last for ever.

I put on an Elsie voice for Tommy, like I'm on the halls, 'Go-orn, man. You know you want to.'

He splutters. And I watch his gaze slide over and away from my belly. He has never touched it, this hard swelling that can be tender as a boil. He turns me over and I gather the pillows under my hips.

It's Jean gives the nod. Adam defers to Jean in everything, I've noticed. Especially since baby.

'A good blow-out, eh, Tommy?' says Adam.

Tommy grins. A party will be a chance to lord it over Adam. Recite his achievements and ambitions once more.

'I'll get started on those fires,' says Adam.

Tommy sits up on his elbows. 'You what?'

'Three fires,' says Jean, matter-of-fact.

Tommy's forehead convulses. He looks to Adam for an explanation.

'Witches are powerful on the solstice, Tom. Once the fires are done, we take a brand and walk the bounds. Best you both join us.'

'Right you are,' says Tommy, his face quite blank again. 'Right, Lettie?'

'Why not?'

Adam plants a tender kiss on Jean's cheek before he peels away to pick up his barrow.

'That settles it.' She pulls on her gloves. 'We'll all of us walk, this year.'

*

I've unhooked the washing lines so Tommy and Adam can drag the tables out between the house and the shed. The tables wobble on the uneven grass, and we're looking for something to wedge them up when Adam stops short and pulls a face.

'Who invited Rosie?'

He's right: the breeze has moved round behind the pigsties, as it often does this time of day.

Tommy sniggers, puts on the pitmatic. 'Aye, fine snap this is gonna be. In bye.'

Adam raises an eyebrow. He knows all about how a pitman takes his meal unpaid, in the same place he shits and pisses: there's been no escaping Tommy's marra talk out here.

'The orchard then,' Tommy says.

Adam and Jean exchange looks. I never told him about Beauty of Bath, and the others. Jean sets her hands on her hips. 'Well, go on, you two. Lettie's not carrying those tables.'

Jean picks the first of her Royal Sovereign strawberries, specially. They are softer and sweeter than any of the others. She shows me how to nip the stem through with your nail, and then lay the fruit in the basket without touching it.

Strawberries bruise easily. You don't notice the day you pick, but the next day they'll go mushy.

First Tommy must pour more cooling water on Rosie. We're all to look out for her pushing the straw about with her nose, making a circle. Her first litter isn't likely to be big, but still. He doesn't want her agitated. Sows can attack and eat their offspring if they get upset. The piglets can even be born mummified. He pets her a while, rushes the tables down the path, then he's straight back inside his cucumber house.

Adam took his hat off when he saw what Tommy's done in there. Those cucumbers have grown like they're bewitched. With a proper cucumber house you don't pinch the vine off after two feet; you can let it grow all the way up and train it across the roof so the fruit hang down over your head. Row after row of them, big, hairy saucers of leaves that spill blotches of light all over Tommy as he thumbs off his braces. He's shaded them from scorching with sheets of newspaper and lime and water, syringed for red spider with luke-warm water and dusted with flower of sulphur against mildew. He didn't trust Jean's bees to pollinate them; he went around with a little brush, transferring pollen from the male flowers to the female. Now his cumbers are as long and straight as a policeman's truncheon. Their skins only softly ridged. The straighter and smoother, the better. He'll be able to raise his own from seed in September or October to supply the winter market too.

I rinse gooseberries in the scullery sink. Adam drags a straw bale down into the shade of the orchard hedge and rips it open with his knife. He's stashing the jugs of beer inside to keep cool. I sit on the step to rub in the pastry while he builds their fires on the open patch of grass between the rows and the orchards. One bonfire on their holding, that is almost all bones. Big and small, and all clean. Another on the path, that's half and half bones and wood. And one on our side, just wood. The middle pile is the biggest; the other two won't last long, but I bet they'll smoke for hours. I hope the wind doesn't move round again.

Adam walks back up the straight and narrow. 'All done. Want to keep the right side of witches, don't we?'

I rub the pastry from my fingers. The chickens come running.

'Where'd you get a great pile of bones like that?' I ask. 'Old sweetheart?'

This is how it is with us now.

He shakes his head, starts counting on his fingers: that fox he shot last autumn, a deer—

I giggle. 'Don't forget the tramp.'

He frowns at that. Adam gives as good as he gets when Tommy's ribbing him rotten. But he won't joke about a dead man. It was Jean told me about the tramp they'd found.

Now he's off up the lane to look out his St John's hand. A St John's hand is the root of a male fern trimmed to look like thumb and fingers. He's going to smoke it in one of the fires and then hang it in the house for protection.

Adam will search patiently up and down the lane until he finds the right fern. He'll crouch down and take his knife out his pocket, or maybe a tool, a dibber. After he's dug out the root he'll brush off the dirt and set it on his lap, maybe right there on the verge in the shade, and take the knife to it. That's how he does everything, careful, slow, methodical, like the old countryman he is. Tommy still attacks each task like the devil is at his back, doesn't let up all day, then plunges head first into sleep.

Now the pies are in the oven, I'll have just enough time to top and tail the gooseberries. When I'm peeling vegetables or picking over fruit, I often take it out front. It's getting uncomfortable to sit on a chair, and too stuffy indoors, and I can do with looking at something other than the holding for a change. No one ever comes by; I can lever myself down against the wall of the house, and let my legs fall open to the sun.

I drape a clean cloth over the colander and carry it round the side of the house. Tommy is there, leaning on the gate. On the other side is a stocky little man, no taller than him. Dusty, road-weary, underfed, but big in the shoulders. The cap, pulled straight down. The suit. The waistcoat and the white muffler, snug around the neck despite the afternoon heat.

Tommy's talking to him, in that soothing tone he uses with his pigs, but the man cuts him off. His abrupt, lilting speech jolts me back in an instant. The whoosh and sizzle of fat in the fried-fish shop, boots tromping up the dust, stale beer stink from the open pub door. Breaking glass and shouts from the alley as the light fades.

I back silently round the corner. Then I go inside the house and lock the door behind me.

*

The tables under the apple trees are set. Scrubbed radishes and shelled eggs with mayonnaise; sugared strawberries and raspberries; her cherry pie; my gooseberry fool. Jean grew a first cash crop of peonies this year and I've arranged the best of the leavings in a fruit jar, along with some trefoil Adam brought back for her. The holdings lie silent. The cloths gleam as dusk falls, soft and still. It's perfect, I tell myself. To be outside bare-armed and bare-headed, this late, this idle. After I shut up the chickens early, I put on the lilac frock. I've let it out as far as it will go but the hem still rides up over my knees. I light the lanterns, even though we don't need them yet.

Tommy had hold of that gate like he was pushing a truck. He straightened up and the gate banged open. I was fumbling with the window latch when Adam strode towards them, out of that tunnel of trees, his knife in his hand.

There he is, lighting the first of his fires. I blow out the match and straighten my dress. Jean's on her way down, all lop-sided carrying a heavy basket. She sets it down to talk to Adam. I catch the scent of smoke, sweet and powdery. The wood fire, then, not the bone. Apple and cherry wood, he'd said.

I stepped away from the window. All I could hear was their boots, scuffling in the dust of the lane, and then tramping back down the side of the house, the echo between brick and concrete. The scrape of handlebars and the jangle and tick of pedals and chain. They rode off northwards, in the direction of the station. And then I thought he might have tricked them somehow, the visitor, and be here still, by the house. When I did go out, though, there was no one. The gate hung at an angle and the lane was empty.

I could ask Jean, did you see that man at the gate earlier? That man Adam was talking to? Where have they both been all afternoon? I won't, though. I mustn't say anything until Tommy is back. I walk about among the trees. Feel my frock move against my legs, try and lose myself in the hazy dusk.

By the time Jean steps off the crunching path I'm rigid with fear again.

'Look.'

'Lettie?' She can hear the quaver in my voice.

I hold out my cupped hands. Walking towards me, she dislodges more tiny apples. They bounce off the tablecloth and disappear into the shadows.

'Careful! Jean, they'll all fall off and—'

All that work, all that careful tending, for nothing. Some are just whiskered hips, some are round and smooth, the size of a cherry, even a walnut. They weigh nothing. Have come to nothing. The loss, the waste, feels like my own. It's not the pitman has set my heart pounding now. It's the idea of losing this baby, that I try so hard not to think about. My poor, unwanted baby that can't be stopped, and yet might slip away regardless, whatever I wish for. And when it does come, might ruin everything.

Jean takes three large brown bottles out of her basket and lines them up briskly on the table. 'June drop.'

'What?'

'Happens every year. Nothing to worry about. Unless we get a bad frost next season, at blossom time, and the whole lot go.'

'It's such a waste.'

'This is how you give the best ones the best chance. Same as pricking out the seedlings. And the chicks.'

She scoops the aborted apples out of my hands and throws them into the grass. She looks after them a moment. Then she sits down and takes a bottle between her knees.

'We usually help them along, in fact. Nip out the weakest apple in a cluster. Onesing the pair, we used to call it.' She pushes firmly at the clasp. 'Believe me, it's the only way you'll make any money.'

When the birds started eating the young crop, Jean got her shotgun out. She saved a couple of pigeon, a magpie and a bullfinch to hang above the glasshouse doors and on posts in the rows to keep them away. She drove six-inch nails through the very plumpest part of their breasts and the tips of their wings. I saw her face as she stood back to check they were level. She could have been pegging sheets.

The carcasses rotted, and they stank for a while, but they still haven't fallen off those nails.

The bigger her belly swells, the more imperturbable she has grown. Jean's ruthlessness is not random. Something must be sacrificed only in order that something else might live. Those other babies were just the weakest in the cluster. This is the only one that counts now. But how can she be so confident this one will live, when she wants it so much more than I want mine?

Her thumb slips and the bottle slides, unopened, into the long grass.

Of course she doesn't want reminding. Any more than I do. I find the bottle before she does, and open it for her.

It takes me a few sips to recognise the dark, foaming liquid. 'Dandelion and burdock?'

She nods. 'Good for the blood.'

'They used to sell this back home. D&B, we called it.'

To distract us both, I tell her about the temperance store that opened up next to Crampton's soon after I started there. Didn't last. Methodists, they were. Our people want a proper drink, when it comes down to it. Gin. Lots and lots of gin and a good old knees-up. We needed iron, we got it from nails in a jug of water thank you very much.

It always helps, somehow, to make her snort, see her face crease up like a walnut.

'You needn't waste your money. My mother taught me how to make it. We'd dig the roots up and knock them clean and they'd pay us so much a stone for them.' She takes a deep breath, another sip. 'Gleaning we used to go too. That was our summer holiday, it was gone gleaning.'

Us St Clement's kids snuck down the cliffs to pick sea coal, penny a pinnyful and every penny went straight in the sweetshop till.

'Gleaning?' I say. 'Tell me.'

Her face brightens. 'I used to enjoy it, I did. Although—' She twists about in her chair to glance down through the trees.

Even the thought of that scarecrow, hidden now by the high hedge, riles her. Those villagers will be out gleaning themselves in that field before long.

'Tell me, Jean.' I'm hungry for her memories.

She turns back with a sigh, her eyes deep and dark. 'Those women, with babies on their backs, they'd give them something to keep them quiet. Because they was working for the master, see, and he had to have quiet.'

It's what they'd give the poorly infants at St Clement's, the ones who wouldn't stop bawling. Laudanum, on a tea-spoon of sugar. I was glad of it, couldn't wait for them to shut up. I'm about to tell her so, when she adds: 'Sometimes they gave them too much, of course.'

She bows her head. I sit silent, remorseful, until a whiff of something acrid catches in my throat and makes me cough. Adam must have lit the bone fire.

'Tell me about the gleaning, Jean.'

'Well.' She gives a small, grateful smile. 'We started ever so young. We'd sit with the older women and listen to their stories until the church bell went at nine. No one went out until the bell rang, or after it rang at six o'clock at night, so's everyone could get their fair share. I'd sometimes be sorry to start because that was the best part, before. Mother showed us how to make bags and tie them round, stick a safety pin in the middle so we'd have somewhere we could push either side. And after, Father would have it threshed.'

The lilt in her voice is stronger than ever. Mother. Father. This is the first time she's ever said those words in my hear-ing. I'd decided that her silence about her own family was

Jean's brand of tact. Perhaps now we are both about to have families of our own she thinks it won't matter any more. Maybe now she'll tell me where Adam came in.

'We'd pay the rent once a year. We'd glean the rent.'

'Mother used to shout at me, *stoop your lazy back!* And when you got a lapful we used to shout—' She holds her belly and out comes that cawing field call. '*Are you ready to lay down?*'

The answering shout that comes down the path makes me jump. I reach out to squeeze Jean's hand, to make sure of her before they reach us. But she is already up, one hand on the table to steady herself, and peering anxiously up the path. Everything is smothered blue and black up there now the sun is gone and the fires are lit, even the glasshouses. They come walking out of the darkness, each with two jugs of beer, both flushed and scrubbed, fresh shirt, hair combed in close ridges.

The change in Tommy when he scrubs up proper is always a shock. Clean inside his ears, to the roots of his hair. His skin is shiny with soap, his bleached hair smoothed with oil. But his face is so tense I can see the ridges of bone down the sides of his nose.

He sits with legs sprawled, his knee knocking against mine as he pours the beers. If it had been nothing, I'd ask him straight off: who was that were you talking to at the gate? But I don't.

'Right ready to lay down, I am.' Adam rests his hands on Jean's shoulders, kisses the top of her head. He has on a waistcoat I've not seen before, and a drooping dark red kerchief tied about his throat. His hair is oiled back too, a dark helmet. 'Don't you listen to her, Lettie. It was all walking, endless miles up the road home. Like this. Watch.'

Adam heaves one of the jugs up on to his head and

tries to balance it there. Tommy downs his beer steadily, watching.

'Idiot,' Jean says softly. 'You know nothing about it. You were leading the horse.'

She stands up, balances the jug on her own head, adjusts it, then slowly lowers her hands and spreads her strong bare arms for balance. She looks like a priestess, the lamplight running all over her.

'See? Get it right, you could walk miles and miles.'

It's a three-gallon jug, full to the brim, but she wears it like a straw hat.

I watch Tommy pour himself another. His foot never stops tapping.

Adam gazes at Jean. 'Takes me back, that does.'

She reaches out a hand to him, without turning her head. Her fingers find his collar, and he closes one hand lightly about her wrist.

Tommy pushes back his chair and walks away from the table. He lights up, and gazes out into the shadows under the trees. Adam and Jean are taking up plates and forks and inspecting the dishes. Only once we are eating does Tommy talk back. He leans his elbows on the back of his chair and starts to recount the latest from the Fox – fisticuffs again with the locals down the Anchor. The four of us talk shop for a bit: the packing-house rota, the flimsy new bean crates, the seed order. I pop strawberry after strawberry into my mouth. When Tommy finally sits back down, he drapes his arm over my shoulder. I smell his fresh hot sweat, wild garlic through the carbolic.

The Dells sit alongside each other, feet planted solidly on the ground. Upright, like king and queen. I hoist Tommy's heavy arm up and duck out from underneath, arch my back, shake my head and fluff up my hair. The lamplight makes it a mass of golden threads. Adam is watching. I dart a look back, straight back, quick as a flash.

That's four jugs they've emptied and we've not started on the tarts. Tommy's taught Adam one of his drinking songs.

> *Here's to good old beer!*
> *Mop it down! Drink it down!*
> *The stuff that makes you queer!*
> *Here's to good old beer!*
> *Drink it down! Drink it down!*

On and on they go.

> *Here's to good old brandy! . . .*
> *Good old cider . . .*

I've never seen Adam drunk before. These two've done their drinking down the Fox. He rocks back and forth, roars out the words, bares his glistening teeth. He's lit up. He leans into Jean, his muscles warm and loose. Adam's a large, heavy man, his legs reach a long way across the ground.

'And she said to me, she did—' Adam drums his heels. 'Lettie, listen to this. She said, "You got a cockerel in that cupboard, ain't you, Adam Dell?"'

Jean chuckles, looking away towards the bottom field. The air around us is cooling, settling, damp and still.

Pour drink into Tommy, and it's like filling up a water butt. Takes a long time before anything overflows. I need to get him away and inside the house. Up to bed, before anything spills out that shouldn't.

'All right!' Adam claps his hands together. 'It's time.'

Jean stands up, gathers her collar under her chin and shrieks like a girl. Behind her, the moon has risen high and full over both our houses. Its silver light burnishes the slates, sheens our hair and shiny-plates the glasshouses. The shadows are walls, ink black, the path a shining rail. Adam crunches away to the middle fire. He walks around it once, then squats to tug out a smouldering branch. Jean joins Adam to tug out another. Tommy draws in his breath and folds his arms.

Adam comes back with the branch. 'Here you go, Tommy.'

I stand up. 'I'll take it.'

Jean is holding her branch high so it casts its flickering light over all of us. 'Ready?'

Adam takes his time, tucking in his shirt, pushing back his hair, like they're off to church. He folds his fingers over hers and they raise the branch high between them and walk off through their low-hanging trees. I realise that since he and Tommy came down the path, Jean's not addressed a word to me. She's only had eyes for her childhood sweet- heart.

The flickering light from their branch disappears behind their glasshouses. A cloud passes slowly across the moon and the darkened sky above our heads is huge and heavy. I have to hold on to our branch with both hands, hold it high and steady so sparks don't leap on to the tablecloth.

'Right then.' I make my voice bright. 'Don't we need all the luck we can get?'

Tommy swears under his breath. Then he twists up, and storms ahead of me, past the bean rows and into the dark. His boots tear at the invisible growth. He's not steady on his feet. If he doesn't slow down he'll trip, and fall.

All evening I've watched him, and told myself this is a good sign, this is Tommy letting off steam. That we wouldn't be having this party if that pitman was bad news. But Tommy shuts his eyes to what he doesn't want to see. He pretends until he can't pretend any longer. He's as good at fooling himself as he is others. He's won card games on sheer bluff.

Maybe that man was only a tramp. Maybe he wasn't, but they sent him away with a flea in his ear, and Tommy's drinking out of sheer relief. Maybe he's only now realised the danger he was in. But what's to stop him coming back? And if one pitman can find us, who's to say others can't?

I sit back down, and prop the branch between my knees like a fishing rod. I watch the bark blacken and curl, the flame lick up and around, and the sparks launch themselves into the darkness. How long would I have to sit here, I wonder, before he would come back to me of his own accord, before the branch would burn down to my hands?

Low down, deep in the hedgerow, I catch the glint of marble-green eyes, steady and unblinking. Two pairs of eyes, close by. Fox cubs, at the start of their slinking, secret lives out here. Watching us, at night, snuffling around the boundaries of our lives. Always just out of sight themselves. Until, fully grown, they pounce. There's a scuffling sound, the tiny twin lamps snuff out, then silence.

Silence ahead too. No movement there. Tommy is invisible to me. The Dells are far away, and noiseless, moving steadily along the hedge behind the glasshouses. The flame they carry is constantly chopped and magnified by the glass, a series of silent, repeated explosions of light. But when I blink the flame has disappeared. For a long moment the strafing lights remain. And then I am alone again.

I steady the burning branch, lift it high and inch forward through the beans until I see the shock of Tommy's head. He stands very still. I take the skirt of my frock in my other hand and pick my way towards him. I will make my voice light and gentle, lay a loving hand on his shoulder. Then I'll wait. Here in the dark, just the two of us. If it was nothing, just a tramp, he'll be able to tell me. And if he can't, then at least I'll know, this will be it.

Tommy has the branch. Orange sparks shower everywhere. He throws it in a great swooping arc over our heads, over the hedge, with a force and speed that shrink the flame until it lies cringing and blinking on the ground. I watch, helpless, as its glow dulls and then dies slowly until it is indistinguishable from the darkness all around.

'It's a joke, this is, a fucking—' His breath blasts my face up close, rank and yeasty.

If I move, if I speak, he will be at my throat. I needn't have risked any of this. Something was badly wrong out there at the gate, I knew it. I should have waited by the gate and not let him back in until he told me everything. The last lantern is far behind me on the table; there's no sign of Jean and Adam. I'm trapped between him and the hedge, all the way down here in the dark.

'Bit daft, isn't it?' I have to put my hand to my jaw to stop its tremble. 'Tell you what, pet, let's give this up, shall we?'

He doesn't reply.

'Pet? This was a silly idea, I'm worn out. You must be too. I'll go up now. I think I'll clear up in the morning.'

Nothing.

'See you in bed, then.'

Only when I'm certain he's not going to reply, or move, do I turn away. I don't waste time fetching the lantern. I feel my way through the rows, stepping high and slow, and invisible. Only when the cinders cut into the soles of my shoes do I let myself breathe. I keep to the verge so I don't make a sound, all the way up the path.

After Tommy had gone out that night, I'd barely slept. I never did, when the marras went out, to raid a potato field or poach a rabbit, he'd never say. I knew it wasn't as risky as cutting a drift and selling the coal on the side, but not by much, and that didn't stop my head splitting all the same. I waited until I could see without a candle before I came down to wet a cloth for my forehead. He was back in the yard.

He was watching the gate to the alley, and he had his knife open in his hand still. His cap had come off, and his face was shining wet and pale and drawn, like worn china. I saw him wipe that knife against his thigh, again and again.

They'd been locked out nine months by then. They'd fixed and sharpened and cleaned and collected and sold and rallied and protested; even the fellowship dinners were bowls of soup, and then little more than bowls of dirty water. Out they'd gone, him and his marras. I'd come to recognise the smell of it on him when he came to bed. Leaves and bark and soil. And blood. And I'd go to sleep at last: whether he'd sold what they'd caught or brought it home, I knew we'd have something with our bread and marge.

He'd not gone with his marras that night. He'd gone with another lot up to the Harrington estate, where they kept a flock of sheep. A keeper had said he'd look out for them, if they looked out for him. At least that's what I heard, later.

I saw the flash of that knife and I went straight back upstairs and lay down before he saw me. I closed my eyes, but I could still see the fear that had been in his face.

He'd changed into his other set and was gone again before I came down. There was nothing hung up in the scullery for me. I never found the knife. I found what he'd been wearing, stuffed behind the settle. I washed the shirt and I dashed the trousers. Nothing but mud and burrs and bits of hair. Wool. I brushed and pressed them. Laid them out on the back of his chair. He came back and saw them. I served up his fried bread, like he'd never been out. If he'd thought there'd been nothing to find on them, he'd have asked: why'd you bother? He couldn't thank me for what I'd done, any more than he could tell me what had gone wrong.

I can keep an ear out with the best of them. Walter, that had been his Christian name. Walter Turnbull. Him that had the bike shop out of his shed on Deries Street, who'd set up the cycling club. When we were first married, he'd pop in with a new part for Tommy, the smell of rubber and polish off his blue overalls fair knocked you out. He'd shut down for good not long into the second lockout.

Walter Turnbull, the only one that didn't make it back that night. No one dared go up to look for him. He had no family to speak of, but it wasn't that he wasn't liked. There'd been more than two dozen lads and lasses in that club of his. No one wanted the authorities involved, either. We'd just to wait, and hope he'd got himself lost, or was injured, and he'd make his own way somehow. It was rough land up there, with steep woods and streams. For a while they were for blaming the keeper – turned out he was one of the Elford cousins – saying he'd set the lads up. Saying he'd caught Turnbull himself. Scented the whiff of rubber and polish, perhaps. But there was no word from the estate, or the authorities.

Talk swung round to who'd been with Turnbull last. Who'd left him behind, in the dark, like that. And why. And there was talk, finally, about going up there, and what they might find. By then four whole days had passed. Tommy sat on indoors, silent, smoking, staring into the fire like nothing was wrong.

It was after tea and it was raining, but out I went. Going up the Cut, I passed half a dozen men coming back, each with something or other in a sack or a basket that had cost them nothing but time and sweat. It hurt to see them, my stomach was that empty. I'd have rather they hadn't seen me either. Because I clocked Andrew Brister and John Poile straight off, from the Guardians' suppers, cycling club men both. I felt guilty then, for what I was about to do. Once or twice, those two had brought their own allotment produce along to the Guardians to share, and not just with the cycling lot either. I turned off so they'd think I was going to the Baths, then doubled back. At least I knew I was headed the right place.

When I got there, even I could tell things were winding down for the winter. Those poor fellows had stripped their plots near bare. Didn't feel that sorry for them then, they'd more than we had. There was one plot, though, right up under the embankment, with a couple of heavy fruit trees, one apple, one pear. Brambles starting to arc across and the grass untrodden. No bonfire, no freshly dug earth, but every inch planted up and row after row still in the ground. Yellowing, tops gone over, wilting in the ground. This must be Turnbull's. Rather than take it for themselves, those fellows were going to leave what was in the ground to rot until he came back or not.

There were loads of blackberries. It had been hot for days and they smelled like jam. I popped one into my mouth. It tasted like a dog had pissed on it. I sat behind a wall till they went home, then I dug up some carrots and onions and tugged out some weeds with my bare hands so it looked more tended, and scragged some apples and pears and ate the apples on the way home. Never said a word to Tommy about where I'd been. Just showed him the Association leaflet I'd pinched from the window of the butcher's in Argyle Street that morning. No, I hadn't shown him, I'd left it on the table. Let him think he'd worked it out for himself. I left telling him about Turnbull's allotment until the day of our interview.

After that, it had been easy as falling off a wall. Yes, Lady Sanders, I said, Tommy's family came over from the good old country, indeed yes, don't they miss the old farm still, the mountains and the lake. Oh yes, Lord Sanders, he chimed in, my old da had me spreading pony muck on our allotment since I were this high. Want me to take you up there?

Our house is dark and empty, wide open to the breath of the fields. I shut the windows and go back out to the doorstep, breathe deep the peppery scent of the Dells' briar rose. Next door is dark too. Chimney dead, door closed. They must be in bed already. And down in the orchard, the lantern on the table has gone out. The moon is rising over the ash tree, but nothing else moves.

I don't need to know any more than I know. Turnbull went out with them that night and never came back. Sanders turned out to be a lazy bugger and he took Tommy at his word: the man drove straight off to spend the night with his good friends the Harringtons, never went near Turnbull's allotment. I'd got Tommy away before Poile and Brister or anyone came after him. They none of them can know which settlement we went to. And whatever became of Turnbull, who knows? Tommy'll never tell a soul, I know that much. A stranger came to the gate and, whatever he came for, whatever was said, about Turnbull or lord knows what else, he only got as far as the gate and now he's gone. We gambled and we won. Tommy's safe still.

I ease myself down on the step and tuck my hand into the warmth under my belly. Nothing. Not even when he tossed the branch and my heart hammered fit to break a rib. But I only need watch that moon for a minute, and I see her rise still, her slow escape from the trees' grasp. Soon she will launch herself overhead for all to see. This baby is growing. He's seen Tommy, that man can come back any time he likes. No, my pretending has been as foolish as the Dells thinking they can ward off witches with roots and bones.

Under the nettie door, a thin half-yard of light has lodged. A faint skittering thud rolls across the grass, rhythmic and repeated. It's Tommy. He drums his feet in the nettie to keep himself company, a habit from when he was a boy alone underground.

I wade a little way out into the damp grass. Abruptly, the drumming stops. He's in there to hide. To hold on to himself and his secrets. Hoping someone else can make it go away. Is it Adam, this time, who can rescue him?

As I turn my back on him, I see a light burning in the cucumber house.

It's slow going across the long grass; plenty of time to change my mind. The foxgloves and lupins, nettles and dock and cow parsley that have erupted either side of the gate stand watch, moon-bleached and silent. I slip inside the door and catch the night breath of the leaves. My head collides with the hard hanging fruit. They sway on, tugging at the vines, and set the leaves rustling. The vines blot out almost all the moonlight.

'It suits you, Lettie.'

The light at the far end wavers and grows. Adam emerges, holding the lamp.

'That frock.' His voice is thick with drink still, his eyes huge and dark. 'I was looking at you.'

'What are you doing in here, Adam?'

He sways slightly. 'Might ask you the same, Lettie.'

My longing is not for Adam, never has been. That fevered night in the glasshouse was about something else entirely. He sated my hunger, but it had never been for him, it was for the life I never knew I wanted. And ever since, hope has been growing inside me, tiny tendrils of hope, attaching me to this place. And now I'm fastened tight. I can't uproot myself again. Not now.

I pick my way down the narrow, rutted aisle. Hairy leaves scrape my arms. I make my voice neighbourly, confidential: 'Who was that earlier, at the gate?'

He clicks his tongue.

'I saw him, Adam. Talking to Tommy. I saw you too.'

Adam sets the lamp on the ground at our side and straightens up in my face. 'On the tramp, wasn't he?'

I am careful not to let him touch any part of me. 'What did he want?'

'What they all want.' The harsh reek of bonfire drifts from his hair. His face is all shadows. 'Food. Shelter. Directions.'

'And you sent him away.'

'Well, yes. Can't take in every waif and stray, now can we?'

He touches his fingertips to my hair, my cheek, my chin, like I'm sacred, fragile.

'Baby too,' he says.

'What?'

'Baby suits you too.'

It excites him to put his arms around someone so dainty. I feel like a child to him. He doesn't touch me like a father should, though. The span of his fingertips hardens both my nipples at once. I hold myself away.

'What has Tommy told you?'

'What have you told him, Lettie?'

He reaches out and touches the mound of my belly, lightly, with his fingertips.

'Thought so.'

I let him wrap me in his arms, until I'm wearing him like a coat. Very gently, he cups the underside of my belly. I let his hand rest there, where Tommy never touches me now.

'He was a tramp, Lettie. He'd heard talk in the doss-houses. About Turnbull, you know. But yours was just the first gate he came to. He didn't know nothing, not really.'

'Didn't know nothing about what?'

A helpless jealousy tightens my throat. So Tommy has told him about Turnbull. Told him more than me. Adam must think I know what happened up there. That I only want to know what went on out in the lane. I want to know everything, now.

I lean back into the mass of leaves, out of reach. 'What's up? Somebody found a body or something?'

'Lettie,' he says with a lilt, as though I'm joking. When I don't speak, he waits. He's not like Tommy, is he. Adam would let me question him till kingdom come. I'll still not get any answers.

'I don't think you know as much as you think you do, Adam Dell.'

'I know what I want.'

'Tommy's right there.'

'In the nettie. I know.'

He puts his arms about me again, confident, waiting. Down we could go, his hands cushioning my bare flesh against the cold concrete. I could perch like a doll again, wide, wide, wide. Lean back and think of that scarecrow in the field at the bottom of the orchard. All the stuffing poking out of her, her clothes awry and bleached by the sun, but still there, still stuck on her post. Think of the warm secret places the fieldmice will have hollowed out inside her. Risk everything. And still he might not tell me what I need to know.

I back away, my arms raised to fend off the hard truncheon fruit, the scratching leaves. I make my way up the concrete path, towards the pale broken gate. He doesn't follow.

At my side Tommy lies heavy, hot, and sour with beer. I listen to the blackbird start up, and after a while, the robin. Then the wren. As daylight grows, the thrushes will join in, the cockerels, the wood pigeons.

I rip back the sheet and clatter down the stairs. I don't care who hears me. By the time the song thrush starts up, I've lit the fire, although it takes a few goes. I kneel there a moment to ease my belly, until the nagging chiff chaff gets too much. I go through to the scullery and pump his shaving water. I set out his things and pull on my boots. When I open the door the wood pigeons thump with alarm and flutter from the trees. There's only Tommy's bike there now, propped up against the wall.

Down in the orchard, the hedge is rimmed all along its top with pink. Rags of mist snag at the trees and our table is a pale sliver dragging heavy with dew. The cloth's been pawed half off, the bowl of fool knocked into the long grass. Jean's peonies have overturned and scattered and there are scratch marks in the pie dishes. A thrush thwips loudly overhead as I scrape together what's left for the pigs, stack the rest of the silver-trailed crockery. Then I peel away the sodden cloth, its thread work snagged and torn, and clumped in places, like it's been chewed.

Jean opens her door just as I reach the top of the cinder path. She rubs at her forehead with the back of one hand, as though the sight of me is too much. Jean always looks her worst in the mornings, her eyes bagged, the flesh hanging off her cheeks and jaw. But this morning she gives me no more than a glance, her face heavy with hurt and resentment, before she goes round to her girls.

Voices carry in the still of night. The glowing tip of that hurled branch would have caught her eye, as it flew high over the hedge *a fucking joke* Tommy can't hide what he thinks of their country ways at the best of times. She is upset with us is all.

A deep envy tugs at me, at the thought of her boundless country innocence. Even last night, by lamplight, she wasn't beautiful. That solid build may be handsome on Adam, but not on her. Nor the thick neck and heavy brow and long, curving nose. Her eyes are hooded and her cheeks are lined and her brows are thick and springy. Not a face to desire. But to admire, yes. Regular. Strong. Full of certainty. Jean has no – ways. She's never been near a picture house or a department store or opened a weekly. Never covered up, never conned anyone or visited a quack stall. She can't imagine anything might come between her and her child-hood sweetheart.

I stack the bowls roughly in the sink and pile the ruined tablecloth on top, take up the scrap bowl. Then I follow her round to the henhouse.

This northern side of the house feels dank, uneasy, out of bounds. I've never come this far into her territory. Rearing up in front of me, on eight sturdy posts, is the tarred bulk of her henhouse, at least twice the size of ours, stranded in a swirling flock of white and brown bodies. Her girls have flooded out into the enclosure to greet her. She cleans it out religiously, but the acrid stink still makes my nose and eyes water.

They press close as she crouches awkwardly, raising one arm to fend off her leaping black cockerel. I have to walk right up to the wire before she hears me call her name. The chickens shrink back around her, then surge to peck at my boots, make frantic, tentative stabs through the wire.

I hold the scrap bowl high over the fence. A peace offering. 'Not much left, I'm afraid. I should have cleared up last night.'

'Thanks.' She doesn't move to take it.

'Tommy's still sleeping it off. Adam was out early, though? His bike's gone.'

'Oh yes.' She gives me a flashing look, possessive and flaunting. 'Ads can take his drink.'

I watch her flock surge before her, grateful and jostling. Even if she knew anything about the tramp, she'd not confide it now. Not after Tommy's display last night.

'Gone to the bank, then?'

She turns away, to face the lane. She points: 'Look at that.'

Low over the fields across the lane, where the weather always comes from, is a mass of heavy grey cloud, its scudding dark underbelly pregnant with rain. A steady wind is getting up, pithy with grain scent.

Our broken gate scrapes open. She takes the bowl from me and tips it up. 'Shame. Raspberry will have to wait.'

Over the squawking, I hear their door slam shut.

'There he is now. Just in time. Shame about your raspberry, though. Raspberry wait for no one. They ripen behind you.'

*

Tommy's shaving water has cooled, clear and untouched, on the scullery windowsill, leaving only an oval trace of steam on the lowest pane. Rain drums hard overhead. I listen to the stillness upstairs and down. He waited for me to leave before he went out. Or for Adam to come back. I take down the Crampton's tin, cut a slice of parkin, then another, and and wrap them in a tea towel. Then I put on my mackintosh.

All the wide open spaces of the holdings have shrunk, the long views choked right up with growth, and the rain has laid a gauzy grey curtain over it all. It's impossible to see inside any of the glasshouses any more, packed full of plants and coated in condensation. The cinder path is a snaking, narrowing trace. Eventually, in the tomato house, I see the flicker of leaves as they are pressed against the glass, revealing their pale undersides.

It's hard to slide the door to, everything has grown so. We planted too close to the sides. The clatter of rain on the roof and the thousands and thousands of leaves almost muffle the squeak and splatter of Tommy's spraying. He only found the latest infestation Sunday evening and it could have been here for days. He sprayed everything thoroughly then. Now the leaves are dripping wet again. He always sprays twice as long as recommended, just in case, till they droop. But these plants are drenched.

Cascades of green and orange and red globes bump against my arms as I work my way towards the wheeze of the pump. The air is bathhouse thick and my head starts to thump. Tommy is at the very end of the aisle. Seeing me, he stands at bay: legs braced apart, torso bare and slick under the heavy knapsack strapped across his solid shoulders. The muscle is back on him all right.

He makes a play of shaking off the spray head, pumps it clear, inspects the nozzles.

I hold out my parcel. 'Brought you some bait.'

'You can leave it on the side.'

I unfold the tea towel and show him the two slices. 'Thought I'd join you.'

He looks suspicious. 'Lady of leisure, are you now? One party not enough for you?'

'No, I just thought it would be nice—'

'To come spy on me?'

'Course not, Tommy.'

'Adam send you, check how much I'm using, eh?'

I refold the tea towel. 'Fine. I didn't mean anything.'

'What did you say then?'

'Nothing, Tommy.' I look back at him.

Tommy stops fiddling with the spray head. 'What do you mean, nothing?' he says, louder.

'Tommy.' I hold my ground.

'I'm asking you what you mean? Didn't you just say something?' He steps forward.

I shake my head. 'I didn't say anything.'

'What? Didn't you just say something?'

'I did.'

'Yes or no?

'Yes.'

'*Pfft.*'

'I just thought . . . I didn't mean anything.'

'Yes you did.'

I raise my voice too. 'It's pointless, it's a waste is what – you hide in here, Tommy, and—'

He's sprayed everything there is to spray. Now he sprays the same drooping plant, up and down, over and over. His eyes are tight shut. There is no air left, nothing but the sharp reek of tomato and the fizzing sherbet haze.

'What sort of a wife are you?'

I look at him.

'What was I thinking, marrying you. Why didn't I find myself a proper pitwife? Don't you see how much there is to do? No, you want a fucking party. I'm out here, doing everything I can for you and your—'

'We wouldn't have this place, Tommy, if I hadn't, if you hadn't—' I fold my arms and look away.

He's struggling out of his harness. 'Don't you talk back, Lettie, not to me. Do you want to starve, Lettie? Do you want us to go back? They'll hang me, Lettie, they will, if they can. Who will look after the poor little orphan then?'

'What happened, Tommy? I've never once asked, but, my god, Tommy – that man at the gate—'

He stares at me, breathing fast. 'You don't know a good thing when it's staring you in the face, do you? This is my chance, do you hear? My chance, and I'm not letting you ruin it. You shut up, you keep quiet, you don't say a word to anyone about anything, and you do as you are told. I run this place, my way.'

'Fine.' I wait for him to catch his breath. It's all talk, he's not laid a finger on me, I remind myself. It'll be all right. 'I wish I hadn't opened my mouth.'

'But you did, Lettie. I hear you, you and Jean, wittering away like bloody sparrows. You go on and on and then you throw a fucking party right when we need to work all hours, and now you say you're sorry. Well, just don't open your mouth then, all right?'

I keep my eyes on the floor.

'Pass me that canister.'

He won't touch me now. Still, I must be very polite. 'This one?'

'Yeah, that one.'

I hand it to him. Then I take up the folded tea towel. 'I'll save this for later then.'

'Yes, you do that.'

He straps the knapsack back on. 'Eat for two, why not.'

'You go on and on and then – I get confused, Tommy, when you get like this, you know I do.'

His mouth pinches. 'I'm sorry,' I think he says, but I have to close my eyes. I'm on the merry-go-round, lights flashing by, steam engine thumping. There it is again. I put my hand to my belly. A bubble rising, a fish in a pond. A gasp, a life. This is what Jean meant. My baby is waiting. All alone in the dark.

I hear Tommy unstrap his knapsack and drop it on the ground. He takes me by the shoulders and peers into my face, his pupils huge and dark.

'Lettie, what is it?'

I rest my forehead against his hot, slick, sweet chest.

'Lettie? What's up, Lettie?'

Quickening. It's just a word, at first. I watch it seed, and blossom in his eyes. His mouth seizes up. He can't hold this in. I say it again.

'No,' he says. 'No.'

I've won a prize. A tiny fish, swimming round and round a small glass bowl. Swimming for its life. It's far too late now, isn't it, for anything else to matter? The pitman, Turnbull, spin into the distance. Baby is real. Here. Now. Baby will grow and grow and one day Baby will look me in the eye. I must be good, very, very good.

There it is again. Coming up for air.

Tommy holds on to me, tight. Too tight for me to breathe. Oh but Tommy, you have no idea. We have never been further apart. I let my lips rest like a kiss against his neck.

'Yes, Tommy, yes. Don't worry. We'll be all right, I promise.'

'You promise?'

'Yes, of course. I'm fine.'

He takes a shuddering breath. 'It'll be worth it.'

'Of course. Of course it will.'

He wants to believe it so badly I could cry. He wants to forget them too – Turnbull and the pitman, Rosie and his mother. He wants me to cradle him in my arms like my own child.

I stand close, we breathe the same air, but inside I know I am moving away, floating in the same element as Baby. Poor Tommy. He keeps pushing me away, again and again, always believing I will come back.

A muscle flickers in his jaw. 'All right,' he says.

'All right. Tommy?'

As he releases me, I turn away. 'Tommy, what I came to say: that gate's come loose. Best mend it, before Bridgewater sees.'

He splinted the frame and screwed the hinge back that same morning. But near every other job since he has left undone. Rather, he's been doing needless double shifts in the glass-houses, right through the heat of the day and beyond. I glimpse him through the choked panes, parting the leaves as he moves down the aisles, stunned, drenched and mute. And what I feel is nothing, compared to Baby, turning about in the dark.

I told Jean about the quickening too, in the end. I want someone to be happy for me, I think. She started counting on her fingers straight away.

'Was that the first time you felt it? Are you sure?'

There was a hot, deep reddening in her leathery cheeks.

'What?' I said. 'What is it?'

'Me too.' And she giggled. 'You know what? I've felt it too.'

'When?' I asked her.

'Today. Yesterday, perhaps.'

I looked at her. At her torn dungarees, the secateurs in the pouch, the sweaty rag. I wanted to be able to see her stomach, to touch it, to be sure. I didn't, though. Never have. I don't want her to touch mine. I took her hand instead.

'What are you counting?'

'November. I was right. It will be November.'

'Really?'

She giggled again.

6 Nov. It could be Adam's.

'You're sure?'

She shrugged.

'What, the same day?'

She pulled a face. That's not very likely, is it? Don't worry, we'll get Mrs Bamber in. You know this means we've both got all winter to get back on our feet. Aren't we clever?'

I've not told Tommy what she'd said, about the due date. Of course. When would I? As if he's not left enough undone, half the time he's down the Central, angling to get on one of the Covent Garden runs. The Association lorry stops off – unofficially of course – and sells direct to hotels and restaurants along the way. He's right, of course. It's easy money, he'd be a fool not to go along.

Since the birds went on to full lay, he's been getting regular orders at the pub too. I iron him a shirt, he polishes his shoes, puts on a tie and wobbles off to the Fox with a crate of eggs or tomatoes or a strangled old pot-boiler. Next morning I check the pocket of his trousers, sliding heavy with coins. We're not supposed to sell independently, you get thrown off if they have proof, but he says it would be criminal not to, everyone does it. Everyone but the Dells. But the Dells won't tell. *Why not?* I wonder. If they've noticed him pedalling off, they don't say anything.

If we ever stop, if we ever talk, we talk about the holding. Everybody wanted lettuce some weeks back and we had twenty more boxes to send down to the packhouse for a very good price. We thought we'd be lucky to get ten boxes but we cropped nearly as many as the Dells. He's been wound up about our soft fruit yield, though. The Dells only pick on a waning moon if they can; they say the fruit keeps better. Tommy and I have picked all month, but even with the spraying we've been running neck and neck. Although we'll have more tomato. And the cucs of course. See how easy it is?

*

Dusk is here, the cooling air still sweet with scythed grass. I lumber up to the bedroom to pull on a cardie. Through the open window I can hear Jean's girls squawk as she approaches. I do up the top button only, like a cape. My belly is warm and round as a new egg, and the throbbing between my legs is just sweet enough to bear. I'm glad to see the jut of my hips soften. I feel fond of my body for the first time. I was always proud of what my body could do with Tommy, from the beginning. But not fond.

Then I hear the Association lorry rumble out of the tunnel of leaves and judder to a dusty halt outside the gate.

*

That fruit was immaculate when I shut it in the store last night. Grade one. Now the blackcurrant are dull and soft. The cherry wrinkled, split and bleeding. It's the whole of yesterday's soft fruit crop, our biggest yet, dumped in the lane.

'What's this?' I ask.

No one answers me. Jean stands sentinel at Adam's shoulder. They're watching Tommy, the other side of the pile.

I've folded my arms across my chest. That's what pit-wives do. I unfold them. 'Tommy?'

Tommy stares off over my head. The tawny owl hoots and makes us start.

'There's a glut on.' Jean keeps her eyes on Tommy. 'It happens this time of year. Depot's taken as much as they're going to be able to, without the price dropping too far.'

'They just send it back?'

'We're lucky to get it back. Often they just dump the lot.'

'What about everything I just picked?'

'Get it there early, you get in under the quota.'

This is how it works everywhere. Tommy used to say the weighmen could find a stone in a 10cwt tub of pure coal. And we've had produce sent back before. Maybe a box or two of cucs, or a dozen surplus lettuce. But never this much. And Tommy knows to be at the depot first thing. It has to be there early, anyway, to stop it spoiling.

Then I remember his face this morning. His blind, sleep-bloated face. These days he's working so hard and so late, he'd belch and roll over and go back to sleep if I didn't open the window wide, bang the kettle on the hob. I went to let the chickens out, Jean called me over to get that pair of secateurs she'd had sharpened and I never saw him leave.

'What time did you get it there, Tommy?' My voice is sharper than I intend.

When his mouth turns down like that and his cheeks hollow out, I know I need to be away, even just the other side of this pile, with Jean and Adam. If I even move towards them, he'll think I'm swapping sides. When Adam steps between Tommy and me, I have to stop myself reaching out for him.

'Not anyone's fault, Tom,' says Adam smoothly. 'It's the way it goes, this time of year.'

Very slowly, Tommy turns to look at Adam. And for all his height and sinew Adam looks exposed, as though Tommy could go for his throat. It's the first time I've seen them together for, what, days? Weeks? And for the first time

I see just how much Tommy has come to resent Adam and his fatherly manner, his well-meaning interventions. Sometimes I think all he's ever wanted is just not to be told what to do. Is it that he knows, deep inside, what Adam and I did? Or is it that pitman? And for one ridiculous moment I want to to get it over, and have them fight it out, right here, in the lamplight, slip and roll over in a sticky scarlet mush until one of them wins and the truth is out. Better now than later, after Baby is born.

Jean appears round the corner of the house, holding three stacked baskets held high over her belly. I know we can't just leave this here. But there's no space in the store either. Tommy takes his chance to retreat. He spits on the ground, stalks off. She sighs.

'Right then, Lettie. Best get this lot on the stove.'

I stare at her. 'It's spoiled, Jean. It's been left in the sun all day.'

'Lucky I save those June drops, then. They'll thicken it up nicely. Stir yourself, Lettie. And bring round all the sugar you've got.'

*

We tip bag after bag into her preserving pan. Torrents of white, that dissolve into sharp-smelling red soup, creamy foam and sweet mist. I crook my finger greedily into the soft, melting mass. The heat wakes stray bluebottles, who bombard the growing pile of discards. Even the rank smell of Jean's kitchen on hot evenings is drowned out by the trumpeting sweetness.

She sluices out jars with a quick wipe of the fingers and a shake, then stacks them straight on the table for the kitten to prowl and sniff.

'Don't bother drying them. Why don't you sit?'

I straighten my aching shoulders, then shrug. I don't want her to see how happy I am to be here, with her. Adam took Tommy down the Fox in the end, but they're both long since back, silent and swaying, and up to bed.

'He'll come round, you know.'

I flap one hand to fend off the moths and gnats and midges lured by the glut of sugar in the air. 'Can you shut the window?' A small grey moth scalds, shrivels and drowns. I chase it with the spoon. 'This was his fault, Jean. He'll not match you on soft fruit now, will he? All he cares about, and he can't even get up in time.'

The tremble in my voice makes me furious. I've never done Tommy down in front of her, anyone, not ever.

'Oh I don't know.' Jean wipes her hands on her thighs, all brisk certainty. 'He'll make it up on the raspberry, I'm sure.' She gathers together a piece of parchment, the rolling pin, a saucer and a pencil. 'What I meant was, Tom'll come round about the baby.'

'Tommy's over the moon about the baby. You know that.'

'Oh, Lettie.' There it is again, that old charitable expression of hers that makes my head throb. She rolls the paper around the rolling pin one way then the other, to flatten it, then clears a space on the table. 'Come on.'

I let myself sink down next to her, and the dragging pressure in my belly and legs eases. 'He made a mistake on the delivery. He's over-tired. We all are.'

'Lettie. It just takes them longer is all. You can't blame them. They don't feel the growing, do they? Should be sorry for them, by rights.' She starts to draw circles around the saucer, then stops. 'Be nice to him, Lettie. He's working hard.' She hands me the scissors. 'Tom's a good grower, chemicals or no. He deserves his success.'

An obscure disappointment settles in the pit of my stomach. Jean can see more than I thought. But she can't see through Mr Radley – jam-loving pitman, dedicated grower – to the Tommy I know.

I line up the scissors with her pencil marks, ease the jaws open and snap out a jagged circle that's far too small. I screw it up and start on the next.

Or am I too close to Tommy to see him, and how he might have changed? Before the lockouts, he worked harder than anyone, no matter how scared he was. Yes, we tricked our way on here, but that was my deception, not Tommy's. Maybe he told me nothing about Turnbull because there was nothing to tell, just the unfair suspicion. That man at the gate was just a tramp trying his luck. Tommy's earned this tenancy fair and square. It's Baby that's thrown him. He deserves to do well. It's a wife like myself he doesn't deserve.

I try to free myself of the scissors, but the handle has trapped my thumb, hot and red and sore. 'Oh Jean. He thinks Baby will ruin everything, you see. How will I work, when it comes, what if I—'

Jean eases them from me. Then she lays her hand on my belly, as if it were her own. 'You let Tom get it out of his system. Remind him how lucky you both are, that your first one will be coming in the down season. Come spring, we take them with us when we work. Babies are no trouble in a basket. You must help him, Lettie, encourage him. With his own holding and his own family, he'll be happy as anything come Christmas. I promise you.'

I let her hand move down to support my belly, feel its cool strength.

'Lettie, you're overwrought is all. This is your first baby.' Jean starts to gather up the rustling circles. 'You don't know how lucky you are. By the time—'

By the time I'm her age. I see the worry etched deep in her face, the worry that will never leave her.

'Come on.' She heaves herself back to the hob. 'This has to be done, then we can sleep.'

Before we know it the air has thickened. The scarlet soup spits back, daring us to come closer. Once, twice, three times, Jean tips her wooden spoon to the saucer. We rake our hair from our foreheads. My neck and back and belly and feet all ache.

I open her windows wide again. Then I work my way back round, fists on the table, to sit heavily and wait. The pigs, who have dozed all day in the heat, root and rub up against each other. There's the barn owl again, screeking. I'm awake so much now because of Baby tumbling around I know these and all the summer night sounds, and the order they come in, right through to the blackbird before dawn.

Jean stands and reaches for the saucer. 'That's it.'

The ruby oval wrinkles under her forefinger like water before wind. Setting point. At Crampton's we had a thermometer: Thread. Soft ball. Firm ball. Soft crack. Hard crack . . . What would I do without her? I stretch up to kiss her hot cheek. She rears back.

'Magic,' I say, brazening it out.

Her eyes widen.

'It's magic,' I insist. 'You're magic.'

But she shies away. I reach my arms up to clasp her to me, my belly hard against hers.

'Here,' she says, after a moment. 'You hold the jars and I'll pour.'

By the time we've spooned the last of the jam into the jars the condensation has run from the windows. Moonlight is pooling on the floor.

Next morning, when I let myself in, I count thirty 2lb

jars on the table, sealed tight. The jars are smeared and sticky, the lids crunchy with sugar.

Jean opens the stair door, her face puffy with sleep. 'What?'

I peel off a fly and hold it up by one wing.

I tie an apron on her, then me. When the water is warm enough we dip a cloth each and wipe the jars clean in our laps, turning their smooth, heavy roundness over and over. I clear the windowsill and polish the panes and stack them up carefully: four rows of four, staining the morning light purple and scarlet.

Jean turns. Tommy fills the doorway.

'Look,' I say. 'Look what we made.'

He picks up a jar, weighs it in his hand. 'What can we ask for this, Jean?'

'We're not selling it.' We'd make back some of what we lost on the soft fruit. What he lost. But this is my jam. My first.

Jean sits up straighter. 'No one will be buying jam, Tommy, not this time of year. It's yours to keep.'

'Yes,' I say. 'We've space under the stairs. We can eat it ourselves.'

'We can always keep it here for you,' Jean adds.

He gives us both a steady look. 'Do what you like.'

Michaelmas

I should start on the layette. All summer I've told myself I'm too busy, there'll be time enough when the work eases off a bit. When the evenings get longer. But not just yet. I get a pain all the way down to my bad foot if I sit or lie still too long these days. I lever myself off the bed and go over to the window.

The birds have fallen silent. This morning the sky was hazy with grey, churning cloud. It seemed to be brightening earlier, but it's thickened again. Everything is tinged with yellow. I watch George and Georgina peck their way across the shorn field beyond the orchard: Jean beats a gap in the hedge every Michaelmas and shoos them through at dusk, to gorge themselves on gleanings before the villagers get them. 'Scarecrow or no scarecrow,' she says, all chuckling, sly defiance.

Adam and Tommy are up and down with their wheelbarrows, clearing old growth. Our side is a sorry mess, nevertheless: half-pruned hedges, piles of browning cuttings and empty nests spilled where they fell.

A crack of thunder makes me jump. The sound rolls round and round the holding. The leaves start to quiver on the hedges and the quick beat of the falling rain finally reaches me. That's what the pressure in my head has been.

I flatter myself I know now what the weather will do almost as well as Jean and her bees, but this has taken me by surprise.

A thunderstorm always used to make me want to go out and dance in the street. Even did it once or twice, in high summer, to rouse Tommy as much as anything – tore off my hat and dared the lightning to come down from the hills and strike my bare head. I stroke my belly and wait for that feeling, but it doesn't come.

Downstairs is so dark that I light the lamp before I settle myself back in at the table. Nothing soothes me now like sitting down with the almanac to make plans for next season. I understand it now, the alchemy of our success. Soil, sun, water and spray. We order, we sow and water, feed and till, tie in and tweak and spray and tend, and there you have it. A cash crop. And because we own – what is it those commies call it, the 'means of production' – the profit is ours to keep, to invest how we like. We have capital, for the first time in our lives. We'll work as hard as we like, as long as we like, because we're smallholders, not shift workers, and we're making money hand over fist. This will be yours, Baby, to keep. And no one need know what we had to do to get it. No one need know anything.

There's a sharp burst of rain, hard as hail. I jump, and the back of my hand jolts the lamp. Baby flinches. If the lamp fell and smashed, fire would spread like water, across the table and on to my lap. I would put it out with my bare hands.

*

George and Georgina are back, and sipping at puddles. Six o'clock, and the light is as rich and thick as it was in high summer, only washed clean and clear. It comes streaming across the land and straight through the open door. Jean has cooked us the Michaelmas supper she promised us back in the spring. She wouldn't let me help, not even peel the veg. This is for you, Lettie. For all the luck you have brought us.

She opens the door, a massive swirl of printed cotton, red spots on cream. 'Pretty, isn't it? Ads got a woman in town to run it up. He chose the print too. Look, they're tiny apples.'

Each one with a little dent in the top, for an imaginary stalk.

'I've never, you know – I've always just carried on in dungarees, letting out the straps. But this time, well—'

'This time's different.'

'Mmn.'

The men come in, wet-combed and ruddy. But neither of them looks like they belong indoors. The sun has grooved Adam's neck like old wood and there are tawny flaws in his irises I've not seen before, wiry hairs springing from his eyebrows like the bristles on the oak tree. Tommy's so dark his eyes look wrong, pale bits of ice. His fair hair has bleached to brittle straw, hat or no hat. I see why the locals put up a new scarecrow every year. The sun and the wind and the rain wear them out, worry them to bits.

We've had to squash up indoors because the grass is sodden and everything stinks of the onion we've been lifting. The cloying smell of hot goose fat, on top of the fusty smell Jean's kitchen always has, makes me want to gag. Those ants, on the windowsill, keep going in and out, up and down, round and round. I sit up straighter, try and catch my breath. 'Did the clamps get done?'

'Pfft.' Tommy leans back and stares out the window.

Of course, you can't clamp roots once they get wet, they'll rot. But that's another day gone. And he knows he'll be needed back at the Central before long. Jean busies herself at the hob, all sizzle and clatter, humming under her breath.

'Rosie got out again,' says Adam.

'No!' I half turn to look out through the door. Rosie could do a lot of damage in very little time.

'Surprisingly strong necks, pigs. Get their snouts under a fence or a gate, they'll lift it easy. Just walk out.'

'Nothing wrong with my fences.' Tommy is terse. 'Or that gate.'

'You want to pen her in proper. Barbed wire, six inches above the ground should do it. Even better, that electric wire.'

Jean towers above us, blocking the light, the glistening goose held high in a shimmer of steam. Tommy's face is inches from her belly, and all the little apples printed on her frock. I see her belly button pushing out, like a tiny, answering face.

'Rosie just had her little adventure. Now mind yourselves.'

Adam smacks his hands together. 'How's that for a stubble goose?'

'Twenty pounds if she's an ounce,' says Jean.

Tommy curls his lip. 'Twenty-pound green goose?'

A green goose is culled while there's still grass. But no one raises green any more, not commercially. Adam and Jean are running three dozen Sebastopols. He thinks they're foolish. We're running half that in Chinese, all for Christmas. I'm glad that's George and Georgina still sipping at puddles out there.

'This one was too big to bleed. I had to use the broomstick, see. Break the neck. But she'll be lean and sweet, mark me.'

'If you're eating goose at Michaelmas you know you're set right for the rest of the year,' says Adam.

Jean smiles fondly. 'Used to pay our rent at Michaelmas, didn't we? With the gleanings.'

She keeps telling us the same stories.

'No one can rear a green goose like Jean.' Adam takes up the big knife and fork and starts to carve. Mushy wads of apple and black strands of prune spill out of the cavity. 'Wait till you taste her Michaelmas pie—'

'Think our Chinese will make this weight, Tommy? I'd bleed the lot tomorrow, the amount of stinking green you-know-what I've slipped in.'

The Dells chuckle, on cue. They love to remember townie Lettie, turning up with her button shoes and posh hat.

At last we're all served. Jean raises a glass. 'Now here's to the Radleys, who have brought us luck, and made their own luck along the way.'

'To Tom,' says Adam, raising his. 'May your next season be as good as your first. Association is minting him a medal, you know that, Lettie?'

He's cropped more than any Special Area newcomer to date. We won't have the final figures for a while, of course, but his first season already looks to have 'exceeded all expectations'. There's talk of Bridgewater coming back with the photographer.

Tommy twists his head away. *Pfft.* No answer to that, is there. I'm embarrassed for him. His sullenness is suffocating.

I summon the dimples. 'To the Dells,' I say. 'We couldn't have done it without you.'

*

Jean draws her Michaelmas pie out the oven, exclaiming. Adam talks him through the fine pies she has baked over the years. I watch Tommy pick up his spoon, rub it on his shirt, and put it down, pick it up again. Baby kicks and kicks. What little I've eaten has lodged just below my collar bone.

I swallow hard. 'That's a beauty of a pie.'

And it is, golden, smooth and perfectly crimped. Jean gives me her proud, heart-breaking, little smile, and rests the tip of the knife teasingly on the centre of the pie.

'How many minutes, Lettie? Ten?'

'Oh no, five will do me.'

Jean has never cooked so well. I can't get much down, but I can feel it doing me good. Doing us good.

'That's beautiful, Jean, thank you.'

Baby's foot pushes back against my palm and Jean glances at my belly. She sees everything, after all.

Adam tips cream over his crust. 'Never been so well provided for, have we, Jean, going into winter?'

Adam puts one hand on Jean's arm and leans over to me. 'We used to take kit's chance, you see.'

I raise my eyebrows politely.

'What we could get. Kit's chance. Then sometimes nothing, all winter long.'

'February.' Jean nods. 'That was the longest month. Ads had to go out too often to tell.'

Adam taps his nose. 'Never got caught, my darling, not once. Well, I don't need to tell Tom the tricks. Famous for it, aren't you, you Special Area boys? Catapult and a borrowed whippet. Cosh down the back of your coat. Aren't I right, now?'

Tommy gives him a fleeting smile.

'You lot can see in dark. Nowt gets past you pitmen.'

Tommy rubs at the back of his spoon. 'No,' he says. 'No. It doesn't.'

'You'll have more cream, Tom,' says Jean.

Tommy watches the thick, steady flow of cream spread over the crust, spill over the filling, begin to pool on the plate. Jean wipes her finger across the lip of the jug and sucks it clean. I lift my spoon to my mouth and scalding juice spills from the pastry on to my lip.

'Ow,' I say. 'Ow.'

Jean passes me a glass of water. Tommy stirs his cream into the black and purple juices on his plate. It looks like marbles, or the paper inside book covers. He bends over his plate, tilting it to chase up the jammy juices with his forefinger. Then he sucks his purple finger clean and wipes it on his bib.

'More, Tom?'

'Why not, Jean. Why not.'

I keep my head down. Wish he'd just make an excuse and go. Whatever's going on between him and Adam, he's no call to spoil this for me too. Unless it's to punish me for Baby. God help me when it's born.

Jean rears to her feet. 'It's late,' she says. 'We need to get our girls to bed, Lettie.'

I let her lead me, out into the twilight and across the cool, wet grass, and I breathe deep, heady with relief to be out here, just the two of us. That kitchen felt like a bottle of pop, about to explode. When the door opens we are careful to look only at each other. It's Tommy, off to the tomato house, to pull down old vines.

She hands me the bundled tea towel. 'Here, before I forget.'

Jean and I get through her soft, nutty lettuce as fast as Tommy gets through Woodbines. We've set up trays in the upstairs room again, there's no room in the glasshouses. As I pick out a handful of choice leaves Jean winces, puts one hand to her belly.

'Jean? Are you all right?' I step towards her. There's a crunch underfoot, and my foot slides, throwing me off balance. Right next to the path, two of their Dutch lights have been smashed flat, frames splintered, shards of glass nestling in the soft, dark outer leaves.

'What's this?'

'Rosie, remember?' She smiles. 'Adam will have it fixed in the morning. Come on over when you're done with the birds. We've something for you.'

*

Adam shuts the door behind me, brushing past my belly, the way you'd brush past a coat, without thinking, or even noticing. My belly, that Tommy studiously ignores, is as knobbly as a poacher's pouch these days. All hard curves and little, nubby bones. Baby kicks hard again.

Oh yes, Baby knows what's right. And what's wrong. Each time I come in here there seems to be less and less space. If Tommy were here too, I don't think I'd be able to breathe. He looked up as I went back to the house, but he didn't stop pulling at the vines. I could feel him watch me, though, up the straight and narrow, to their door. Let him watch. I'm doing nothing wrong.

Jean looks about, frowns. 'Did you move it?'

'Here.' Adam bends down behind the table and brings up a long wooden trough full of water. Part submerged in it, weighted with a half-brick, is a pale sheaf of wheat stalks complete with ears.

Jean dips her fingers in the water to rummage through the stems. 'You've some wild oats in there too, even better.'

'We've a little something for you, see,' Adam says. 'And we thought you'd like to see how it's done.'

Jean spreads a clean cloth over one end of the table, and

sets down a fat reel of red thread, a pair of scissors and a small ball of galvanised wire. Adam lifts a handful of stems from the trough and shakes the drips off before wrapping it in the cloth. Then he takes out his knife and starts to cut the stalks into lengths. The cut ends smell of grass and butter.

Faster than I can follow, Adam strips off a filmy outer layer, and sorts the stalks with ears into one pile, those without into another, and discards the rest.

Those dollies up there, he made for her. Tied the red threads tight round their throats and wrists. Each one darkening over time, from golden to bronze.

Jean has seen my face. 'She's after a dolly of her own, Ads.'

He shakes his head. 'We've more than enough of those.'

'True enough. Foolish old custom. You'll not be making any more, will you, Ads?'

'No, I shan't.'

Adam puts down the knife to rummage in his pocket. Two smooth, grey oval pebbles click and slide from his hand into hers. He selects straws, counts and shuffles. He grips and ties with wire and thread, wraps and snips. Then he splays and waggles the straws into a bouquet of blades and starts to plait. First he forms a tight little curl, that bellies out into a starry poke no bigger than an eggcup. Then he drops one pebble inside and plaits on, but tighter this time, until the pebble is trapped inside, invisible. Before I know it, he has tied off the end; a snip, and it's done. Nestling in his palm, a seed pod on a stalk, trailing red threads. Still damp, the straw darkened like wetted hair.

He tips it into my cupped hand. I hold it lightly, gauge the weight of the pebble as it shifts. I don't need to ask what it is. My little finger barely fits through the curl at the end. I shake, as gently as I can. The pebble shifts about like a shadow. I listen intently for the noise it makes. Rustle, thud, rustle, thud.

'Thank you, Adam.'

'You're welcome, Lettie.'

Jean squeezes my shoulder. Adam sorts through his straws and begins on another rattle.

As I pass between their door and mine I see Tommy in the tomato house. He's pulled down so many vines the light of his lamp spills out clear on the ground. He sits silhouetted on a stool in plain sight, smoking. Whether he can see me out here in the dark or not I've no idea. I can't see his face.

Safe upstairs, I take the rattle out of my pocket and hide it in my suitcase under the bed. If Tommy saw it he'd only kick off. Tomorrow, Jean and I will start on the layettes.

18th October

Our summer is over, at least in the mornings. Mist lies low on the furrows and there's a reek of pickled nuts. The bonfires smoke and crackle day and night. The grass is lush still, but there's a yellowing. And spiderwebs, everywhere, catching in my hair and on my goose-pimpled arms. This morning, I pulled on a cardie and boots for the first time in months. The wool itches and my feet are swollen and clumsy. But the mist burns off and by mid-afternoon it's as blithe and warm as spring, with a blue haze over the fields, and I bare my arms again.

Tommy and Adam plant up the Dutch lights, take out everything that's gone over, clear dead leaves and burn the lot in case of disease. Then they dig, before the frost comes. Tommy can dig just as well as Adam, now. Better. He digs like a demon.

Last Thursday a heavy fog came down and the leaves fell off the chestnut and sycamore within the week, laying a bright yellow and red carpet that mushed down to brown slime. Now you can see all the way through the orchard, to the hedge with its rosy studwork of haws and sloes and hips, and the ploughed field. The dew is heavy as rain, and when the sun shines it's hazy all day, like there's thick smoke in the air. And when it doesn't, a chill sets in.

'Now that,' says Jean, easing herself down on to her stool, 'is the last bit of outdoor sowing I'm doing this side of Christmas.'

I look at the ranks of filled trays on her potting bench, the brush neatly slotted into its dustpan and the tomato plants hung upside down to ripen along the crossbeam. The whole glasshouse is swept and neat and clean. Her house is as unprepared for Baby as it was when we arrived. Bluebottles stir as you step inside, there are brown smears on the lino, cat hair on the dishcloth and that familiar, fermenting smell.

Baby turns over, presses gently up into my ribs, and lies still. Up against the fat little booklet that came with yesterday's Co-Op delivery, that I've been carrying around in my bib pocket all day.

Motherhood

is all it says on the front. Smiling out from inside the cover is a cut-out photograph of a baby wearing an ermine-trimmed crown. Underneath is printed

'Motherhood is the noblest calling in the world.'

I hadn't wanted to read it, but I did, sat on the nettie after tea, holding it up to the last of the light through the slat Rosie broke. When I got to *Geoffrey Nash, aged 4, adjudged the most beautiful child in the 'Hairdressers' Fair Competition', 1932*, I put it back in my pocket. Shiny lips and curly hair and pretty as a starlet in his matinee coat.

Later, I'd got it out again. *Some Danger Signals* and *Care of the Breasts* and *Souring of Milks*. And then *Feeding Schedule 'A'*. *Feeding Schedule 'B'*. A whole chapter on crying. My dreams were full of shrieks and moans and what woke me was a howl, an animal howl. I'd been handed a little punnet of horrors: naked squibs trussed at the ankles and wrists with red thread.

'This came with my delivery. Did you order it, Jean? It says it costs a shilling.'

Jean rubs at her belly and mine starts to itch too. I have aches and twinges all over, like I'm coming apart at the seams. Jean has a permanent furrow between her eyebrows. But she never complains.

'They give it out for free, I think, if you're expecting.'

'Really? How do they even know?'

Jean blinks. 'Who wouldn't know by now? Ads will have told them down the Central, the Fox, the bank—'

I try to imagine having the sort of husband who would proudly announce such news, who would have filled in the '*Motherhood*' coupon for his wife.

'Bound to be yours then.'

She hands it back. 'No, you hold on to it. It's your first time.'

Indeed. Back and forth I'd gone, all the way through, but it ran straight from *The Expectant Mother* to *The Nursing Mother* with nothing in between. I flex the smooth sugar-paper-blue covers between my hands. 'We've had a good growing season, yes?'

'Yes. The best.'

'Don't you think we could run to a doctor? If we needed one.'

'Give that here.' She turns it over and shows me the back cover. 'Look, Cow & Gate. They're as bad as Ferguson's and the rest. They'll tell you nothing. Just want to sell you stuff, powdered milk and rusks, all that nonsense. Anyway, doctors cost a fortune, you know that. You'll be fine. Don't go getting above yourself.'

'What about that handywoman, in the village?'

223

Had Jean ever mentioned her name? She had, hadn't she? My brain is softening. Even my fingers don't grip as well.

'As if that lot would – Do you not trust me, Lettie, is that it?'

I drop my eyes. Where are her babies now? Dead. Buried. Unbaptised. Unconsecrated. Under the first, seventh and ninth trees in the first row, the third and fourth in the second. She's awake in the small hours too, and when I get up to open the back door for air, often as not I see her lamp down there in the orchard again.

'A doctor's bill could wipe out Tom's profit for the year, you do know that, don't you?'

I look at her big, raw knuckles. 'Jean,' I say. 'Jean, please.'

'Mrs Bamber. She doesn't charge, you take her produce.'

Then she places both hands on her belly, as on a table-top. 'But it won't come to that. You're young, you're strong, you're healthy. It's your first time.'

It's your first time. Jean says this every time I cry at some new cruelty here. I cry when I see a spider trying and trying to spin a web, and they're everywhere. I used to just squash spiders in a bit of newspaper. Flush them down the scullery sink. Throw them on the fire.

I look up at her. 'It's not, though.'

*

Jean sits beside me until dusk falls. When she reaches out a hand, I can't help myself, I flinch. She pulls me to her and kisses the top of my forehead. When she doesn't let go, I let my body sink into hers, soft as a pillow.

Tommy's at the door, a black shape against the orange-streaked sky.

'Lettie? Is that you?'

'Oh, hello,' I say, sitting up and pushing at my hair. I feel dizzy and my eyes won't focus.

'What's wrong?' His voice is loaded with fear and antagonism. 'Jean? What's wrong?'

She fingers my hair back from my ear, her breath warm and steady on my cheek.

'Nothing,' I say. I don't want him anywhere near us.

Tommy takes hold of either side of the doorway. 'Jean?'

If she gives me away, with a movement, something in her voice, if he kicks off, I don't know what I'll do. What he'll do.

'I stand up, straighten my clothes. 'It's nothing, Tommy. I fell asleep.'

Jean stands up too, one hand pressed rather theatrically to the small of her back. 'It's quite natural, you know. Not long now. You get back to work, Tom. And let's get you back indoors, shall we, Lettie?'

The evening air helps, but inside the house is warm and stuffy and I have to sit down on the third stair. 'Nearly there,' says Jean, taking hold under my arms. 'Watch your step now.'

It's just the two of us again. At last. I can catch my breath.

'Here we are, love. Your own bed. Look at your preserves, through there. Look how prettily you did the apricots. Quite a knack you have, with ribbons. That's not damp up there, is it, there in the corner? I'd get Tom to look at the roof, if I were you. You know they never felted it, Adam was shovelling snow out of the loft last winter.'

After she's got me into bed I hear Tommy coming up the stairs. Jean holds a cup to my lips. The freshly pressed juice is thick and sweet, almost fizzing.

'Spartans!' I say. I recognise the toffee taste. Slowly, Tommy goes back down.

'Very good,' she whispers. 'Drink it all.'

*

I must have slept a little because I feel like a new person. Like everything inside me has dissolved and reset. I stare at the sloping ceiling, at the evening shadows thickening. Jean lies beside me, in Tommy's place, wheezing softly, like the cat does when it sleeps. She swallows and wakes. Her throat must be as dry as mine.

'I'll put the kettle on,' she says, and squeezes my hand tight tight tight. Her fingers have swollen too, like mine. I shift, touch my forearm to the warm wall of her belly. There is a pulsing, like a heartbeat. But nothing moves.

'Baby sleeping too?'

'Hmm?'

'You're lucky. Baby seems to wake up whenever I go to sleep. No wonder I'm tired. I'm awake half the night.'

She props herself on one elbow. It's clear she's been crying too. 'You didn't know what you were doing, did you, Lettie. You mustn't be ashamed, though, promise me. I know about shame, see. I thought I was unnatural, or evil, diseased even. Born to be barren. When we first came here, a woman said it to my face: green fingers, black womb. I've never forgotten that. Over and over, I've let Adam down. I don't deserve him, really I don't. He's been that patient.'

I reach for her hand again.

'But that's in the past now. For both of us. I know I go on about your hair. But you're our angel, Lettie. Believe me. You'll never know how grateful we are.'

'Jean,' I say. 'You're too good to me. Everything you've done for us. It's me should be thanking you.'

Now I've embarrassed her. She swings her feet to the floor. 'Up we get.'

She lights the lamp on the mantelpiece and watches me pull on my cardie, slip on my house shoes. 'You know what this means.'

'What?'

'You're due later than we thought.'

'I am?'

'First babies quicken later, as a rule.'

This is why I need Jean. Who ever would tell me such things? Not *Motherhood*.

'Probably more like end of November.' Her sing-song lilt is stronger than ever, like she's already rocking the cradle. 'Maybe even December.'

December. I go to the window and draw the curtains. And then I have to grip the edges tight and I can't let go. Because if Baby is coming later, if it's December, chances are it will be Tommy's, won't it.

'Which is good.'

'Yes?' Then I realise what she means, and turn to face her. 'Oh Jean.' I let the relief flood my voice, pretend even to myself that it's gratitude. 'If you're due before me, you can be with me when it's born. And we won't need Mrs Bamber.'

I know I should move towards her, but I can't. Jean stands stiffly by the door. I see her blink back tears.

'Why, yes,' she says. 'There's that. I was thinking, though, you won't have to pay the Association to slaughter your geese either. We'll be able to do it ourselves. Keep the feathers too. You can get as much as two shilling and six a pound for body feathers. And the down is worth twice as much.'

227

20th October

First, though, it's the pigs' turn. Overnight there is a hard frost, and we wake to heavy fog. Adam brings over his thermometer to show us. He's not been anywhere near our door since before midsummer, let alone inside, but he doesn't knock. Just walks right in.

Tommy sits back and clasps his hands behind his head.

'It's a very good killing temperature, is what it is,' says Adam, placing the thermometer on the table in front of him. 'Well below forty-five. Cold enough for rigor mortis to set in. Looks set to last a few days too. If you hold off feeding your lot tonight, Tom, we could get them out the way by Friday easy.'

I wish Tommy would see that this is a gesture of goodwill. Most settlers have to send their livestock off to the slaughterhouse, even though it can cost as much to get a pig slaughtered and butchered as it did to buy it as a weaner. Adam's been butchering since childhood. And this way we get to keep the offal.

But when Rosie farrowed, she only had six in the end, and two stillborn, he'd stayed up all night with her. And when, to make the most of her milk, Adam gave him three of his own, little pink wriggling things with their ears folded back, Tommy had all them in the house; he didn't come to bed again all their first night. Once they were up on their feet he followed them around, afraid they'd get lost or a fox would get them.

Tommy presses his lips together. At eight weeks, his pigs were heavier than Adam's, and they're easily market size now – he's been feeding them on fishmeal, like the Association recommends. But it's adding up. Rosie's already been put to boar again, she'll have even more come the spring.

Adam tells Tommy all he has to do is starve them, string them, show them a bucket of feed, put a spade to the back of the neck. Snap the spinal cord. One jab, they don't feel a thing. They'll squeal, of course, they're pigs, but it's not painful, not like it sounds.

'See it as a kindness to the pigs. They don't know what's coming.' Adam flashes his confident grin. 'Meat tastes better if it's not scared.'

Tommy purses his lips.

'No? I'll do it. If you'd rather. You can watch.'

He has reared those piglets, his and Adam's, like they were his own. There've been times I've been jealous of them myself. Had he had it in him all along? I can't tell any more. But I can read his face. He's stringing Adam along. I already know what he'll decide. And I'm glad of it. The later Baby comes, the more certain I can be that it will be his. And I want to be glad of that too.

'No,' Tommy says, with the smallest twitch at the corner of his mouth. 'I want it done right.'

The night before they go off the weather is still hard. They've been mired in mud up to their bellies, mud so deep you'd think it could never freeze, but it has. Adam comes round one last time. He lounges in the doorway, letting the frost roll in, and holds up a gleaming spade, freshly sharpened. Perfect weather. Last chance. Think of the profit.

I look at Tommy, and it's like his flesh has curdled. His pale hair is sticking up and there's a nasty rash on his neck where he's been scratching in his sleep. He's more upset than I realised.

He pushes back his chair. He shakes his head one last time and shuts the door on Adam. *I want it done right.*

I go up behind him and wrap my arms around his shoulders. He smells of soil and Lysol. I can't remember the last time we touched. It feels chaste and awkward. His spine pressing against my belly makes me feel a little sick. When I pull back, he clears his throat and goes out.

In the middle of the night he wakes with a jerk. I seem to have been awake for hours. These last few weeks, sleep has come in shorter and shorter shifts: two, four hours at most. I listen to his ragged breathing until he goes back to sleep. His jaw tightens and his fingers curl and flex. I put my hand in his and stroke his fingers until they soften.

There was the one dream he used to have, that he'd told me about in the dark, that kept coming back. When he's fourteen again, knocked up at four with his da and down the shaft together and he's walked a mile to his station. He's sat there on his own in the dark and the silence, listening out for the tram, hearing it come closer and louder and faster down the roadway that dips one in forty.

It's Tommy's job to open the trap and he has to do it at the very last minute and close it again sharpish, because unless the trap's shut air won't flow through the mine properly and the men will die. He's not quite sure where his da is working but he knows it's down below, far down below, where the air doesn't reach unless the traps are doing their job.

And in the dream the tram is coming closer and closer and faster and louder and he opens the trap smartly and through it goes. But then he can't shut it again. The tram's long gone. Tommy's alone in the dark, tugging away at the trap. And all the good fresh air is being sucked up and out of the mine and away from the lower roads where his da and his marras are working. Tommy has to decide: does he run a mile back to the shaft to get help? Or head on down and try and warn his da? Only he finds he can't move either way, his head is growing thick and his legs heavy—

Tommy has rolled on to his back. His breathing is very shallow. When I place my palm on his chest, he lays his hand over mine. *Firefly.*

Just a few more weeks, Tommy, you'll see. Breathe deep. This good fresh air isn't going anywhere and neither am I. We're safe now. We have capital, we have land, we have friends. That tramp never came back. We don't have a choice, we will be tied together, tied to here, but that's all right, because this is your baby. Our baby.

*

Early morning he goes down to his pigs for the last time. They bound out of the shelter through the sleet, thighs and bellies so thick and bulging they're obscene. Rosie licks feverishly at his wrist. Faster and more desperate than usual, as though she knows they don't have much time left. He bends over her and scratches her ears. The others nudge for his attention. Only one still has its curly tail. The others are completely unwound and hang like rat tails. He stays out there for the longest time.

The slaughterhouse man arrives just after eleven. Adam helps Tommy guide them into the trailer with boards, one after another. It doesn't take long. To be honest, they seem pretty keen. Adam stands at the gate and waves them off with a cheery shout, but Tommy withdraws just inside the door of the cucumber house, to pull on a tab. I've some cocoa ready to heat up, with sugar. Once he's that inside him, I might coax him back upstairs. I want him inside me, for the first time in a long time. But by the time I take his cup, Adam's got him on to his bike.

They stand astraddle, the other side of the fence. Tommy's never looked more in need of a drink.

Adam waves. 'We're off to the Fox. Tell Jean, won't you?'

I take Jean the cocoa instead. We watch the sleet start to settle on the empty pen.

The days keep shrinking and the nights expand some more. The sun has moved right round, it rises and sets over the beech tree at the end of our hedge to the south. As soon as it touches the hedge the air turns chill. Darkness floods out of the earth and drowns the light from the sky. The fields are empty and silent. There's only the moon, pacing across the sky.

The hens have stopped laying and Jean's put the mouse guard across the entrance to her hives. Vermin don't dare enter in summer but in winter, when the bees are sleeping, tightly clustered together, they can do serious damage.

We retreat inside her kitchen, build up the fire, and the cats stalk over and claim what's left of our laps. When we're done tearing newspapers for the nettie, we iron the rest for paper pads, cover them with sheeting and brown paper and stitch them together. I've bought an extra kettle, hemmed dozens of napkins. I've cleared out the bedroom, washed the spare blanket and wiped the bedframe and every single spring with Jeyes. Jean still won't clean, or dust. After tea Tommy settles in at ours with his papers and I go to sit with Jean, and we knit, and knit. Adam starts going round to join Tommy, says the clacking annoys him.

I start to feel I'm living by lamplight. Drowsy all day and awake at night, suddenly so wide awake and jazzed I'm propelled out of bed and down to the back door for air. It's hard to walk, as though Baby's head is wedged between my legs already. And often as not I'll see a lamp burning in the glasshouse and I know it's her. Sometimes I imagine this is how it will happen. Out there, in Jean's lap. But each time, by the time I reach the glasshouse, the twinge has passed.

Even at night, the air inside the glasshouses is warmer than outside, the earth underfoot eking out summer heat. She's sowing again, though she said she wouldn't.

Jean leans against the potting bench, wiping off her soil-stained hands.

'Purslane?' I say. Neither of us can get through the day without the stuff. My mouth waters just thinking about it.

'Broad beans.'

'Sow more purslane,' I tell her. Get ahead, for after Baby.

We contemplate her rows, six of them, in varying degrees of readiness. Now that the daylight has seeped away and the colours drained, they seem to glow even brighter, the unearthly lurid green of that first night.

'Can't sleep?'

'Can't sleep.' I try to bend down, rub my ankles, give up. 'I'm – I don't know. Everything's – tight.'

But it's not that. Not just that. This past week or so, I feel electrified. A thrumming buzz runs through me day and night, sometimes jolting and sparking, making my swollen fingers jerk straight open. Everything feels open.

I nap with Jean now. There's just room on my bed. Neither of us can bear to lie on our backs any more. I face the door as she settles herself around me: I'm the egg, she's the spoon. It's the only time I really let myself sleep. We are lying like this the first time my belly clenches, pulls tight like a drawstring. I cry out. She kneels up in an instant and we both put our hands to either side and hold it. It is hard as a shell. My heart drums. The blood wooshes in my ears. She stares down at me, a small smile on her face. Everything seems to float. But then it is over. It hadn't even begun.

I shut my eyes tight so she can look me over. I want her to know, to share each minute.

'Hmm. Me too.' She puts her swollen hand over mine. It's very hot.

'Might start cleaning up the house tomorrow,' she says.

I want to smile. But that jazzed feeling is rushing through me and my legs are weak. 'Mm,' I say.

'Ready?'

I nod. 'More than ready.'

Tommy leaves the scullery sink in a shocking state. Soap scum, bristles and tab ends. I shake out the Vim and give it a good scour, and the metal legs too, unhook the little curtain I'd hung between them for a wash and reach into the corners, where the lino is fly blown. Rolls of dust come away one after another. I jam a hairpin down the plughole and pull out hanks of pondweed. There are brown drips down the wall by the sink and the windowsill and fly spots on Tommy's mirror. I bend over to flip the doormat and it's as though cords tug tight from ribs to groin. My head spins. I feel my way into the kitchen and sit down to catch my breath. My breasts and thighs roll slick with sweat.

I sit and wait and breathe. But it doesn't come again.

All night I'm ready. I listen to the rain, worry about the state of the lanes. Soon as it's light I make myself go out and get the sheets back in. Don't bother with a coat, just boots, cardie, nightie. No chilblains this year. I'm stoked up warm inside.

I'll miss that.

7ᵗʰ November

The spits of rain hurt my doughy skin. I'm afraid of the huge clouds, the wind-whipped branches, the sudden rattle of glass in putty. And out of nowhere I'm remembering the Gala helter-skelter. What it was like to sit in that midget doorway at the top, with the edges of the coir mat bristling in my clenched palms and rain on my face. To look down the steep, curving grooves of those polished wooden runners. No going back.

I miss that life again now, more than ever. I don't want to be back among the pitwives, but I have a fierce urge to be running through the crowded fairground and the clattery streets, with their lights and noise and shops. And the smells of the people, wet wool and burnt sugar, fried fish and tobacco and coal smoke.

I get the sheets in, hers as well as mine. The tightening comes as I'm picking up the laden basket. I have to squat, bend over, and I can't keep the corner of the sheet out of the mud.

10th November

Once, early in the morning again, then nothing. It rains all day. Tommy's in and out to the tool shed, sharpening. Or he's cutting broken glass from the Dutch lights to fit the seed boxes. He's in and out far more than he needs to be, I reckon. Makes a pantomime of having forgot something, claps his hand to his forehead, that sort of thing. He doesn't ask, and I'm glad of it. I want to reach out for his hand as he passes, but I stop myself. Time enough. I keep remembering him down the pen, with his arms around Rosie. *I want it done right.*

Jean pops in with a covered plate when I'm not over for tea.

'Everything all right?' she asks.

'Right as rain,' I say. 'You?'

She smiles mutely. She's been scrubbing the stairs, I heard the brush knock on the treads well into the night.

If we talk about it, it won't happen.

I wake up cross with the bed. I pull it out from the wall and try to clean behind it, but I can't fit. And the door won't open with it in the middle of the room the way *Motherhood* says it should be. My heart is hammering. There it is. And again. I'm halfway downstairs and then it stops. I'll go back up and lie down and wait for one more to be sure. Then I'll call her.

One more. One more.

It's dark already. Tommy has the wireless on below. He must have charged the accumulator at last. My eyes fill. I don't recognise any of the dance tunes any more. One New Year's Eve long ago we were at a party up in Bambergate and a woman danced her baby out, had it halfway up the stairs.

Brace. Stand. Baby rolls and settles heavy like a bowling ball between my legs. My head hits the eaves because I forgot I moved the bed. Come upstairs, Tommy.

On and off all day. It's not as strong as it was, more like the start of my monthlies. I keep checking, but there's nothing. And if I get up and move around, the pain goes. Jean's not been round, and I'm glad. It's good to know she's there next door, but I don't want anyone in the house. I'm sinking back inside myself and there's nothing I can do. Around three this afternoon I came upstairs into the small room and opened a jar of pickled eggs. Monica's friend, Mrs Gooner, six children she had, her husband would tell anyone who'd listen, and not a labour pang with any of them. Never missed getting a meal on the table. She had a passion for pickled eggs.

However many times I swallow, it feels like the last egg is stuck solid in my throat. And look how dusty and sticky the jars are. It takes ages to wipe them off with my pinny. Putting them back takes even longer. I space them out neatly, labels to the fore, until I find the last one doesn't fit and I have to shunt them back together. It's getting dark and my fingers are clumsy and I'm terrified of one slipping out of my grip and shattering on the floor. I light the lamp and go round collecting the dead spiders in my hankie and shake them out the window.

The fresh air makes me dizzy so I sit down with my back against the door and put the lamp down so I can have another look at the fruit basket. I've made it up with my prettiest shawl. I chose the basket with the biggest handle so I can carry it about on my forearm and have my hands free. I'll be able to take it everywhere with me. Into the glasshouse, up and down the rows.

Baby will never be alone.

15ᵗʰ November

Nothing.

Nothing.

17th November

Nothing.

Even when he was full grown they'd send young Tommy into seams so narrow he had to crawl on his elbows and knees. He had special leather pads, and a special small pick. I imagined his shoulders wedged, his head craning, legs waving, like a tortoise. How did you turn round? I'd ask. To go back?

He'd just laugh and slide up on top of me like he was on runners, slippery and hot.

18ᵗʰ November

I let myself in. Jean is bent over an empty table, motionless; her forehead, forearms, palms, fingertips, pressed to the scrubbed bare wood. The red apple dress is stretched high and tight over her raised hips. When she rolls her head slowly to see me, her face is pale and bloated, with the gleam of raw fish. There are shadows like bruises under her eyes.

Wiping sweat from her upper lip, she straightens. 'Association say they'll come for the geese,' she says quickly, as though she's been waiting like that just to tell me.

I ease myself down into a chair. It would feel cruel to speak. There's nothing to say. If she was starting, she'd have let me know. Jean's circled date has come and gone. She's been avoiding me too.

She reaches a hand for the kettle.

'No, don't. I'll just need to go again.'

There's no room left inside me. I don't bother with the nettie, empty the pot out the window. This is the first time I've left the house since Wednesday, I reckon. Tommy's been doing everything there is to do outside, and some.

She winces, and presses one hand to the small of her back.

'Jean?'

'A minute—'

She's gone inside herself too.

'Jean?'

'No,' she says finally, wiping her gleaming upper lip again. Breathless, she rests against the dresser, stately no longer. 'I think – I don't know. I must have got my dates wrong.' She forces a rueful smile.

I've never known Jean admit she's got something wrong, not ever. I can't bear it. If Jean can be wrong, then—

'You look shocking, Lettie.'

Her familiar bluntness makes me smile back.

'Well, thank you.' And then my eyes prick and I have to swallow. 'I keep – I'm always – I just want it over with.'

'You do?'

I nod. 'Yes! Don't you?'

She looks at me intently. Then she takes a deep breath. 'Will you let me help?'

'You mean—'

She nods. 'Yes. And, well, I'm a way off, I'm sure, so – then I can be with you, can't I? I'd like that.'

'Really? You'd do that? For me?'

'Yes. Yes, Lettie, of course.'

I nod again. 'All right.' Relief floods through me. I don't know why I've hidden myself away. I should have come round long ago.

'Good. Good.'

'You'll be with me?' I can't tell her how much I've dreaded doing this alone. Cried for my mother: alone with me on the stairs, in an alley, a barn, a high, lonely bed. Because she must have been alone, with no one to turn to. She wouldn't have done what she did otherwise, left me at St Clement's; trussed up like a parcel, they said, with paper and string. Not because she hadn't wanted me. If only my mother had had a friend like you, Jean. But I can't let myself think like that.

'I promise, Lettie.'

'Oh, Jean. Thank you.'

My fingertips are tingling. How many times have I sat here and watched her lift down jars and open tins, scald the pot. And soon, soon, we shall both be sitting here with our own babies. On the dresser, one of her hyacinths is so far on that its heavy head of pink blossom has toppled the pot. I prop it up with the iron.

She sets a cup down on the table between us. I've never seen it before. It's a shiny blue and very small. The surface is choked with small brown twigs and leaves.

'Down in one, if you can.'

The taste is rank. I think of the sticky brown juices that seeped out of the baby birds the cats caught almost daily in July, and left on the paving down the side of the house. If I didn't pick them up straight away, maggots crawled out. It needed a pail of carbolic and hot water to rinse the smell away.

I almost lose my nerve then.

'I can't—'

'Try some honey. I have lots of honey.'

It's been a bumper year for the bees too. She has six jars, high up alongside the corn dollies; there's nowhere else to put them. Lettie Radley and her sweet tooth. I add one spoonful, then two more, stir and sip.

'Yes, that's better.'

'Good girl. It'll be all right, I promise.'

She sits back. Her hands stroke either side of her belly, like she used to stroke Flo before Jean grew too large to fit her on her lap.

The burning in my chest fades, and I come over all shivery. 'It felt like snow out there. It can't snow, can it?'

'It might. But not for a few days.'

'How can you tell? Your bees are fast asleep.'

She winces, and drops her head.

'Oh, Jean.' She can't have lost those bees. Isn't it a bad omen? 'All of them? What was it?'

'I don't know. The guard was still there.' She rubs at the crease between her eyebrows. 'It's happened before.'

'Still. I am sorry, Jean.'

I look about for distraction. There's a copy of *Woman's Weekly* on the table in front of her. I pick it up and see she's slipped her almanac underneath.

'Ads brought that back,' she says. 'Someone was throwing them out. Thought it might help pass the time.'

I look at the date. I'd stopped buying it long before then. It's from a different world.

'Shall I read to you, Jean?' I try to shift myself up straighter in my chair, then I can prop the magazine in front of me and reach my cup. '"What they ask Matron?" Or "The Shadow of the East", by E. M. Hull?'

'"*I have ridden almost without stopping night and day—*"'

We both hear the choke in my voice. We look at each other until I am ready to go on.

'"*The British Government will not distress itself about me,*" he said dryly.'

Jean takes both kettles out to the scullery to fill. My voice slows, and then speeds up again. My mouth gets dry, and she hears that too. I can't face more of the tea. She hands me a cup of freshly drawn water instead, but that's too cold.

Adam comes in with two pails of coal. As I turn to greet him a cramp comes. When I see his face again it's as though a chunk of time went missing.

'Fetch some more, would you?' Jean's voice is tight and high. 'Just leave it by the door.'

'Settling in,' he says.

I think he means us, until I see the scud and blur of snow on the window. It's gone dark already. Jean hands him his Woodbines from the mantelpiece. She's come out in another sweat.

'Right then.' A little smile plays across his face. 'I'll be next door if you need me.'

He goes out, and excitement floods through me. Thrills run up and down and round my belly and shoot into my thighs. The words dance.

'Oosh,' I say.

Jean watches it pass, then takes the magazine from my trembling hand. That one scared me a little.

They've turned the wireless on next door. Tommy'll open that packet of Woodbines. They know to stay there now, for as long as it takes. Or maybe he'll go out to the cucumber house. He'd be better off out there, I reckon. I'd rather he did that. I don't want him to hear anything. Or they could always turn up the wireless. That's a carol, I know it from chapel, but I can't remember the words.

'It's snowing, Jean.'

She fusses over the kettles. 'Tea?'

I feel a bit sick.

'I've had enough for now, I think.'

'Well then. Pass me the mag. You walk about a bit, and I'll read to you.'

I walk right to the end of 'The Shadow of the East' and take a breather for the start of 'The Genie of the Ring'. It's just words. Round and round.

'Try "Household Expert".'

Coal Dust on the Carpet. Washable Walls. To Soften Hard

Water – The room whirs and I'm thrown off the merry-go-round, but I don't reach the scullery in time. Vomit comes up my throat with a noise like pumping a plunger. My nose stings. I need air. My legs have dissolved and my knees slip on the lino. I rest my chin on the cool lip of the sink.

Can't smell, can't see, can't speak. I'm being pulled apart like a cracker. Vomit one end, shit the other. It's abject, violent, unstoppable. Jean, where are you?

Cold air. Hands. Everyone is talking at once. I'm slick, steaming. Up you get. My buttocks are cold. They can't see me like this. Pain reams through my thighs, my back. Give her a minute. I smell frost, coal smoke, rot, but I'm locked inside.

'Oh God,' I laugh. 'I can't do that.'

I'm standing in a puddle of clothes and she's wiping at my face, my legs.

'Here.'

She holds out my nightdress, the one with the green ribbon.

'Not that one.'

It dances away across the fields, chased by a pair of overalls.

That dark little bike shop on Deries Street, a shed really. It must be the mackintosh sheet I can smell. It rucks up all funny. She's shivering too. Oh Jean. I put my hand on her forearm and feel goosebumps.

She puts the bowl down by the bed.

'Do you think you're going to be sick again?'

'Oh, Jean.'

'Oh, my lovely. Do you want them to turn that wireless off?'

I throw back the covers and go to the window and open it. 'I need air.'

A juddering chute opens up inside each leg.

'Ah,' I say. 'Ah.'

After that, it takes me inside. Only my hand is over-ground, reaching round for something to hold on to so that I'm not dragged under completely. Sometimes I can hoist myself up to the rim, rest on my elbows. Jean's face, calm, close, untouchable. I hold on to her hand. But it's rising again. I learn to take a deep breath and let go of the sides when it comes thundering down the tunnel because if I resist it will slam into me and I will shatter. I let it surge over and around me. But I don't let go of her hand.

And I'm out again. Time to catch my breath. There's the lamp. She spoons jam into my mouth. Strawberry. I want to explain how each time the tumbles and turns are different, I can't learn these steps before we're on to the next ones. And we're off. Further and further down I go.

It's all right. I remember how good I am, at submitting. When you let go of the sides you don't know how many twists and turns there will be on the way down, but you always land somehow. And I'm not the one who's afraid of the dark.

The bed, Jean, the room, they've spun away out of sight. Here's the corner of the sheet tethering my hand, that's the iron dowel of the bedhead against my scalp. What a huge excavation is going on down here inside me. Level after level. The pain keeps on flooding up out of the darkness. The sides clamp tighter and tighter. Up there, Jean is holding the light steady. How long will it take to get back to the surface? I'll have to ask her. I'll ask her when I've dealt with this one.

This one's a wild, ravening beast, all teeth and claws. It comes out of nowhere and takes hold of me, pins me down and doesn't let go. I don't panic. I know to play dead. There is smothering pain, and pain sharp as knives, and the grinding, pulverising pain of clashing rock. They roll on and on together.

I've let go of her hand. It's dark. And I'm down here alone.

Growing Season
No. 2

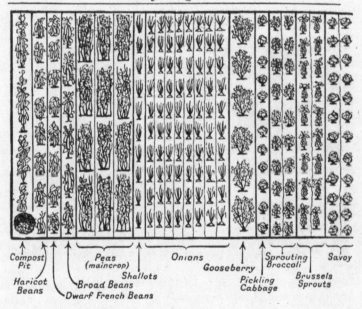

Plan for Vegetables

Compost Pit · Haricot Beans · Broad Beans · Dwarf French Beans · Peas (maincrop) · Shallots · Onions · Gooseberry · Pickling Cabbage · Sprouting Broccoli · Brussels Sprouts · Savoy

I am still. Stilled. A clock stopped, no movement left in me. My legs lie seeping, one on top of another. Hands together now I lay me down to sleep. My head rests deep in the pillow, one ear to the cold, blessed silence. Because I did it, I did it, I did it. Oh. The screw, the sting, the force of it. The squirm and slither of release. Couldn't even lift my head to look. Good girl, she said. You rest.

It's all over, and it's all to come. *I'm still here, Tommy. I'm still yours.* Sleep buries me again. It fills my mouth and my eyes. Blankets have been piled on top of me, heavy as turf and smelling of carbolic. I breathe, deep in the warm, soft whorls of my body.

The cold ear flinches. It could be anything. Anything at all. It locks me tight. Seizes my breath. There is nothing else except this alarm, this instant alert. But I am deep, deep buried. Fingers, feet, arms, legs, they connect to nothing. Nothing, nothing, and then a heaving pain. A sick sleeting. Upright I am a bucket of guts sloshing in cold daylight. My belly sways, marshmallow soft. My only solid parts my breasts, cabbage hard and hot and huge.

A cry. Shrill, unearthly. Tiny. It rakes over me, blasts passages, shatters stillness and reclaims me entirely.

It's two steps from the bed to Baby's room. My legs are

soft and useless as liquorice ropes. Odd pains ratchet up and down as I fumble the latch and peer into the dimness. There are my stacked jars, gleaming, the square of curtain I quilted, drawn snug, the fruit basket and the shawl I folded and the rattle I placed on top.

I hear myself whimper.

Back to the bed I must go. I peel away the blankets the sheets the pillow oh so carefully but I know, I *know*. The grate is full of ash. Someone has lit a fire but it's gone out. I hold on to the edge of the mantelpiece. Fine ash on my fingertips. There. Dear Christ. Faint, but there. Through the wall. The world is crying. The room is crying. The stairs. The kitchen. What a time it is taking. My legs hang loose like an old teddy bear's. Outside is crushing huge and ragged white with fog. If I could just pick up this useless body and run with it.

Their latch stings, sticky with frost. But it's up, it's open. I step over *Woman's Weekly*, splayed in the passage. There are pails and bottles and a loaded ashtray. The chairs have been left any old way, a mackintosh sheet, and the preserving pan of water on the hob still. The air is warm and awake, soaked through with Lysol and Woodbines, and the door to the stairs wide open.

My belly sack nudges each steep tread. The crying grows louder and louder. A hot wetness spreads between my thighs and my head is a black buzzing.

Their bed is a high old brass thing, layered with linen and blankets and a trailing plum-park eiderdown. There are photographs, hangings and crowded whatnot shelves. Brass lamps and a fire crackling and Jean, sitting up in bed in a pie-frilled nightgown. Her hair curtains her face and brushes the pink crown of Baby's head, where the little knitted cap has fallen back.

A pause, a hiccup, a whimper, and oh my goodness here we go again, as loud as bells in the churchyard. That wail, that rising, twisting, wrenching wail.

'I'm here, Baby.' I hold out my arms. 'I'm here.'

All that heavy hair swings away. Jean's eyes are huge and dark and look right through me. 'Ads,' she says, as though testing the air. Then again: 'Ads!'

Baby's cry chokes off, then squeezes out again.

Out comes Jean's cawing, carrying field voice. '*Ads.*'

It blasts me, furious.

'*Ads!*'

Adam thunders up the stairs, huge in his black winter coat and out of breath. Jean tugs the cap back on to Baby's head. I hold out my arms again.

'Sleepy time now,' Jean says, in the same high voice. 'You too, Lettie. Back to bed.'

Adam takes my elbow.

'Cover her up, Ads.'

Adam reaches round me to take a folded blanket from the foot of the bed. As he drapes it around my shoulders my nightdress gapes open. I grab at the collar.

He gives me a queer smile. 'Now listen, will you?'

The fire crackles. The bedclothes shift and settle like sand. Baby is quiet. I can't see Baby any more. No Baby. There's just Jean, huge in the bed.

'All quiet. That's better, isn't it?' Adam backs down the stairs ahead of me. 'Come on now.' He beckons, firm, but distant, as though I'm a wandering stray, a stranger walked in off the lane.

There are clots of mud and grass on the treads that weren't there before. Near the bottom, spots and streaks of purple and scarlet, thick as yolk. And across the kitchen floor.

Outside, the fog glare dazzles my eyes. Too late, I see the wrinkled wad of muslin on our doorstep, bent like a saddle, stained rust and ochre and gleaming wet. He's cuffing it away with his boot, away from the house into the fog.

I get myself behind the door. 'I can manage, Adam, thank you.'

'Good girl.' His voice is tight and neutral. 'You get yourself back to bed now.'

I shut myself in the scullery. I can feel the hot trails down my thighs, a huge heaviness inside. Someone has washed out a load of muslins and hung them over the sink. They're still wet, and brown in circles like tea stains. I raise my palms and rest on the back of the door. The blanket drops from my shoulders and the updraught brings with it all the butchery smells that have collected inside my nightdress.

I'll have to take this one off, won't I, find the other. And then, when I've cleaned up, I'll make myself another pad somehow. I'll need to rest a little. Then I can put a coat on at least, something on my feet. Go back round. I'll call from the bottom of the stairs this time. I should get the fire going again in here before I bring Baby back. Clean that floor for them, at least, those stairs. I'll clean myself up, rest, then warm this place, the little room, clean up for them, and get her to bring my Baby down to me. We can start again.

Adam's the other side of the scullery window. He ducks his head and I hear the click and rasp of his lighter. My head is sleeting again and I'm very thirsty. There's no air in here.

Fog dulls the crunch of boots on cinders, but I know it's Tommy, moving fast. He says something I can't make out and Adam says, who knows? Adam goes back indoors and up the stairs. He's taken his boots off this time.

*

Tommy knocks lightly on the scullery door. Again and again. I sit on the floor, shivering hard.

'Give me a minute.'

'Ah, Lettie.'

It's the voice he had on him whenever one of his ponies had to go to bank.

'You go on, Tommy, I'll be there in a minute.'

'Best come out, Lettie.'

I close my eyes.

'What is it? Tommy, tell me.'

I open the door. He backs away until his head touches the underneath of the stairs. Tommy's nose always goes red in the cold, and his eyes water; it makes him look much older than he is. 'I'm just going to have a bit of a rest, Tommy.'

He wipes at his cheek, his eyes wide and staring. 'Yes. Best you get back to bed, Lettie.'

All those stairs, Tommy. All those stairs.

'Go on now. I'm right behind you.' He keeps his distance all the way up. Shuts the bedroom door behind him quiet as he can.

'Best you lie down, Lettie, quick now.'

That voice. All those done-in ponies of his, gone to bank and never coming back.

No, I'll stay sitting on the side of the bed, thank you. I must get this straight. I must be patient with him.

'Tommy?'

'Ah, Lettie—' He makes a noise like he has his knuckles in his mouth. 'I'm very sorry, Lettie. We're—'

It's there in his voice. I watch his face. His eyelids, flickering.

'About Baby,' I prompt, for his sake.

Can't he see me falling? Falling and falling. I wait for him to sit down beside me and catch me, but he just stands at the foot of the bed. I hold myself tight, tight, tight.

'Please, Lettie.'

'What?' I can't hear him for the sleet.

'It was no good.'

'What do you mean?' Everything's taking such a long time.

He bends over me. He takes my hand. Here it comes.

'It never drew breath, Lettie.'

Nothing.

'I don't understand, Tommy.' I'm waiting still, such a long, long time. I could wait for ever. But he's opening his mouth again. Here it comes.

'When you – it was already—'

How long have I got? I need him to open that window. I need to sit up. I need to stop his mouth. No. No. No.

I hold my hand up, palm out. He shakes his head.

I think about this for a moment. Calmly, on a rising note, a woman who can cope with anything, I ask, when, exactly. Was it before—

'Like I said, Lettie, it never—'

'Oh, Tommy—'

'It's all right, we've dealt with it, Lettie. You don't have to see it or anything.'

Unstoppable, then.

'Yes.' I look at the back of my hand, splay out my fingers. 'Thank you.' I feel the air between them. 'Oh silly me.'

'Lettie?'

'So that's—' I try to wave at the mantelpiece, my hand that doesn't even belong to me, but my whole arm is shaking.

'That's right.' Tommy clutches at his cheeks with both hands, pushes the flesh up, then down, presses his eyes with his fingertips. He emerges blinking, stricken, furious with relief at having got through to me. 'That's right, see. That's their baby in there. Jean's baby.'

*

She comes in head bowed, as though she's the penitent. She sets her lamp on the mantelpiece and the light makes pale petals of the eaves. They fold together over our heads.

'Can you sit yourself up, Lettie love?'

It's in the lilt of her voice, it was in those few light steps of hers across the room – no, even before that, it was in her neat tread up the stairs. She's not as I last saw her, not as I've ever seen her. That frightful frock she's wearing, all sunk in and sagging, it's done its job. That strapping, lumpen body, it managed in the end. She is done, complete; and it is all true, every last aspect of it. This is how it will be.

'Take your time.'

Her face dissolves into wrinkles. Jean can't hide this happiness, not even from me. She eases herself down on the end of the bed and clasps her long, veiny hands together. They look tiny for once, in that broad, emptied lap. Her face stills.

'I am sorry, Lettie. There was nothing you could have done, nothing anyone could do, you see? It never drew breath.'

It never drew breath. The words come out, one after another. If I can just stack them one on top of another, in the right order, it will make sense.

'We did everything that could be done. You must know that. If there is any comfort, Lettie, let it be that. There was nothing that could be done. I should know.'

I did have a baby. But it never drew breath. And now I have no baby.

'I know, I know, it's a terrible, terrible thing. We couldn't tell you before. You've been in and out for days now. I made you up a bottle of something to help you rest. You must be feeling better now? Seeing as you've been out of bed. Lettie?'

It never drew breath. I want to tell her about that man on the corner. Some days he couldn't get his dummy to work, couldn't manage the levers. I suppose he was drunk. Or there was something wrong with the mechanism. Either way, he carried on. He made the sounds himself. People still gave him money. I press my hand against my closed-up mouth.

'You said you'd stay.'

'I did.' She looks alarmed. 'I promised. Don't you remember? You were in my kitchen. It was me brought you up here.'

'When?'

'Days ago, Lettie. Only—'

She ducks her head. When she looks up again, her face is drawn every which way.

'I started too. It couldn't be helped, you do understand, don't you? I stayed with you as long as I could manage. Mrs Bamber, the weather, she'd have taken an age to reach us, even if— There was nothing she could have done. That's just how it was, Lettie. I'm sorry, sorry, sorry.'

She tucks the sheet, tries to smile. 'You're young, Lettie. Another baby will come along soon enough.'

I try to sit up then. But my arms have no strength and the sheet traps me tight. 'Where is it?'

I feel the crying, like a pause in my heart. She does too. Then its echo: the high, wavering wail through the wall. I watch the changes in her face. The alert. The pull. The gratitude.

I'm too ashamed to ask her to stay. She should take my suitcase. It's just under the bed, here. Have everything in it, you can never have too much.

Jean doesn't move her hand. But I can feel her pulling away. And so I let her go.

Tommy slips *Motherhood* out from under the pillow and tucks
it under his arm. He pours three spoonfuls. I swallow one
after another. The cork squeaks as he forces it back in. He
puts the bottle and the spoon back on the mantelpiece, the
booklet in his pocket and sits down on the bed with his back
to me. The cabbage leaves he puts on the foot of the bed.
Every day, twice a day sometimes. *Until your milk dries up.*
Jean's idea, Jean's words in his mouth.

Poor Tommy. He'll go back outside in a minute. He
doesn't know what to do with me, any more than I do.
He smells of fried bread and fortnight-old shirts. He should
be scrubbing down the glasshouses with that Sterilizal he
likes, repairing the broken panes and giving them a coat of
white lead, not keeping house and spoon feeding. I should
be out there sowing seed: radish, salad, cabbage, beetroot,
broad beans, chard . . . There'll be hundreds of plugs due.
Thousands.

They're agreed. Best Lettie doesn't get out of bed for a
while. Considering. Tommy's eating with us, it's no trouble.
Jean actually feels very well. Considering.

She's left me a second pot of egg white mixed with
brandy, a sort of paste to get the milk to stop coming, to
stop it hurting at least. I've told her it's working, but that's

only to get her to go away sooner. I want my breasts to hurt. They're not my breasts, anyway; all this milk, it belongs to my baby. What did I do wrong? Did I not push hard enough? Was I not strong enough? Anyway, I know what I did wrong.

I can't look at her. I nod and I smile and I'm grateful, but I can't bear the sight of her. The flush in her cheeks, the unearthly shadows around her eyes. The milky smell on her. That small, flickering smile, between pitying and smug. Then, when she's gone away, it's even worse. Sometimes I press on my breasts, that must be as big as hers now. Sometimes the pain is so bad I think I must faint. I wish I could.

Besides, the milk is all I've got left. I squeeze it out, soak it up, so that it keeps on coming. Taste it. My own sweet, warm milk. Going to waste. My long, deep-familiar pains are fading too. My belly flattens by the day, it feels like a piece of tripe. There'll be nothing to get hold of before long.

The mornings are hardest. I open my eyes, stare at the blankness of the pillow. I've retched into my hand, some mornings. I got up and tidied the house, burnt everything that wouldn't wash out. I didn't open the door to the little room, or the suitcase under the bed, but I sent back the mackintosh sheets. Ordered a new mattress, even. Now I lie deep in the pillow, one ear open.

Crying is Baby's only language and the mother must learn to recognise what he means by the different kinds of sounds. The three principal kinds are . . .

'You're still alive, you know. Have you thought of that? You could have died, Lettie. How would you like that?'

I lie very still. I would. I would like that. Anything but this.

'Be grateful for what you've got.'

'I know, Tommy, I know.'

'Well, then.'

'Well, then. I'm ever so grateful.'

Tommy puts on a bright smile. Now he'll tell me what the hens have been up to. He'll do that funny walk of Nancy's, when she knows you've got food behind your back. I'll want to sit up then. I'll start to say something, and then have to stop.

'Speak to me, Lettie. I'm not angry. Lettie? Don't drive me crazy, I'm talking to you, chatting like a human being, for crying out loud.'

He goes to the door. Sighs. 'Come down, Lettie. I'll fill the trays. All you need to do is sprinkle the seeds. You can do that, can't you?'

'Tommy?'

I've tried to remember. That would be something, at least. I lie quite still, but it doesn't come. None of it, after Jean's kitchen, and the bedstead and letting go of her hand. I like the wooziness, but it does make everything foggy.

'Tommy, where's our baby?'

He stands, shoulders stooped, as though the roof has fallen on him too. Oh for that bright smile again, full of want.

Oh, to tell him all my wants. Did he see our baby? Hold it? Was it a boy? A girl?

'Don't.' He thinks I can't see him if he can't see me. 'I swear, Lettie. Don't ask.'

18th December

The village men are out ploughing. Tommy's talking to them through the hedge; never mind what the Dells think, he never could stay away from horses. Rain cleared the fog before noon today and I can see our winter cabbage, still not lifted. The thick, dark outer leaves have fallen back, leaving their pale hearts open to the sky.

He told me in the end. I didn't have to ask again. He explained, laboriously, why it couldn't be the churchyard. Stillborn. Unconsecrated ground.

'Under one of your mulberries. We thought—' He looked hopeful. *She's showing an interest.*

They dug a hole and they laid it to rest, covered it with turf. Adam would have known how deep to make the hole, to stop the foxes digging. Shown Tommy how to tread the earth down, with their heavy boots.

Every morning I drag myself over to the window. Sometimes I'm too early, there's too much mist. I think I've worked out which tree it is. I can't ask him, about anything. They leave me alone up here for hours and hours. Tommy must still be sleeping on the settee. I go through Baby's suit-case. Hold every little garment. Fold each one away again.

Pick up the rattle and put it down before I hear the rustle inside. *Another Baby will come along.*

*

Jean goes outside. On and off all day she's out there in her dungarees. Striding about. Just a shape, in the glasshouse, hard to tell her apart from Adam already, but I know. You'd think those precious plants could manage without her. He could take over for a bit. Years, they've waited, the Dells, but look at them, business as usual.

Next time I see her, she's carrying a basket down the straight and narrow. If she has her baby in that basket I'm not sure that's a good idea. It's still very cold out there, however sunny the sunshine is. Much better to wrap the baby in a shawl, tie it on; she did her work perfectly well like that before it was born. She's carrying that basket with just one arm, not even holding it close to her body. She sets it down, on the cold, bare earth. Turns her back and gets on with her work.

I don't understand. It's far too cold to leave a tray of seedlings outside, let alone a baby, a tiny little new baby like that. I opened the window just to check and there's a nasty wind you wouldn't expect. Exactly the sort of thing *Motherhood* advises against. Adam's nowhere to be seen. I was going to call out. I went down to open the door to say something. Only she picked up the basket and went into the glasshouse and slid the door shut.

'You're up, then?' Tommy's in the scullery, rinsing out a cup.

It should be warmer in there. At least she's shut the door. She can see what the temperature must be perfectly well, the thermometer's hung on the middle strut so you can see it from anywhere. No condensation, though. I don't think their boiler must work as well as ours, it's older, for a start. Adam should take a look at it.

'Is their boiler broken?'

He leans heavily on the rim of the sink.

*

After dinner she's out again, with a spade and a pail this time. She looks tired. She'll go back for the basket, surely. Anything might happen. Adam's down by the canes. The basket could fall off the table. The cat might sit on it. The baby might cry and cry and cry, and would she hear? The other morning her baby cried ever such a long time, and did she come? I was halfway down the stairs, I was holding on to the walls, I'd have gone round in my nightie and not cared, only Adam came hurrying up the straight and narrow. All he did was stand outside and yell for Jean. And now look, she's gone and dumped the baby's basket on that bale it could easily fall off and she's nosing about the place like one of Adam's sows, not a thought in her head.

Anyone would think she hadn't had a baby.

Hours of it, that creaking, buzzing, coughing sawmill wail. It drills right into me. On and off, all night, night after night. Loops and spurts and creels. Sheets of crying, buffeting walls of it. Tommy sleeps through it but I'm awake even before it starts and then I can't get back to sleep. And Adam's voice, rising and falling; nothing from Jean.

When Baby cries, mother should go quickly over the possible causes . . . She should make sure that he is not in pain or ill . . . If he is not thirsty, or if it is not time to feed him, she should just let him cry for a little while.

He will probably stop if no fuss is made of him.

This morning, when their latch went, and Jean came out, it was to tether that nanny goat of hers. I watched her duck into the shelter and tug it in after her. Even with the rain I could tell she was in a bit of a state but I wasn't going to feel sorry for her. Leaving that poor baby on its own again. I put my forehead to the cool glass. She scurried back up the path, holding a can covered with a cloth, careful as, and the crying stopped, for a bit.

It must be after midnight, but it's not the foxes. It's never the foxes. She's out there in the dark, striding up and down the glasshouse, swinging that basket. That's her voice, quavering up and down the aisle. That's her baby's cry, straining through the glass. I walk with her. My feet could be glass bottles for all the feeling left in them. She needs to hold that baby close, between her breasts, like this. Rock baby, up and down, like this, in time with my warm, beating heart. That's it. And slower, slower. A pain cleaves down from my breasts to between my legs. My nightgown clings to my nipples, hot and wet.

'Lettie.' Tommy's voice is muffled. I stand very still.

'Stop it. Lettie. I'm warning you.'

It's as though he hears the wind blowing or the geese calling. How can that be? It's as though he doesn't believe in babies, the way other people don't believe in ghosts, or witches. I come back to bed and turn my back on him. He doesn't move or speak.

When the crying next wakes me, I feel it in my own throat, my own chest. It's right next door now, in their bedroom. And a low, choking growl, thick from Jean's throat, forcing its way through clenched teeth. She sounds like a cornered dog.

I'd forgotten all the little sounds there are inside a glass-house, the creaks and ticks and taps, the scrabble and moan of the wind. Every time I do a pot – tap out the plug, shake off the roots – I stop and listen. Just in case. Nothing. I want to press my face back into my pillow, gather this earth and stuff up my ears.

Tommy was right, though. To strip back the blanket and shout at me one more time to dress myself and pull on my boots; right to take me by the elbow and march me out here. I knew they'd be listening next door, and I was right, there they were on the doorstep, watching. He prodded me in here. I thought he'd have another go but he just stood and looked at me. He almost staggered when Adam clapped him on the back. And he took an age to sort his pedals out before they set off for the Central.

I brushed off the bench, I lined everything up, I'm careful not to scoop too much or overfill. This I know how to do. I label each tray and fold over the packet so that no seed spills out. I check the spout, clean out the rose, before I fill the can. I've only half-filled it, I'm holding it with both hands, but it's wobbling all over the place. None of it's sinking in. Water pools in smooth lozenges, hot toffee on parchment. I keep pouring till it brims over and gushes down the sides.

More pools on the bench. They spread and spread. Green fingers, black womb.

Jean's hand is huge and clammy over mine. She tries to tip the can back, but I force it up in the air with a flourish, for the very last drops. Dozens of plugs are floating adrift, their leaves battered with water and crumbed with soil. The waste of it, the pointless sacrilege, is thrilling.

'Lettie, you mustn't, please. Let me—'

With her hair scraped back like that, under one of those muslins we sewed together, her face is harsh and huge. She's been chewing on her lower lip, there's a big purple berry of a sore. She looks lost, in that big, flapping dress.

I raise both hands and wiggle my fingers. 'Take over, why not. Go on, Jean, show me how it's done.'

Jean sets the can down on the floor, steps out of a spreading puddle. 'It doesn't matter. It's probably too early. For you to be out here—'

'Too early? For me? What about you, Jean? Out here all day long, leaving that baby to cry its heart out, anyone would think you hadn't ever had a baby before. Oh, that's right, you haven't, have you?'

Her face is kneaded with pain. I have so much space in my chest I might never need to draw breath ever again. It pours out of me and it doesn't even touch the sides.

'Lettie, stop. Please stop. I've tried. I have. Please, Lettie. We need you. Please come.'

*

Baby is in my arms. My empty, empty arms. A bundle of pillowcases, ripe apricots, curd cheese, Rich Tea, everything and nothing like I've ever imagined. I tuck Baby into the crook of my left arm, but there's no time. It's tiny face is red and hard as an apple and squirming with want. Its eyelids bulge, its lips quiver at the slick and spreading patches on my bodice.

Quickly, quickly, my fingers work the last button. I lift out my left breast, hard ridged and hot and pumpkin huge, take the stalk of my nipple between my fingers and brush Baby's pale, rindy mouth. Its eyes open, unseeing, dark and deep, and its mouth unclasps, a pink-hinged purse. There is the tongue, thick and spongy. My milk seeds all over my nipple. And then Baby's tongue spoons me inside. Its mouth clamps down. Silence, and a pull, deep in my belly, that of a plant being tugged up from the ground.

Jean watches us both, down to the very last drop, until I am soft and empty and done for. Until Baby's mouth slackens and its head falls back, eyelids stilled.

'There,' I say softly.

Jean presses her fingertips to her trembling mouth and shuts her eyes. 'Yes. Baby likes that.'

She eases one hand underneath the crook of my arm to shift it, ever so slightly, as I do up my buttons. Baby breathes fast, like a bird. My other breast burns and throbs, and shooting pains come and go between my legs. My tongue has cleaved to the top of my mouth. I'm very, very thirsty.

Jean grinds the heels of both hands into her eyes. 'Thank you.'

'Yes, yes, of course.' It hurts to swallow.

Jean grimaces. She goes to the scullery, pumps as quietly as she can, stops when it squeaks. Baby and I are alone together, replete and whole. It's heavier already, I swear. Its cheeks are pinker. I feel the tug and release course through me.

Jean hands me the cup and sits down again. She flattens both hands into a mask over her face and rocks back and forth, silent and terrible. I empty the cup in one draught, but it doesn't touch the bottom of my thirst.

'Maybe if I drink more water, that's it, isn't it?'

Her voice is high and wavering. She's gazing at me the way she did that first day, craven, abject, like a kicked dog. And I wish I'd held the water in my mouth so I could spew it back in her pleading, pathetic face. Babies don't wilt silently if you ignore them, Jean. You don't leave them lying around, or carry them about like produce. They can't peck out their own food or be shut away at night. At St Clement's the nursery was two floors up and we could still hear their cries, in gusts, like the wind in the trees.

'I've never – I don't know—' I hold myself tight, impassive, and gaze down at those magical, translucent, flickering eyelids, as Jean's urge to confess unstoppers.

'Baby wouldn't feed, Lettie. I tried, I really did. Nothing came. I tried everything. You know I've been dipping my finger in the brandy? I've been so scared, Lettie. Not this, I thought, after everything, after so long, I don't know what I thought it would be like, but I never thought – And then when I saw you out here at last, I saw—' She puts her hand to her own sagging chest.

'You should have brought Baby sooner, Jean.'

Soon she will reach for Baby, and I shall have to give it back.

'Lettie,' she says. 'What are we going to do?'

We, I think. We?

I smell him before I see him. Sharp, feral and throat-thickening. Adam, streaming the stink of frosty manure on the doorstep. Jean has already put herself in front of me as I lay Baby in her basket.

'Here's Lettie, look, Ads, come to see how we're getting

on. Baby's a lot better.' Jean speaks too rapidly. 'Isn't that good?'

I see for the first time how Adam has aged. His greying hair lies in lank curls on his collar, and his chin is mildewed with spots of stubble. His eyes tighten. The room must be filled with the smell of my hot, sweet milk. It's swollen Baby's cheeks, and smoothed its eyelids. It seems to seep through Baby's skin; a sheeny bloom.

'Isn't it nice to see Lettie up and about at last?'

Adam inspects me. My nipples are hard and big as thumbs. I remember how he checked Rosie's teats, flicking them to get the milk to come. I remember how he sucked my small breasts into his mouth, one then the other, and how my nipples grew spongy and dark then too.

He clears his throat. 'Up and about at last, eh? That's good.'

Jean stays close. 'You're feeling much better, aren't you, Lettie?'

I do feel incredible, warm and sated, like I've been licked and pulled inside out. I say the first thing that comes into my head. 'Do you have a name for Baby yet?'

We'd talked about it endlessly, Jean and I, towards the end. Not one of the old varieties this time. That had always been Adam's notion, she said. No, this time she wanted Walter or Annie, after her parents. I'll wait until mine's born, I'd always say. Then I'll see.

Jean's eyes flick away, back to Adam. He nods.

'Hope,' she tells me. 'We've called her Hope.'

*

They told me Baby's name and I said but of course and that's nice and a minute later I'd forgotten it and had to wait until Adam said it again, and how it was grand to see me up

276

and about and making a start on things. Hope. I still can't seem to get it into my head.

They told me they were taking her to be baptised the very next day. Hope Elizabeth Dell. Elizabeth had been Adam's mother's name. That's nice, I told him. I hadn't known that. And Hope because no one can beat Jean when it comes to good old-fashioned sentimentality.

I stay in bed until I hear them go out the gate. They walk down the lane the other way, in the direction of the station. There's a church on the hill there, that I've never seen.

Tommy comes up in his stockinged feet. He grips the edge of the door.

'What's all that mess in the glasshouse?'

I shrug.

'You'll have to clear it up, you know. I've not the time.'

I shrug again.

'Lettie—'

'All right,' I say. 'All right.'

'Don't you all right me.'

I close my eyes.

'Lettie,' he says. 'Lettie?'

Then he goes away.

Jean comes up to check on me when they get back. She's pressed that apple dress. I can smell the scorch. Pulled it in with one of Adam's belts, given herself a waist of sorts. Screwed into her earlobes are ruby-red, glass teardrop earrings. I never knew Jean owned earrings.

Hate flashes over me, like sheet lightning. And I tell her I'm fine, I'm just very tired, please leave me alone. Because I am, up about the house now, if not outside, same as before, when Baby was still in my belly. But now I know. My belly is empty, my breasts are weeping again, because I know inside and out what it is to hold a baby and the relief of Baby's mouth; when I sit down the ghost of my baby is there in my lap, its weight, its warmth, its scent. It stills me, utterly. I could tear my insides out. Rip my breasts off.

All night her baby cries. Hope cries. Off and on. I lie rigid, on my back. My breasts pulse with pain. I have terrible, terrible thoughts. That dark, twiggy drink she gave me to make my baby come. She never said what was in it. I never asked. I said yes, give it to me. And I drank it.

And then I remember what else I've drunk. Deliberately. Knowing what it was and what it would do. What it did. There's no one to blame but myself.

The next morning, after the boys go off to the Central, I hear her door bang open. She has her baby with her and Baby is crying again. Right under my window. She stands there an age. And then I hear her go on, into the lettuce house, and out the other end, and she comes back to the house without the baby crying and gets another basket, full of washing, and starts to peg out. All the while I hear her baby alone and wailing in the lettuce house. She pegs ever such a long time, hidden by the big sheet. Then she goes back into the cucumber house and comes out with the crying baby in the basket, and this time she looks up to make sure I can see them both from the bedroom window.

Later, when I go into the scullery with the empty cocoa cups, I see a lamp in the lettuce house. I open the door a crack. Baby is keening. Hope. On and on, like she's been crying all her life. Luckily Tommy is already upstairs. I go out there and shut the door and I take the stool a little way from the lamp, behind one of the struts, so no one can see. Baby doesn't latch on straight away. Jean comes to stand in her doorway. I manage it. She stands there a while anyway. Then she leaves me to it.

7ᵗʰ January

I bring Baby in our own glasshouse now, when it's at its warmest, before I get tea on. It's good to sit down. There's no one to see us. My breasts are soft and ample and my bleeding's almost gone, just a rusty stain. Night times must be tricky. I don't know what she does then. I don't hear Baby cry much; maybe my one big feed is enough. I barely see her. I tell myself it's not Jean's fault she's too old and has no milk. Anyway, I'm not doing it for her. I'm doing it for Baby. For Hope. I don't know why I can't be happy.

No, I am happy. Balanced on the potting-bench stool with a crick in my neck and my arms aching and my feet going numb. This I can do. This I am good at. Baby plugs away like a pit pump and I keep refilling. Full to the brim, a magic porridge pot. At first, when it still hurt quite badly, all sorts would go through my head: useless rubbish like did my mother get to do this, they told me she went away after I was born, but I'd never thought to ask if she'd fed me. Who did feed me? And how do I know how to do this and Jean doesn't? That sort of thing. Nonsense. Now, each time Baby latches on, I could be feeding myself. It's as though a blanket of snow comes down and muffles everything.

Afterwards I have to splash my face and wrists with cold water. My eyes are huge and dark, my mouth slack. If

Tommy or Adam saw me now, they'd think I wanted them inside me. I could be sealed up down there and I wouldn't care. This place could blow down about my ears and I wouldn't blink.

19ᵗʰ February

'Goodness, is that Mrs Dell?'

It's a long time since I've heard a wireless voice like that. Making allowances but judging all the same. She's a brisk, stocky woman, and she doesn't wait for an answer, walks right in. Shuts the door behind her. Hangs her sopping mackintosh on Tommy's hook.

'You gave me quite the shock, Mrs Dell, sitting there in the dark.'

I'd drawn all the curtains before I sat down. Over-cautious perhaps: Tommy and Adam are long gone. But it's bitter cold out, and there's a plug delivery due at three, so it's our first time in the house. Jean went down to the orchard, I'd been turning the wash on the horse, and there it came: that thin trickle of sound, coming and going and almost lost in the rain. High, insistent, alone. Calling.

Mrs Dell indeed. But why not. After all, Jean's not here to correct her.

I say, in my dainty voice. 'I'm just feeding Baby.'

Unchastened, she struggles out of her gloves. 'Never mind me. Miss Deering. Lawford Hall. I do think you people should have been provided with porches. Where do you keep your galoshes? And no front door. Where's your through draught?'

Miss Deering wafts face powder and setting lotion as she leans over me to tug back the curtains. I tuck myself in, best I can. My throat's terribly dry. I always forget to fetch myself water. When she unlatches the window, a cool green breeze washes the back of my neck. With it, the soft percussion of drizzle on the new growth.

The rain may have done that hat no favours, but she has a rosy flush on her poreless skin, and sound, even teeth. She beams down at me, the picture of trusting, respectable health. I smile back. She's seen me now. She must have no idea what Mrs Dell really looks like.

Miss Deering straightens up, discreetly tugging down the skirt of her navy gabardine suit. When she stands back to look at Baby, pride floods through me. I adjust Baby's bonnet and gown. How she's grown, these few weeks. Look at those cheeks, plump and pearly pink. Baby smiles before she can even see me, you know. My breasts prickle when she's near. See her curl those tiny fingers around mine, even as she sleeps. She won't let go, not for anything.

'Baby *is* a dream boat, I must say.'

I adjust Baby's bonnet to show off the fine, girlish curves of her brow and cheek. 'She's called Hope.'

'Yes, I know.' Miss Deering slips a bag off her shoulder, a shiny brown leather bag, big as a doctor's but with longer straps, and sets it down on the table. There's mud, in splatters on the back of her sturdy calves. A nasty run in the stocking too. A bicycling lady, then. With documents. Do-gooders like this never used to make it over the doorstep. I've gone soft. Dangerously soft.

'Now, Holding 95, you weren't actually scheduled until April. However, since the vicar announced your good news, Mrs Dell—'

Miss Deering has a penetrating voice. Baby flings up a

splayed fist, bat, bat, over my heart. Miss Deering averts her eyes and fiddles with her papers. Miss Deering could well be more nervous than me, I realise, for all her posh talk. The same age. She sits up straighter.

'I represent the Women's Support and Advisory Sub-Committee of the Foxash Estate Welfare Committee, set up by Mrs Hodges – the doctor's wife, you know – specifically for our women settlers.'

Gratitude. Mute, docile gratitude. Until I know what she's about. 'Pleased to meet you, Miss Deering. Very kind, I'm sure.'

'Don't mention it. You see, we ladies think you settler wives have been out here for far too many years, on your own. Naturally, we must put the men first. But we women *do* need company and colour, don't we? There should be no shame in admitting it.'

'Yes,' I say. 'No.' What I want to say is, look, this is new. You've woken her up. She's trying to stand right up on her toes. Admire her, and then please, please go away.

'Consequently, we are planning a friendly reception for you all. And then a weekly social club, once we have a venue. What is really needed, of course, is a village hall. A focus for estate life. We hope to convert one of the billeting huts. We are also making arrangements for you to borrow books from the County Council Branch Library. Well-wishers have made donations, and we are collecting for a wireless in the first instance. You Special Area people do like a good dance, don't you?'

Miss Deering has clearly delivered this speech many times before. Baby puddles at my thighs with her hard little goat feet. Dance, little baby, dance. Miss Deering stares down at her papers.

I say: 'That sounds marvellous.'

'And now perhaps,' Miss Deering says, a little primly, 'you might put Baby down now. If you start to play with Baby, he will soon expect to be fussed over after each feed. How are you going to manage to get your work done, if you have to spend extra time with a little one who refuses to sleep?'

Baby launches her own silent, slurry protest. Her bottom swells, hot and soft as a fresh boiled pudding. Miss Deering crosses her ankles and grows quite pink.

'And now you appear to have missed the moment to put Baby on the pot, Mrs Dell. We can't say it to you people often enough: if you don't begin in the right way now, you will find you have many mistakes to undo later on.'

Now she's looking around for a pot. She'll clock the wireless. I filch a tea towel from the hob rail to tuck under Baby's bottom and unpin the soiled napkin, breathe in her warm cake-batter fug.

Miss Deering barricades herself behind her bag. She's trying not to look at the soggy napkin, balanced on the arm of my chair.

'I see you've no pram, Mrs Dell. We must remedy that. The only reason for keeping a healthy baby indoors should be an east wind. Or fog.'

I look at her eyes, round and staring and eager, keen to be of assistance. Her pudgy hands stroke the flank of her bag, nestled between her sturdy knees and her high young breasts. She would pluck Baby out of my arms if she could. And then: oh God, not her too? Dreaming of her own little dancing man.

'Once you are done with the napkin, you should not take Baby up again. He will like this, and next time when he awakes he will cry *in order to* be taken up.'

'Baby's not crying now.' I say. 'Baby never cries when—'

The outside door bangs open. Jean, huge and streaming wet in her mackintosh. 'Lettie!' she shouts. 'Lettie!'

In two strides she is in the room with us. Her face is pale with rain, her mouth an awful gash. When she sees Miss Deering, I watch Jean's face soften and her body shrink, until she is a sweet, harmless, bumbling country thing again, wrinkled and shy and unassuming. She tugs off her hat, spraying raindrops.

'Ah, welcome! You're from the Welfare Committee, aren't you? I saw your bicycle out there. Do forgive me—'

I've never seen her act this wee timorous beastie with anyone else before. Miss Deering's is the first new face to appear since mine, all those months ago. We must share the same instinct: to smile and appease a stranger, at least until we can get the measure of them. But it's clear Jean knows who this woman is, and where she is from. She is afraid of her. And angry.

Miss Deering gets to her feet, tugs down her skirt again. Her face is quite pink. She is looking at Jean the same way I did, all those months ago: taking in her mannish shoulders, her matted hair, her leathery cheeks. When Jean thrusts out her hand, it's clear it's only breeding makes Miss Deering proffer her own too.

'You're Mrs Dell?'

Jean shakes her hand vigorously, smiling hard. 'Glad to see my neighbour has been entertaining you. Thanks ever so, Lettie, for watching Baby.'

'Oh, you're welcome. I've just changed her.'

Jean smiles on at Miss Deering, reaches out blindly to take Baby from me. Her fingers fumble through the folds of the shawl and close about mine. One quick, reassuring squeeze, so brief I might have imagined it.

*

She does us proud, Miss Deering, in the end. She sits back down and keeps right on talking. On and on and on, sucking the fresh air out of the room until Jean and I are stupefied by politeness. *Do, do forgive me. Of course, it's right here, Mrs Dell is Holding 95. Mrs Radley is Holding 94. Entirely my mistake, terrible handwriting, how foolish.* She is our eternal friend.

But what might Miss Deering write in her notes, once she's away? Report back to the reverend, the doctor's wife, Mr Bridgewater, about the strange set-up down the end of the lane? She knows perfectly well that if Jean hadn't come in when she did, I'd have let her go away thinking I was Mrs Dell.

We follow her out, to her bicycle propped by the gate. The rain is evaporating, the geese are racketing about, and the baby birds are cheeping their heads off in the bushes.

'Oh, I am a silly!' She struggles to turn herself and her bicycle around at the same time. 'I forgot the very best news. The Association has decided that you women really should have one whole day a year away from the estate. And so we have arranged an outing for you. You people love a charabanc, don't you? We thought Clacton. At Whitsun. Sea air and sunshine, just the thing.'

She turns her best charitable smile on me. 'Mrs Radley, you must accompany your friend, if only for her sake. She will appreciate the help with her baby. It will be good practice. I doubt you will have your hands free for long, Mrs Radley.' She titters politely.

'Oh, yes,' I say. Jean shifts Hope in her arms, as though she's suddenly much heavier.

Miss Deering sets her sights on the long, rutted lane ahead. 'Marvellous, simply marvellous. I shall rest easier in my bed tonight knowing I have brightened your day a little. And look, there we are, a patch of blue sky at last!'

*

Jean never said a word after Miss Deering left. She took Hope straight back to hers and shut the door. Baby will be all right now for a bit, anyway, feed-wise. And Jean did squeeze my hand. It's the shock, probably. I'd gone too far, bringing Baby into the house. Of course it's going to look strange, to outsiders. To the Association.

Only those were the boys' bikes just now, crashing down any old how outside the cucumber house; their boots, heavy and quick on the path. They must have passed Miss Deering of Lawford Hall on the lane. Raised their hats and brought her to a wobbling halt, no doubt. Exchanged words. It's the three of them I can hear, Adam and Tommy and Jean, their voiced raised, back together round Jean's kitchen table.

I have to sit myself down. And then I can't get up again. The room is fugged with milk still and the scent of Baby's dirty napkin. I should tidy myself up. Splash my face at least. But here is Jean, back already. Her eyes are wide and staring and she keeps wringing her hands. Adam and Tommy crowd in behind her.

'Sent home early today.' Jean is out of breath. 'There's an audit.'

She folds and unfolds her arms. Tommy sits himself down at the table, dazed, as though he's been hit in the side of the head.

Adam has the basket. Adam has Baby. 'This has got to stop, you two, do you hear?'

His voice is pure steel. I try, later, to remember if I'd ever known Adam angry before. He says it again, louder. I will

Jean to look at me. She's in tears too. Adam's tirade slices through the air. We are disgusting, Jean and I. Unnatural.

'Unnatural!' Jean bursts out, in a sort of squeal.

He holds the handle tight and close against his chest, with both hands, the way Miss Deering held her bag. He's not shaved for a while, and his five o'clock stands out like filings. Jean hangs her head.

Adam elbows her aside. 'And you, Radley,' he says to Tommy. 'You want to get your wife under control.'

Tommy is pale. He runs his thumb across the corner of the almanac, riffling the pages. Jean mumbles something about the nanny goat and Adam wheels abruptly around.

'No!' The windows rattle. 'No! We get it weaned!'

Baby doesn't stir, although Adam is holding her basket close up to his booming mouth. She's fed, she's warm and dry, and she's fast, fast asleep.

Slow and loud, I say: 'Your baby would be dead, Adam, if it wasn't for me. We've enough dead babies around here. We don't need another one.'

My ears ring. There's more, much more. I can feel it rising up inside me.

Adam stares, open-mouthed. He gives Tommy a furious look and Tommy gets to his feet. Adam takes Jean by the elbow and propels her out the door. And later, I think: I should have walked out after them. Headed round the corner and through the gate and then down the lane, fast as I could go. Found that Miss Deering and told her what sort of mother Hope really has. What sort of father.

Once the Dells are outside, I turn to face Tommy. Always safer, to keep him in sight. He takes my arm and drags me up to the small room and kicks the doors shut behind him on the way, loud enough to be heard. Pushes me so I'm hunkered down under the windowsill, where no one will see, or hear us. There's a little moment when he's struggling to straddle my knees and I see that fleeting look, bewildered, hopeless.

Sorry. I say. *Sorry sorry sorry*. Although I know it won't help. The ghost of Baby is between us. Tommy knows it too. *We've enough dead babies around here*. He sniffs, and wipes his nose, and takes his hands from about my throat. But he tells me proper.

Stay away from Hope.

And Never. Ever. Talk to the Dells like that again. Never.

*

It wasn't too bad. It was over before I knew it, and no marks. I was out of line. Tommy had to say and do something, even if just to keep face with Adam. And we do have to live together, get along. The four of us, out here all alone. You can't go round saying stuff like that and not expect people to take offence.

Afterwards, though. Afterwards.

I can't stop thinking about what tumbled out of Miss Deering's mouth when I handed Baby back to Jean and was sat there, folding my arms over the damp, clinging patch on my blouse.

You're not the mother, then?

For all her manners, she couldn't keep a note of accusation out of her voice; seeing as I'd gulled her, led her on, although I can't see how she ever gave me much of a chance to say otherwise. I shook my head and smiled an apology.

I couldn't argue with her. Not then. But, if she'd known the truth, if I'd told her then about my own baby, what could she have said? What would she have written in her notes then? Mrs Letticia Radley has had her own baby too. *It never drew breath*. She has a baby, a baby she can't let herself think about, that still exists, down there in that place beneath the mulberry tree she can't think about either, let alone go and see. Lettie Radley never saw her baby, or held it, or named it, she doesn't even know if it was a boy or a girl; it came out dead: how could she be its mother? She once had another baby too. One that was never born.

You're not the mother. How can I be, without a baby to mother.

There is a name for every loss but this. I've been an orphan all my life. I've been a wife four years, and if Tommy were to die, I'd be his widow. Lose your parents, lose your husband, you still exist; there's still a name you can be called. But what can you call a mother who has lost her baby?

*

That very evening, Adam has Tommy make up a bowl of pobbles. Pobbles wasn't anything we'd ever had at St Clement's. It's what mothers make up for their own babies. His ma had made it for his sisters, then Monica made it for him. And you're to come with me, Tommy says, slowly tearing the buttered bread into bits and dropping it in the hot milk. This is his punishment as much as mine and Jean's.

There is Jean sitting silent at the table, with Hope on her lap. We are all to watch. Tommy and I stand, our backs to the dresser. Adam's grown a bit of a moustache over the winter, and when he blows on the loaded spoon to cool it, bits of yellowy crud get stuck in the longer hairs, that are coming out a foxy red. He pokes his tongue out between his thick, purply lips, and I want to gag.

See, he says, furious to his core still, when she gulps it down hungrily. That's what she needs. How he gazes at her, the way he used to gaze at Jean. Can he feel it all the way down there, as I do? Hope is everything to him.

Solemnly, he weighs her in the produce scales and writes down the result in one of his little books. Jean has to feed her the same amount every day. Hope's to put on seven ounces a week. And Jean's to bring her nowhere near me.

'You remember Beatie Hix?' Adam says.

'You remember. Beatie Hix. Nobody wouldn't go with her husband.' Jean shakes her head.

'Her husband? The cripple carpenter?' Adam titters. 'Hix could never get away with anything, poor devil. You know why, Tom?'

Adam takes up a pair of spoons and walks them across the tabletop like stilts, dragging the right behind, thump, thump, thump. It leaves a trail of dints. 'We always know where Lettie's been, don't we? So you keep her well away from our Hope, you hear.' Jean covers her face.

She obeys his instructions to the letter. She stays away from me, she doesn't speak to me, or even look at me. She carries Hope out under her arm and plonks her down on the path at arm's length and then sets to work. Hope can look after herself. Before long Hope's over on her belly, I don't know how, and she'll stay like that, although she grunts and groans, and if Jean sees her and does put her on her back she rolls over again. When Hope sees a bird or a worm or something, she stops moving altogether and watches it, like the cats do. She pushes her bottom into the air but she doesn't get far because she can't get her chest off the ground. Her face is in the dirt and she grumbles a lot and sometimes she cries. You can't leave a baby to scrabble in the dirt like that. Jean should put something under her chest to lift her face up, and then she could get her arms out at least.

How hard Hope works to get someone to notice her. To talk to her and pick her up and play with her. I itch to get out that rattle Adam made and take it to her, just to see her clasp it in her hand. At least she'd have that.

Jean never forgets about Hope, though. She may not pay her any attention, but she is never parted from her, not for a moment, whether Adam's about or not. I can be safely in the glasshouse, and Jean just has to catch me glancing in their direction, and the next time I look they've both of them vanished.

I try to stick to the cinder path. I try not to walk on the soil or look behind myself to see what marks I've left. What a mess I've made. Nothing's going right. I'm still not done setting out the Dutch lights – I keep dropping my end and breaking the glass. I can't get rotations straight: Tommy had to hoe up a whole row last week. I forget to water, or I plant too deep or too shallow, I don't know. Trays of plugs have had to go on the bonfire because I've not got round to planting them; dozens more I've had to rake out because they wilted and turned to slime. The other day I let the bonfire go out. He had to be out there for hours to catch up. He's not said anything. He's not come near me. I don't think he trusts himself. I tell him all the time I'm sorry, about the bonfire, that the beans were where the onion should be, and all the rest of it. Feeding Hope. Baby. I'm sorry about all of it, everything. *Sorry sorry sorry.*

Tommy, I think, oh Tommy. He raises his chin and stares me out. I won't let him see me cry.

Today was their last day at the Central until the end of the season. I knew Adam wouldn't be taking Tommy down the Fox to celebrate tonight. They've had to put in an extra week or two pruning the orchards there on account of this weather, so we're doubly behind. It's not just they've to be up first thing, to catch up to where we should be by now. It's that he'd not leave Jean and me alone this year, with Hope. But I didn't expect him to walk straight in and pull out a chair when I'm about to dish up.

He gathers up Tommy's chit tins from the dresser, pushes back a setting and empties them out. The table's a fluttering patchwork of pink and blue. He hands Tommy the almanac. Tommy runs his hands through his hair, once, twice, his face impassive. Then he cracks open the almanac and props it up against the butter dish. At a nod from Adam, he reaches behind me to switch on the wireless.

I'm walking through clover, a young man croons, *a romancing rover* . . . The thin trail of the young man's voice, jaunty and fervent, propels me to the table. Tonight, it's about Tommy. I may as well not be here. I set down our plates on the table-cloth of chits. Never mind grease spots. It's curious, really, how little I care about the housekeeping these days. How little I care about anything worth caring about.

Tommy hands back the plates. 'Leave that for now. We'll be wanting a fresh pot.'

Back home it was a wife's job, handling the accounts. I wasn't bad at it. But I wasn't a bit sorry to leave it behind, the juggling, the endless nagging worry. Association keeps track of the big stuff, Co-op bills go straight on our account, and Tommy has a little red book that he writes everything else in, on a string in his shed. I've not handled as much as a ha'penny since Tommy's off-sales last summer. Adam's just throwing his weight around. Association gave Tommy the Best Newcomer medal, for heaven's sake. I put the hot pot in the top oven and take myself off to get in the washing.

By the time I go back through, the chits are back in their tins. Tommy is chewing on his lip. Adam finishes totting up columns on a scrap of paper and hands it to him. Tommy barely looks at it before folding it in two and stuffing it in his trouser pocket. His neck reddens slowly.

'Pass us those tabs, Tom.'

Adam blows a perfect smoke ring. Tommy's taught him that. He fixes his eyes on me and starts to whistle, out of time with the jolly fellow who's taken over on the wireless: *'Oh I do like to stroll along the prom, prom, prom—'*

I've tried to imagine myself, stepping out of Miss Deering's charabanc, holding on tight to my hat. The beaches where we scratted sea coal were as grey as the streets and twice as windy. Down south, the sand is a bright custard yellow. And the sea is royal blue, with meringue-white waves. I saw those Sunshine Coast posters, on the mainline: those sands, huge and open and spacious. With maybe a game of cricket, a kite, a woman in a bathing suit, under a parasol.

I've seen the newsreels too. Proms and piers get choked with people. Trippers clog up the steps and they swarm over the empty sands to claim their own little patch of heaven, and they sit there shoulder to shoulder, all baskets and spades. There are children everywhere, digging holes and waving flags and shrieking. And babies, hot, red squalling babies.

I refill the teapot, one hand supporting its warm, heavy bottom. When I tug the cosy back on, the rim is sopping wet. I reckon Whitsun can't come soon enough for Adam. He'd like me to get on that charabanc and never come back. He watches out for me, scans the holding, but these days it's to keep me at bay.

Adam should be heading back before long in any case. Hope's due her evening feed. He's taken to weighing her every night beforehand as well; I've seen him through the window, on my way back from the chickens. Jean helps him undress Hope and slip her into the cold metal scoop they use for the soft fruit. Hope cries then, all right. A squalling, desperate punnet.

Adam stands up and drops his tab in his cup. It sizzles. Tommy drums his fingertips against the side of his cup. Adam reaches in front of Tommy and turns the wireless right up, just as the brass section begins to blare. 'Night, all.'

'Night, Adam.' He waits until Adam's out the door and then he snaps off the wireless, but he doesn't turn back to the table. He sits there hunched, face averted, as though he's been dealt a blow.

There's nothing wrong with his chits, is there. Adam has no right to go through them. He's not helping Tommy out, he's punishing him for what I did. I watch Tommy sink back into himself, into his silence. *I've done this*, I think. *And now I'm losing him too.*

The very next day, two men come for the wireless. And another two arrive not long after, in a bigger van, for the three-piece, the standard lamp and the sewing machine. There's thick, low cloud and a gusty wind: the fringe on the lampshade comes away as the men carry it through the gate, flapping like a scrawny wing.

I go to show Tommy the pieces of paper, but he shakes his head and turns away. He watches proceedings from inside the cucumber house. Only as the van lumbers up the lane does he venture out. He keeps his hands clasped at his back till it's out of sight. Then he leans heavily on the gate and lights up.

'I told them straight,' he says, when he hears me behind him on the path. 'Sideboard's stopping here.'

This is the first time he's opened his mouth since Adam left last night. It might be the first time we've stood out front, together, Tommy and me, with nothing but the lane for company. No one to see us, no one to hear.

'Well, that's something, isn't it?'

Tommy turns to look at me. 'We'll have that wireless back soon enough, don't you doubt it.'

He comes to stand next to me, in the lee of the house.

He rubs his hand up and down the rough brick, looks up and down the path.

'Then we're all right, Tommy?'

I can't keep the question out of my voice. Wireless, three-piece, standard lamp, sewing machine. All gone. I don't care a whit about any of it. Not any more. They can take the lot. I'd wrap myself in a clippy mat and sleep on the floor. But something's gone badly wrong.

'It's me signed the contract, not you.'

He brushes past, heading for the sanctuary of the cucumber house. Inside, the air has the dry, acrid stink of used-up compost. The hotbeds are dry and cracked. The untethered remains of vines hang overhead on sagging ties. The light's dim and watery, through the greening growths on the roof panes. I follow him down to the far end, where there's a scattering of tab ends at the corner of the hot bed, like someone's emptied out an ashtray. Or stood there smoking, day after day, letting time and money slip through his fingers.

Tommy lights another tab. He picks at stray tendrils and reattaches them to the wires, as though they might start climbing again. His fingers pause and stretch, like a cat flexing its claws. A gust of wind buffets the cucumber house and sets the panes rattling, and the tendrils he's just attached to the wires loosen and sag.

I am very tired. There is nowhere to sit. All I want is to be back indoors, listening out for Hope. I can't miss her cry. Can't think beyond her next feed.

'Oh, we're all right, are we?' he burst out, high and cruel. 'I tell you what, Lettie. Look at you. You're not all right, are you? Nothing like.'

I have magnified his rage, just by being here, the way a pane of glass focuses the power of the sun on one small patch of grass.

'I know, Tommy, I know. I'm going to really try now. You'll see. I am trying. I am sorry. Truly.'

'Pfft.'

I know better than to touch him. I never want to touch him again. 'All right?' The weariness in my voice ignites him again.

'You need to pull yourself together, Lettie, I mean it. If we don't catch up, if those plugs aren't in, we haven't a hope in hell of getting that lot back.'

That's Hope's thin wail already.

'Lettie!'

'Oh, I will, I promise, Tommy. I'm all right, really I am.'

I'm rinsing out the cups for our cocoa, in a scullery that is cramped and chill after the fug of the kitchen and the echoing, empty space there is in there now. I've turned the table about to take advantage, and moved the rugs to cover the rips in the lino. No amount of India rubber will shift the hulking shadow of the wireless engrimed in the wallpaper.

Down in the dim orchard, Adam is moving back and forth with a barrow under the glowing white balls of blossom. Tommy's tried to bring ours on with a good dosing of the Bordeaux treatment, he's turned what blossom there is blue as forget-me-not. Last season he sprayed so much of the stuff on the tomato, the leaves turned blue.

All through dinner and tea I've kept cheerful and encouraging. We've had a week or so of basking warmth: washing left out night after night and come to no harm. This morning's wind blew itself out before noon and the sky has been cloudless, the waning moon has risen sharp and clear. We've time, still, to get the cucumber up and running. Catch up on the trenching and lifting, and the plugs. Maybe tomorrow, I'll take a look at those chits myself, when I've more of a head. Maybe it's been good, to be thinking about something other than Baby.

Tommy comes through and peers over my shoulder. He was in the cucumber house all afternoon, ripping down the dead vines, digging out the beds. That's a good sign, surely. He opens the back door and looks out. A wave of dense cold air flows inside before he shuts it again and goes back to the kitchen.

'Where's that cocoa?'

I set his cup down at his elbow. 'Tommy? I'll take mine up, if you don't mind.'

He nods, and reaches for his tabs.

Sometime in the night I wake, smelling smoke. Tommy's side of the bed is cold. I go to the window and see all three of them down in the orchard, fuzzy silhouettes with barrows and rakes, and three low, red fires. I hold a lamp to the thermometer in the scullery. Twenty-five degrees at most. When I sit down on the doorstep to tug on my boots, my fingertips grow numb instantly. Dew has frozen on the grass in tiny spurs.

Tommy shouts and waves me away. I'm to get back to the house right now and fill the coal scuttle. Adam yells no, I'm to take over tending the fires, they need to siphon oil from the glasshouse tanks. Jean starts to drag over another incinerator. We have to warm the air before the frost rises and takes the blossom. We have to keep the air as warm as we can until dawn comes. Because if we lose the blossom, we lose the crop.

Now we have seven fires to their eleven. They snap fitfully at the dense air. Smoke has thickened around us like mist, in choking layers. Adam keeps barking orders at Tommy. Our trees are younger and smaller, we have far less blossom, and it's closer to the ground, and lower down the slope, where it's coldest. Rather than build more fires, waste more fuel, Adam wants to cut away the hedge our side, to let the frost flow out into the field. Tommy covers his face with his hands and coughs and coughs.

We need tea towels to fasten over our faces. Damp handkerchiefs. I won't be a minute, I say. Get that bloody coal, Tommy shouts hoarsely. Near the house the air clears, and I can see the Dells have left their door open a couple of inches. And a lamp burning. Back in the orchards, a low wad of smoke has settled. Beneath it, only patches of orange flame, flickering quietly.

I push open the Dells' door. Their kitchen table is stacked high with dirty dishes, seed packets, boxes, basket-work jugs from the Fox that should have gone back long ago. No, those are their corn dollies, propped up in a circle. And that's Baby's basket, tucked in the middle.

This can't be where Baby sleeps. The Dells must have reckoned she'd be better off in here, away from the smoke and the frost. They'll have set her on the table so they can see her, and the dollies must be to distract her if she wakes up, or to stop her getting out. They left the door ajar in case she cries. But they won't be able to see her, or hear her, from down there. It's freezing cold, and there are foxes about.

I walk up to the table. There she is. Sitting straight up, sturdy and pink. Can she sit up by herself now? And she looks twice the size. I gaze at her cheeks, her arms, the creases at her wrists, her tiny hands, soft and plump and rounded. No cardigan, no mittens or shawl to keep her warm; just a cream knitted bonnet tied under the chin with red ribbon and one of the smocked cambric robes we sewed. But there she is, sitting in her basket. A big, silent baby with big blue eyes, looking right back at me.

*

I shan't say anything to the Dells. Or Tommy. I shan't tell them I looked and I looked and then I picked her up and held her and breathed her in all sweet and malty. Her arms were cool as cucumbers straight from the cold store. I kissed her stubby fingers warm. One of her fingernails was peeling. She smiled at me, she did. And she gurgled. Yes. A burbling sort of sound I'd not ever heard her make before.

They wouldn't have been able to hear that, down there among the trees. I wanted to build up the fire for her, or at least tuck her in with a couple of tea towels round her shoulders. But they'd have known I'd done it and I couldn't risk that. I held her in my arms and walked her up and down and sang to her, *Raspberry, gooseberry, apple jam tart.* Just for a short time, I knew I couldn't stay any longer. I laid her down in her basket and watched as she curled herself up and put her fist to her mouth and went to sleep. And then I latched the door behind me, so she'd be safe from night creatures. The Dells would think it'd blown shut. If they even noticed.

Tommy will be awake soon, needing a cup of tea. I can't find the coal, must have left the scuttle down among the trees. Outside, the air is blue and hazy and sour with ash, but warmer than it was. The wind has got up again, from the east. Lucky it wasn't blowing last night. I let a gust catch my hankie and when it scuds to a stop several feet from their kitchen window I crouch down and fetch it.

The Dells are at their table, just the teapot between them in its blue and maroon cosy. Adam has Hope paddling on his thighs and he's holding her under the arms. He must be saying something to her because I can see that new grey beard of his wagging. Jean watches, stroking her straggly locks over her shoulder.

Adam grasps Hope by the wrists and lifts her up so her head bobs higher than his. Then he lets go quite suddenly and she drops into his lap. Jean doesn't move an inch, but her smile goes crooked and stiff. Adam catches Hope about the waist and lifts – no, throws her – back up in the air. She shrieks, and twists and turns, her little skirts puffing out like a mushroom. He does it again, and again. He's not hurting her. She's not crying. He catches her each time, and she doesn't make a sound. Jean shifts in her seat. I pluck up my handkerchief and hurry on down to the orchard.

There was a man came to St Clement's who used to take the littlest ones on his knee and bounce us up and down. He'd come into the dormitory after his hot dinner, whiskery and loud and smiling. We could shriek and giggle with him as loud as we liked and there was never anyone came to tell us off. *Ride a Cock horse, to Banbury Cross*, we'd shout, when we played it ourselves in the yard or sitting on the edge of our beds after. Even when we were quite big and our bony bottoms would bounce off each other's bony thighs.

My heart is tumbling about in my chest, like an apple tossed in a basket. Baby wanted me to come to her last night. She did. Just like she wanted me to see her now. I know, because every time Adam threw her up into the air she twisted round to see me through the glass. Every time he caught her, she twisted round just so she could see me again.

24ᵗʰ April

Soon as the sun is up proper, Adam and Tommy head down to inspect the damage. Tommy keeps stopping on the path to cough. The morning light floods my gritty eyes and I can't tell from here what has been saved. Much of the blossom has fallen in thick drifts, confetti and ash.

There it is: Hope's yelp and gurgle, loud and clear through the wall. That gurgle from last night, that's new, that's for me. I hurry back to the kitchen and tuck my chair close to the range, press my forehead to the wall, feel that joyous thrumming inside, stronger than ever. *I'm here, Baby. I close my eyes. I'm here. I'm listening.*

'Lettie? You up?'

Jean walks in. She has Hope on her hip, dressed in a royal-blue knitted jacket and matching bonnet. I sat with Jean while she trimmed that jacket with red wool. And crocheted the strings for the bonnet, and made the pom pom. I'd found her the pattern, in *Women's Weekly*.

'I've brought you something.' Jean pulls a slim brown stoppered bottle out of her pouch pocket. Hope's head swivels and I glimpse her rounded, downy cheek as she reaches out one small hand, dimples at the base of every finger, that tiny crescent of fingernail still loose.

Oh isn't this everything we had let ourselves hope for: an

305

excuse to pop round, baby on hip, to mirror and wonder, share and delight. *Hasn't she grown? Did you sleep? Thought you might want this* — Jean shifts Hope's weight on her hip so that she has to sway back round and press her face into Jean's shoulder. If I can't see you, you can't see me. But I can, and you shouldn't be here, either of you. I might dissolve with grief for all of us.

'Tommy's coughing again.' Jean's tight, anxious face makes me even more nervous.

'Yes?' I make my voice a hard, bright shield against the pain. 'Well, that'll be the smoke. And the cold. Thought you didn't have frosts this late down here, anyway.'

'It sounded bad, so I thought—'

Hope's little head is turning back and forth as we talk. I dodge her gaze and take the bottle, place it on the windowsill.

'That's kind, Jean, thank you.' I keep my back to the light.

'He'll want two doses. Morning and evening.'

She knows full well I can't have her here. But then Jean always was thick-skinned. She's not even noticed the wireless has gone.

'Right you are.'

Jean touches the back of a chair. 'Can I?'

Hope turns her gaze on me once more. And the thrumming starts up again. *Firefly.* This, then, is what it is, to have a baby in the house. This singular, shining new life, that is impossibly alert, fresh and warm. It arouses and softens and defies sense. I have to look out the window. Adam and Tommy are still way down in the orchard, squatting in the blossom.

I pour another cup of tea, keep my back turned while Jean settles Hope on her knee. As I sit down and hand Jean her cup, Hope swivels her head to watch. Her pale blue eyes are entirely round and lashless. She stares and stares. Then she arcs her back to slide off Jean's lap and lands on her bottom on the rug. Her moist little pink mouth pouts, and those marshmallow cheeks quiver.

'Oof!' I step back. 'Bumpety bump!'

Hope stares up at me. I feel weak. Those eyes. Like invisible ink. She reaches forward to clasp at the clippy rug. Her fingers close on the patch of poppy red, from our first curtains. Hope twists so she can see me again. I breathe carefully in, and out, and make myself look at Jean.

'Oof!' says Jean, too late.

Hope sways back and forth. I want to put out a hand to stop her toppling back.

Jean doesn't take any notice. She doesn't touch her tea. She glances out the window. 'It'll be turning wet from tonight, that's got to help. With the cough, I mean. And the blossom. Although, maybe tell Tom, not so much Bordeaux this season.'

'He's worried about fire blight.' His words, my mouth.

Jean nods, then bites her lip. 'But he risks the fruit russeting. Adam can always show him how to scrape the bark instead, that should do it.'

'Tommy does it the way he's been trained.'

Jean adjusts her cup in the saucer.

'And we had more blossom to start with, this season. You know, the June drop.'

'Listen, Lettie.' There's that familiar furrow between her heavy eyebrows, that frown of knowing concern. 'The second season is always the hardest. Once you're on your own, you've got to have kept enough back to get through your second hunger gap—'

Hope is swaying again. This time I put out my hand, low

enough that Jean won't see, close enough to catch her if she topples. My turn to look out the window. Jean's right about the weather, there's a faint drizzle misting the panes already. Adam and Tommy are still way down the orchard.

'And this year it's been so wet we've not been able to spread muck, or plough, or plant up. Everyone's behind. Even so, it's rushing to seed – the leek, the cauli, the broccoli, the salad – but we'll likely not cut our first lettuce until Whitsun.'

The hunger gap. She talked about that when she took me to see her strawberries. Oh so long ago. Did I know this, and I've just forgotten?

'You know the Association stop Tommy's dole money from next week, don't you? The allowance stops too.'

Had Tommy known this? Perhaps he sent the HP furniture back himself.

'And you've to start paying back your loan.'

'What loan?'

'The capital—'

'Yes, our capital—'

'You've to pay five shillings a week, Lettie.'

'Ah.'

It's been so long since I've had to think about figures it's hard to get them straight in my head.

'Five shilling?' I shrug. 'Then we're all right, aren't we?'

'Well—' Jean adjusts her cup in the saucer again. 'Adam reckons Tom'll have to ask the warden for short-term credit as well. At least until Michaelmas. If Central Office approve it, that is. And he'll have to yield at least £2 a week to keep his head above water.'

'I don't understand. We had the best first season of any Foxash newcomer. They gave him a medal, remember?'

'Yes, you outcropped everyone, even us, but Tommy's outspent everyone too, didn't you realise? Adam—'

'Adam,' I spit back, 'can keep his nose out of what doesn't concern him, if you ask me.'

The swell of resentment moves deep in my stomach. Time to go, Jean Dell. There's more where that came from.

'All right.' She bites her lip. 'All right.' She nods and pushes back her chair. 'You know we none of us have no security of tenure, don't you? We don't own this land, not really. Everyone's on three months' notice.' She flushes up. 'I don't want you to have to leave, Lettie.'

She swoops down to pick up Hope, too sudden, too fast. Hope throws up her arms in alarm and I hear the soft pat of her hand hitting the range door. Hope's face flushes crimson. Her mouth opens, but no sound comes out. Jean grabs her and sinks down on the rug, folds her deep into her lap.

I scoop a pat of butter from the dish and join her down there, where Hope's yells of distress thin the air, dim the light. Jean has her corn dolly rattle in her hand, and is nudging at Hope's huge, quivering mouth, only it's dark and moist and misshapen and there are small hairs on it, something gooey attached to one of the ribs.

'Here, here!' Jean prods the rattle right inside Hope's mouth.

Hope bites down. The thick glaze of tears in her eyes brims over. I take her wrist and I dab the butter over the hot pink skin on the back of her hand. It runs clear between her fingers and collects in the three tiny dimples at their base. And I breathe in the tang of her scalp, the hartshorn odour of her damp linen and the biscuity scurf that has settled in her creases and crevices because Jean doesn't know how to keep anything clean, and safe, not even her own baby.

Hope chews, a bit of dark fluff stuck to her upper lip like a stubborn fly.

'There.' I wipe my glistening fingers on my pinny. 'Just a minute.'

Upstairs, I kneel and rest my forehead on the cool satin edge of the eiderdown. I pull out the suitcase from under the bed and open the clasps, and I hold my breath until the lid is shut again.

The rattle is sweet and pale, its plaited ribs smooth and cool and intact. I shake it, once, twice. Now the straw has dried, the small grey pebble rattles more brightly. When she sees it, Hope's mouth opens wide. She lets her soft, mangled rattle drop. It slides off Jean's knee on to the rug. Hope reaches out. Go on, Baby. Take it in your mouth. Go on. It's clean, and crisp and fresh. It's yours.

Hope nudges the tip to her lips. Her eyes close and open again, silent and glazed.

'Lettie?'

I look up at Jean. We can both hear them, crunching back up the cinder path.

'Go on, then,' I say. 'Go.'

*

I wake myself up crying. I press my hand over my mouth, but I can't stop. Water rushes and gurgles through the down-pipes and bubbles on the ground outside. It's dropping out of the sky in gouts, in torrents.

I fight my way out of bed and make my way downstairs and retch over the sink, knees trembling, until my throat is sore and my stomach aches. I let myself think, just for a second, of Tommy's expensive little sacks of sherbety powders. It wouldn't take a moment, to sneak out through the rain and scoop a handful or two. It could hardly hurt more than this.

My fingers are trembling so hard I need both hands to take a cup off its hook. I put it down in the sink while I pump the handle, and wipe my mouth. I pick it up and hold it under the spout and I see Baby's face at the window.

Her small, luminous face. Eyes round and mouth open. Her warm breath fogs the lowest pane. I lean forward, slowly, slowly, until my breath meets hers. She reaches out a hand, white fingers splayed like petals against the glass.

I breathe lightly, but the fog of my breath keeps spreading. I pull back and watch the hazy patch shrink. I stare for a long time into the streaming, empty darkness. Then I lift the latch and open the window.

All the smells of night and wet earth and vegetation pour in, sweet and thick and piercing. The rain is louder than ever. My bare feet slip in the puddled mud and the rain sprays fresh and cool about my head and shoulders. I duck back inside to light the lamp. It brings the darkness to life. It picks out the trailing slugs as they climb the walls, it conjures the raindrops into dancing silver beads and turns the mud to soft brown velvet. But it doesn't bring Baby back.

25ᵗʰ April

I make myself wait until I can see the ashes of yesterday's fire in the grate. Then I pull on my boots and go out. The sky is heavy with cloud still. Rain has lashed away most of what's left of our blossom. Water has run off the Dells' rows across the path and down the slope into a long, brown pool that spreads out along the whole southern side of our holding, dammed by the hedge. Tommy never did dig out the ditch. Another smaller, shallower puddle laps at the doorstep. There are no footprints to be seen. I look at the scullery windowsill, beaded with rain. Inside it is level with my waist; it's even higher outside.

It was dark. I was in a state. I could have seen anything. My own reflection. She couldn't have got herself downstairs and let herself out. Let alone stood upright, or been able to reach the latch on the door. Or touch the window. Impossible.

When I come back inside, there are muddy marks on the lino. My knees go weak. I get the lamp and kneel down. The marks are too big; they must be the unsteady tracks my own feet made last night, coming in for the lamp and going out and coming back in again. But there is my cup on its side in the sink. The window, ajar. I hang the cup back on

312

its hook, but I struggle to close the latch. The frame must have swollen somehow. Then I see it.

There, on the bottom-right-hand windowpane. A small, impossible smudge, the size of a bantam egg. I touch it lightly with the tip of my own finger. It's on the outside. Splayed petal fingers. Feathery palm creases. The tiny whorls of Baby's fingertips.

*

I never was one to give up. Hope had never been something to be kept alive. I just had it. Because what else was I to do? St Clement's, Mr Roberts, Crampton's, Tommy, all the way through the lockouts, I never asked anyone for anything. Didn't sell myself short. Didn't pawn my ring. I managed. I held my tongue. I did without. *Never drew breath.* Before, I always had hope. More than Tommy, at least. And this is how I've let him down the most, these past few months. Without his firefly, he's lost and blind. All Tommy ever needed was for me to believe in him.

Well, now Baby needs me more.

I've polished every pane of every window in the house for her. Twenty, front and back, upstairs and down. Buffed so clear your hand could go straight through. Now it's dark, they are shiny and black as gelatine prints. I watch myself, waiting. Me and my clean, empty rooms. I mopped those footprints off the lino, and now that's shining too. Taking up the rugs, I found Baby's old rattle where it had rolled under the table. I have it safe for her, here in my pinny pocket.

At teatime, Tommy brought his little red book into the house for the first time. He flattened out its spine and propped it up against the butter dish. He's still going through it, page by laborious page, totting up columns in the margin of the newspaper and crossing out the totals and starting again. In the hallway, drips from his mackintosh land on wet newspaper. He coughs, tight and rasping.

'Lettie,' he calls. 'Cocoa.'

I pick up Jean's bottle and show him.

'Go on then.' He closes his eyes and lets me dose him. Two spoonfuls, or was it three? As he swallows, Tommy makes small, trustful noises. The sooner he stops coughing, the sooner he'll sleep. Perhaps there'll be something in it to help him sleep.

He lights up. Then he sits very still.

I must have been smiling straight through him, straight through the window.

He catches hold of my wrist, and for a moment I think he's going to pull me down into his lap. His arm goes rigid. 'We'll be all right, Lettie.'

For once, it sounds like it's me he's trying to convince, not himself. I nudge his shoulder with my hip for reassurance anyway, out of habit. 'Course we will.'

Anything we want, we might have.

Tommy drinks his cocoa, staring into the fire. He doesn't cough again. When he goes up, I work my way through the mending basket. I listen to him turn about, and then I listen to the rain hammer on the roof and drip off the eaves. I feed the fire.

Around midnight, the latch bumps open. I lift my head from the table just in time to see Baby crawl over the doorstep. She makes straight for me. When she reaches the rug, her gleaming white gown tangles and she sprawls flat on her face. Before she can make a sound I fold her up into my arms.

Baby is perfectly dry and warm and light. Helpless, I stare back into her violet eyes. I let myself touch my lips to her silky forehead. I press my nose against hers, its nubby softness. She takes a small, shuddering breath. I fold my fingers around hers and hold on tight. After a while I can't feel anything, and when I open my eyes Baby's not there.

26th April

All night, all the next day, I hear a sort of humming chorus, soft and steady. Every so often there's a run of higher notes, along the top, a sort of unfurling. Then a pause, and we're back to a low thrum. I keep having to look at myself in the mirror. My eyes are brighter, maybe. There is an ease behind my temples, a liquid smoothness when I blink, as though I have woken from a long, long sleep. I clean the house again, and then I go out and sweep the glasshouse too. The day takes an age to pass, although I never seem to tire. As soon as I've dosed Tommy and he's gone upstairs, I build up the fire and settle myself in with one of the rugs over my knees. In my dreams all the plants are singing at once. The green air is still and warm as a bath.

I feel a tug at my pinny. Baby is taller, standing taller than my knee. Her cheeks glisten like pearls. She's brought my fresh rattle with her this time. It's smaller than I remember, no larger than my little finger. Each time I hand it to her she throws it down in my lap and her face crumples up. I pick it up and shake it. She bats it out of my hand and gurgles. Now we have a game going. I hold the rattle up to my nose and wait for her to grab at it. I hold it over my head. I shake it. What's that noise, precious? What's that?

I cry for a long time. She is very patient. She puts her hand over mine on the rattle and pushes it towards me. Then she laughs. Because it's not hers, is it? It belongs to my baby. That's what she's come to tell me. She keeps giving it back to me because she knows it's not hers. She wants me to give it back to my baby.

*

The ground is driest close up against the base of the mulberry. I set down the lamp and prop Baby against the trunk, double over the blanket and tug her bonnet snug to her face. It's much colder down here, this close to the hedge. I start to dig. I try not to nick the roots. I can't bear the judder of the blade and the gleam of their pale, stringy insides. In the end I kneel and use the trowel. It takes a long time to make a hole anything like deep enough. I sit back, panting slightly. Above the hedge the sky is paling. Next to my mound of earth I have placed the large chunks of flint, and some smooth black pebbles, just out of her reach. Don't want Baby popping one in her mouth. Be patient, little one. I check for the rattle, safe and dry in my pinny pocket.

I dig eight or nine holes, all around the trunk. Some deeper, some shallower, all empty. It gets lighter and lighter. A blackbird has started up. I use my hands. Still there is nothing to feel, or see. I gather up the empty blanket in my arms and look about.

The sky is heavy and swimming with cloud. It is lighter than it was, but there is no sun. One after another, the holes are filling with muddy water. I leave the mounds of earth where they are. Tear up hanks of grass and wipe the trowel and the spade clean and put them back in the tool shed. As I walk up the cinder path I see my hands and arms gloved in wet dirt, sheeny as black satin. I plunge them into the overflowing water barrel, the rainwater shocking cold and soft. I splash my face, over and over, until my eyes sting and my cheeks go numb.

Tommy whistles for me. He's standing on the doorstep in long johns and bare feet. I wrap the blanket around my shoulders and arms as he strides through the dewy grass to meet me on the path.

'That blossom doesn't look too bad,' I tell him.

He sees the smears of dirt up above my elbows and on my neck. His breath comes in puffs. You can't see the holes I dug from here. The mounds of earth could be mole hills.

'Lettie.' He takes both my hands in his. Gently, he buts his forehead against mine, turns his head from side to side. 'Lettie, Lettie, Lettie.' It's that familiar voice that's just for me, that choked whisper, when he doesn't want anyone else to hear. The fog of his breath warms the air between us.

I look down at his naked toes, white with cold. They flex on the cinders as we rock together. It's just the two of us out here. I could ask him to show me. Why haven't I dared? He could show me. We could give Baby the rattle together. That would be something at least.

I pull the rattle out to show him; only it's the gummed one, the dark and misshapen and foul-smelling one Jean left behind.

Tommy steps back. 'What's that?'

He starts to cough, hard and loud. He can't stop. Finches and sparrows burst chattering from the rowan by the nettie, and the geese honk back as Tommy barks out cough after cough after cough.

From the house comes that cawing, carrying field voice of hers. 'Tommy? What's up?'

Jean stands in her open doorway. She holds Hope close on her hip. Tommy straightens up immediately. Before he can wipe his mouth on his shoulder, Jean shifts Hope to the other hip, turns quickly and goes back inside.

I have her rattle tucked safe back in my pinny pocket before the latch slams. My heart is jumping out of my chest. Because Jean heard Tommy, but then she saw me. Because she's never let me see Hope without her bonnet before. Never let me see her hair, that bright halo of hair, pale as the moon. Hair that stands out in a white-blonde puff, a full two or three inches. Each strand spun gold, impossibly pale and fine. Dandelion hair. Candyfloss hair. Hair that might glow in the dark.

Tonight Baby is sitting on the hearth rug when I raise my head from the table. She doesn't startle, or make a sound. The fire has died, there's no moon tonight, I've no candle or lamp. By rights there should be nothing but empty darkness. But here she is again, sitting up straight between my chair and the range, her fingers worming about deep in the clippy rug. Her pale eyes darken as she sees me, and her cheeks flush. Her hair stands up like thistledown. I can see every stitch in the smocking of the gown that covers her feet, every strand of hair. She is luminous.

Baby clambers up into my lap, her rattle gripped in one hand. Silently, she shifts and shunts herself into position. Her shoulder and knees and hip press into my ribs and my belly, as vivid and vigorous as when she was inside. Warmth spreads through my belly and thighs. When I lower my head to feel the tickle of her hair against my nose, she catches me round the neck with her tiny, soft fingers, and nests her head snug between my breasts, nestling herself down back where she belongs.

*

After holding Baby in my arms for so long, Tommy's head feels huge, his shoulders massive.

'Come downstairs, Tommy.'

I hold the lamp high. He rubs at his face. His hair, slicked to near invisibility by day, sticks up in pale tufts too, fuzzy with sleep. I want to laugh out loud.

'*Now*, Tommy. Come on. Be quick.'

'Downstairs?'

'Yes. Come and see.'

I leave him the lamp and feel my way back down. I know, with absolute humming certainty, that he will follow me.

At the foot of the stair all is dark. I wait for him to raise the lamp high. Light tilts up the walls and lurches out over the ceiling, spreads itself across the walls, picks out the shelves and the shapes on them, the table set for breakfast, the laden drying horse, the filled scuttle, the banked-down range, the waiting chair, the empty rug.

I cry out, I can't help myself. It would have been much easier, for him to have seen her, held her himself. But it doesn't matter, it really doesn't. I can explain.

Tommy sets the lamp down on the table. His chin sags, all stubble and creases. My poor Tommy, walking blind all this time. But he's seen that Baby's not happy with her. He's seen how she doesn't care for Baby, not really, not how she should. He knows she can't even feed Baby herself. She's too old, anyway. It's too late. Perhaps she wanted a baby so badly because a baby was the one thing she couldn't grow. Who knows? I reach out across the table for his hand. And the words birth themselves.

*

They've fooled us? He keeps repeating it. He won't listen. He won't sit down. He won't come anywhere near me. Up and down he paces, with his hands clamped to the back of his head, out of harm's way. He bends over and hisses in my ear. *You think those two fooled us?*

I keep my voice low and steady. 'You saw Baby's hair, didn't you. You've seen Baby's eyes. Anyway, Baby knows herself she is ours. That's what she's been trying to tell me. For days I thought it was something else she wanted me to do, because she brought my rattle back, look. I have it in my pinny pocket— Well, never mind, that's her old one, but anyway, I got it wrong, because—'

He won't look at it. Or at me. He's up against the window, gripping the sill, his forehead pressed against the cool glass. Just the other side is solid night, thick darkness. Nothing else exists. But we're not alone. Plenty of time until dawn.

It was their baby that died, not ours, I tell him. They tricked us both. They took our baby and gave you theirs to bury. Their babies always die. But remember how sure they were, all summer long, this one would live? When the Dells realised I was going to have a baby too, they couldn't believe their luck. If their baby died, they could just take ours.

Tommy makes a small, forced sound behind his clenched lips. He makes himself sit down opposite me and he hinges his hands on to the edge of the table as though he's about to overturn it, but he doesn't, he just sits there, pulling in the air through his nose as though there's not much left of it. But it's making sense, now he can help me, because I can't do this alone.

'Lettie,' he says.

'Yes?'

'Stop. You've sat on your backside too long. You've let your mind run away with you. Leave them alone. And their baby. It's none of your business.'

'Come round there with me, Tommy. Once it's light. You only need to see Baby without her bonnet. She's got my hair, my eyes – anyone could see she's mine. If Bridgewater could see her, that Miss Deering—'

'Stop,' he says. 'Please, please stop.'

I ask him. 'Where's our baby, Tommy?'

He looks up then.

'If you buried it,' I say, 'where is it?'

He shakes his head. 'I didn't bury it. But his forehead furrows right up. And then, so I can hardly hear: 'I couldn't.'

He tells me that Adam brought our baby out to him in the cucumber house and told him what had happened. *Never drew breath.* Told him that meant it couldn't be buried in the graveyard. We could bury it down in your orchard, under a tree, he said. Which one would be best?

'I couldn't do it, Lettie. Dig a hole for it, and put it in the earth, and cover it over. Leave it down there, in the dark.'

That's all right, Adam had said. And he told Tommy to go back to the cucumber house. He'd do it.

Tommy's shoulders hunch miserably.

'Did you hold it, Tommy?'

He shakes his head.

'Did you see it?'

'It was wrapped up.'

'But did you see it?'

'In a blanket.'

'What did Adam do with it? Did you go with him? Was it the mulberry tree, Tommy? Did you see him bury it?'

Tommy clasps his hands between his knees and rocks. To and fro, to and fro. The lamp glares huge and bright on the table between us. If I were to knock it over now, fire would run like water, flames would lick up the walls and smoke us out. I turn down the wick and cover my eyes, but I can't stop the jagged lights.

I stare at Tommy's hunched back, the muscle and

the bone. And I listen to the blackbird's song all the way through, and again. And after a while, the robin. Then the wren. As daylight comes, the thrushes will join in, the cockerels, the wood pigeons, but Tommy won't say a word about our baby. He never spoke of it when I thought she was dead, and he won't now. He'll neither confirm nor deny what he's done or not done. This, Turnbull, anything. He never will tell because he thinks not telling keeps him safer. Don't I already know this about him, as well as I now know all the night sounds, and the order they come in, right through to dawn and beyond. I watch as daylight – thin, hard, unforgiving – extinguishes the light from the lamp as surely as if I had reached into the glass shade and put it out with my fingers.

When I pick up the rattle to put it back in my pocket, it makes no sound either. The ribs are so chewed and mangled the pebble must have fallen out. I go to find my pinny, hanging on the back of the door, and I root about inside the pocket, pushing out the seams. There it is. But when I hold it up to the light, I'm holding a baby apple. A June drop. I can't keep anything straight.

I try to ease the apple back inside the cage of straws, but it keeps slipping out. The whole thing is coming apart in my hands. The red threads that hold the handle together are loosening, their ends tangled and stiff with dried spit. It smells of stale breath and rotten teeth. Like I've put my hand over my own mouth. I lay it on the table to smooth them out and retie them. I straighten the straws, very gently, tug the ends until they look neat and trim. It's only when I retie the threads and pull the knot tight that I remember where I've seen red threads like these before.

Whitsun morning

Jean half rises from her chair, her face a startled mask of good manners. One hand holds a rag, the other wears a brown heeled lace-up, as though it's a glove. Its twin sits polished, pungent and upright on a sheet of newspaper, facing me. As Jean unsheathes her hand and stands up tall, the swell of her breasts is clearly visible in her apple-print dress, freshly pressed. Her skin has paled, over winter, and this morning she has parted her hair and rolled it tight and smooth at the nape. She looks like a giant, crazed porcelain doll.

Baby kicks her legs in a chair pulled up to the range. She is dressed up too. More little girl than baby, in a green knitted bonnet, and a thick brown cardie I've not seen before. She shrieks and stuffs her fists in her mouth, arches her back, and I see that Jean has tied her to the chair with a binder that is knotted under her arms. Baby sucks and slurps, her eyes wide and pleading. She arches her back again and stretches out her arms.

Jean and I both watch her for a moment. Then Jean tries to unhook a clothes hanger from the top dresser shelf. My lilac frock, worn thin under the arms and faded across the yoke.

'There you are,' she says, in a tight, wound-up voice. 'I've pressed it for you.' She holds it out in a jerky movement that is timid, yet desperate. She tries a smile. 'Tommy brought it round. Wasn't that nice?'

'Tommy?' I say.

Adam thuds down the stair. As he swings through the door and sees me, he clamps one hand on the doorframe to steady himself. In the other he is holding a small brush, like a paintbrush.

'Hello, Lettie!' he says, jovial yet formal, the way he speaks to Bridgewater. As though he had been expecting me, although maybe not here, at the foot of the stairs, in his kitchen.

To distract him, I point at the brush he is holding. 'What's that for?'

Then I look over his head. The corn dollies are right there, up on the top shelf in the corner. It's a grey, overcast day, but with the front door open I can see every strand of every cobweb, every speck of dust on everything they store on those shelves except their shining, cherished corn dollies.

Last summer, Adam had said he wouldn't be making any more. Because we Radleys had brought them luck. He made rattles instead. A leap of faith. A gesture of hope. One for each of our babies. Only, one of them was never needed. I'd kept mine hidden in my suitcase, clean and dry, bright and pale as the day it was made. Some of their corn dollies have darkened a little, over the years, but not much, up there in the shadows. And they are just as clean as my rattle was: not one spider, not one speck of dust has been allowed to settle.

Adam looks to Jean expectantly, as though she's missed her cue. She's still holding the dress by the hanger, glancing from me to Hope and back again. Three strides. Maybe four.

'The brush, Adam. What's it for?'

Adam can't resist sharing knowledge, it's a reflex. 'Well

now, Tom's asked me to help him do his cucumber. Since Jean's lost her bees.' He wags the brush airily, like a tab. 'I told him he'll have no crop this season otherwise. And he asked me to help. We operate cooperatively here, if you remember?'

I smile back. It's an old joke. But the dimples don't come.

Adam wags the brush one more time as he crosses leisurely behind me to pull on his boots in the hallway. He casts a chiding look at Jean. 'Give it to her then.'

I still don't understand why Jean's dressed up, or why she's got my frock. It's been hung up next to the green tweed, behind the curtain in my bedroom, since the end of last summer.

'Ridiculous, really, the Association fixing on Whitsun for you ladies to go off gadding: they know it's the busiest time of the year. Jean certainly can't spare the time. But, well, we thought you could do with some sea air, Lettie.'

Miss Deering's Whitsun charabanc outing is today. *Sea air and sunshine, just the thing.* Our one designated day a year away from the settlement. I've not even left the holding since I arrived. In over a year. I've only known Jean step outside the gate once, for Hope's christening. And that was with Adam. Has she ever been anywhere, I wonder, without him right there at her side.

Jean hooks the hanger roughly over my forefinger. Before she lets go, she gives my hand a quick, meaningful squeeze.

'You always looked lovely in that, Lettie.' There are tears in her eyes.

'Come on then,' Adam says to her. 'Let's take a look at you.'

She straightens the skirt of her dress and stands, arms awkwardly out, looking anywhere but at him. 'I took it in, like you said.'

Adam taps her on her shoulder. As she swings around full circle on the spot, he runs his eyes up and down her figure. It's all wrong, I think, even her bust looks false, like a pantomime dame's.

His moustache quivers roguishly. 'You won't scare the birds.' She stares at her large, strong feet, and I see she is wearing stockings for the first time.

Adam tugs on his hat. 'You'll make sure Lettie's ready in time?'

'Of course.'

He wags his brush at me again. 'You enjoy yourself, Lettie. Blow away some of those cobwebs, eh?'

Jean goes to the door, ready to shut it behind him. Stiffly, she lets him peck her on the check. 'Bye, Ads.'

*

I've already got one finger right inside the knot in Baby's binder. No time to unwind, it, but one more tug and it will be loose enough for me to reach inside with both hands. If I can slacken it a bit more, I can get my hands around her midriff and tug her free. Already Baby has her arms tight around my neck, and she's not letting go. One final heft and I uproot her and her legs swing loose.

Oh but she's heavy, twice, three times as heavy as I remember. I almost drop her. Her body is big and soft and unwieldy. Her neck smells of blossom and bacon. There's a mesh of scurf beneath the spongy foam of her spun-gold hair, scaled like dried mud. Later. I'll clean that up for you later. I lower my face to her head and breathe her in. Just the two of us, at last.

'Hello you,' I say softly.

You've never left the holding either, have you, Baby. *You must accompany your friend, if only for her sake. She will appreciate the help with her baby. It will be good practice.* We could show you the sea, the sand and the crowds gadding all over the pier, and the prom, and the pleasure gardens. Find you a dry patch of beach and watch you run sand through your fingers. Tear off a skein of pink candyfloss and watch it melt to scarlet on your lips, the shock of sweetness widening your eyes. We could curl up in a deckchair with its back to the wind and doze to the thrum of the band as the shadows grow long and Jean's head nods. And then away we'd slip, Baby, just the two of us, before the sun drops behind the rooftops. *Oh I do like to be beside the seaside, Oh I do like to stroll along the prom* . . .

'No. No, no, no, no. Lettie—'

Jean tries to prise my fingers away. Her knuckles are white. Her eyes are closed, her face flinching back from Baby's flailing fists.

'Mine,' she says, from deep in her throat. 'Mine, mine, mine, mine.'

A child's spell, the sort of thing you say to yourself when you cross your fingers behind your back and hope.

I jerk Baby from her grip, remembering to cup my palm against her puff of hair before her head snaps back. Oh, that tender white stalk of a neck. She presses her forehead hot against my cheek, close enough, real enough, to speak to me with her hectic, snuffling breath.

'Give her back!'

'Oh no,' I say to Jean. 'You stop. You stay right there.'

I back away. I put myself between her and the door. And now at last I can count them properly, those dollies up on the shelf in the corner by the door to the stairs. I give them the names she gave me.

'Beauty of Bath.'

Jean's whole body contracts.

'Norfolk Pippen. Wyken Pippin. Tom Putt.'

She shrinks away, curls up as though lashed.

'Peasgood's Nonsuch.'

Watch that tongue of yours, Lettie Radley, they told me. But with each red-threaded figure named comes a sweet release. Five names, for each of Jean's dead babies, lined up there on the shelf. Only there's one more, unnamed, at the very far right of the row. The smallest, shortest one. Its straw is the palest, freshest gold and the threads about its wrists and neck are the brightest scarlet.

'What's that doing there, little one?'

Baby's head swivels right round to look. She gurgles.

'That's right, there's one more, isn't there? There at the end. What's *that* doing there? What's *that* one called, Jean?'

Jean stares, helpless, as though I've struck her across the face. I can't stop now. I've stepped out into the shaft and now I'm plummeting, because it's real, all of it. I've never seen her so pale. So scared.

'All right. All right. I'll tell you.' She holds out her arms. 'Just, give her back.'

Baby lets out a little cry and I hold her tighter. Baby knows what she's done. All this time. And Jean has kept us apart and lied and lied and lied to me. The anger comes surging up and consumes me.

'Oh, stop!' I want to spit in her face.

'No! Please, Lettie, it's not how you think—'

'Stop. Stop now. I'll tell you exactly how it was, Jean. Right from the week I arrived, you had it planned, didn't you? You knew about that night in the lettuce house, didn't you. You told me those drinks would get me back on my feet. You knew what they'd do to me, they'd make me want more than the lettuce, when you wouldn't let me have them any more. When I've never once been with anyone but Tommy, never once. Never even thought of Adam like that. You waited until you knew I couldn't wait any more and you sent him out to the lettuce house that night – And then—' I have to stop, gulp for air. You pretended you were my friend. All those months. And then – and then you took my baby from me. Jean—'

'Please, Lettie.' She wipes her eyes. 'Please stop.' Her face is a ruin, blotchy and red. Her hands are trembling violently. So is her jaw. 'All right, Lettie, I can explain, only – please, please, just give her back.' Her voice rises and rises, and in it I hear my own wild panic and desperation and longing, mirrored and amplified.

'You're right,' she says finally.

As soon as she says it I want her to take it back. I shake my head.

'Only it's not what you think.' She makes a sudden move towards me and I snatch Baby out of her reach.

'No. No. I won't take her, I promise. Just let me, please, let me show you. I won't take her. Let me undo this button on her bonnet? Can I?'

I hold Baby tight to my chest.

Jean reaches in and undoes the button that fastens the chin strap under Baby's right ear.

I look at her nimble fingers, her worn, wet cheek, her fine profile. We could have been friends still. Mothers. Neighbours. Helping each other out.

'There. You hold her still.' Jean's eyes are soft and very dark. 'Now let me just—' She takes hold of the bonnet and gently pulls it away. 'I'm sorry, Lettie. Truly I am.'

Baby's hair lies crushed against her skull like trampled wheat, hot and damp. Jean peels a strand from where it has stuck to Baby's forehead. It stands up, a colourless tuft, almost transparent. Baby's eyes gaze back at me pale and clear.

'Look at her again. Who do you see?'

He'd spotted Tommy straight off the truck, that dark winter afternoon. The stump of a man that he was by then, all bone and stubble. He'd seen Tommy thump his chest and gasp for air, fumble for his hankie. That one's desperate, he'd said to himself. He's walking blind. Younger than the rest too. He told Jean the same. We're desperate too, aren't we?

Tommy was their last chance. They were old enough to be grandparents, and not one child living. Everything else had failed. Even the wife before me at Holding 94, done in by the kids and the work: Jean had offered to work their holding for free, for ever, if only she'd let Jean raise their littlest as her own. They did a flit that same night, went straight back to her mother's. And then the Association had announced that new families were being allocated to the central holdings only.

Tommy was desperate. Half starved, no work for years, and far from home for the first time. No wife or sister to confide in or lean on. He'd everything staked on Foxash, could never go back. And along comes Adam, all smiles and ease, father and brother and marra rolled into one. Adam would have seen straight off that he'd pulled some trick – he couldn't tell one end of a plant from the other.

After they'd been fed, and shown their bunks, Adam beckoned Tommy outside, into the country dark. Told him how competitive the scheme was going to be, how many men ended up being sent straight back home. How would he like to be sure of getting his tenancy, and be guaranteed the most productive holding on the estate, by the end of his first season? A long, healthy, profitable future above ground, all sunlight and fresh air? His own name on his produce crates: Mr T. Radley, established grower.

Pfft.

Tommy would have thought about it, for sure. Calculated the odds. Tommy had never been unfaithful, not once. And he had no reason to trust this man. *He did say no, Lettie, that's something, isn't it?* Adam had to get him drunk. Pour drink into Tommy, and it's like filling up a water butt. Takes a long time before anything overflows. Adam's a patient man. He had a hunch there'd be something worth waiting for.

She says Tommy ended up telling Adam about Turnbull. Jean doesn't know that Tommy's never told me what happened, does she. That I've never asked. What you don't know can't hurt you.

The keeper came at the two of them with a flashlight. Tommy had his knife in his hand and he'd swung out at him but somehow he'd got Turnbull instead. Turnbull fell into a gully. Tommy remembers a tumble, and a splash. The keeper chased Tommy, only he got away. But he never went back for Turnbull. And Turnbull never came back, that night, or the next. And Tommy had to leave before they found Turnbull's body. Because the keeper had seen him wield that knife, and if it came to it, he'd give Tommy up in a flash, if only to save himself.

My Tommy, who never tells anyone his business. Not even me. Oh but, Adam Dell, with his sing-song way of talking, grinning like he's your best marra. Who stands much too close, like he already knows you inside out. Adam would have put his arm around Tommy, offered him a way to keep his head out of the noose for good. Or maybe waited till the next morning, for Tommy to realise what he'd given away. And then. Promised him the earth. His own little Eden, in exchange for one moment in the dark. Whether a baby came of it or not, Adam swore he'd keep his end of the bargain. And he did, didn't he?

Tommy'd have worked out the odds. It would solve everything. He'd be safe. What were the chances of a baby, anyway, if it was just one time? At their age. They'd not tell. No one else need ever know. And he's good at not knowing, is Tommy. Or telling.

It was only supposed to be that one time. Jean keeps saying that. One time, before I ever got here. Just before I arrived. That's how long it took to persuade him, she says, as if it's a compliment. And it was Ads chose him, not her. Jean didn't even meet him until it was settled. Although once it was agreed, she made up her Special Area specials, and Adam took them to him in barracks. To get him ready.

The day before I arrived, Adam got him drunk again. He shut him in the lettuce house, without a lamp. No moon, shuffling on his knees in the earth, only his blind white fingertips to show him the way. Even though it was dark Jean kept her eyes shut the whole time. Oh but her face that first evening, flushed and smiling.

She's not blushing now. She's root pale.

I could never have done it if I'd known you'd be such a good friend to me, Lettie. I only did it for Ads. All our lives he's wanted us to have a baby of our own and I'd let him down over and over. I love him.

And for what it's worth, the green drinks, that night

Adam came to the lettuce house? Tom never agreed to that. We didn't tell him. Ads only thought of it after you came. He thought it might be a good idea, in case—

She wets her lips. And anyway. It made it fair.

I am still sitting at her table, my back to the dresser, the way I always used to. And I still have Baby in my arms. Tommy's baby.

'Lettie?' Jean stands up and goes over to the corner by the stair door. She doesn't need to stand on a chair. She reaches up with both arms and takes it down. The smallest dolly. She tucks it neatly into the crook of one arm. Its sheaf splays out prettily over the tiny apples of her frock. She rocks it in her arms, to and fro, to and fro.

'I would never have taken your baby from you, you must believe me. I know what it's like, don't I? To lose a baby. I was sure your baby would live, Lettie, whether he was Adam's or Tom's. You're young, and strong and – I don't know why he didn't, I swear. And I knew you wanted your baby, really you did. I thought, if I could keep him for you, safe, at least you could hold him, when you were ready. It's always helped me.'

She sets the dolly down on the table to face me, settles it upright. She smooths the sheaf together and adjusts the red threads to hang neat and straight. 'Here he is. Quite safe.'

I look away, hold Baby even tighter.

'He's lovely, really he is. Go on. You should hold him. I know you think you don't want to, but it helps, Lettie, really it does.'

I look down at Baby instead, sitting huge and silent in my lap. Jean's telling me this is Hope. Their baby: Tommy and Jean's. How can that be? I feel her as my flesh and blood. I can't tell where I end and Baby begins. Baby is as much a part of me as my hair, my tears, my breath. Look up at me, Baby, please. But Hope's staring straight ahead, at Jean's corn dolly, there on the table before us.

Its straw ribs are cool and dry to the touch. It might be one of those basketwork jugs from the Fox. When I take it by the waist and pull it towards me, I feel a drag inside. I lift it, there's a sucking sound, and something drops an inch from beneath its stiff woven skirt. Something wrapped in parcel paper, thick and brown and smooth, the same as Jean and I used for our paper pads. Wrapped neat and thick, the way you'd wrap a pair of shoes to send in the post, or bring a vase home from market, well wadded. And tied about with double and triple lengths of dark red wool.

It might be a vase. It weighs no more than a vase. It smells like the neck of a vase, dark with the debris of stems. It smells how Jean's kitchen has always smelt, beneath the hyacinths and the jams and the chutneys and the roast goose. Only stronger.

It rustles softly, settles upright again, threads swaying, as I push it back across the table.

'My baby?'

Jean nods. 'The same as the day he was born. I promise you.'

I look at her. There's a sick thudding in my chest. 'That's not possible—'

She laughs, almost. 'I know. We don't know why. Oh Lettie, we were so young. We didn't know anything. And Beauty of Bath, she came before we knew it. She was so beautiful, Lettie, I'd never seen anything so beautiful. I couldn't let go of her. I wrapped her in a cloth and hid her behind a rafter. I was in one attic with the other girls, Ads was with the men by then, over the barn. And then, well, we had to move on, so we took her with us. And oh Lettie, when I unwrapped her she was perfect, a little lighter perhaps, but just the same. I looked her all over again. She'd been born with this little dimple on her back, at the base of her spine, that was all that was wrong with her, and even that was still there. You just have to keep them dry, that's all.'

I look up at the shelf again. All of them. The Dells did this for all their babies. Bundled them up in straw and lined them up and kept them there. For years. And now they've kept my baby boy there, secret from me, all these months. And never once told.

'Jean, it's disgusting. It's – cruel.'

She gives the faintest toss of her head, dismissing the thought with maddening certainty.

'You all told me you'd buried him. You lied to me. Over and over.'

Nothing moves behind her wide, unblinking eyes. Her mind is a dark cold store.

Then, with the smallest of pouts, she says: 'I shouldn't have to explain this to you, Lettie. I saved him for you, Lettie. If you'd only unwrap him, you'll see for yourself. He's just as he was. He just never drew breath.'

*

They had the right idea at St Clement's. What you don't know can't hurt you. It's never how you think it's going to be. You think you want to know, but you don't really. You think it's going to hurt less, when you know. But the truth can be something much worse than you ever suspected.

Knowing hurts far more than not knowing. And there's no going back.

Jean pushes one of her grubby handkerchiefs into my hand. Crouches at my side, pats my knee. She keeps asking me just to give her Hope, and hold my baby.

That sturdy little straw figure stands up straight and alone in the middle of the table. I'm starting to gag. How can that be my baby in there, curled up the way he was inside me?

She sits back on her haunches and runs her hand over her jaw, as though she's tried her very best. 'Maybe later. I'm sorry, Lettie, really I am.' Then she ducks her head to look anxiously out the front window.

'Look at those trees,' she says, in a different, breathy voice. 'It's getting gusty out there. I hope it won't be too windy.'

I'd thought this was just the way her kitchen smelled. Come to think of it as something friendly, and warm. Comforting. I'd ended up barely noticing it. I'll never be able to stop smelling it now. It's inside me, my nose, my mouth, my throat, it will choke me wherever I go. Nothing will blow it away.

'Why tell me today, Jean?' The words rise up like vomit.

Her eyes brim over. 'Because you came for Hope, didn't you. She's mine, Lettie.'

The fine-spun web of Baby's hair is catching my tears as they fall. They hang there, suspended, like shining, spangling beads of light. Baby is still in my lap: warm and damp and impossibly, immovably heavy.

'I'm not giving her back, Jean.'

She looks nervously at us both. Then she wipes her eyes and picks up my frock from the floor. She dusts it off and knocks out the creases.

'The charabanc will be here soon, Lettie. A day away from here, some sea air, you'll feel a lot better about everything, I'm sure.'

When she holds out the frock once more, I dash it away.

'You think I'm going to the seaside now. With *you*.'

Her face grows weary and bewildered. 'No, no, I'm not going.'

'You're dressed up, though.'

'Lettie, please.'

'What is it?'

'Go. You have to.'

'No, I don't.'

'Lettie, please, I need to get Hope strapped back in, and—'

'I'm not giving her back to you, Jean. No. Do you really think I'd leave her here with you? With those—'

Jean bundles up my frock and clutches it to her stomach. 'Oh, Lettie, I can't tell you.'

'Jean,' I say steadily. 'You have lied and lied to me. Just tell me the truth for once.'

I kept my voice low, because of Baby, but she looks terrified, as if I'd bellowed in her face.

Jean nods. Nods again. 'All right. Ads has taken over the cucumber house. The Association would have called in the debt this month, on top of everything else. Tom will get the profit, if there is any. You see, he never did anything with the cucumber seed last season, so Ads has paid for plugs again. He's helping Tom, which means—' She stops.

'Jean? What has that—'

Her face contorts. 'You're my friend, Lettie. I think you're the only friend I've ever had. I wish it were different, I really do. But this way – this way, everyone's happy, Ads says. He'll be happy. Finally. There were eight of us altogether.

He was the only boy. Don't you see? Now we know it can happen, with Tom, we'll try again.' She takes a breath. 'Ads has always wanted a son, you see.'

*

Hope sits very still in my arms. Her legs dangle down like a rag doll's. But her face is alive and watching. All I can hear is the tick and whoosh of the range. The rising wind outside sweeps through the grass, and shakes the branches, scours the glass.

Somewhere far away, down the lane, a low rumble has started up, regular and mechanical. The whine of a distant engine straining over the ruts, and the splash of tyres in the puddles. The thunk and scrape of branch and twig against metal. Nothing bigger than the HP van has come down that lane all winter.

'Jean,' I say. She turns back to look at me, her eyes glazed, her hands fretful. 'You're not my friend. You never were my friend.'

Faintly, from just outside, there's the smash of glass. Jean's chickens flap and chunter. Whatever it is, it's set the geese off, honking in rounds. A shout on the wind, abruptly shut off. A flat twang, and then a crunch, as of a vast puddle of ice mazed by a boot.

Jean drops my frock and hurries to the door. She scans the holding, then she sets off round the corner towards the cucumber house.

There's a sharper, louder crack. Another yell, and the sound of many tiny fragments raining down on to leaves and stalks and sliding off.

Hope shrinks into my side. Her heart is beating even faster than mine. I watch her skin as it pales, tender and delicate and pierceable as a petal. I can't take her out there with me.

I cover her eyes until the last minute and heave Hope into her chair by the range. When she arches her back in protest, I tickle her toes and butterfly-kiss her face, and draw the binding up around the back of the chair and fasten it across her chest so she'll be safe. *Wait for me, little one. I'm not leaving. I'm coming back, I promise.* And the thought comes like an echo: are these the words my mother said to me? Hope blinks slowly. Her pale, trusting eyes track me to the door.

Round the side of the house, over the path, are showers of glass, like sea spray. In the roof of the cucumber house, in three of the large panes of glass nearest the ridge, are huge, splintered holes. And there, directly below the nearest of them, his head bare to the opened sky, stands Tommy. He's looking away from me, facing the door, still gripping the vent pole before him like he's raising a banner. Down his right temple and on to his cheek unspools a fine scarlet ribbon of blood.

I see you, Tommy. Oh I see you now.

Ahead of me, Jean hitches up her skirt. She skids and crunches up the path. When she slides open the door she looks down the aisle and stops dead.

'Tommy!' I shout.

That pole's not half as long as the glasshouse vent pole. I've never been able to manage that one, I always had to call Jean to do the top vents for the tomato. But then the cucumber-house roof is lower and its panes of glass much bigger. Twenty-four inches square. *Imagine that*, he'd say.

'Tommy!'

If he can hear me, he doesn't show it. He sucks in his breath and takes a step forward. A terrible sound starts,

343

deep in his chest. Even from out here I can hear it. I see his mouth, wet and open. He bends at the knees, just a little, in preparation. And then he ducks his head, takes a high, short step forward and rams the pole up once more into the roof.

Jean screams.

I run to the door to pull her away from the falling glass. And that's when I see what Tommy stepped over. Adam, huddled on his side, halfway down the aisle. One arm is flung over his face and his legs are sprawled and motionless amid the shards and splinters.

Jean tries to turn her face into my shoulder. I push her away, tell her to stay right where she is. As I walk down the aisle, I see the tiny vibrations my footfalls set off in the leaves. I could be walking back into last spring: the place is warm and light and open again, with a clear view of the wide white sky overhead, the air rich and soft. The hotbeds are packed with bristling young plugs. Tendrils climb the wires and twisted yellow flowers are opening.

Something has rekindled deep inside me at last. I am pure and mighty and roaring, like a chimney caught light. There's a rushing in my ears, like there was on the platform at Durham, when the mainline train came thundering in.

Tommy faces me square, resting the end of his pole on the ground. He is lit up too. It's Tommy versus the world. Always was.

'He deserved it, Lettie, all right?' Tommy's voice resounds as though in an alley, funnelling back from the side of the house. That bullying tone, thick with the pitmatic, that always got me sick to my stomach. Not now.

Jean has come out of nowhere to push past me. I have to catch hold of the splintering side plank of the bed to keep my balance. She ducks under Tommy's arm and throws herself down beside Adam, her bare feet scrabbling for purchase in the shattered glass. As she tries to tug him upright, his head lolls and I see the dark stain spreading from the puncture on the front of his shirt.

I've been a child, sticking my fingers in my ears. What was it Tommy said when he came back and smelt the Jeyes? Had a clean-up? That's right. I've dealt with it. I got rid of our baby boy, for him. I've never let on. I went and found this place for him. I never once asked him about Turnbull. I lied through my teeth for him. I gave up everything, for him. For us. Jean's lies are nothing to this. That pain, that ravening beast inside, all teeth and claws, that birth, that loss, even – it was nothing compared to knowing this. This is butchery.

'You are a piece of work, Tommy Radley.'

'She's told you then? Thought so.' A strange little snicker escapes him. 'You know he's her fucking brother, did she tell you that, Lettie?'

Setting the pole firmly in the ground, he wipes his right temple on his fist and I watch his forehead crease right up.

But then he looks at me, implacable. 'Anyway,' he says. 'You're one to talk.'

Oh he's good at this, my pillar of stone. A matter of feet between us and it may as well be miles. If I were to beat him with my fists, I'd break my own bones.

Tommy shakes his head. 'Don't bother, Lettie. Adam told me himself, just now. What you've been up to.'

He takes up the pole again, like a cricket bat, weighing it in both hands, and gives me a half-cocked smile. 'Think we're done here, don't you? Call it quits?'

He wipes his face once more and starts to thrash the pole to and fro across the aisle, from bed to bed, tearing the young vines from their strings. I jump back before the hooked end catches me. He builds up speed.

'Stop it, Tommy!'

'It's rotten, this place. It's no good, I tell you, any of it. We're no good, they're no good—'

I back up the aisle, reach the door. 'That's the charabanc coming, Tommy. They'll see. They'll see Adam—'

Panting hard, he changes his grip on the pole to ram it into the side panes. But he's too short to reach that far. He has to half scramble up on to the bed with his elbow and knees before he can crack one pane. He throws the pole down anyhow on the crushed plants.

'Let them. You know it was all for you, Lettie, don't you? I can't even—'

Locking his fingers about the back of his neck, he looks up through the jagged holes to the open sky. Then he turns on his heel, steps over Adam and Jean and strides rapidly to the very far end of the aisle, where his tab ends litter the ground like blossom, and he hunches up, gripping his elbows, the way they all used to stand about on the corner of the street, day after miserable day. Shifting their weight from one foot, to the other and back again. And I'm back with the other pitwives, watching through the nets.

Out in the lane the droning is louder, slowing to a dense judder. The high, shiny snout of a charabanc, painted thick maroon with a dull gold trim, heaves into sight. There's the driver in his peaked cap, clutching the wheel and staring straight ahead. One by one they appear, hazy behind the fogged-up windows, the women's ruddy faces, their trimmed-up hats and tarnished brooches and faded scarves, mouths open but silenced. They gaze out at the punctured glass. A pale glove reaches forward to jab the driver's shoulder.

Jean has pulled Adam on to her lap somehow. His eyelids are closed but flickering and the heel of his right boot makes short, jerky ruts in the earth. She's bent over his chest, sobbing, her hair swung across her face.

'Jean,' I say. 'It's all right, Jean, they're here.'

The faces sway forwards and then back as the charabanc comes to a halt at the gate. They're packed in close, moving their heads, their hands, the way women do when they're together. One starts to squeeze her way to the back. The driver stumbles as he jumps out at the front, nearly loses his peaked cap.

'Leave him, Jean,' I call. 'Come away.'

A cry, a high, unspooling, eye-opening cry threads through the air and snags me. It breaks on a moment of silence but then it comes again, and again. It echoes against the walls, pours in through the smashed openings, floods my ears. Even the driver comes to attention.

'Jean!' I shout. 'Jean!'

Jean rocks silently on. It's as though she hears the wind blowing or the geese calling.

The driver's having a great deal of trouble opening the gate. 'Oi there!' he blusters when he sees me. 'Oi!'

He's tall and erect and broad-shouldered, more of an officer than a driver, although there's something wrong with one side of his face. And here she comes behind him, Miss Deering to the rescue.

Oh hadn't she just known what was going on down this end. She's no fool, our Miss Deering. She'd known it the minute she walked in the door and found me in the dark, with the curtains drawn. Hadn't she seen them in church that day, this tall dark couple, this matching pair. Wouldn't she have seen them slip off the baby's bonnet and wet that halo of shining hair?

She shoulders the driver aside, her pale gloved hand quick as anything with the latch. One glance down the aisle, and she's quite taken in the whole situation. Those powdered cheeks are flaming pink and she is quite out of breath herself.

'Come away,' she beckons to me. 'Come with us. Be quick.'

Leave Tommy, rooted to the spot in his shattered house. Leave the Dells, entangled there in the scuffed earth. Leave them all.

And there it comes again, that unspooling cry, that snags my heart and tugs me back to Jean's stuffy kitchen.

Wait for me, little one. I'm not leaving without you. I'm coming back, I promised.

Outside, the wind gusts low across the holdings and plucks at the puddles winter has dug. Nothing reflects from the glasshouses, whitewashed by cloud. It's less than twenty yards back round the corner of the house. A matter of moments, unless you're pushing a loaded barrow, or carrying full crates or whatever. But even in those few yards everything can fall into place. More often than not, whatever's in the barrow or the crates that you think you might have overfilled and is likely to spill out has settled by the time you set it down. It all fits. That's why the Association always measures our produce by weight, not volume.

The door is wide open, as I left it. And she's watching for me. Of course she is. I can't look away either, not for a second. I know to brace myself before I lift, and how to keep her balance. I know the damp heat under her arms like my own. The flex of those soft, small ribs.

I have Baby's weight against me. Baby's cheek against mine. I can stroke her cheek, put my lips to her, again and again, there's no one to stop me. I don't know where I end and Baby begins. I lower my head and it's like going back into the glasshouse. Living in her breath, sweet and warm and steady as the breath of plants. Lips soft as petals. I want to live like this for ever.

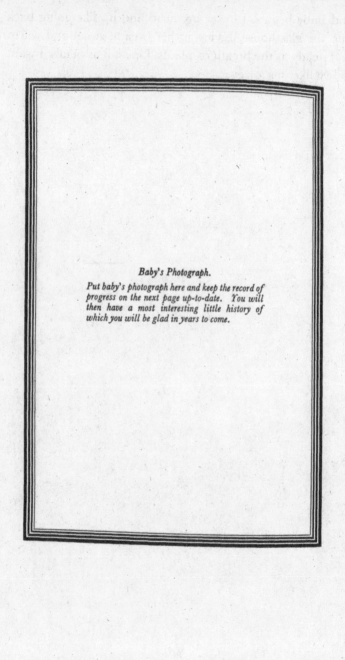

Baby's Photograph.

Put baby's photograph here and keep the record of progress on the next page up-to-date. You will then have a most interesting little history of which you will be glad in years to come.

A RECORD OF BABY'S PROGRESS

Birthplace_____

Time_____Date_____Day_____

Names_____

Where christened_____

_____

Clergyman's Name_____

_____

Godparents_____

_____

_____

Weight when born_____

Birth Marks_____

Colour of Eyes_____

When Baby cut First Tooth_____

When Baby sat up_____

When Baby crawled_____

When Baby stood_____

When Baby walked_____

When Baby first spoke_____

The Land Settlement Association

In 1934, at the height of the Depression, a British Government-backed body called the Land Settlement Association began to buy up farms all across England. It selected long-term unemployed industrial workers – mainly miners, but also shipbuilders and labourers – from so-called Special Areas, where unemployment was high: Glasgow, Tyneside, Lancashire and South Wales. It trained them in horticulture and livestock rearing, and settled them in cooperative colonies from Carlisle to Chichester.

The LSA was the biggest and most expensive of the interwar 'back to the land' movements. Over a period of five years it acquired more than 11,000 acres, developed 1,100 holdings on twenty-one estates and trained more than 1,700 men.

While *Foxash* draws heavily on my research into the LSA, its practices, personnel and ideals, and the colonies at Foxash in Essex and at Newbourne in Suffolk, the novel is in no way a record, portrait or critique of the LSA project itself, or of those who came to live on the settlements, or of those who have lived there since.

The Dells grow a range of varieties of lettuce for the London market and for home use, including winter purslane or miner's lettuce, and lamb's lettuce, also known as Rapunzel lettuce, a salad green of the valerian family.

MINER'S LETTUCE

Claytonia perfoliata (syn. *Montia perfoliata*), also known as miner's lettuce, Indian lettuce, spring beauty, or winter purslane, is a flowering plant in the Montiaceae family. [. . .] The common name of miner's lettuce refers to how the plant was used by miners during the California Gold Rush, who ate it to prevent scurvy. It is in season in April and May, and can be eaten as a leaf vegetable. [. . .] Caution should be used because wild *C. perfoliata* can sometimes accumulate toxic amounts of soluble oxalates (also present in spinach)

– '*Claytonia perfoliata*',
Wikipedia, Wikimedia Foundation, 22 June 2022,
https://en.wikipedia.org/wiki/Claytonia_perfoliata

'"You are cooped up in this miserable place, without fresh air, without sunshine, without exercise, and without vegetable diet. You will die, the last man of you, if you don't get out of this place." [. . .] "Now" said I, "I'll tell you what will cure you. On those sand-hills back of the city there grows a kind of wild lettuce," which I described to them. "If you will go out and gather that lettuce and use it, with a little vinegar, it will cure you."'

– Revd William Taylor's account of using
miner's lettuce to treat scurvy: Taylor, William (1860).
California Life Illustrated. New York, New York, USA:
Carlton & Porter. pp. 230–231

Valerianella locusta, called mâche or mache; common cornsalad; or lamb's lettuce, is a small, herbaceous, annual flowering plant in the honeysuckle family *Caprifoliaceae*. It is native to Europe, western Asia and north Africa, where it is eaten as a leaf vegetable [. . .] Common names include lamb›s lettuce, common cornsalad, or simply cornsalad, mâche, fetticus, feldsalat, nut lettuce, field salad. [. . .] In some areas of Germany it is known as rapunzel.

– '*Valerianella locusta*',
Wikipedia, Wikimedia Foundation, 22 June 2022,
https://en.wikipedia.org/wiki/Valerianella locusta

One day the woman stood at the window looking into the garden, and she saw a bed which was planted full of the most beautiful lettuces. As she looked at them, she began to wish she had some to eat, but she could not ask for them.

Day after day her wish for these lettuces grew stronger, and the knowledge that she could not get them so worried her, that at last she became so pale and thin that her husband was quite alarmed. 'What is the matter with you, dear wife?' he asked one day.

'Ah!' she said, 'if I do not have some of that nice lettuce which grows in the garden behind our house, I feel that I shall die.'

– 'Rapunzel', *Grimm's Fairy Tales. A new translation by Mrs. H. B. Paull. Specially adapted and arranged for young people.* (London: Frederick Warne and Company, 1868), n.d p70.

Acknowledgements

I am extremely grateful for advice, support & encouragement from the following:

My muchly esteemed agent Veronique Baxter, & Sara Langham & Laura West at David Higham Associates; Sarah Bower; Rhiannon Bull; Kathryn Burton; Chloe & Zara Chancellor; Steve Cook, Katharine McMahon & the Royal Literary Fund; Elizabeth Davidson; Ruby Dawson; Peter Gant & the Manningtree Museum Local History Group; Helen Garnons-Williams; Lynne Goodwyn; Rose Helm & Joanna Mudhar at Newbourne; Christie Hickman; Tobias Hill; Charlotte Hume; Peggy Hughes & the National Centre for Writing; The Museum of East Anglian Life; The Museum of English Rural Life; The Living Museum of the North, Beamish; Clare Kemsley; Aga Lemieszewska; Jonathan Myerson; Petra McQueen & The Writers' Company; Lisa Newman; Kate Pryor; Bethan Roberts; Nick Siddle; Dina Southwell; Imogen Taylor, Rosanna Hildyard & Tinder Press, Headline; Sue Ward-Booth; Annie Watts; John & Iris Worsley.

I thank Arts Council England for awarding me a Grant for the Arts & the National Centre for Writing for my Escalator Literature Development Award, both to support the writing of *Foxash*.

I also thank Ethel Cook & John Crawford for sharing with me their memories of growing up on the real Foxash settlement. I drew heavily on the oral histories contained in *Tommy Turnbull: A Miner's Life* by Joe Robinson (The History Press, 2007) &

Fenwomen: a Portrait of Women in an English Village by Mary Chamberlain (Virago's first non-fiction book, 1975), both essential accounts of British working-class lives.

Foxash is fiction, of course, but as ever, any historical inaccuracies are mine alone.

Most especially, I thank James, Alex & Luke.

You are invited to join us behind the scenes at Tinder Press

TINDER
PRESS

To meet our authors, browse our books
and discover exclusive content on our
blog visit us at

www.tinderpress.co.uk

For the latest news and views from the team
Follow us on Twitter

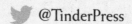 @TinderPress